It's All Love

It's All Love

BLACK WRITERS ON SOUL MATES, FAMILY, AND FRIENDS

Edited and with an Introduction by
MARITA GOLDEN

BROADWAY BOOKS
New York

Published in the United States by Broadway Books, an imprint of
The Doubleday Publishing Group, a division of Random House, Inc., New York.
www.broadwaybooks.com

BROADWAY BOOKS and its logo, a letter B bisected on the diagonal,
are trademarks of Random House, Inc.

Permissions acknowledgments appear on pages 400–403.

BOOK DESIGN BY JUDITH 'ABBATE/ABBATE DESIGN

Library of Congress Cataloging-in-Publication Data
It's all love : black writers on soul mates, family, and friends / edited and with an
introduction by Marita Golden.—1st ed.
p.   cm.
1. American literature—African American authors. 2. African Americans—Literary
collections. 3. Love. 4. African American families. 5. African Americans—
Attitudes. I. Golden, Marita.
PS153. N5I87 2009
810.9'3543—dc22
2008025496

ISBN 978-0-7679-1686-8

PRINTED IN THE UNITED STATES OF AMERICA

1 3 5 7 9 10 8 6 4 2

First Edition

This book is dedicated, with thanks, to all the individuals who have provided moral and material support for the mission and work of the Hurston/Wright Foundation, and to the next generation of Black literary voices, who will make a new and better world.

Contents

Nonfiction

Fiction

PART TWO: TIES THAT BIND

Poetry

Nonfiction

Fiction

A LETTER FROM THE EXECUTIVE DIRECTOR OF
THE HURSTON/WRIGHT FOUNDATION

*I*T HAS BEEN SAID, if you are able to utter only one prayer a day, let that prayer be thank-you. This is a letter of thanks and praise to the ancestors and the many people and organizations that have supported Hurston/Wright for the past nineteen years.

The first person I wish to thank is my partner, Hurston/ Wright cofounder, fellow cultural worker, friend, and inspiration Marita Golden. It was because of her insatiable desire to give back to the community that Hurston/Wright came to be. If it is true that the future exists in language, Marita has not only helped to speak Hurston/Wright into existence but she has also been the keeper of the faith. And keeping the faith is the one ingredient essential to building an institution.

Thanks in part to my and Marita's mutual commitment to social change, Hurston/Wright has become an institution recognized for its contribution to the development and cultural continuity of African-American literary arts. As a nonprofit institution, Hurston/Wright strives to continue the literary traditions and achievements of generations of African-American writers from Frederick Douglass and Gwendolyn Brooks to James Baldwin and Dudley Randall, as well as the renowned namesakes Richard Wright and Zora Neale Hurston.

I feel grateful and privileged to have helped direct the process that honors and preserves the genius of Black people and our magnificent story for the past nineteen years.

As a natural progression, since its inception the organization has experienced exponential growth and development of its programs. In order to accommodate this expansion we have refined, broadened, and updated our mission and goals.

The mission of Hurston/Wright is to preserve and advance humanity through the acquisition and dissemination of knowledge and information through literature, with a specific focus on literature by and about people of African descent. We accomplish this mission through programs that discover, honor, and develop writers of Black literature at every stage of their development.

This mission does not tell the whole story, however. The story is the continually unfolding narrative of the individual readers' and writers' lives we have touched, by offering unique opportunities to them for fellowship and to pursue shared interests.

Another important part of the story includes our gratitude for the support of the publishing industry, especially Random House, which has so generously invested in our work for many years; the many individual and corporate donors who have underwritten our programs; and the committed literature lovers who have served on our board of directors and our advisory board. It is evident, these individuals and organizations have provided Hurston/Wright with financial and intellectual resources because they understand the valuable contribution that Black literature has made to civilization.

Of course, the whole story would not be complete without a blueprint for the future, which includes the enhancement of our programs for young people. In keeping with our mission we will continue to provide services for aspiring, emerging, and published writers, and for readers of their work. Our annual programs, including the Writers' Week Workshops, the Award for College Writers, and the Legacy Award for Published Writers, and soon to be developed Online Workshops, will continue to be offered.

Based on the requests of participants and attendees, we have begun to expand our programs to include a younger age group—middle and high school students. This program, the Hurston/Wright Creative Writing Intensive, is a year-round tuition-free reading and writing program that complements the students' formal schooling—a finishing school for the literary arts. All students in the program will be given the opportunity to develop skills in their chosen genre while at the same time being exposed to all forms of literary art, including poetry, fiction, playwriting, nonfiction, public speaking, and debate.

Adding the Creative Writing Intensive to our program mix completes the cycle. Our adult programs will ensure the development of a pool of good writers from which to recruit writing teachers for all of our training programs, including the middle and high school classes. As is the case in the life of successful people and organizations, Hurston/Wright is involved in sustaining and perpetuating itself while simultaneously taking steps to advance.

I was once told, "There is no hovering in life"; you are either going forward or crashing. With the continued support of people and organizations that understand literary arts, which are powerful platforms for sharing our collective history and culture, healing our communities, and assisting us to become agents for change, Hurston/Wright will always remain in flight and on course.

—CLYDE McELVENE

For more information on the Hurston/Wright Foundation, please visit our Web site at www.hurstonwright.org.

Introduction

LIKE ALL THE BOOKS I've written or edited, this anthology is an effort to answer a question. The question is: Where is the love among Black folk? The question arose, haunting and obsessing me, against the backdrop of the following:

A *Washington Post* article headlined "Marriage Is for White People" popped up in my e-mail one day. Making the rounds of the Internet, the article sparked outrage, jokes, and considerable embarrassment. The article included the quote "Marriage is for white people," a statement made by a twelve-year-old sixth grader in southeast Washington, D.C. A first-person account of writer Joy Jones's visit to an elementary school to speak to a class about future careers, the story recounts how the boys in the class thought it was more important to be a good father than to make a lot of money but saw no correlation between fatherhood and marriage.

The article discussed the extremely low marriage and exceedingly high divorce rate among African-Americans. I know the dominant family profiles of the community these youth live in. Many of these young men live in single-parent homes, and they may see more married couples on television or in the movies than in their neighborhood or extended family.

The import of the beliefs expressed by these young people

concerned me for a multitude of reasons, among them that as half of a bedrock-solid marriage, I am keenly aware of the multitude of types of love and commitment a good marriage can produce. The attitudes of these youngsters also was searing evidence of the instability so prevalent among Black families, the result of generations of racist social policies, as well as a deeply entrenched trust and commitment phobia among Black men and women.

Then I kept reading about the "drop" in the urban homicide rate of the major urban areas, a decline that annually, however, still leaves too many mostly Black men dead at the hands of other Black men. The fact that African-Americans are 13 percent of the population but 49 percent of the country's murder victims is proof that the supposed decline is mostly an illusion.

On the personal front there was the news that hit me one weekend like a meteor: that three longtime married couples who were friends of me and my husband were divorcing. I began to wonder if those students were right.

As we say among ourselves, I was suddenly *too through* with my people. Increasingly, I began to feel assaulted by a steady bombardment of negative, soul-sapping pronouncements, discoveries, and statistics that seemed to declare, "Black love is dead."

But I was determined not to deliver a eulogy until there was an actual funeral, so the optimistic realist in me took a deep breath, put on my reality-check glasses, and adjusted the picture.

I realized that searching for evidence of the presence of Black Love in the images produced by mainstream popular culture was like looking at myself in a fun house mirror. By their very nature the purveyors of popular culture—magazines, newspapers, the Internet, television, movies—are at odds with representations of resiliency, strength, and love in the lives of African-Americans. Dedicated to the easy answer, the disposable lie, the half-truth, the thirty-second answer, the arresting image, the quick sale of a product or an idea, the media hemisphere that surrounds us like oxygen makes pitifully little breathing room for dimensional representations of the good and the true.

When I adjusted the picture, I could see that the *Washington Post* story was merely titillating and designed to sell newspapers. I also remembered that love and commitment can flourish without a wedding ring. Neither a ceremony nor sharing the key to the same house is a guarantee of readiness to give of oneself and to be fully open to another, which is what the bonds of real love entail. Quiet as it's kept, love is not easily defined, quickly mastered, or nonchalantly tossed aside.

So I began talking to friends, colleagues, and my fellow writers about love and specifically Black Love. Because I believe so fervently in the power of the written word, pretty soon I had an idea for a book.

You are holding the answer to my question in your hands. *Don't believe the hype.* Surely that is one answer to the question I posed. African-American history is so much more than the Middle Passage, assassinated prophets, a catalog of the dead and dying, the imprisoned and the failing among us. The human spirit is never summed up or adequately captured by a litany only of its weakness, confusion, and fear. So once my fellow writers began their dialogue with me through the pieces in the book, I could see with the same old but made-new eyes: the work of a group of women in Washington, D.C., all mothers of young men who had been killed, joining with the mothers of the young men who killed their sons, in an act of mutual forgiveness and support and love, love so deep that it took the mothers of the dead youth to prison to visit and offer forgiveness to the men who had killed their sons. Friendships and unbreakable bonds have formed between these remarkable women whose grief did not close their hearts to life and redemption.

As I traveled around the country, lecturing and speaking, I became more aware of and attuned to the willingness of young African-Americans to ask themselves tough questions in seminars, at conferences, on panels, about everything from colorism, sexism, hip-hop, politics, and the future of the world they are preparing to govern and rule. These conversations rarely show up on the popular culture radar screen. But they are taking place all over the country and the world and are embedded in love of the search for truth, love of community, and love of self.

Love is all around me. In the eyes of my three-year-old grandson. In the pride I feel as I witness my thirty-year-old son's spiritual and emotional quest to consciously become a "grown man." In the prayers I offer up each morning for my family and friends. In my dedication to enlarging my students' intellectual horizons. In the work I have performed for nearly two decades, creating and expanding opportunities for Black writers through the Hurston/Wright Foundation, work that will benefit from the sales of this book.

It's All Love is divided into two sections, "That Lovin' Feeling" and "Ties That Bind." These wonderful, often wondrous expressions of love are affirmative, but never sentimental, and wrenching in their honesty.

Dwayne Betts's meditation on his eight years in prison and his reconciliation after his release with his long-absent father in "Learning the Name Dad" is a deeply moving essay about courage. Kim McLarin in "Love Is a Verb" excavates the heart and soul of the complexities of a mother's love for her children, how often it is tested and tried and what makes its endurance possible.

In "Loving Johnny Deadline," Lisa Page writes of how she met her husband, journalist Clarence Page, and the new birth they gave to each other at the beginning of their romance and continue to give each other in a long, serious, and loving marriage. Sonsyrea Tate Montgomery recounts her victory over the naysayers who said a good Black man could not be found, as well as her own demons and doubts, as she remembers how she learned to write her own love story in "One Hundred Days of Bliss." W. Ralph Eubanks, in "A Shared History," writes of his White grandfather's absolute devotion to his grandmother, a woman he married in the South at a time when interracial unions were illegal and how he made a universe of love for her where despite the insanity outside their door, she was safe. And she knew she was loved.

Working on this anthology was an honor. The spirits of these writers have enlarged and restored me, my faith in myself and in Black Love as a living, breathing source of strength that is real and resilient. I sincerely hope you, the reader, will be renewed.

I also want to thank my editors, Janet Hill and Christian Nwachukwu, Jr., and Doubleday for their continued support of my projects and the Hurston/Wright Foundation. This book was made possible because they all believe in the foundation, they believe in me, and they believe in love.

Marita Golden

PART ONE

That Lovin' Feeling

Poems

♥

Wedding Night

A. VAN JORDAN

John

let's strip off our words
to speak without our tongues. let's
try to tongue without
saying a word. let's turn speech
back into struggle tonight.

MacNolia

no, in the middle
of the night, afternoon, or
morning, let's pull up
our voice, our moan, yes, our song.
at 3:00 A.M. bring back words.

John

why bring words when we've
waited so long for silence?
why bring light when we've needed

to knead heat from our shadows?
when dark rooms call out our names?

> *MacNolia*
>
> in the shadow's heat,
> in the dark's light, in the night's
> promise of morning,
> there's always a language born
> out of the struggle to touch.

John

I don't know if I
have the words to touch the back
of your knees, the small
of your back . . . brown lines in your
palms . . . what language can frame you?

> *MacNolia*
>
> our language frames us
> as we resemble our words.
> the words we speak when
> an open window carries
> our new language to rooftops.

John

and here I thought I
was teaching you! now, you show
me a mirror in
which I see a stranger, how
good it is to meet *me* when—

       MacNolia

       when we are standing,
       nose to nose, as my wedding
       dress falls to our floor.

A Black Wedding Song

GWENDOLYN BROOKS

First dedicated to
Charles and La Tanya,
Allen and Glenda,
Haki and Safisha

I

This love is a rich cry over
The deviltries and the death.
A weapon-song. Keep it strong.

Keep it strong.
Keep it logic and Magic and lightning and Muscle.

Strong hand in strong hand, stride to
the Assault that is promised you (knowing
no armor assaults a pudding or a mush).

Here is your Wedding Day.
Here is your launch.
Come to your Wedding Song.

II

For You
I wish the kindness that romps or sorrows along.
Or kneels.
I wish you the daily forgiveness of each other.
For war comes in from the World
And puzzles a darling duet—
tangles tongues,
tears hearts, mashes minds;
there will be the need to forgive.

I wish you jewels of black love.

Come to your Wedding Song.

Autumn Poems

NIKKI GIOVANNI

the heat
you left with me
last night
still smolders
the wind catches
your scent
and refreshes
my senses

i am a leaf
falling from your tree
upon which i was
impaled

Haiku

KWAME ALEXANDER

If I am your heart
Imagine me inside
Beating, pumping, loving

Kupenda

KWAME ALEXANDER

I have never been a slave
Yet, I know I am whipped
I have never escaped underground
Yet, the night knows my journey

I have never been to Canada
Yet I've crossed your border

If I were a poet in love
I'd say that
    with you
I have found that new place
Where romance
    is just a beginning
And freedom
    is our end.

Untitled

E. ETHELBERT MILLER

On your left hand
a paper cut near your thumb.

I notice small things
because I love you so much.

After Midnight

JALAL

For Milton

When opportunity knocks
I open my door
After midnight.
You appear
First in a line
Of homeless men standing
Outside a shelter.
You enter my apartment
Unannounced.

The neighbors on my floor
They come and go
They stand between the elevator
And my door,

Waiting for a way out,
They curse me,
"That Black faggot bitch got crackheads coming up in here."
Peering through their peepholes
They don't love us
Or even know how the pairing of two Black men
Is so much greater than the rumors they've reduced us to,
Rumors I hear when I enter the bar
Where no handsome stranger flirts with me,
Rumors that litter the streets we walk
And pollute the eyes around us
With self-disgust and self-pity.

When opportunity knocks
I let you in,
You open
My refrigerator door,
You take
Sacrifices packaged
And ready to be eaten
I run your bath water, wash your clothes
Lie in my bed with clean sheets,
But there are places within me
French kisses and erections cannot reach.

When opportunity knocks
America sees shiftless garbage walking
Through my door—a crackhead, a killer, a thief,
Another nigga racing past them in disgrace.
I live beyond the expiration date men
See stamped on my face.
I'm a forty-year-old Black gay man
Living a life challenged by HIV disease.

What makes me different from those who would
Exploit you,
Knowing you are
Unemployed, homeless,
And a crackhead on call who sells his body
For a rock, food, and shelter?
I worry about you
You don't have to fuck me
Or get fucked in the mouth for a meal.
I won't wet your appetite for self-destruction
With my cum,
I won't buy you crack
Or give you money.
I will grieve each time
You tell me you can't stop
Smoking crack
And that you like your life
Just as it is.

When opportunity knocks
You fuck me with the sincerity and passion
Of a condemned man in prayer.
Isolation binds us
Soul mates locked in Hell's hotel room
And this is our wedding night.
Am I liberated or lonely,
Lucky or reluctant
Free or afraid to be hurt again,
Discarded by men
ISO (in search of) personal ad playmates
Wanted—Black men, must be younger, must be lighter, must
    be darker, more

Muscular, more masculine, more status conscious, more
    attractive than . . .

After midnight,
When opportunity knocks,
I want you to find a way station of comfort
Not at the bottom of a beggar's cup
I want us to give more to our lives
Demand more of ourselves
Than despair.

Nonfiction

♥

Lamu Lover

DOREEN BAINGANA

I AM ON AN ISLAND in the Indian Ocean. The sun is strong and constant; it is holding me up. There is wide blue water to soak in, salty and warm. Spicy Swahili pilau and fish, cold beer, and a warm man. A slender young man as dark and smooth and supple as the sun is bright. Issanda is lemony sweet. I am so far away from my life that regular rules do not apply. We are here, with our bodies, what can't we do? What can we do?

Seduce each other. He was in my workshop; I was the leader or facilitator. It would no longer be unethical for us to venture closer, the workshop is over, no grades were given, and now, on this island, Lamu, we are all writers here, together. But just last week I acted like I had the knowledge; since I was published, I pontificated and was in charge. He listened, not exactly at my knee, but close to that position, it may have been easier to impress him. When he walked into the workshop on the first day, my mind went *yummy,* but hid it in the very back corner of my mind where thoughts that pop up unbidden are stamped down and locked away. As the workshop continued, I couldn't help but admire his physical beauty, his eyes that were sharp with intelligence, though a little red from the dust, bright sunlight, or late-night drinks, who knew? I noticed with secret delight his sharpish-flatish nose that is a bit like mine; and his neatly cut toenails that are a tawny color that matches perfectly the coffee of his feet and the even darker leather sandals. I was amused and impressed by his effort with English, which he is still learning, and which comes out with a French accent, not a Congolese one, as I expected. His ability to make jokes in a foreign language, betraying a sly humor that belies his boyish face. His tiny teeth shielded by lips a little too large, a little too much, but by whose standards? I asked myself. Musing about that was pleasurable too. I was also genuinely moved by his writing, which would have struck me even if nothing else did. Thank goodness it was not wrong to voice admiration for his words. To the contrary. It was easy then to enjoy the nurturing that is part of teaching, of both him and my other students.

And now he is no longer my student. About fifty writers and I came from the United States to join about twenty African writers at a seminar in Nairobi. After a week, we flew from the Kenyan capital to the Indian Ocean coast, an hour's quick trip, for a writing retreat on the island of Lamu. We land on a dusty airstrip by the shore, with a long low shed for an airport, and, walking, push through a wall of hot humidity, across long brown elephant grass to a wooden, rickety pier. At the end of it are two dhows ready to take us across the water to Lamu. Yes, dhows, those age-old wooden boats that plied the route between the East African coast and the Persian Gulf for centuries and led to the intermingling of Arab and African that became the Swahili people, culture, and language. We will live among them for a week, soaking in the sweet and spice of their hybridity that is clearly revealed by their skin color. The islanders are a kaleidoscope of browns that recall the word for *brown* in my language, Runyankore—*itaka*—which means the earth, mud, loam, or soil.

On the dhow, a giant creaky brown bowl, under a huge khaki-colored flapping sail, between the wavy carpet of dark blue water and canopy above of brilliant blue sky; stroked by the half-understood Swahili shouts of half-naked sinewy sailors; brimming inside with beginning-of-foreign-holiday excitement, as tingly as the salty breeze, amid all this, somehow, even more: Issanda is standing next to me. The jokes we shared in class continue, or perhaps the flirting starts. He says, "My favorite teacher!"

It is time to make it clear. "I am not your teacher anymore; I am your friend." We go silent. I can only guess what he was thinking, and that is the scary thrill of another person, an *other*. I cannot enter his mind nor he mine, but I wouldn't want it any other way. My mind is a place of private little plays, where my character adopts the scene by having me emphasize *your friend* with a bold and meaningful look. In reality, I look out over the blue expanse to hide my face, too embarrassed to make a deliberate pass. Still, I feel a tremor of flirtation between us, that nervousness of wish that is a reaching out, hesitation, and prickles of sweat. Something not yet, but could be and is becoming, or not.

Our group more or less writes in the mornings, eats lunch and swims at the beach in the afternoons, has dinner and talks into the wee hours of the night on various rooftops overlooking the wide ocean. We take dhow rides, explore the surrounding islands, shop, meet with writing mentors, or lie around and read in clusters large and small, or alone. Bliss, in short, but my body wants more.

One afternoon Issanda and I are part of a group that takes a boat to Manda beach. He does not spend much time in the water, but wades out in loose white and red swimming trunks.

I note his lithe body and hairless chest with approval, and his solidly dark arms that are muscled in a natural, not exaggerated, steroidish way. His legs are spindly thin, but by now anything that could be a fault is a plus: a confirmation of his uniqueness and my uniqueness too, because it proves I am not shallow. I can stare freely because everyone is half dressed and in full view of one another, but I would not be surprised if he felt my stare like bores through his back. I am sure even he takes this chance the beach offers for full-body scans. We are half naked already but protected by being in public.

The top piece of my aqua blue swimsuit covers my rather flabby forty-year-old belly, but something about this island makes me unself-conscious. Who cares about knock-knees, thighs rich with cellulite that would be more useful on my boobs, and hair that puts the dread in dreadlocks? Unlike Dutch courage, Kenyan courage is a heady brew of sun, sea, and the confidence I gain on (well, near enough to) the black soil I grew up on, with a topping of extremely smart and funny writers who admire my work, and I theirs. Potent stuff. I swim in it and, with each stroke, reach for more and relish the reaching.

I follow Issanda out of the water after a few minutes so that it is not so obvious I am after him. My inner cat is prowling, sure-footed, as I join him on a canopy made of roughly hewn poles covered with beige sisal matting, sandy on the skin.

"You didn't swim much."

"I don't swim very well." He is shy about it, which is so sweet.

"I'll teach you."

This is a role I relish. It is an opening I want to enter like a man. The others join us in the shade, and we joke and laugh and are generally relaxed. Issanda remains in the background, a little silent. The resident clown fuels his performance with vodka straight from the bottle. I take sips of it, and it shoots straight to the center of my head, making the play in my mind sparkle and squirm to get out, get real. The salt water drying my skin gives me a good excuse; I take out my sunscreen lotion and hold it out to Issanda with too coy a smile.

"Can you spread some on my back please?"

"But of course, Doreen!" He moves over quickly. Oh, the accent, the willingness, the way he laughs at himself because he is so obviously willing. The guys laugh approvingly; the girls giggle. A man can be publicly willing and as lustful as he wants to be; in fact he should be lusty if he is a real man. A woman must be coy, act unwilling, must woo by running away, but not too fast, of course. Thankfully, I am beyond all that, liberated by past frustration.

His touch is surprisingly soft. The cream is deliciously cool as he spreads it over my shoulders and back, but it is not a sexual caress. His hands are polite, and my skin, all smiles and relief. I am glad for the tentative tiny steps, for time. Skin and skin greet each other, saying more because we say nothing, and nothing is perfect right then. Still, I want more and desire is pleasurable too.

A little later. "Okay, it's time for your swimming lesson."

We get back in the water, I in the lead. He sputters and splashes around like a little kid, which makes me laugh out loud. He can swim but not well, so I show him how to move his arms better, how to breathe, showing off some too. Isn't that what teaching is? We enjoy the focus together on something else besides each other, which paradoxically is one of the most intense ways to be together. I see that he must learn to trust the water, so I ask him to lie back in it and float as I hold him up. The water gives me a perfect excuse to wrap my arms beneath and around his body.

"Relax, I have you. Let the water hold you too," I say. He

does. I turn him slowly around in the warm seawater and tell him to empty his mind, all is clear. To simply float between the blue sky and blue ocean. I turn him the other way slowly, as I was taught was a form of water shiatsu. We are silent together, all feeling. The play in my head and reality are meeting; they are becoming one. We switch positions, and this is no longer a lesson: Class is over, and a serious game has begun.

We find an excuse to leave the group; the lunch offered at the beach is too expensive, we say. We prefer to go back to Lamu and eat at a basic and very cheap nontouristy restaurant. We are joined by the only other Congolese among the writers, who has become Issanda's buddy. This makes it less obvious to everyone else and to us that this is an escape, and we spend the rest of the day a threesome, talking, eating, drinking, laughing. We wander through narrow ancient streets that are more like tunnels, squashed and shadowed as they are between four-storied walls. Small stall fronts add to the claustrophobic feeling, as they are packed tight with similar cheap colorful plastic items and hairy brown coconuts, grayish cassava, pink onions, and other vegetables and fruits that are smaller and drier versions of the ones we have back in Uganda or the large shiny engineered ones in American stores. We skip over open sewer streams, pass by little raggedy children with large soulful eyes and shy smiles sitting on doorsteps or dodge them as they scamper through the streets. Bearded men mill about wearing long white gowns with Muslim caps and beards or shirts and colorful *kikoi* cloths wrapped waist down. The women are completely covered from head to toe in black *bui-bui* or wear long dresses and cover their heads with shiny, slippery scarves. All you have to look at, as they avert their eyes, are their feet, decorated with intricate henna patterns and sparkly nail polish, hinting coyly at more. The culture permits men and children to be friendlier than women to strangers, and so they greet you with a welcome *Karibu Lamu* and a smile.

Issanda orders our lunch in Swahili, and we sit on metal tables and chairs and share our food with large flies. A television flickers faintly and unhappily in the background as almost everyone ignores the blurry football game. The fried rice and meat stew is mediocre; I would have preferred a tourist restaurant on the busy street along the water, but I want to be with Issanda, and I am. I want to touch his arm as I talk to him and watch him eat, completely engrossed, but I cannot. Not yet. We three move on, taking over the empty third floor of Lamu's famous Petley's bar. We spread out on huge, beautifully carved mahogany chairs and cushions covered with brightly colored cotton cloth that obeys an unspoken law on African design: It must blind you with brilliant colors and wildly exaggerated patterns. The vast blue ocean outside provides a pleasant contrast, and we open wide tall windows to let in the strong wind and sounds from the busy pier and settle down to more talk, more drink, and more laughter, our rising flirtation buffered by his friend.

What do we talk about? Congo, America, Kenya, our various journeys, writing, our workshop, and more. Issanda is the interpreter, as F does not speak English and I do not speak French. He relishes his role, and we go back and forth, striving to understand each other, laughing at the effort and mistakes, getting frustrated, then rising yet again to the challenge, showing off like birds in heat, mental jousting replacing the fluttering of feathers and trill of song. It is a primer for the possible physical engagement to come, that sweet struggle and strain. The air breathes with our hidden and tremulous anticipation, perhaps, perhaps, oh, please.

Despite us, I cannot ignore the hugeness of the ocean outside. It seems to be an arm's length away as it charges forward and falls back in that constant and infinite rhythm. Ours are mere words and mortal wants, but over and all around us, long before we existed and long after we will cease to exist, the ocean will come crashing to the shore and slide back into itself, relentlessly. The thought soothes and silences me. As the sun recedes, something shifts in the room, and our talk subsides. The wind gets louder; we close the windows. F decides to leave us, saying he is tired, perhaps of being the proverbial third wheel. We are alone, we are on an island. The sky turns as dark as the ocean.

We can only move forward by walking back through the narrow streets. They are dark, but it is safe, a cocoon, a womb. I am with Issanda and that is enough. The good Muslims do not drink and carouse late into the night, and so the streets are ours. They are now narrow winding corridors in an immense gray, dusty house, and they all mysteriously merge into one. Issanda and I, tipsier than we thought, cannot find the way back to our separate hotels. We turn small sharp corners and end up where we began, giggling at our silliness but not at all afraid of this strange place that has become one of Calvino's invisible cities. We leap over the same sewage drains, squeeze past the same donkey that refuses to budge from the middle of the street but simply stands there, head bowed dejectedly. To be lost with Issanda is magical. Everything is. How to express this initial thrill of attraction that makes anything you do together special, imbues it with a sharp and sensuous quality? Even cutting our fingernails together would be unearthly because it would be *our* moment.

Issanda says he does know the way to *his* hotel, and I give in so easily. He is not a person to resist; there is simply no place for negativity. We turn, hold hands, and walk to his dark hotel, bang on the heavy carved wooden door until someone opens, climb up steep curving uneven steps, pass the courtyard with bushes and cement stoops made for chats, but also perfect for mosquitoes. The beds have mosquito nets, and Issanda's has a top of green and white *kanga* cloth attached to swaths of white net curtain that surround the bed, giving it a bridal feel with a Swahili flair. I creep under the curtain into his bed fully clothed. I am suddenly shy rather than lusty, as if anticipation were better or at least safer than what was anticipated, because it brings everything closer to the end. This has always been my fear: the end, even before the beginning. I cannot explain this and do not even try. He does not insist on anything, and so we sleep.

Only a day later, lust grows stronger than fear. His lips are the largest I have ever kissed. He uses them delicately. He says my name with every sentence. I act like a man, demanding and impatient. He takes it with confidence and more than enough lust and thrust for me. Dare I confess that after white lovers, the pure blackness of his skin is heightened pleasure in and of itself? I have taken delight in the contrast of dark skin entangled with white, but that has now awoken me to what I used to take for granted before: the beauty of black on black, and how skin turns in the light or dark to coffee, loam, red soil, lava rock, all sorts of tea colors, on and on. I luxuriate in the constancy of Issanda's color, doubly aware that it is mine too. I am greedy for his smooth, almost childish hairlessness, the feel of his supple young muscles moving under my palms, the way we move together. Much later, when he slips his jeans up over his slim hips, my belly jolts with lust all over again.

And we talk, of course. I tell him I have always felt I was too much for most people, but not him, for some reason. When I was about eight, my father called me Kamabati because my constant chatter was like the clanging of rain on metal roofing, *mabati*. I laugh too loudly, dance *and* sleep too much; I am much too opinionated for a woman. Issanda says he can take it, which of course is the right answer, but I believe him. I want to be myself with him, instead of trying to be someone else, as I usually do with men I fall for. This is different, perhaps because I am more than ten years older than he is. I feel he is attracted to me because of my experience, my accomplishments, my opinions, even when I am being a smart-ass. I wonder why for so long I have tried to fit into a fake female mold, to be demure, to assume the position of lesser, to not want to outshine my partner, especially in public. Not this time. Or perhaps not yet, since I do not know him enough, but I can't help but hope.

Issanda does not take me lying down; he is razor-sharp and ironic and funny and melancholy all mixed. He must be even more so in French. I want to tell my friends everything he says, like how one evening he pretended to be Senegalese, but then we were regaled with Senegalese stereotypes (that are not worth repeating) for hours on end from some beach boys. Issanda whispered to me, "I chose the wrong country," and I could not stop giggling. I know, I am like a mother so besotted by her child that she finds his every move fascinating. But we go deeper quickly. He tells me about his move by necessity from Congo to Burundi to Senegal, and I tell him about mine, almost by compulsion, from Uganda to Italy to America and back. He says he is not at home anywhere, and may not want to be. Neither am I; we are ambivalent about the places we have chosen to live and the countries that claim us. He has seen the dark sick side of human nature, in the war in western Congo, things he has yet to tell me but has hinted at. There is so much more about Issanda that I need and yearn to learn.

I jokingly tell him seducing me was so easy, all it took was one night of no. It was I who pursued him; I deliberately turned longing and the play in my head into reality, instead of having him chase and catch me, thus making me a prize worth having, as women usually do. He disagrees, saying *he* pursued me but was so subtle that he tricked me into thinking I was the one on the chase. We laugh and harvest yet another precious moment of mutual appreciation and satisfaction.

But. Great sex and the springing up of a new friendship on a tiny island of paradise do not a relationship make. We may be foolish to try to build on that fantastic (in all senses) foundation. He is back in Senegal, in school as well as teaching, and I am back in the United States, working and writing. No amount of phone calls, e-mails, and IMing changes the fact that we are not physically together, getting to know each other in a concrete and everyday way. Perhaps not being with each other is what makes this so enticing. Is this just a drama of longing?

We almost could have been neighbors once. He grew up in eastern Congo, and my ancestral home is in western Uganda, but both of us are so far from there now. We don't even speak the same language: He speaks French and Swahili, and I, English, because of a colonial accident or, rather, colonial grab and takeover. I could have spoken Swahili, but don't, having spent too much time in school immersed in English and having considered Swahili an instrument of terror, as it was the language of Idi Amin's army and all the ones that have followed since. Our mother tongues belong to the Bantu family, but we don't speak them well enough and might not have understood each other even if we did. So near, geographically and culturally, and yet so far because of history. Once, as we struggled to understand each other, he said, "Look at what they have done to us," and we laughed at our mock victimization that is based on truth.

He can speak some English, thank God, but my French is nonexistent, and now my love project is to learn it. I tell him to speak to me in French because it sounds so romantic; who am I to resist clichés? It is also not the language I argue in, fend off creditors, talk to my boss or worry in; it is not part of my real life. French to me now represents something budding and beautiful, like the word *bisous,* little kiss, which to me is a bee buzzing around a flower, then zeroing in for a delightful sting. French is Issanda's voice down the phone line, telling me how much he misses me. It is the memory of long French kisses.

But. I am forty-one, he is twenty-nine. Despite my confidence when we were together, my age gives me low-level trauma, while his age, I admit, is something I want to get drunk on. Yet one more reason why I enjoy his young supple body is that I am acutely aware that mine won't stay this way much longer. He does not need to work up energy or try to store it, and he takes being physically flexible for granted. I don't. Can I compete with nubile young babes? I'm told by many, including Issanda, that I do not look or act my age, but when that is said to reassure me, it underlines the issue. More practically, I want a child, and it is now or never for me, but not for him. But we hardly know each other. I would like us to have a few years all to ourselves. When I tell Issanda my exact age, months after Lamu, he says, "Then we have to make a baby soon." That is about the dearest thing I have been told by a man. Whether it is sweet talk or genuine longing, I am not sure, but I love him even more for saying so.

Can the beauty of how this began be enough to conquer the obvious obstacles? The island and color and lust and spark and skin? After that peak of pleasure, we are now in a vast plain that is months of distance. What is on the other side? How do we get there? We all know that love, or infatuation, fades, but what can grow is friendship. Do we have that? Not quite. Not yet. How can we cultivate it? How can we make fragile frothy feelings become farmed land, as steady as the seasons? Solid, fruitful, full, and into the future?

We could have let it remain a delectable liaison on a tropical island, let it become a delightful memory, and I would not regret it, oh, no. We did not have to complicate it by taking it out of Eden with us, but we have. We rubbed beautifully against each other and birthed a living fire. Now we must keep on blowing, dreaming, and making it real, just like we did on Lamu.

After She Left

WILL BESTER

THERE ARE THINGS you understand when a woman you love has walked out the door. If you are awake and alone, you understand that it takes eight hours to get from 3:00 A.M. to 4:00 A.M. There are phone calls I could make, visits that might momentarily dull the pain of her absence, but I convince myself that if I am to learn the lesson before me, I must give birth to a new me without anesthesia.

I am a good Black man, one of those brothers who we perennially lament are in short supply and high demand. I am tall and attractive. I have an advanced degree from a premier university; I have good credit and I give back to my community. I live in a city where there are at least three eligible Black women per every eligible Black man. And I am completely alone.

My friends see my story as a success. Raised in a home rife with violence and substance abuse, I have never raised my hand to a woman in anger or used an illegal drug. My two brothers have battled lifelong addictions. I have a law degree and the respect of my peers. People frequently tell me that I am an inspiration. It has become increasingly difficult to accept that compliment without feeling like a fraud. The truth is that some of us simply hide our scars better. In one of my earliest memories, I awoke to the sounds of an uncle and his wife fighting late at night. The next morning as I left for school, I found my uncle lying on the couch, his shirt stained crimson from where his wife had stabbed him with a pair of scissors, a wound that would require surgery and weeks of recovery. This was not the only time I witnessed such episodes. On the surface, I appear to have escaped unscathed.

The woman who loved me knew better. She knows that I do silence the way my brothers did coke binges—starting off in small fragments of time, believing that this is a momentary lapse only to find that hours or days have gone by and you have been trapped in the same unhealthy place. She knows that I am intelligent and the law comes easily to me, but away from the public world where I thrive, I am emotionally dyslexic. The paradox is that I am exuberant about the accomplishments of the children I tutor and open and encouraging to the people in the community who need my services. But alone with a woman whom I love I am as expressive as a television on mute.

A friend once told me that shutting a woman out is nearly as bad as hitting her. His words stayed with me, they told me that even though I never raised my hand—or even my voice—I had carried on that tradition of violence in my home. I came by the silence honestly. The men I looked up to as a child were uniformly reserved, brooding figures. They withheld themselves from the world—and especially from those closest to them—and kept themselves exiled behind furrowed brows. I remember my uncles whose yeses held the gruffness of other men's noes and who grunted appreciation for some act of kindness from their wives. I wondered why it was that men seemed so unhappy and assumed that it was part of the unfolding mystery of adulthood. I assumed that when I was a man, I too would learn to keep the world at arm's length. My story is not unique, generations of Black men have literally internalized this lesson. Solemnity has become the cornerstone of our manhood. It was no coincidence that both of those uncles died of cancer. Their deaths were tragedies and metaphors.

My woman left because of the silence. She tearfully told

me that she was tired of being alone even when we were to-gether, tired of waiting for me to show up and summon the courage to smile and be open to her. In a moment of painful introspection, I admit to myself that each woman who has ever left me has done so for the same reason. I have come to un-derstand the difficult truth that even with the ever-dwindling numbers of available Black men, a woman who values herself will not settle for the cruel quiet of a man who is only partially present. I have been taught that eligible and available are not necessarily the same thing.

Still there are times when the facade cracks. A few months ago I was playing with my eighteen-month-old cousin in my basement when his mother called him up to dinner. He be-gan crawling up the stairs. After he successfully mounted each step, he would turn and wave good-bye to me. By the time he found his way to the kitchen, I was in tears, overwhelmed by the purity of a gesture from a Black male soul too young to have calluses. Had I been able to admit the beauty of that mo-ment, to call my woman and share it with her, maybe I would not be alone. But I held back.

So this is where I am, in the dark distance between 3:00 A.M. and 4:00 A.M., waiting for late to become early. Listening to my own silences and knowing that I would sleep if she were here again curled up with her back pressed against my chest. It is the middle of the night, and sleep is miles in the distance, so I make use of my time and offer a prayer that my little cousin never sees in me what I saw in my uncles, that he never learns to hide himself from himself. I pray that it is not too late to share my soul with a woman who has walked out. And I pray that God makes my heart as open as a child waving good-bye as he climbs up the stairs.

Loving Johnny Deadline

LISA PAGE

*T*HIS MORNING I lay next to my husband in bed, the way I have so many times before, listening to him breathe. It was before dawn, and the room was dark. I listened to the ticking of the bedside clock and to the sound of the freight train several blocks over, rattling through the inky blackness. I listened to the man snoring next to me and wrapped my arm around his body. His fingers intertwined mine automatically, even though he was asleep. I forced myself to pull back the covers, knowing I would fall back to sleep myself otherwise. I got up and found his shoes in the bathroom, black and polished on the white tile floor, found his keys on the sink, his tie slung over the towel rack. I went downstairs to grind the coffee.

This is my life with Clarence.

We have been together for over twenty years, but as I write this, it feels like a lie. I feel like he was always in my life—feel like I was always in his life too. There was never a time we led separate lives, had childhoods, other relationships. We've always been together, even as I know that's not true either. We live in this old house, outside Washington, with its wraparound porch and its high ceilings, like we've always been here.

But there is evidence to the contrary. Our son, for instance, is only seventeen. We have not always been married. The past is full of people who are long dead—Clarence's parents, an ex-wife, and old friends. We led single lives once, loved other people, and made mistakes. Whereas today our lives are made up of ink stains and coffee rings, newsprint and talk radio playing in the background. But it wasn't always this way.

I FIRST SAW Clarence doing a stand-up on local television in the early 1980s. He was in my living room, via satellite feed, holding a microphone that read "Channel 2 NEWS." He wore red-rimmed glasses, a bow tie, and suspenders, and he sported a mustache. In those days it was a rarity to see a Black man reporting the evening news, and I remember thinking, Who is that guy?

CBS had hired him away from his job as a reporter for the *Chicago Tribune* and made him its community affairs director.

I was in my twenties then, trying to make it as a writer myself, working as an editorial assistant at *Playboy* magazine. I spent my days transcribing tapes by Hunter Thompson and fielding telephone calls from Roy Blount, Jr., David Halberstam, and other journalists who wrote for the magazine. In those days *Playboy* was still trying to be *The New Yorker,* even as it was a skin magazine, with photos of naked women sandwiched in between choice fiction, interviews, and major features. I cut my teeth there, learning about layouts, dummy books, and bylines. And in my spare time I wrote for weeklies and an arts magazine.

The columnist Bob Greene was a friend of my boss. He wrote about a character named Johnny Deadline, a sort of superhero reporter in a trench coat. In those days it seemed like reporters were everywhere.

Chicago was on the precipice of major change. Harold Washington had become the first Black mayor in the city's history, and doors were flying open in corporate offices everywhere. In a city with a reputation for the worst segregation in the country, there was a feeling of opportunity electrifying the atmosphere. The media reflected this: The head of CBS was a Black man, and Black editors were at the Chicago bureaus of *Time, Newsweek,* and *Playboy* too. I myself was promoted at *Playboy* nine months after being hired by the magazine.

But there was a dark cloud amidst all this good news. Leanita McClain, the first Black female member of the Chicago *Tribune*'s editorial board, committed suicide. This was a woman with her own column in the paper, who was garnering national attention, when she died. She had also been married to Clarence Page.

This was front-page news. Leanita McClain had grown up in the projects and climbed into the upper middle class, only to take her own life at the age of thirty-two. She wrote about her identity crisis as a token Black woman in a White male world in a column titled "The Burden of the Black Middle Class": "I have a foot in each world, but I cannot fool myself about either. I can see the transparent deceptions of some Whites and the bitter helplessness of some Blacks. I know how tenuous my grip on one way of life is, and how strangling the grip of the other life can be." Her eloquence echoed what many of us felt at that time. She was also brutally frank about the racism she found in her White colleagues during Harold Washington's mayoral campaign. Mike Miner's *Chicago Reader* profile mentioned her divorce from Clarence Page, two years prior to her death. The piece included Clarence's description of his late ex-wife—how he first noticed her freckles, light complexion, and hazel eyes when he met her in the *Tribune* offices. Reading it gave me chills—he could've been describing me.

While I had never met Leanita, I was touched by her death. Her struggle with depression, a secret she kept throughout her life, was suddenly public information. It was a story that rippled through Chicago's publishing world.

And at *Playboy* magazine she was a hot topic of conversation that went on for weeks, especially among the sisters. The editorial department was abuzz with innuendo. How could she have had so much outward success and still been so unhappy?

Six months later I met Clarence for the first time. The *Tribune* had lured him away from CBS with the promise of his own column and seat on the editorial board. He effectively took Leanita's place. When I asked him, some years later, how this made him feel, he said he saw the situation as a "blood stripe."

"What?" I asked.

"It's a term I learned in the army. You get a blood stripe when you replace someone who died in combat."

OUR FIRST MEETING happened at a party hosted by *Chicago* magazine, celebrating the Nelson Algren literary award. I'd gone completely on the spur of the moment. *Playboy* had a nonexistent dress code, and I'd gone to work in jeans and a sweater. Friends from the fiction department told me there was a party at *Chicago* magazine, and I initially refused to go, knowing I was underdressed. But I knew many writers would be there and so relented and went to the party after work.

Chicago magazine's offices were alive with writers, that autumn night, ones I'd met before like novelist Leon Forrest and poet Sterling Plumpp. I had so much fun, working the room, sipping white wine, I completely forgot I was so casually dressed.

Eventually I recognized Clarence Page across the room, wearing a suit and tie, and staring at me.

I smiled and shook his hand.

I said, "I think you're wonderful! I just read your piece on Louis Farrakhan." Clarence had written an exquisite profile for *Chicago* magazine that included interviews with Minister Farrakhan and Malcolm X's widow, Betty Shabazz, among others. We talked about it before I made my way to some other section of the room and realized he was following me.

"Might you be available for lunch sometime?" he asked.

And that was the beginning.

I should say here that in all honesty, I knew Clarence was asking me to lunch in terms of a date. But I ignored this at the time. I was married to someone else then, a guy I'd known since I was sixteen years old. And being married was extremely useful to me, even as I was unhappy in my marriage. Working for *Playboy* meant men got ideas about me when they found out where I worked. I often flashed my wedding ring in those days.

But when Clarence found out I was married, he surprised me by wanting to be my friend. I fed him stories about *Playboy* that he used in his column. He gave me suggestions for ways I could pitch my own stories to other magazines. We met for lunch, for drinks, and occasionally for dinner. I liked him because while he loved to talk, he also really listened. *Playboy* had promoted me into its circulation/promotion department, and I was doing publicity junkets and writing press releases. I could tell him about my new life, about the trips around the country *Playboy* sent me on. I could tell him about O.J. Simpson buying champagne for the Girls of Texas, in Houston one wild night, about the Library of Congress censoring the Braille edition of the magazine.

I could not talk to the man I was married to. My professional success rubbed him the wrong way. I had stories for days that he didn't want to hear. So I saved them for Clarence and told myself it was okay to do.

Clarence needed a friend. His mother had died shortly before Leanita killed herself. He'd lost two of the most important women in his life in one year. His stories about his marriage became a touchstone between us. He called his former wife Lee and talked about their years together, about how alone she felt early in her life. I learned she'd left the projects for Northwestern University, on full scholarship, and had won one award after another, once she began her journalism career. But the awards and the recognition only served to fuel her sense of alienation and despair. I learned she was suicidal, even during her college years, before she ever met Clarence. And during their short marriage she tried to commit suicide several times. He had been at a loss as to what to do. She begged him to send her to a mental institution, a request he refused, thinking she was mentally coherent—how could she consider herself so emotionally unstable? Finally, after their divorce, she went into therapy and went on medication. But it turned out she was saving up the pills, and one rainy night she took them all.

These stories cut me like a knife. I had a mentally ill family member myself. I knew what it was like to live with a person who suffered terrible bouts of depression in secret. I understood the burden of leading a public life where you pretended everything was fine, all the time knowing the opposite was true. Where friends of mine speculated about Leanita's suicide and how she'd been driven crazy by Chicago politics, Clarence described a different story of loneliness, confusion, and despair. He'd clearly been in love with her and was devastated by her death.

But on occasion he'd take on a different persona, where he smoked More cigarettes and jauntily referred to her as his "ex." He talked about his "Bachelorhood #2 Phase" and told me I looked "adorable." I'd recoil—this seemed so out of character from this man nine years older that I was becoming so fond of. Seeing my reaction, he would eventually relax into the man who was my friend.

Meanwhile, a *Playboy* editor named Walter Lowe had assigned a feature about the Atlanta child murders to the writer James Baldwin. That magazine story became a book called *The Evidence of Things Not Seen*. I set up a meeting with the editor and Clarence, resulting in another column. And we were both introduced to James Baldwin.

We talked about other writers too, like Ntozake Shange, Michelle Wallace, and Gwendolyn Brooks. Clarence discussed Alice Walker and the male characters in her novel *The Color Purple* on national television. He debated novelist Ishmael Reed on *Good Morning America*. Much like Ntozake Shange's play *For Colored Girls Who Have Considered Suicide When the Rainbow Is Enuf*, *The Color Purple* was deemed a feminist diatribe celebrating female empowerment at the expense of Black men. Clarence thought that was ridiculous and said so. This led to more national attention, more TV appearances, and a higher professional profile. And in response, he started to physically change. He shaved off his mustache and got rid of the red frames. He got rid of his bow tie and started wearing tortoiseshell frames, silk ties, beautiful suits. It seemed like he was better-looking every day.

Then one Friday night, after drinks at Riccardo's, a famous watering hole for journalists, Clarence walked me to the subway at Grand and State. As we said good-night, he kissed me.

It was such a romantic moment! I was completely surprised. But then I had to ride the train north and make the walk to my apartment where I knew my husband was waiting for me. I had to go through the whole weekend, pretending like that kiss had never happened. I felt like I was falling in love with Clarence, but I had to act like he was the farthest thing from my mind.

I decided I couldn't see him again, except in the daytime. We could only meet for lunch from then on. Clarence understood. He said he was content to be my friend. He didn't want to be a problem in my life. He would do anything to keep our relationship alive, and if it could only be platonic, so be it. And while I let on that my marriage was unhappy and had been for some time, he said, "You ought to give it the old college try."

Two months later I left my first husband.

THAT WAS OVER twenty years ago. Clarence and I have been together ever since. Between the deadlines and the sound bites, we have forged a life. Our kitchen is full of bills and correspondence that pile up between the fruit bowl and the Rolodex. The front page, the jump, and the op-ed spread themselves like cloths on the table. Blogs and Web sites, e-mail, and dates on the calendar make up small talk, while background noise is supplied by NPR or the *Tom Joyner Morning Show*. The newsprint stains our fingers, as we crack our boiled eggs and taste the coffee. And other equipment is at the ready, including the laptop, the trio, the cell. (I remember when he was a Filofax man. Those were the days.) Our house is full of remnants from our travels that are displayed in every room: stained glass from Chicago, a starfish from Cozumel, batik from Zimbabwe. Our son wanders in, a red iPod in his ears, and gets ready for school.

In the evening, after work, Clarence has a cigarette on the back deck, where he goes with pen and paper, and I can see the first gray hairs sprouting on the back of his head. The smell of the smoke gives me pleasure even as I close the door and go back to the stove and check the burners, shake the salt. I can see him through the window, flicking ashes into a flower pot as he puts his feet up on a garden chair. The land behind our house spreads out below him, an expanse of lawn and shrubbery that leads to the back woods some yards away.

Is it always this idyllic? By no means. We've had our share of ups and downs. But our strength is conversation and the time we take to share it. Listening and talking are two things that go together, but sometimes voices are raised and feelings are hurt. Getting bent out of shape goes with the territory, I've learned. We are both strong-willed people with fierce political beliefs. We have our differences. We need our space. But so far we always come back to talk about the details of our day. The argument fades. The place mats are set.

I grew to know Leanita McClain's parents and her two sisters. Clarence compiled a collection of her columns and published them in a book entitled *A Foot in Each World*. His own columns were nominated for a Pulitzer Prize. He won in 1987. That was how we came to Washington—he began doing so much TV here, including the *MacNeil/Lehrer NewsHour, The McLaughlin Group,* and *Lead Story* at BET. The *Chicago Tribune* transferred him to its Washington bureau in 1991, and we've been here ever since.

Clarence got to know my family too. They embraced him even as they were initially surprised by our relationship, because of my first marriage. In time they adjusted.

Our son is already a writer. While he is still in high school, he has a byline on a student newspaper and is working on his first novel. Now all three of us fight for the floor when we have political discussions, and sometimes I throw up my hands and give up. The two of them are so alike, I need to take them on separately.

I have cobbled out my own career and forged my own space. That's been important to do, in terms of having an identity of my own. So that when we come back together at the end of the day, I've got my own stories to tell.

This is my life with Clarence.

One Hundred Days of Bliss

SONSYREA TATE MONTGOMERY

TO: god@universe.com
FROM: sonsyrea@peace.com
SUBJECT: Many Thanks

Dear God,

You know I've wanted to write about a beautiful love
since I was a little girl. I've wanted to write about the
wonderful men in my life who weren't like the men in the
Black classics I read—molesting a child and beating wives
like in Alice Walker's *The Color Purple.* I wanted to write
about men I knew—even as a little girl—who were different
from the men in Zora Neale Hurston's "Their Eyes Were
Watching God," men who drained women of all their value.
You know I wanted to write about men who didn't torture
women like the men in Ntozake Shange's *For Colored Girls
Who Have Considered Suicide When the Rainbow Is Enuf.*

God, You know I wanted to tell stories different from
the ones my grandmothers and aunts told: that most men
ain't worth a damn, but if you can luck up and get yourself
a good one, make him marry you and hold on for dear life.
I was even determined to put to paper something other than
the hard-luck stories I shared with my girlfriends in our
early twenties and thirties.

Even though I went through men like pairs of jeans we
outgrow or trade up, and even though I lived some of the
scenarios in Terry McMillan's *Waiting to Exhale,* I hoped I

could someday present a better narrative. You know that my first marriage was monstrous and that when I later lived with a man I loved dearly, we each had so much maturing to do we nearly tore each other to pieces—those times when I set all his clothes, suits included, outside our apartment in trash bags or I left him, taking everything I owned, including the chickens out the freezer and the bag of broccoli too. The time when he set my furniture in the middle of the street, and the other time he jacked me against the wall to make me drop the knife I tried to cut him with. Madness. But those growing pains are in the past, and God, I thank You for that. If I learned nothing else from it, I learned that men's feelings are as real and strong as mine and they too must be honored.

God, You were there when I succumbed to the drone of women's cries, calling their husbands "dumb-ass, asshole, the goddamned devil." It's a wonder I wanted to get married at all, my heart and head filled with these dire warnings. God, You know my friends and mentors with all these horror stories stood like sentries around my heart. Hell, You probably sent them to test my convictions about and real commitment to love.

God, I thank You for delivering me from those dark days and for guiding me to write in the light and to write about the light. Only You knew I deeply craved the love of a loving, strong, complex man like my granddads, Dad, and my uncles. God, do You even remember this prayer? Only You knew how I wanted to be able to write about this man in my own personal story.

I still can't get my hands around how it happened; it seemed so fast. But I can see now how You were working this as a grand plan all along.

I clearly remember Mike telling me about when he saw

me standing before a small audience reading from my first book. He thought I was the sexiest woman he'd ever seen.

"I was wearing a baggy suit!" I reminded him.

God, only You would send this gentle spirit in the form of a police officer moonlighting as a security guard at the Oxon Hill library where I read from my debut memoir, *Little X,* in 1997. Only You would have him join the librarian ladies who took me out for dinner afterward, having first made these librarian ladies our mutual friends.

I remember Mike sitting at the other end of the table, but I had no idea he was interested in me personally, and God, You know, for my part, I was only interested in promoting the current book and writing another one—and holding down some kind of mindless job to make ends meet in the meantime. But You would have it so that just a few months later Mike would show up at a reading one of our mutual friends hosted in her home. Did You mean for me to be so oblivious? I had no idea this fine brother was scoping me out.

You know we laugh about it now. Mike says I was wearing a dress the second time he came to my book event. He says I sat off in a corner like I was scared or nervous. I don't remember it quite that way. I remember feeling outside of myself, like I was not me onstage. This business of being a celebrated author was new to me. I had yearned for it, and it was thrilling but also a bit scary. And I didn't even realize my girlfriends hosting book parties for me also were secretly inviting eligible brothers trying to make a love connection.

It's funny how the next several years would find me nibbling on relationships just enough to take the edge off my hunger as I pursued a publisher for my second book. Interesting how those years would find Mike dating and marrying a librarian, not realizing he was fulfilling one of her life's goals just shortly before she would be diagnosed with cancer and called home to be with You. You know I consider it no small coincidence that she would leave him a trove of autographed books, many autographed by famous authors.

God, how many times can I thank You for that fateful day in June when You sent me to Avis so she could redirect me to Mike.

God, I remember the day when I arrived at the right place at the wrong time to report on an event for my job. That was You at it again, wasn't it? You had me arrive at the Lake Arbor Country Club to cover an event so I could meet Avis, who would put me and Mike together again, didn't You? I still remember the thrill of learning someone (Mike) had given my book to a friend for Christmas. God, I thank You for giving me enough gratitude and good humor to call him and thank him for gifting my book. But let me ask You this, God: Why'd You make a sister so dense? Why'd You make a brother so shy? I mean, I called him and jokingly told him he was one of only five people who bought my book so I wanted to thank him personally. He appreciated the humor and invited me to lunch. I accepted the invitation, but I thought it was work-related. I was a reporter, who needed reliable "sources" within the police department. He was a police official. I thought he could use a few good friends in the media. Talk about going through life with blinders on! God, I just didn't get it, but I see You had it planned all along. My last engagement didn't work out because You had this marriage in the works. Wow. I mean, thanks!

God, I need to thank You too for dressing Mike in the right clothes when You put us together at Avis's

Christmas party. That's where the lightbulb came on. It was his Kangol turned backward, his black leather jacket, and very sexy walk that did it. Whoah. I mean, the white shirts and expensive ties he wore to lunch were fine, and they reminded me of the security I'd felt as a little girl in the presence of Nation of Islam soldiers who wore white shirts when they protected the Temple. But the pristine white shirts and straitlaced ties Mike wore didn't turn on my womanly wiles. I hate to admit it, but God, You already know some part of me still longed for the thrill of a bad boy. So thank You for sending Mike to the party in cool-ass gear. A good boy with bad-boy flava. Yes!

I still remember him walking me to my car. Brother had a pimp and a coolness that blew me. It's a wonder I made it home that night. I felt too dizzy to drive, and You know it wasn't from the one rum and Coke I had.

God, You knew I wouldn't have cheated on my fiancé, but I'm glad You put the temptation there at least. Finally I realized the man I was engaged to wasn't the right one. I mean, if seeing Mike in his coolness could make me dizzy, maybe the man I was about to marry wasn't going to maintain my interest for a lifetime. God, I love Your subtlety.

Thank You for moving my fiancé out the way without drama or trauma for either of us. That was lovely. The way You eased Mike back into the picture was brilliant. Sending Avis to make it plain was a blessing.

I have been extremely happy with this brother. I mean from the time we started dating in May 2006 till the time we got married seven months later, it's felt like a hot minute. The fact that we met ten years earlier, and have seen each other in so many different situations and configurations, gives what we have now more depth, and we have a more mature perspective on ourselves and our love. Over the years You were preparing him and preparing me, right? I mean, the whole courtship and first year of marriage felt like an extended day at an amusement park. You know I consider this period my hundred days of bliss though technically, it was more than a hundred days. I call it a hundred days because it's been 100 percent fulfilling in ways I had not even imagined.

God. I used to meditate on Whitney Houston's "One Moment in Time," and I must've moaned a hundred bars of Sade's "Please Send Me Someone to Love," but when You were ready to bring it to me, You brought it in a mighty way.

You know the whirlwind romance was necessary because if I'd thought things through like I usually do, I wouldn't have gotten married before I was about fifty and feeling financially secure. That was my grand plan.

You remember Mike's response when I told him that plan? "I'll help you get there," he said. Wow. Here I was explaining why I wouldn't consider a serious relationship with him at the time. I'd wasted too much time dallying around, and now, before it was too late, I would focus all my concentration on my work and building financial security. "I'll help you," he said, and he meant it! I mean he stepped up offering to help in ways I certainly did not expect. God!

It totally surprised me how we got to talking about marriage so soon. I remember riding in his car, coming from house hunting in Baltimore one evening, and I was discussing buying a house big enough for both of us in case we found that we'd want to get more serious in the future. Mike had a house big enough for both of us, but I was determined to do my own thing because, still bruised from the past, I was convinced I simply was not good in relationships.

God, I can still remember us walking and talking around the Lake Arbor Country Club, me telling him, "I'm real good at friendships. I have some wonderful friendships with men, and they're really good men. I'm just not good in the romance department. It never works out." And he said, "Maybe it's not you. You just hadn't met the right man."

You remember the smile that spread across my face as my insides warmed? "Maybe it wasn't me?" God, You were awesome to send such a message at such a time. I remember sitting under the pavilion near the Lake Arbor Country Club pool chatting through the evening like I could sit there forever. I remember feeling like this man was "home." At that moment I knew I could be anywhere with Mike and it would be the perfect place to be.

God, it's amazing how You made Mike decide to propose to me on a day of personal significance to me. He called for a date on Wednesday. He had it all planned. We'd go to a fancy restaurant to celebrate my new job teaching journalism at one of the top J-schools in the country. His invitation was tempting because the brother took me to the finest restaurants, but I was sticking to my schedule. I needed to go straight home from my full-time job running a small newspaper, take thirty minutes to eat leftovers, thirty minutes to power walk around the block a few times, two hours to work on the epilogue for my new book, and an hour to work on a syllabus for the class I would begin teaching in a couple weeks. But those were just small details in Your grand plan. He asked about Saturday, and I declined, planning to spend the whole day working on my book. But God, You, in all Your brilliance, You had another plan.

Remember how I went back and forth from my computer to the window because the weather was too nice to stay indoors? Remember how I frantically called Mike, telling him I could go out after all and telling him I wanted to go to a free concert in the park to hear Blue Magic rather than go out to a fancy restaurant? Remember him asking if this park was safe enough for him to drive his BMW and me telling him to drive the Matrix instead? "I'm not tryna get a brother jacked hanging with me in the hood," I joked. I'm still impressed he was able to pull together a complete picnic dinner on such short notice. I was glad my big plaid yellow and white blanket was clean for the occasion, since I used it whenever I went to the park to relax with a pen and a pad.

It brings a smile to my face, God. Just remembering that day makes me smile. Mike came through the door handing me a greeting card, as usual, and I gave him one in return. I remember melting as I read the one he gave me: "Love is a Mess! It messes with your schedule and your personal space (not to mention your house). It messes with your head and your good excuses and your better judgment and all your previous resolutions. Love messes with your hidden stuff and your lost hopes, your common sense and your sense of direction." Then his scribbled note: "Looking forward to making the mess of a lifetime with you."

I remember my surprise when I turned back to face him and he was standing there with a tiny black velvet box.

"Well?" was all he said. There was a moment of silence.

Everything was still for a moment. God, You know if there was dust floating in the air between us, it froze. He opened the box. My eyes popped. He extended his hand. I nervously accepted the box and plopped down on the sofa and sighed, "Wow."

God, You know why I was surprised. I mean, when we looked at rings that once, I figured he might plan to propose in a year or so, certainly not before Christmas. And You remember, the diamonds I'd asked to try were much smaller than the one he bought. "Wow . . . um . . . wow." I didn't know what else to say.

"Is that a yes?" he asked.

"What else would I say?"

God, I get a smile every time I think about that day, him cupping my face in his hands to seal the deal with a kiss, me feeling goofy and giddy the rest of the evening.

You know I enjoyed more than 100 days of bliss between the time he proposed and the day we got married. And You know in our first 365 days of marriage, I enjoyed more than 100 days of bliss. I cried once or twice—but wouldn't let him see it. And I upset him a few times too. But it's been in no way as tumultuous as in my younger years. God, I'm thanking You for my growth. I've learned to love again, trust again, and bond again. I learned to surrender to Your will.

Just yesterday I was looking at our wedding photos, amazed again, at how You pulled it off. A destination wedding on an island, coordinated in a matter of months? You really are an awesome God. Bringing his family and friends together with mine for a four-day nonstop party was delightful, but the wedding at the oceanside with sunrays spilling from above and clear blue waters crashing ashore was a blessing beyond my expectations.

Having my mother sing Barbra Streisand's "Evergreen" for us, then Mike telling me Streisand was his first wife's favorite singer, was added confirmation that You had Your grand design on this union all along. You know, I had suspected something the first time I went to Mike's house and saw that he had kept his beloved late wife's autographed books. Never mind that he simply had not known what else to do with the books but keep them. It appeared to me that he valued books as much as I had. It appeared to me that he had been prepared to be my partner. God, do You remember how delighted I felt learning of his love for jazz since my father is a jazz musician and our relationship had grown apart? Talk about restoration! So much restoration was unfolding here.

God, You know when love shines in our life, it illuminates our darkest spaces, corners where our valuables have collected dust. With this burst of love between us, I fell in love with my own family again.

I was reminded of so many pearls of wisdom from my mother. You know Mother used to tell my sisters and I that we could have a fairy-tale marriage like the ones we watched on *The Brady Bunch* where the mom and dad never fought, never even fussed. But we'd have to work hard for it.

God, this first year of marriage felt like a fairy tale unlike any I'd seen on TV or read about in books, and I thank You. I realized Mother was right. I worked hard at settling into Mike's home and adjusting to my new life as part of a couple, but the "work" was so much fun it didn't feel like work at all.

I knew it would be important to spend quality time together especially in the first years, and I knew I would have to make this marriage my priority, but doing so did not feel like work because it was all so playful.

I enjoyed the cotton candy–coated banter we enjoyed many mornings.

"Good morning, my beautiful wife," he'd begin playfully.

"Good morning, my wonderful husband, with the deep dimples."

"Good morning, my beautiful wife, with the pretty eyes and the skills to run a whole newspapah—even if it's full of typos!"

"Good morning, my wonderful husband, with the deep dimples and pretty gray eyes who can pay the mortgage laying home all day on his ass—'cause he put in his time!"

"Good morning, my beautiful wife, with the pretty eyes who can run a whole newspapah—never mind the typos—and be a best-selling aufah cause she gon be on the *Ofra* show!"

> *God, I thank You for the scents of our first year of marriage—the cinnamon or berry air fresheners I used to make our home welcoming as we entered, the smell of his favorite cologne or my favorite scented soap, the scent of waffles or fried potatoes I cooked Saturday mornings or pulled barbeque chicken he prepared for a special occasion.*

I thank You for making our loving more than sexual. Isn't it funny how my attempts at sexiness tickled him sometimes? He laughed at my striptease.

"You can't do a strip dance cheesin'," he'd say.

God, I could go on thanking You for days—for small gestures and huge transformations. I could thank You for moving me to a space where I could joke about not having to fight over toothpaste because he could have his on his side of the double sink, and I could have mine on my side. I could thank You for not having to argue about whose turn it is to cook because we can afford to eat out as often as we want or need to. I can thank You for the total transformation in my life.

I thank You for teaching me to measure a man by the depth of his happiness and the extent of his joy rather than by the size of his professional or financial success or by the intensity of his sexual prowess. You know for the longest time I thought sexual chemistry was sufficient, but Mike came with that and so much more. He makes me laugh often and You know the laughter makes me feel better than I have since I was a kid.

Some days I feel so good, and so blessed with this wonderful man, I want to call his mother or father and say, "You done good." But I don't call because I don't want to sound like a suck-up. Some days I call my girlfriends to testify, "This brother is the bomb." I share this joy with them so they can remind me of it when we are faced with the inevitable storms.

Many days I count the blessings; I write them down too. I used to pray Sade's lyrics, "If it's not asking too much, please send me someone to love." But God, You sent a lovable man who could also love me! I thank You for our ordinary meals and our birthday feasts. I thank You for the gifts we exchange on holidays and presents we pick up for each other while out shopping. I thank You for our silly mornings and even the somber days that make the other days that much brighter.

What a mighty wonder You're working in my life. God, You know life was serious business for me up until now since I grew up believing life is one long test of faith in and obedience to You. I thank You for this reprieve. I thank You for Mike, and for a million more days of bliss.

A Shared History

W. RALPH EUBANKS

WHEN A RESTAURANT on the Eastern Shore of Maryland made an attempt to refuse service to my wife, Colleen, and me less than twelve hours after I slipped an engagement ring on her finger, the message was clear: A Black man and a White woman should not be together. The White waitress's pursed lips could barely disguise her disdain. The Black kitchen help shot stern "You should know better" stares with their folded arms. A deafening silence hovered over the room.

In spite of it all, we demanded service that morning, and we got it. That moment served to bond our love rather than fulfill its intended purpose, which was to chip away at our relationship or at least make us question moving forward with it. Years later this incident is part of our shared history, something remembered on anniversaries or recounted to our children. Someday I hope to tell our grandchildren about that experience to remind them of the strength of the love my wife and I have for each other.

The slings and arrows faced by my wife and me pale in comparison with those faced by my own grandparents, who were also an interracial couple. The assumptions, accusations, and stereotypes were stronger and more dominant in American culture in 1915 than they were in 1988. On that steamy July morning of our engagement, at least we had the right to demand service in that restaurant. Faced with the same circumstances, my grandparents probably would have faced jail or a beating. In spite of it all, the marriage of my grandparents, Jim Richardson, a White man, and Edna Howell, a Black woman, endured for over twenty years. Now, two generations later, I'm trying to figure out how their love survived, what bonded them to each other given their life in the Jim Crow South.

Jim and Edna's story is one I want to know better and want my children to understand. They need to know that their parents didn't get the freedom to marry on their own. There were people like my grandparents, their great-grandparents, who paved our way. But no love letters or diaries survive that document their life. It's through family stories and oral history that I have begun to piece their life together. As I stitch together the stories, at the same time I have to pick through the judgments made by those who tell the stories, since remnants of the cultural labels of the past are still very much with us.

Until I decided to find out more about them, I knew my grandparents only through what I overheard family members say about them. My grandmother died when my mother was seven, and my grandfather left this world exactly six months before I was born. For most of my life, my grandparents were spirits rather than flesh-and-blood people with day-to-day lives. Consequently, the stories I overheard spoke of these two people in deified tones. They weren't real. With no pictures to imagine them, I made up my own. Of course, in my mind both of my grandparents were Black like me, perhaps one light and one dark, like my own parents. Then something happened that made my vision of my grandparents change.

Late one Friday night, when I was sixteen, when my parents thought I was asleep, I heard my father say to my mother, "The hardest thing I ever did was to ask a White man to marry his daughter." Then there was a pause, as my father took a drag on his ever-present Salem cigarette. "And I'm not sorry that I had to do the asking. It's all been worth it."

The two of them laughed tenderly, which I felt in their voices since I could not see the expressions on their faces. At the time, I was an innocent sixteen-year-old, lying awake in a room filled with boyhood toys, model airplanes, and blanketed by naïveté. Though I tried to listen in as my parents talked into the night about how they had forged ahead with their marriage in spite of different backgrounds, I remember almost nothing of their Chivas Regal– and nicotine-fueled discussion. Rather, puzzlement filled the air of my room like the smoke from my parents' cigarettes and crept into my brain as I attempted to process that my mother's much-loved father was a White man.

My puzzlement that night more than thirty years ago led me to make assumptions about my grandparents and what their life and relationship must have been like, much like the people I encountered in that restaurant soon after my engagement. And like those people on the Eastern Shore of Maryland, I based my assumptions on the racial lore of the South: stereotypes of White men who held Black women in subservient positions and sexual bondage, Black women who were victims, and the "tragic mulatto" children born from that relationship. The traditions of the South were molded by the dominant White culture and passed on to Black culture to instill fear. Up until that moment they were tightly instilled in me, though in my innocence at the time I did not know it. Even as elements of cultural imprinting flooded my mind, somehow I knew none of those assumptions that sprang to mind about my grandparents' life were true. The truth lay somewhere in the stories I had heard while I was growing up.

All my life I had always heard about how much my grandfather, Jim, loved my grandmother, Edna. And I knew that when Edna died, Jim held the family together in the best way that he could. When I learned he was White, the same cultural code I had been taught told me that my grandfather could have easily escaped his responsibilities to his children. Instead Jim broke the code. Out of love for Edna, he stood by his children and brought them up to adulthood.

Today my grandfather Jim Richardson stares at me from a hand-painted photograph that hangs in my house. When I was a child, this same portrait was kept in the closet of my parents' bedroom, since keeping it out in the open in Mississippi in the 1950s and 1960s could have led to questions about my mother's racial identity. Sometimes I think my mother gave it to me in an act that spoke of her desire for me to feel some pride in this mysterious man and the life he lived. But perhaps I have this image of Jim so that I can piece together the puzzle of his life with Edna that still lies unfinished in my mind.

In the photograph, Jim is dressed in a blue serge suit, with a fedora tipped back on his head at a rakish angle. To judge from his unlined face, he is all of twenty-one years old. Yet his facial expression says he's a man who knows exactly where he's going and what he wants. Don't get in his way or stop him. And as I track down stories about him and my grandmother from the few people left who knew them, I'm learning that that's exactly the type of person he was.

Lately I've found myself staring at this portrait a great deal as I try to piece together my grandparents' lives. Although I have no pictures of Edna, the photograph of Jim serves to help me conjure images of her in my imagination, especially since I found that it was taken only a year before Jim married my grandmother, Edna Howell. As I've driven around south Alabama collecting stories about my grandparents, I've learned that Edna was an exotic-looking woman with olive skin and long black hair that stretched down her back. Legend has it that Edna's mother, Adeline, was a Creek Indian. It is more likely that she was a mixture of Black, White, and Native American, as are most people of mixed race in that part of Alabama.

Now that I can bring up pictures of Edna in my mind, I can place her beside Jim each time I look at his photograph. In the picture in my mind, they are a beautiful couple. But I still have more questions: How did they meet? How did they choose to forge a life together, in spite of laws on the books that made their marriage illegal?

People who remain in the small community of Prestwick, Alabama, tell me that Jim probably met Edna through his social network, which largely consisted of Black men who worked in his logging business. Local legend has it that Jim was a fixture at the Friday and Saturday night social functions these men had with some regularity. In all likelihood, one of these men introduced Jim to Edna. But everyone tells me that Edna was a different type of woman: She would not allow herself to be used as a paramour, as many White men treated Black women at the time. She insisted that Jim court her and treat her as he would have treated any White woman in his circle. Edna would accept nothing less.

I also believe it was the life and relationship of Edna's parents that shaped how she chose to forge her relationship with Jim Richardson. Edna's family ties scattered when Edna's mother, Adeline King, discovered that her husband, Gilbert Howell, had another family in a nearby town. After their separation, Edna had few ties with the Howells. Adeline, with the help of her family, the Kings, chose to raise her three girls, Janie, Mollie, and Edna, on her own. Adeline felt wounded and betrayed by Gilbert Howell and consequently taught her daughters to be mindful of men and their promises.

Edna carried that lesson into her relationship with Jim Richardson. Gilbert Howell, though of mixed-race ancestry, lived his life as a Black man. So Edna knew that given the racial politics of the time, a White man would leave her with little or nothing if the relationship did not work, just as her father had left her mother. In her own version of a prenuptial agreement, Edna got a house, property, and household help.

In my search I also encountered a story from a woman by the name of Miss Virginia. Miss Virginia related that as a young man, Jim courted several young women, none of whom met with the approval of his mother. Then he started seeing Edna Howell and became enchanted with her, later telling his mother that he was determined to marry her. Miss Virginia said, "He told his mother he was going to marry this Black girl, and he did. They raised a family. She died as a young woman, and he continued raising the family. Now this wasn't some affair between a White man and a Black woman like you read about in some novel. God knows he loved her."

In the eyes of Alabama law, Jim and Edna were not married. From what I have uncovered, they had a ceremony, but their marriage was not recognized by the state of Alabama. Consequently, all legal documents Jim and Edna held identify them as "an unmarried woman" or "an unmarried man." But they sealed their love with a gold wedding band that served as an outward symbol of their love and devotion to each other. As far as I am concerned, that means that they were married.

As I try to paint an image of Jim and Edna's life together, I always come back to my own marriage somehow. Marriages, like people, are not perfect. They all stumble along the way. I know that I will find the imperfections in my grandparents' marriage as I tell their story, and I am prepared to make discoveries of those failings and shortcomings. Still, I know that marriages also don't survive if the focus centers on imperfections rather than mutual love and respect. In the tough times, it is the memories of the shared history of a life together that can help keep a couple's love alive.

Colleen and I have had our love tested by fire, just like every couple. Just like in my grandparents' lives, race has played a role in some of the tests we have faced. Yet unlike Jim and Edna Richardson, we're not marooned and isolated, left to push through our life together with little support. We have a shared history that binds us together, one that transcends race while at the same time not ignoring the racial realities of American society. We've worked hard to do that, and we have had help along the way from family and friends. The next generation will not uncover documents near the date of our marriage that legally disinherited us, as I have found for my grandfather.

And I like to think we have had some help along the way from Jim and Edna Richardson. Jim, ever present in the photograph in our house, watches over us and protects us. Edna watches over us as well, slowly coming into focus beside Jim.

My Own Happy Ending

MARITA GOLDEN

for Joe

I DON'T TELL the story often. Actually, I usually let it lie se-
creted away like a precious jewel. I'm content to reward myself
with an occasional replay of it. It's a story that is hard to believe,
but when people hear it, they know instinctively that it's true. A
story more fantastic than any of the fictional narratives I've labored over. It's the story of how I met my husband, Joe. It's such a
befuddling mix, charming, whimsical, chilling, affirmative. The
tale of how we met is like some talisman, or a reverse hex, that
lifted Joe and me from the very start into a realm incandescent
and thrilling. We met at a party, and when I saw him walking
through the front door, I knew who he was: He was mine. Sounds
like a scene from a movie, doesn't it? Well, it is. My own.

I'll start with the day we met. I woke that morning knowing that on that day anything was possible. It wasn't a feeling
that set me to trembling or that even filled me with curiosity. I just recall waking to see a slant of late-August sun curving with a precise gleam through the blinds, and feeling that
on this day, I was going to meet *him*. I was a forty-year-old
divorced single mother whose twelve-year-old son lay tightly
cocooned in sleep in his room down the hall.

And as I turned my back to that slash of sunlight invading
my room, I smiled, yawned, and then smiled again. I was due
a miracle after a long dry season without love.

On that August morning I was confident that I would meet the man I would marry at a party I was attending that evening. But woven into the seams of my imaginative knowing were certain things I did not know. He didn't have a name. He didn't have a face. But all that was superfluous. I had claimed him. I would know him when I saw him. He would be my psychic twin, the *one,* but most important, he would be the *right one.* Because now I was ready for him. He was ready for me. We were ready for each other. Maybe half a dozen other times in my life I'd felt such absolute certainty. And here it was again.

The life I was living that August morning was one in which doubt was a word in a foreign tongue I could not imagine speaking. I felt completely grounded, sure of and quite frankly in love with myself. Because not only was I going to meet *him* in fourteen hours (as I calculated after looking at the clock beside my bed), but I also felt this subtle rapture because of who I was, who I had become. What was to take place that night was logical, inevitable. A blessing with my name on it was on the way.

I'd been a perpetual victim of a host of mostly self-inflicted love battle scars. But two years earlier, as I contemplated the publication of my third book (a book based on the life of my mother, a book that plays a crucial role in this story of how I met Joe), I knew that my life had to change.

The handsome but hapless live-in boyfriend had to go. Had I really lived with someone so utterly threatened by the books I wrote, my ambition, and my hunger for life? *Yes.* And now I had decided that I had to find a male friend, a man bosom buddy to talk to (the way I could not talk to the boyfriend) about my dreams and fears, establishing a bond of emotional intimacy that I could create in the next love relationship I had with a man. I had to figure out why I kept attracting misery, wallowing in it, and calling it love.

As I lay in bed the morning of the day I met Joe, bathed in a rare, giddy confidence, I recalled how my most recent novel, *Long Distance Life,* had helped me decide that everything in my love and lifestyle had to change. That book, the writing and imagining of it, drove me into a frenzied but focused re-evaluation of my life. *Long Distance Life* wasn't just the saga of sixty years in the life of a Washington, D.C., Black family. It was my bible. My book of possibilities. And during the long process of its creation, spirits were telling me that I had to grow into the woman who could proudly say, I wrote that book.

While writing that novel and questioning everything in my life, I found a platonic male friend who introduced me to the joys of male-female buddy bonding, an important prelude, I learned, to a satisfying love affair. In a way, it was like making love, a different kind of love with my buddy, a smart, in-touch-with-his-feelings guy who was a computer consultant from New Orleans. I relished being listened to, knowing I was being heard. With my new male friend I was forming a bond of emotional trust and intimacy I was starved for but, I had to admit to myself, I had not normally required of the men I chose. All this was a skill set I had ignored, hadn't valued, preferring to be a high-drama queen, specializing in the following equation, passion + pain = love.

Long Distance Life played a crucial role in turning me into the woman I was the day I met Joe. The story centers on the life of Naomi Johnson, who migrates from Spring Hope, North Carolina, in the 1920s to Washington, D.C., as part of the Great Migration of African-Americans from the South that so transformed this nation. It is the story of her daughter, Esther, who four decades later goes back to the South to work in the civil rights movement; her grandsons, Logan, who strides into the Black middle class, and Nathaniel, whose life choices are dangerous and tragic. The book covers much of the social history of the twentieth century. But more than anything, *Long Distance Life* is a love story. In Naomi Johnson, I honored the tenacious, big-hearted spirit of my mother, Beatrice Golden.

I was writing the book during a time of tumult, yearning, and confusion professionally and personally—bonding with my male buddy and still living with the boyfriend and trying to figure out how to get him out of my life; searching for a university teaching job and trying to figure out why, with two books, I couldn't find one—and my son, Michael, was fraught with emotional needs I wasn't sure I was always meeting.

So *Long Distance Life* became a life raft. A balm. A prayer. There were the hours spent at the Library of Congress researching the lives of African-Americans in Washington, D.C., during that historical time span between the twenties and the sixties, reading African-American newspapers, poring over oral histories, talking to still-living Black migrants from places like Wilson, Asheville, and Palmer, North Carolina, small, sleepy towns where it seemed sometimes that one morning in the 1920s, '30s, and '40s all the Black folks woke up one day and decided to head north.

Because I felt my own life so bereft of the complete love of a good man, I blessed Naomi Johnson with the relationship I so deeply yearned for. Writing fiction is a form of sorcery, and I was working on two tracks, creating the novel but harboring in my mind a place where a man as wonderful as the lover/friend and husband I gave Naomi Johnson could manifest for me.

Rayford Johnson, in the novel, is the love of Naomi Johnson's life, a proud "race man" who worked with Marcus Garvey before coming to Washington, D.C., to teach at Dunbar High School, in the 1930s one of only two high schools for Black students in the rigidly segregated city. He is devoted to Naomi and proud of her business acumen that made her the owner of several boardinghouses (as was my mother). Naomi, after having married and divorced a man too small to march with her into the realm of the big dreams she possesses, knows that in Rayford she has found her matching heartbeat.

As I wrote, I kept thinking that if I could believe a Rayford Johnson into existence for a fictional narrative, since everything wonderful that had ever happened to me had its seeds in my imagination, perhaps I could conjure an actual good man of my own to fill the empty space in the real life I was living.

Writing *Long Distance Life* was as much spiritual quest as creative endeavor. But the most important thing I did during this time, this pre-Joe phase of my life, was to get help. From a therapist. I tackled my broken heart and the rebuilding of my spirit as if it were my own private Manhattan Project, figuring out how to build a Marita I had never before imagined and the likes of which the world had never seen before.

I had cracked my hard shell of resistance partially open before I walked into the therapist's office. So we moved pretty quickly through the unfinished grief I was holding on to over parents who'd died twenty years earlier, through the jungle of resulting abandonment issues, insecurities, the ocean of self-doubt, the unease with the professional achievements I'd convinced myself deep down that I didn't deserve.

DURING ONE SESSION I moaned, "How can I really master the habit of self-love? Isn't it too late?" And even if I healed decades-old wounds, didn't she know there weren't any good men out there? Even if now I was armed with the tools to become the good woman I always secretly thought I was, how would I avoid picking the wrong man again? I was so good at it.

"The kind of lovers you've been attracting won't even come anywhere near you anymore," she assured me with an unnerving calm once we felt I was ready to leave her office for the last time.

"What did you do, work roots on me?" I asked.

She just smiled. It was years before I understood how she could make such a guarantee, after only a few sessions, with so much ease. But during years of watching the earth shift beneath her clients as they sat across from her in that office, she'd heard the rumbles and whimpers of new birth, seen the blossoming of self-discovery. And she had heard and seen in me what I could not see in myself: that I would be okay. In fact I would be, in the end, just fine. By showing up in her office, I had proven that I was not just ready to continue living my life but eager to create a new one. I could have the kind of man I wanted. I could love and accept myself.

A lot of what my therapist taught me was straight-up old-school, lessons we learn at home from parents who love us. I had to forgive the boyfriend, whom I asked to move out after the second session. I had to stop dissing him with every breath. If he was so awful, why had I chosen him? He had loved my son and me the best way he knew how. I had to take responsibility for bringing him into my life, my bed, and my heart. I had to forgive and forget a period I looked on as wasted because it had been so difficult. I had to *move on.*

So on the morning of the day of the party where I met Joe, all that was behind me. That evening I strode into the home of the friend who was giving the party, sublime and content. Unperturbed. Then, at ten forty-five, I glanced at the front door where I saw Joe entering with a friend who was tall and ebony-hued and had an open, friendly face. But it was Joe who caught my eye. I looked at him, and my heart didn't skip a beat. It didn't need to. I knew that I was looking at my man. I nudged my friend Louise, who had come to the party with me, and whispered, "There he is." Earlier that day I had told her about my premonition, my certainty that I was going to meet *him* at the party that night. She had warily accepted this possibility with a stunned, breathless "Oh" when we spoke on the phone that morning. But I suspect that she still thought maybe I had lost it.

Joe entered the house joking, smiling, and hugging Tina, the hostess, who was an old friend. Tina was a member of a single parents' group I had started, and I later learned that Joe wasn't even supposed to be at the party. He'd bought a ticket to the Dominican Republic, but when Tina playfully threatened never to speak to him again if he didn't come, he canceled his trip. Despite the handshakes and greetings offered to those he apparently knew in the room, Joe had seen me, for only a few minutes after entering, he made his way through the crowd to the corner where Louise and I stood. He and his friend Issa, a jovial Senegalese, introduced themselves. But really, no introductions were necessary for either of us. That's how it felt, as I basked in his clear-eyed appreciation of what he saw when he looked at me. I was drawn to how comfortable he seemed in his own skin, how easy he was with everyone around us. His humor and laughter were genuine and sprang from a place of integrity I felt inside his soul. Soon we were dancing. And talking. In the next hour, in Tina's blue light–lit basement, I learned that Joe *was* Rayford Johnson come to life. He taught math and computers at Dunbar, *the same school where Rayford Johnson taught.* Like Rayford, Joe was a proud race man. We talked about everything from Jesse Jackson to our concern about Black youth, to his travels in the Black world, from Suriname to Brazil, and my four-year stint in Nigeria.

He asked for my phone number, and the next morning I called Tina to get a "background check." I knew Joe was mine, but I still wanted to tread carefully, and checking with Tina, who also taught at Dunbar and had known Joe for over a decade, was even better than enlisting the services of the FBI.

Tina said simply, "Marita, Joe is one of the best men in the world. You could not do better."

In the coming weeks we didn't date so much as slip into the fold of what we had both been waiting for. Joe was a forty-four-year-old bachelor who had decided three years earlier that he was ready to get married. Joe told me he had nearly given up on finding a soul mate in the United States and had concluded that his life partner might be in some Black country overseas. When I met his family, I knew I had come home. Joe had long-standing and deep friendships with men in which they offered each other the kind of emotional support I had only seen women offer each other. He had female friends with whom he had established relationships of respect and support, and he was enormously proud of my accomplishments, bragging about my books and writing to everyone he introduced me to. Joe's dreams were as big as mine. On our first date he took me to see the shell of a house he had just bought and told me of his plans for renovation of that house and several others he was thinking about purchasing, as a down payment on his future. I was drawn to his steadiness. I felt within days of meeting him the stirring of a quiet love that ran deep. I didn't fall into it as much as claim it. I could tell Joe everything and I wasn't judged. When I told him about the sessions with the therapist and my love demons, he just kissed me and said, "The next time you talk to that therapist you tell her thank you from me for getting you ready to be my wife."

We felt married from the start, our connection was that soothing and so right. As I lay nestled in Joe's arms one evening, I asked him if he had ever thought seriously about marriage. "To whom?" he asked. "To me," I said. He said yes with a certainty that didn't surprise me at all. We agreed that if we were still together in a year, we would marry. We were and we did.

Then things got interesting, got challenging, and I learned whom I had married, who I was willing to become, and what real friendship and real love are made of, how they are tested, and how they survive. Yes, we are soul mates, but our marriage has not been a fairy tale. My initial intention of being the world's best stepmom was quickly derailed by teenaged angst and jealousy of me, whom my stepdaughter saw only as a rival for her father's affection. It took several years for Keesha and me to grow into a relationship of affection and trust. I had to learn that Joe wasn't going to be a *Father Knows Best* dad to my son, Michael, and accept that Joe would carve out his own way of being stepfather, role model, and friend to my sometimes hardheaded, difficult son, who was as jealous of Joe as Keesha was of me.

I had to learn that no, I couldn't shout and scream and stalk out of the room, slamming the door behind me, in the midst of an argument and expect to make my point. Joe had to learn that, with me, the way he said things counted even more than what he said.

But what kept us together through it all is that we never stopped talking. Ever in touch with his feelings, Joe has never hesitated to let me know when he feels I could have done better by him, or even done better by myself. I have learned that the old adage about never going to bed without making up is a nice aphorism but that in the real world of marriage, a spouse may need a day or two of quiet, sometimes silent healing to get over or make sense of what was done or what was said.

Then four years into our marriage Joe was diagnosed with non-Hodgkin's lymphoma, an aggressive and often fatal form of cancer. Having lost both my parents in the space of two years when I was in my twenties, I initially presented the strong, invincible face to the world that I had perfected in the wake of numerous personal crises. I was calm and optimistic, telling friends about Joe's illness, repeating the details of the planned course of treatment, the prognosis, how he was holding up.

And then finally in the shower one morning I wept bitter, scorching tears of anger, cursing fate for giving me the love of my life only to threaten to take him away so soon. I cried in the shower because I didn't want Joe to see me cry, could not imagine seeking comfort from him when he needed at that moment so much. I sank onto the floor of the shower stall and let the warm water beat down on me, sobbing until I could cry no more. Then I stood up, leaned against the wall of the shower, and whispered with a mixture of resolve and faith into the ear of God that no matter what, Joe was going to live. We were going to beat cancer. I had just started loving him, and I wasn't through yet.

Joe has sometimes said that the cancer, with its eight months of invasive treatments, chemotherapy and radiation, the weakness, fatigue, and the loss of appetite, was a blessing. Like many cancer survivors, he credits the disease with increasing his appreciation for life, for helping him gain a real sense of priorities. And the cancer was not just the difficult, often debilitating treatment. Cancer, which in a sense we both had (I had it vicariously and was a victim of it emotionally), manifested itself in old friends coming back into his life and visiting him for hours in the hospital or at home, sitting by his bed, regaling him with the healing balm of memories and favorite stories. It was five of my sister friends showing up at our house one evening with a week's worth of casseroles they had prepared in order to relieve me of the burden of cooking and dealing with Joe's needs. It was those same friends who volunteered to be with Joe at home on the days I had to commute from our home in suburban Maryland to teach in Richmond, Virginia. Joe and I had no idea we were so loved.

Cancer was me coming upon Joe one day in the bathroom,

shrunken down almost to nothing, his head bald, his skin sagging beneath his arms, and at his hips, leaning heavily against the bathroom sink. He looked horrible, yet I stood silently watching him and feeling his vulnerability and his strength and his will to live and in that moment loving him so deeply and so preciously it took my breath away. Cancer taught me how to love my husband in ways no marriage manual, no best friend, not even your mama will tell you how to love.

We survived cancer. Together. And together we have survived Joe's battle now with diabetes (sparked by the cancer treatments), a family member's more than decade-long sentence to prison, his father's death and his mother's health challenges, our mutual job woes, our children's bad choices, and some dreams turning into nightmares. We have celebrated and shared our grandchildren, our children's triumphs, our dreams coming true, Joe's retirement after thirty years of teaching, the life my writing career has given us, travel all over the world, from Havana to Istanbul, Joe's rediscovery of his passion for playing the piano, performing, and writing music.

This love, this marriage, has been a journey. Some roads we made. Others we were forced to tread. This union is nothing like I imagined it would be. It has surpassed all I dared hope for. I've learned how good I am. How great love feels and that it does not have to be perfect to be love. I know what it means to have a spouse who is your best friend. We are joined beyond the tatters, the tears, the breaks, and the breakdowns. We decided at the beginning and along the way to make this work. Ours is a love and contentment that we earn and create and perfect every day. Who says there are no happy endings?

Fiction

Chinaberry

(FROM *THE HAND I FAN WITH*)

TINA McELROY ANSA

*W*ITH HERMAN AROUND and in love with her, Lena felt for the first time in her adult life that she was truly lucky.

And if Herman's presence on her property was a haunting, then it was the sweetest and gentlest one she had ever experienced.

Most of the ghosts from her past had appeared in terrifying forms: wolves, cats, and wild dogs; headless, footless bodies; decaying bodies with heads facing one way, torsos the other; babies who turned into ghouls. They controlled her in her sleep and drew her into dark and dangerous situations to frighten her. They spoke through her mouth, scaring her and getting her into trouble with her friends and teachers. They tried to pull her into their world.

The worst that Herman did was he wouldn't hardly let Lena conduct any business. All through May and past June, after the wisteria had disappeared and the small white flowers on the jasmine vines had taken over, Herman really got in the way of her duties.

It was not that he forbade her to conduct her regular voluminous business dealings. It was just that his "being" got in the way. His laughter got in the way. His invitations to explore her land got in the way. His way of life, so to speak, got in the way. Herman's yearning for Lena got in the way. And Lena's love for Herman got in the way.

The first few days after he appeared, all Lena had to do was think of Herman with his cheekbones like chiseled Georgia granite for him to appear to her.

She would feel the breeze on her neck and then look over to see Herman sitting on the sofa across the room from her. Or she would feel a tickle on the bottom of her bare feet, and he would be lying in bed next to her. Or she'd see a wisp of smoke escape from a late-night fire he had laid and lit for her, and he would be standing there by the fireplace in her bedroom carving the box for a kalemba.

But after a while Herman did not wait for Lena to evoke him. He'd come sauntering into her bedroom first thing in the morning or be lying next to her when she awoke, watching her, waiting.

Adjusted to living alone, unaccustomed to another body— even a ghostly one—in bed with her, Lena would jump, startled at his presence. But she got used to it.

He didn't seem to need any sleep.

"I don't need no sleep, baby. Other than to run through yo' dreams every now and then so you won't forget 'bout me while you restin'."

"How am I ever gonna forget about you, Herman?" Lena asked sincerely. He was making her so bold.

"I just wanted to hear you say it, Lena, baby."

It still surprised her when she and Herman went out walking on the property and came up on Mr. Renfroe or a stable hand who would look up and wave at her and speak as if she were there all alone.

Herman was so real, so solid Lena had a hard time believing that other folks could not see him. Could not hear him. Could not feel him.

Those first days they just walked and talked and explored her property a great deal when she was at home. Right from the beginning, it seemed to Lena that they spent *all* their time together. But they didn't. Lena had too much else to do. She just thought about him all the time. She got up early to spend sunrise and first light with him before going into town and came home as early as she possibly could to end her day with him out on the deck, looking at the stars through the telescope she had bought him.

It was amazing to Lena, but things worked out without her hand in it. For the most part, Lena's time with Herman was undisturbed. Her cleaning, stable, and yard crews did their jobs while she was at work, and only one or two people ever saw her talking to an empty space or riding Baby next to a riderless Goldie.

With James Petersen safely settled down the lane in his own home and the gardening and stable crew finished for the day, Lena and Herman would lie together in the two-person hammock he had found in the barn and strung between two tall pine trees overlooking the river and watch the sun go down. Sometimes they would lie in perfect silence. Other times they tripped over each other's words talking so much.

Magic happened all the time when they were out together. If it started to rain while they were out walking down by the river, there would seem to be a bubble around them as they raced back toward the house. One minute it was dry and breezy inside the bubble. The next minute it stopped raining outside and only rained inside the bubble. And they'd arrive home dripping wet and refreshed.

The first time Lena and Herman swam together outside,

it was in the waters of Cleer Flo'. They had headed to the river one morning to see what had washed ashore during the stormy night, but when they saw the clear inviting waters rushing past the deck, Herman had suggested, "Let's go for a dip, Lena."

Both strong swimmers, they shed their clothes right there and dove into the green pristine waters of the Ocawatchee squealing like children. The river was full of life. And each time Lena or Herman brushed past a fish or a toad or a tadpole or a crawfish, it sent off electric sparks like an eel, and Lena felt like something from a science-fiction novel.

But Herman did not win Lena over with magic or the manipulation of science. He eased into her heart and took her over with real old-time love and attention.

He slid into her heart so smoothly, so seamlessly that before she knew it he was truly her man.

Lena didn't know when it actually happened. She knew it didn't really happen overnight, but that was the way it felt. It was just that Herman and the day they had planned or didn't have planned opened up to them like a woodland amusement park each morning. There were horses and a swimming pool and woods to explore. There was a river to fish in and gardens to work. There was a flat-bottom boat to snake up into secluded estuaries. Herman was a lot more seductive than her duties in Mulberry. And Lena just didn't seem to have time for her old routine.

At first, when one of Lena's customers or friends or acquaintances called or showed up at her door, needing, practically demanding, some help or intervention, Lena did what she had always done and rose to the occasion. She would rush to the phone or dash out the door with a big pretty peach-colored wool melton shawl trailing behind her and catch a glimpse of Herman out the corner of her eye. He would be stretched out in front of the fireplace with his big sock feet crossed on the table, his drugstore reading glasses low on his nose, a couple of books on the floor, a gooseneck lamp over his shoulder, and she'd immediately regret her decision.

"Shoot," she'd say under her breath as she raced to help the latest caller out of a scrape, "I could be laying up here with Herman." And to make it worse, she would recall the feel of his coarse chest hairs brushing across the tips of her breasts when they made love face-to-face.

So more and more, Lena found herself setting some new previously unheard-of limits. Herman showed up in April, and by the end of May she refused to leave home for any reason before daylight in the morning. By the end of June she would not let anyone draw her out of the house after dark, "unless it's a dire emergency," she told Herman.

Lena tried her best to stop doing so much of the work herself. She discovered that without her at the helm twenty-four hours a day, her money, holdings, and power kept right on working.

She continued her "hush mouth" work because she enjoyed giving. And as Gloria would have said, "Ain't no need to rock the boat right 'long through here." Lena continued signing checks and ordering gifts from catalogs. But more and more, she found herself asking Precious or one of the other assistants at Candace to screen her messages and mail and keep her apprised of important dates and events in the lives of her people.

And she continued sending out blessings to people and households in Mulberry even if she didn't drive past them every day anymore. Lena even heard herself say to a caller, "You know, it's you that your father wants to see at his final moment, not me. He probably doesn't even remember who I am. All you have to do is forgive him and let him forgive you."

Herman would hear her up on the deck talking on the phone.

"Uh-huh, uh-huh, uh-huh. Uh-huh. Of course, I understand how you must feel. Uh-huh. Of course, of course. Uh-huh.

"But I'm still going to have to say I can't do it this time," she persisted, looking out at Herman swinging in the hammock. "I've made another commitment.

"Your father just wants to talk to you. It'll be okay. I'll pray for all ya'll."

Then she would come outside and slide into her space under Herman's right shoulder.

"You know, Lena, Miss Cora—who taught me to read out the Bible after I was grown—Miss Cora say the Lord don't want no sacrificed victims or no burned offerin's. He want yo' mercy and forgiveness fo' each other and yo' willin'ness to he'p each other out.

"Lena, you he'p a whole heap a' folks out all the time. Doin' all kinds a' thangs. You ain't got to sacrifice *yo'se'f* too. You ain't *got* to do nothin', baby. We used t' say back in my day, 'All I gotta do is stay Black and die.' And that's all *you gotta do.* Stay Black and die."

But even when she had done all she could without sacrificing her days and nights to good works, Herman still found her looking off into space with that worried look around her pretty mouth. He'd tell her: "Lena, baby, don't worry 'bout the mule goin' blind. Just hold him in the road." And Lena would have to laugh because she did a lot of worrying about the mule going blind.

He got her laughing most mornings when he awakened her in her bed now that she slept soundly through the night. She could feel the weight of his body on the edge of her wide bentwood handmade bed waken her and she couldn't help it. Before she even opened her eyes in the morning, she would realize Herman was sitting beside her, waiting for her, and she'd awake with a big smile plastered all over her face.

Some mornings, especially as they came up on the nearly hot days of early summer, he woke her with song.

Woke up early this mo'nin'
Sun was shinin' bright
Told ma wife don't fix me no coffee
'Cause I won't be back tonight.

Lena would lie in bed—a luxury she had never allowed herself—and listen to the sound of Herman's rich old-timey-sounding baritone.

Sound like he ought to be singing "Ole' Man River," Lena lay in her bed that smelled like her man and thought with a smile. Then she laughed out loud when Herman launched into the tune from *Show Boat.*

God, he made her happy.

But if she didn't feel like laughing first thing in the morning, he would sense it and respect that feeling too. On those days Lena awoke to the sensation of being nuzzled by smoke, by mist.

She didn't dwell on the fact that Herman was a ghost who appeared and disappeared like dew in the morning. He was so full of life, it spilled out all over him and Lena.

"Hey, Lena, come look what I found in the barn!" "Hey, Lena, baby, let's go see if the fish bitin'." "Hey, Lena, hey, Lena, Lena, baby, put on yo' boots and come here a minute."

He called her all the time. And she never tired of hearing him speak her name. "Hey, Lena. Hey, Lena, baby. Hey, Lena, come see this big old blue boulder I found waaaayyy down the riverbank. We can jump in the river off it. Lay on it naked in the sun. Hey, come see. Baby."

"Lena, Lena, hey, Lena, baby," he'd call urgently from out on the deck. And he would point to the sky with wonder at a flock of long-legged wood storks in from the coast. "Look a' *yon*der."

It was difficult for her to talk on the phone, let alone conduct any kind of business in person, with him calling her name all the time. It was just a whisper in her ear, but it was a summons all the same.

His "calls" to her during meetings and visits and errands and conversations roused her to the point where she couldn't do anything but drop what she was doing and answer him.

He was the familiar breeze that intruded on her business. He was the waves of heat that made her fan like one of the ladies at church and made her want to drop her clothes right there in the bank. He was the frog in her throat that prevented her from accepting the Businessperson of the Year award held at the new Dupree Hotel.

Some days he'd call her on the phone at the Candace offices. When she placed the phone to her ear, Herman would blow into it, sending a swirl of his breath down the tunnel of her ear canal, leaving her breathless. Sometimes he was the short in the electrical system that plunged the windowless center rooms into darkness and threw out the whole computer system for the week. So *everybody* had to go home.

The few times she tried to ignore the calls and continue with the business at hand, he would start *messing* with her. No one else in the business meeting seemed to notice the gentle breeze that suddenly stirred up one of Lena's giggles. It would lift the braids from her neck ever so slightly and brush across the short curly hairs of her kitchen. It coiled itself around her leg like a vine and spiraled up her leg in tiny teasing tendrils.

She could ignore Herman's calls, but she couldn't ignore his touches.

"Ms. McPherson, am I doing something amusing?" Mr. Potter at the bank asked one morning. It was soon after Herman had arrived, and Lena was squirming and giggling in her seat.

She had meant to regain her composure, sternly rebuke Herman in her head for interrupting a meeting that might lead to a home and good credit for one of her mother's friends' daughter and husband, and return to the meeting to finish up business. But Herman slipped up under her dress and inside her pink-flowered silk panties, making her grab the arms of the big oxblood leather chair and guffaw right out loud in the old banker's face. The sudden laughter sounded like something that Sister used to do in college and still did if something struck her funny enough.

Mr. Potter, whom Lena noticed for the first time had a bald head that was shaped just like an egg, large end up, laughed a little too, just to make things a bit more comfortable in the glass-enclosed bank office with the understated gray and maroon drapes pulled discreetly around for the private business of finance.

"Oh, I *did* say something amusing, didn't I?" he said.

The breeze wiggled under her deep-rose satin bra that Herman liked so much and pushed one of the wide straps off her shoulder, tickling her there. And the meeting, for all practical purposes, was over. As Gloria used to say when recounting some story of sexual mischief to Lena when she was a girl, "Sugar, church was *out*!!!"

When Lena got to her car, Herman was sitting up in there in the passenger's seat dressed in a new cotton shirt and jeans she had bought for him, right proud of himself. She tried to be furious with him.

"Herman! How could you do that to me in there?" She spoke to what appeared to be the interior of the car even before she looked around to make sure no one was nearby watching.

"Good God, Lena, ain't you *glad* t' be out a' there!??"

"Stop it, now, Herman. You trying to make it seem like you were doing me a favor."

"Wasn't I?"

"No, you were doing yourself a favor. You just want somebody to rip and run with. You just want me to go out playing with you."

"Uh-huh," Herman readily agreed.

"So, you admit you were just looking out for yourself. Not me?"

"It's the same thang, baby."

"Herman, that was an *important meeting*!" Lena knew he had to know what was going on in there.

"You just holdin' up the weight of the world, huh, Lena?" Herman said. "Lena, baby, those people ain't in yo' hands. They in God's hands. And you ain't God."

He didn't say it harshly or even judgmentally. Herman just stated a fact as he saw it. He thought it was something that Lena already knew. But he immediately regretted saying anything.

Lena wanted to be angry to cover her hurt feelings, but when they got to the next corner, she had to slam on the brakes to keep from ramming into the side of another car moving legally into the intersection. Herman didn't miss a beat as Lena was thrown a bit against the steering wheel of the car, straining her seat belt. He reached out his strong solid arm across her breasts, clutched her forearm and held her safe from impact.

"Hold the baby," he said and smiled at her as the car rocked to a standstill. Lena grabbed her chest. And her arm crossed his.

Herman had sounded just like her mother, her father, her grandmother, her brothers, and everyone else who had ever loved her all rolled up in one when he said that. When she was little, riding the hump in the middle of the front seat of the green family woodie, her family always made sure that her pretty little face would not ram into the big wide dashboard of the station wagon. Whenever the car came to a sudden stop, somebody in the car would reach across her with a protective arm and flat hand pressed against her tiny chest and say, "Hold the baby."

Herman's gesture evoked all the love and protection she had felt as the baby of the family and reminded her just why she loved this man. She had to struggle to remember just what she had been so furious with him about in the first place. And by the time they got home, she and Herman were laughing and playing together.

As his sabotaging tactics escalated with the coming of summer, Herman felt he had to explain to Lena how he felt.

"Baby, it ain't that I ain't got enough t' do to fill my time while you away. It's just that ya missin' out on so much stuck in those meetin's and speakin' lunches and 'do good' visits of yo's. I want you here wid me. I can't deny that. I can't he'p it."

It wasn't that Herman was always up under her. He had slipped quite happily and unobtrusively into life at her house by the river—at his own pace and seemingly with his own agenda. Sometimes Lena would have to go look for *him*. She'd find him busy over some project like building a new trellis off the bedroom deck for her grandmama's moonflowers or repairing a loose board on the deck steps. Or sometimes he'd be taking a dip in the waters of the Ocawatchee.

"Hey, Lena, baby, you miss me?" He didn't give her a chance to be coy. "Hey, Lena, baby, you miss me?" Just like that. He allowed her little or no guile.

"Yeah, Herman, I missed you," she had to admit, stepping out of her high-heeled shoes into the dirt or the water with Herman.

And he'd smile, satisfied.

She'd often come home and find Herman browsing through her bookcases. He was insatiably curious about some things like the environment, architecture, and the human body. Others, such as sports, television, or transportation, he could care less about.

Herman would sit for hours staring at the pieces of the toaster or the microwave or her boom box that he had disassembled in his rampant curiosity.

"Now, how this thang work?" Lena would hear him say to himself as she tried to go to sleep on the green-and-white-striped sofa in her office and still remain close to Herman as he explored some appliance.

"You okay over there, Lena?" he'd ask, looking up from his work from time to time.

Electrical advances and laser discs were no reach for him. All Lena did was turn him loose at her computer, and he educated himself about most of the basic scientific advances since his death. He had a quick mind for a man dead a hundred years.

He told Lena he had seen most of these things in his wanderings, but he had seldom had the opportunity to really explore and learn the intricacies and workings of a computer or a silicon chip or a toaster to his satisfaction.

Lena had watched him with sheer wonder and pride. First, he took the front off the computer and, with the half-frame magnifying eyeglasses Lena had bought him from the drugstore resting down low on the bridge of his wide regal nose, examined the inner workings. Lena had heard him say so many times to himself as he hunched over his work, "Lord, if I 'a had just one lens out of these little cheap set of spectacles, I coulda turned the world upside down." And she believed him. He seemed to be able to do just about *anything*.

He let his gaze rest on the circuit board, lifted tiny plastic-covered wires and examined connections. Then, after an hour or so, he picked up a tiny tool from the shammy bag her computer consultant had left there and closed the machine back up. Lena thought he was through, but Herman was just beginning.

"Hey, Lena, you don't mind if I go in fo' a look, do you?" he asked her as he rolled back from the computer table in her new ergonomic work chair.

She was snug on the overstuffed sofa.

Humpph, I don't mind nothing you do, she thought to herself. But she didn't even get a chance to say it before Herman sat up straight in the comfortable chair, closed his eyes, and became a mist that entered the computer through the disk slot in the same way that he sometimes became mist and entered her.

Lena was always amazed at the knowledge that he brought from the turn of the century. But then, Herman was an amazing man.

He told her that in life he had been an inventor of sorts. "Now, I ain't no book-educated man. But don't need t' be. I'm that kinda person that been shown a lot in life." Then he paused and added, "In death too, come t' think of it."

What he mainly invented were tools. Lena smiled so broadly at the information that Herman found himself smiling too, even though he had no idea why they were amused.

"You *would* invent tools, Herman," Lena said in answer. "Something useful and needed and able to make things easier and faster and better and smoother and fresher and more level. Sometimes, when you touch me, Herman, I feel useful in your hands."

With a smile, he pretended to tip an imaginary hat and bow his head to the side in response to her compliment.

Just watching him handle a simple awl or a small appliance like a coffee grinder, Lena had known that Herman was an inventor.

She had watched him from her bedroom as he discovered a box of Tampax in one of her bathroom drawers. He leaned right there against the counter's edge and read the entire sheet of information and instructions for the superstrength tampon. Then, he took one out of the baby-blue cardboard box and, looking again at the instructions he had laid on the counter-top, tore open the thin smoking-paper wrapper, and examined the tampon minutely until it was just a fluffy puff of cotton, some thread, and strips of white cardboard.

"Umm, right clever," he said to himself, and chuckled.

Herman even had a knack for finding and excavating artifacts of tools on her property. Century-old knives—blades made of gray and black stone and flint; handles of creamy-hued animal bone and deer and squirrel skin—fashioned by southeastern Indians. Small intricate red clay pipes made by Africans and African-Americans before and after the Civil War to smoke the wild tobacco in the woods during a brief respite. A nearly airtight earthen container of rice with the imprint of the creator's small slender hands inside.

Lena was always amazed at what Herman could find or accomplish in any given stretch of time. He never hurried or fretted over schedules and dates. He managed time the way he talked about it.

"*Time,* baby," he said two or three times a day.

It was Herman's answer to many things.

"*Time.*"

He said it with such assurance and peace, sounding like a down-home preacher comforting a grieving widow.

It was his answer to everything she complained about.

"Herman, I don't think these carrot seeds are ever going to sprout."

"Time, baby."

Or,

"If these folks and accountants and everybody don't stop pulling me every which way . . ."

"Time, Lena."

And even when the answer exasperated her, she always found herself later agreeing it was the right answer, the only answer. "Time."

"Now, where did you hear about laser surgery?" Lena had asked one hot day in June as they sat on the cool grass of the riverbank.

"Shoot, baby, where you think I been fo' the last hundred years?" Herman asked back with a laugh.

"Dead!" Lena said with an intentionally dumb wide-eyed expression on her face.

"Well, there's dead and there's *dead*," he said, looking at her over his half-frame eyeglasses.

When Lena paused, pretending to consider what he said, Herman got a bit indignant and asked, "What part a' me *seem dead* to you?"

Lena laughed. "Not one single part," she said as she fell into Herman's lap and seemed to sink right into him as if she were falling back into the waves of the sea or a pile of crisp autumn leaves.

"How old were you when you died, Herman?" Lena had asked in late May as she lay back on the office sofa with his head in her lap.

"I was just a few weeks shy of markin' my fortieth birth date when I died," he answered matter-of-factly.

"Why, Herman, you're not even *forty*!?" Lena squealed. "Lord, my baby's pig meat."

Herman looked at Lena with a sly smile, chuckling at her brazenness and pride, and went back to tinkering with the sauna control box in his hand.

Herman tinkered around Lena's place so much that her household started functioning so much more smoothly, cheaply, efficiently that even James Petersen took notice. The toilets used less water, the shower and taps too.

And it wasn't just in the house that Herman made his ghostly presence felt.

Herman showed Lena things on her property. Stones washed down from the mountains by Cleer Flo'. Trees budding out of season. Relics from previous civilizations and peoples. Jewelry made of animal bone and feathers. Unusual markings on Baby's stomach Lena had never noticed before. Gossamer silver snakeskins discarded by growing reptiles. Lena began to walk on the very earth differently.

It amazed her how easily she forgot the busy little town of Mulberry.

When she walked now, she felt Herman's arm resting lightly around her shoulders, her shoulder tucked perfectly in his armpit like two pieces of a jigsaw puzzle. She was actually taking time to see, *really see,* the earth she was walking on.

"Ya gotta cherish this piece a' earth we been given, we been born to," Herman said as they walked so far afield on her property that she couldn't even see the tops of her chimneys. "The trick, Lena, baby, is to cherish yo' own little piece of earth, but not to get *tied* to it. 'Cause it ain't nothin' but a piece a' dust, like us, our bodies, that's gon' come and go."

When he found a chinaberry tree on her land, Herman was as excited as if he had created it himself. He came and got her in her home office and brought her right to it.

"You know what we used the root a' the chinaberry tree fo', Lena, don't ya?" he said as he smiled a smile that Lena wanted to just lick off his face. He pretended to wait for her to answer as he kicked at the knot on the trunk of the tree just above the rich dark ground.

"Yeah, they used this root to make a potion to make ya hot. Our folks and the Indians used it in ceremonies and rituals. And other folks just used it.

"Guess *we* can pass on this one, huh, Lena?"

Looking around at a squat prickly bush, he continued the lesson since he had her outside.

"And look a' here, Lena. This what we call China briar. My ma usta make a kind a' mush out a' the root. A bread too. China briar was one of the first thangs I remember ever eatin'."

Herman showed Lena all kinds of things. He explored her hundred acres of property as if it were a tidy little backyard.

While Lena was away at work in town, he uncovered treasures and mysteries that Lena had never even thought about being on her land.

One Sunday morning after they had made love, eaten grits and salmon croquettes, made more love, gone swimming, and lain on her river deck to dry in the sun, Herman took her for a walk. She had wanted to grab a piece of pie or fruit before they left, but Herman wouldn't let her.

"*I* got som'um sweet fo' you," Herman said, laughing and patting a bulge in his pants pocket.

Lena tramped out in her new heavy Timberland boots just like Herman's and followed him into the woods with a smile on her face. She couldn't get enough of him.

They walked for a good long time along the river to the east of the house. Lena was becoming winded.

"Maybe we should have ridden the horses, Herman," she said.

"Naw, not this time," he answered over his shoulder.

When he finally slowed down by a big sycamore tree at

the edge of the woods, she thought he would take out a tiny copper-colored G-string for her to prance around in. Instead, he pulled out a pair of work gloves and handed them to Lena.

"Here, baby, I don't want ya to get hurt."

Lena thought she could hear someone humming in the distance as he led her deeper into the woods. Then he held up a bare hand, stopped, and pointed up ahead to the biggest circular beehive Lena had ever seen. It hung from the swooping lower limb of a massive live oak tree like mistletoe. Herman smiled at Lena while motioning for her to stand still. Then he advanced on the golden-colored humming hive.

Herman slipped his bare hand sideways into the bottom of the nest, deliberately, steadily. He only paused a moment with his hand inside the hive, then slowly pulled his hand back out, rotating it slightly to form a cup as it came out. The hive was shaped just like the ones in cartoons she had watched as a child on Saturday mornings in which a hungry old hairy bear would try and try to get that honey. She had imagined that animated honey to be the best, the sweetest, the most golden honey in the universe.

Lena was mesmerized by Herman's performance. It was like a theater piece, silent except for the lazy-sounding buzzing of the bees. Then Herman drew her into the act. Looking very serious, he lifted his right hand dripping with thick dark honey and flecks of waxy honeycomb up to her lips. She took two of his fingers into her mouth and, lifting her chin, sucked the honey off.

It was as sweet as the cartoon honey. The intensity of the sweetness nearly blew the top of her head off when she smacked her lips.

Herman didn't just treat her to honey. He taught her how to survive.

"Here, Lena, tie this cotton kerchief 'round yo' mouth when we out walkin' in the woods," he instructed her, "so yo' breath don't draw those 'squitas and bitin' flies."

And it worked too. Some days Lena and Herman looked like happy bandits loping through the woods or the dirt trails or riding the horses flat out over the rough terrain off the bridle path.

James Petersen back at the house gazing out the kitchen window over the sink would see her head off happily into the woods and chuckle to himself at the sight of Lena outside talking to thin air. "That girl knows she can talk to herself. She got so much on her mind."

Mostly what Lena had on her mind was ways to spend more time with Herman.

One morning Herman woke Lena even earlier than usual. Brushing her face with the breeze of his kisses, he gently roused her.

"Come on, Lena," he urged when she dreamily opened her eyes. "Put on some long pants and boots. Ticks are bad this year. I got som'um t' show you."

Lena sat on the deacon's bench by the door in the Glass Hall and laced up her boots over her pants legs. She was laughing to herself at the many pairs of work boots and outdoor shoes she had acquired since Herman came into her life when he blew in and grabbed her hand. He didn't even bother to ask what she was laughing at.

"Found som'um you might be interested in," he said with a smile playing in his voice, pleased with Lena's cozy joy.

He pulled her down the path to the stables, where he had saddled Goldie and Baby for them to ride. Lena always tried to ride behind Herman so she could watch his shoulders and the small of his back as he rode. Herman—with his near-midnight self—astride Goldie—with her near-sunrise self—was a sight to behold, one that Lena never tired of seeing.

They set off across her property heading south and didn't stop riding fairly hard until they had circled a stand of impenetrable woods and reached a meadow on the other side that looked like something from a fairy tale.

The field was encircled with trailing bramble. Small vines had formed a wall around the dale that was covered with rich juicy-looking spots of amaranth.

Lena could no longer see the river, but she could hear the music of it rushing close by. Pulling Goldie's reins up, Herman sat back proudly in his saddle as Lena took in the expanse of early-bearing blackberries.

Without a word, Herman dismounted, tied his steed to a bush, and, reaching into his saddlebag, pulled out two croaker sacks. He handed one to Lena. "We gon' pick *berries.*

"Lena, uh-uh, baby, don't pick that berry. It ain't ripe. Come here. Uh-uh-uh, you mean to tell me I gotta teach her how t' pick blackberries *too.*" He mocked her with a little tug on her hand, making the underripe berries in her tin bucket rattle against the sides.

"See this here berry? Now, this un ripe," he said softly, acting as if he were stalking some living, moving, breathing prey. "See how when you look at it, especially in the sun, it almost glisten? And see how plump it is? Plump, plump even before ya touch it. And when you do. OOooo. See, 'bout ready to bust. And when you take it, with these three fingers, and gently tug—lightly now, so you don't break the skin. It's real tender—it oughta come away from the stem easy, real easy like it want to come.

"There," he said happily, sated, holding the glistening berry aloft by the bushes. "And ya got yo' berry."

Then he reached over and popped the lone fruit into Lena's gaping mouth.

Lena bit down on the juicy nugget, sighed, and smiled.

Sister was right, she thought. I do have an abundance of blessings.

The History of the World

VERONICA CHAMBERS

IT'S THREE-FIFTEEN on a Wednesday afternoon, and I take my place in the playground at Ninety-sixth and Fifth with the nannies whose dark skin mirrors my own. It's a caste system—Latins to the right, Black Caribbeans to the left, Eastern Europeans where they think they belong, at the north tip of the park.

I could sit with the Latins; it's where my mother would have me. I'm Panamanian, united with my Central and South American sisters by language and heritage. If they're honest, most Latinas are well aware that some Latins are as dark as me; the ever-popular plantation-era telenovela, be my witness. But New York is a tough town, and people grab advantage where they can. You sit on the right side of the park and it's *"Mira, esta negra"* this and *"Ay, los negros"* that. I put them in their place by letting them know that *"Oye, te entiendo bien,"* but in the ever-revolving cast that is the nanny world, there's always a new light-skinned Latina to school. A few years ago I gave it up. My job is raising children. I don't have the time or energy to raise grown folks too.

I live in Brooklyn with my sister and her three kids. Now that movie stars are moving to the borough, Brooklyn Heights and even Park Slope have become acceptable annexes to Manhattan. Everyone says "Brooklyn" in a different tone of voice. But I live in a part of Brooklyn that is so much like home you could set it adrift in the Atlantic and it would not sink.

My Brooklyn—a ninety-minute subway ride from my job on the Upper, Upper East Side, followed by a twenty-minute ride on the bus or a ten-minute gypsy cab ride—is bordered by stores that sell sugarcane stalks taller than any man I've seen. It's a place where beef patty stands outnumber pizza parlors and a double scoop from the ice-cream man means guava and mango unless otherwise stated. It is not all food, but food is the foundation, and the foundation is firm.

The manicurists are all from the old places—Colón, Bocas del Toro, Darién—and they know how to do all the old styles. The hairstylists are Dominican because they make the strongest relaxers, removing any memory of Africa from your hair. The music of course brings all the Africa back. It's how we do it in Panama and in our Brooklyn outpost—bone-straight hair, meticulous makeup and nails, eighteen-karat jewelry in our ears, and nothing but jungle in our hips.

I met my boyfriend, Felix, in a Panamanian club down on Eastern Parkway. He told me he drove a gypsy cab, a fifteen-year-old red Chrysler LeBaron with white leather interior. I liked the way he was proud of his work, proud of his car, with no silly story about how one day he would own a fleet of taxis and be to the livery industry what Donald Trump is to real estate. He was wearing a mango-colored polo shirt tucked in with a leather belt, the way the men out here do. Two things sold me on Felix from the moment he asked me to dance. One, he is a wonderful dancer, lighter on his feet than you would expect a man of his size to be. Two, he smelled like soap—not just any soap, but the kind of soap my grandmother made and carved just so with the knife she kept in her back pocket. She sold that soap in the market, and when I was little, I would sit with her, rubbing my small fingers along the curve in the soap. When I got older, I heard rumors that my grandmother had killed her first husband, a man who dared to raise his hand to her, with that knife. With the aid of a good banana tree lawyer, the charges against my grandmother were washed clean. The banana tree lawyer became my grandmother's second husband, although by the time I was born, he was dead and gone.

I asked my grandmother once, on a day when I woke up with an abundance of courage and an unusually small amount of fear, whether it was true she had killed a man with the very same knife she used to carve soap. She was neither angry nor offended, as I expected. She simply said, "Live long, see much," which I took to mean my grandmother had experienced her own adventures, it was up for me to go out into the world and experience my own.

I learned, months into our courtship, that Felix did not bathe with a bar of homemade soap, curved on top like a pint of ice cream missing the first delicious spoonful. He did not bathe with bar soap at all. He washed his hair and body with a brown liquid soap that he bought at a health food store near the Brooklyn Bridge. It was a disappointment, the first time I visited his apartment and asked to use the bathroom with the express purpose of seeing a soap that reminded me of home. But by then I had already fallen in love with him. His smell, although different in origin from what I imagined, was always pleasing, which is no small thing.

I MET EVELYN PORTER through Felix. His cousin knew the Porters' previous nanny—they sat together on the brown side of the park. The girl, a dark-skinned Dominican, was leaving the family to pursue a degree in nursing. Evelyn was searching for a replacement, someone to teach the children Spanish, and although she would never overtly say it, Evelyn wanted someone Black. The Porters had two children—Nick, who was just about to turn three, and Zoe, who was seven. Styling the girl's hair was a big part of the job, hence the desire for a nanny whose hair was nappy. Evelyn liked Zoe's hair combed and greased every morning before she left for school and then tidied again before dinner. A once-a-week wash and condition, hot-oil treatment, and then blow dry is how Zoe and the nanny spent their Friday afternoons. The blow dry helps to straighten the hair and, in and of itself, takes upwards of an hour.

Upon our introduction, it was evident that Evelyn expected me to be intimidated by their wealth. It's true, it's not often that you meet a young Black couple on Park Avenue living in a stadium-sized apartment with the same marble floors and well-appointed furniture you might find in a bank or an old-money hotel. But there is nothing like working in somebody's home to cure you of the misconception that you would like to step into a rich woman's shoes. Every marriage has its cracks and fissures. Every child causes you grief; even a perfect child will drive you to despair with worry over her well-being. Everyone has problems at their job; no one ever has enough hours in their day. Even on Park Avenue, the working rich dream of getting away from it all. Yet it's sadder somehow. When you are poor, you have the fantasy, the blissful illusion that money will solve all of your problems. You get to know rich people, and you realize that it is never really enough. Summer weekends at the beach, winter holidays on the slopes, an annual February jaunt somewhere sunny and warm—yet they can't keep the bags from underneath their eyes or the rubber band snap out of their voices when they talk to their spouses and their children, the people they supposedly love. Evelyn and Hart were no different.

It became clear, within weeks of my employment, that her marriage was a disappointment to Evelyn. She believed that she had married well; Hart was from a prominent Virginia family,

Black folks whose onion skins extended way back before the end of slavery. But while he had followed in their tradition by attending the top schools, Hart had landed no further than senior attorney at a downtown not-for-profit. It seemed obvious to me that Evelyn had made an error universal to women of the gold-digging variety the world over, mistaking good breeding for raw ambition. Even in Panama, where the families with "big money" had very little compared to the U.S., you saw the same thing. Girls who married hoping for a waterfront condo in Panama City and ending up with a brand-new washer and dryer in Colón. A man's last name and relations meant only as much as *he* valued it, never as much as *you* valued it. But like my grandmother used to say, common sense is not common.

Evelyn was vice president—the first woman, the first Black—at a Madison Avenue investment firm. Hart's parents helped them buy the apartment on Park Avenue, but it was Evelyn who paid the mortgage. She informed me of this at our very first meeting, and she complained about it frequently. There were many complaints about money at the dinner table, but they had the kind of distant reasoning of people in warm places complaining about the snow. When I first began to work for the Porters, I feared for my job whenever I heard Evelyn talk about things being tight and how she was "sick and tired of trying to make a dollar out of fifteen cents." I even began, discreetly, to put the word out in my old park that I was open to a new position. But then Evelyn would ask me to work late, because she and Hart had tickets to a benefit to raise money for the Costume Institute at the Met or Alvin Ailey or the Studio Museum in Harlem. These tickets, I saw, never cost less than a thousand dollars each. Nothing in Evelyn's social life cost less than a thousand dollars—not her dinners, not her dresses, not the expensive treatments she had on her face and her legs. Her shoes, always Louboutin with their flash of red sole, were the only discounted thing on her body. The price tags on the boxes inched toward a thousand but never superseded it. I stopped looking for a new job.

Zoe and Nick were easy children to take care of, no more spoiled than any other children whose parents could afford full-time help. At three, Nick had his father's easy affability, which I suspected might someday turn into a streak of laziness, but his future was Evelyn's problem, not my own. Zoe had been given the impression from far too young an age that she was a great beauty, and you know what they say, pretty is as pretty does, which in the end isn't very pretty at all. Zoe liked to call me by my Christian name and seemed to be allergic to the words *please* and *thank you*. I suspected that it was the constant hair combing that led her to believe I was not her child care provider, but rather more like a lady-in-waiting. Her mother expected me to attend to her toilette like she was a teenage queen of England, not a seven-year-old little girl. But this was where Zoe being Black and my being Black worked to my advantage. The little girl may live on Park Avenue, but her hair was as thick as any little girl in the projects. Zoe soon learned that my combing hair could be easy or it could be very, very painful, and soon enough, she began to behave accordingly. In the end, the children were just that, children. It was Hart and Evelyn whom I found endlessly fascinating. Perhaps because, while Felix and I could not be more different from Evelyn and Hart, we were ourselves on the road to marriage. I was curious about marriage during the time I worked for Evelyn and Hart and anxious to learn from their mistakes.

"He's all Black," Evelyn whispered to me one day, as her husband stood ironing a shirt for work. "But there's an awful lot of milk in his coffee." I think she thought I had been admiring Hart physically. He had the kind of fair skin and Roman profile that women tend to admire. This, however, was not what had caught my attention. It still surprised me to see a man doing his own ironing. It was not how I had been raised nor had it been the practice of my previous employers. Evelyn had let me know that while they had a housekeeper who came twice a week, she expected me to pitch in and help with the children's laundry whenever necessary. She would, on occasion, ask me to iron a blouse for her if she was running late for work and behind on her dry cleaning. But Hart's clothes were off-limits to me. "You're here for the children, not for us," she said whenever I offered to do something for her husband. So we stood together, on many occasions, watching him iron a shirt, or a pair of pants, or a handkerchief for his jacket pocket. As we watched him, I knew we were feeling very different things. Evelyn thought of Hart's ironing as punishment. If he made more money, he would not have to iron his own clothes. But I thought of his ironing as a kind of love letter. In my eyes, a man who ironed his own shirts, who did not expect you to do it, was better, stronger, kinder than a man who bought you flowers and chocolate on Valentine's Day but expected you to act like his scullery maid the other 364.

One day, when Hart was working late, Evelyn told me about the day she had fallen out of love with her husband. Those were her exact words: "I am going to tell you about the day I fell out of love with my husband." I was anxious to leave. It was nearly seven o'clock, and I had been in the Porter household since 7:00 A.M. The children had already eaten and were watching a movie in the den. Evelyn invited me to have dinner with her. It was a request without the expectation of a reply, as she did not expect that I might have other plans. I was not meeting Felix that night, so I called my sister and let her know that I was going to be home late.

I sat at the kitchen table as Evelyn made dinner. To watch her cook was to have some small glimpse of how she was in the workplace. She did not change out of her silk blouse or pencil skirt for the task. She seemed as comfortable in her work clothes as the other women her age in the building seemed in their cashmere sweat suits. While I did not envy Evelyn her apartment, her designer shoes, her black tie evening gowns, I did envy her body. She had a body like a track star; you could see the muscles ripple under her skin like a river carved out of stone. Every once in a while when I found myself feeling haughty, as if I were the mother and Evelyn were the hired help, I looked at Evelyn's muscles, and I reminded myself that she might be petty, but she was not a woman to be trifled with.

Evelyn informed me that she was making us a mushroom risotto for dinner. Again, this was not a question but a statement. She did not ask me if I was allergic to mushrooms, and I did not want to give her the satisfaction of letting her know that I had no idea what risotto was. I was relieved when she took out a box of Arborio, and I could see that this dish consisted mainly of rice. She cooked the rice, slowly, methodically in a big copper pot that was itself a thing of beauty. I thought then of Felix, and of our future, and hoped that a pot like that might someday grace our kitchen.

The story that Evelyn told me went back some fifteen years. She was still in business school; Hart was a year out of law school. They did not yet live together, as that would ruin all prospects for a marriage Hart's family would approve of. Hart lived in Gramercy Park, in a sublet arranged for him by a friend of the family. Evelyn lived in Columbia University student housing with three other girls she could not stand.

One Saturday afternoon she and Hart had arranged to go to the movies. But Hart was at the office, preparing a brief. Evelyn arranged to meet him there. She was shocked to find that his office was a pigsty. "I do not exaggerate," she said, chopping exotic-looking mushrooms and tossing them, as she chopped, into the rice. "There were papers everywhere, unopened mail, old magazines, dirty pizza boxes, empty Chinese takeout containers full of mold." Hart noticed her horrified expression and laughed. "There's a method to my madness," he said, trying to reassure her. "But the office cleaning woman won't even empty my wastepaper basket anymore. It's a trip."

Evelyn was shocked. How could Hart not know what a travesty such a filthy office was? How could he not know how badly this reflected on him, the only Black first-year associate at this powerful firm? That was the day Evelyn knew just how far Hart would go, which was not, in her estimation, very far. She looked around his office and wondered how he had missed it, the essential message of their children-of-the-dream upbringing: Be impeccable, know that you'll have to work twice as hard to get half as far. She did not know that Hart had been trained, ruined maybe, by his White friends, who moved through the world as slippery as fish. The confidence, the gift of these boys, was their inherent confidence in the fact that they were born with gills. They took the spoils of their privilege as easily as the rest of us take in air.

Evelyn served us both a plate of risotto and poured each a glass of white wine. She had never offered me wine before, but I sipped it without question, admiring its cool, crisp taste and how well it paired with the cheesy, slightly soupy rice. I noted the name on the bottle and imagined making such a meal for Felix. By the time she had poured me a second glass I was bold enough to ask the question that had been gnawing at me since her monologue had begun.

"Why did you marry him then?"

She did not, as I expected, take my question seriously. Instead, she continued her story. "The day I went to Hart's office, I was so horrified that I spent the entire day cleaning it. He kept offering up false apologies about being busy with the brief. But what I remember most is him tapping away at the computer while I spent hours sorting through the papers and throwing away empty food containers that looked like after Hart was done with them, rats had had a run at them as well. Each layer revealed a nastier level of filth, and by the time I was finished, I was so angry I could barely speak. But what could I do? He hadn't asked me to clean his office, I volunteered. So I begged off of dinner and went home, determined to break up with him."

"What happened then?" I asked, worried that if I did not hurry her along, Hart would come home and she would think twice, the next day, about finishing the story she had begun.

"The following Sunday he asked me to meet him for brunch. After we ate, he took me to Tiffany's and bought me this ring."

She waved her hand at me, five thin brown fingers, each immaculately polished in a pink the color of cotton candy. On her ring finger, a Flintstones-sized gem sparkled. It was of course a ring I had seen many times before.

"It's a big diamond," I said appreciatively.

"It's a *big-ass* diamond," she said, laughing. "Emerald-cut. Double channel band. It cost sixteen thousand dollars, and Hart bought it as easily as if he were putting a quarter in a gumball machine."

As if on cue, we heard Hart at the front door. Evelyn rose, her story not finished but finished enough. She kissed her husband and then urged him to check on the kids. "They've been curiously silent," she said, waving him off.

To me, she said, "It's late. You should take a taxi." This was unusual. She had never offered me taxi fare home before. But I took the two crisp twenty-dollar bills and was pondering whether I would actually take a taxi or save the money and take the subway when she reached out for my shoulder. Once again, she flashed me her ring. "Tiniest handcuff in the world," she said, laughing, without any hint of a smile in her voice.

I took the subway home that night, and the following weekend I made Felix a dinner of risotto and white wine, using the money Evelyn had given me for a cab. I spent ten dollars on the Arborio and mascarpone, a cheese I'd never heard of. Then I spent another ten on a bottle of Pinot Grigio. I reserved the second twenty, in case dinner was a disaster and I needed to run to the corner for two orders of curried goat and rice. But I followed the instructions I had found in one of Evelyn's cookbooks to the letter, and dinner was perfect. Felix had never had risotto and asked me if I might make it every Sunday night. This was not likely. The risotto had required 'round-the-clock minding, and I think, ultimately, I preferred my rice with less liquid and no cheese. But I made a mental note of Felix's flexible palate and vowed to surprise him with new dishes as often as I could.

HART NEVER made partner at the law firm where Evelyn had spent an afternoon cleaning up his office. He wasn't fired exactly, but it was suggested that his talents would be better used elsewhere, and so it was he'd taken a job at the NAACP Legal Defense Fund. He had been there ever since. Evelyn saw him as a man fallen from glory, and in her mind, this was a fact that would never change. Her diminished expectations were understandable enough, but my grandmother had taught me the one constant in life was change. I could feel it in the Porters' house, and I often wondered what it might be. Might Hart meet another woman down there at the NAACP, a nice Black girl, half Evelyn's age, with no Park Avenue aspirations and an abiding passion for ironing Hart's shirts? Or would Evelyn be the one to leave, abandoning Hart and the children for one of those European robber barons who would relish the thought of a smart, wealthy Black woman as his second wife?

As it were, change came not in the form of infidelity as I expected, but under the guise of friendship. Hart had a good friend from childhood, a man who was a regular houseguest of the Porters whenever he was in town, which was often. I had met both him and his wife on a number of occasions. Like Hart, the man was dedicated to "fighting the good fight," which Evelyn took to mean he had chosen a career path in which he would never make any money. Evelyn was none too fond of the wife, although she did a decent job of hiding it. The woman, who lived in Chicago with her husband, was pretty enough but modest in her dress and demeanor. Behind her back, Evelyn called her Ann Taylor because the woman bought all of her work clothes there and regularly tried to bond with Evelyn over news of an upcoming sale. Evelyn, who bought her work clothes at Bergdorf's, preferred labels that went by one name, not two: Armani, Escada, Valentino.

Sometimes it seemed that it was one of Evelyn's few pleasures in life that as low as Hart had sunk, they still had much to lord over this couple, who were, in terms of race and breeding, their closest peers.

"Have you ever been to Chicago?" Evelyn would ask me, moments after showing her husband's dearest friend to the door.

I had not.

"It's so provincial," she said. "And they don't even live on the Gold Coast. They live in this itsy-bitsy house in some god-forsaken suburb. I mean she actually thinks Ann Taylor is a bona fide designer."

It was always like that when the couple came to visit. Evelyn was always cutting them down, despite the fact that Hart and the man were more like brothers than friends and the couple had two girls who were exactly Nick and Zoe's age. One year Hart suggested the families pool their resources and rent a house in Jamaica for the winter vacation. Evelyn complained about it for weeks.

"They've never even been to the Caribbean!" she said. "I don't think either one of them has been out of the country since they met in Africa, working for the Peace Corps."

"That's very impressive," I said. "I've heard about the Peace Corps."

Evelyn rolled her eyes at me as if I should know better than to open my mouth unless invited to speak.

"Please," she said. "Travel in college hardly counts."

This hurt my feelings more than it should have. Much to my own surprise, I was wounded by her presumptiveness. She seemed cruelly unaware what I would have given to have gone to college, how much more I would have valued a chance at the Peace Corps over a lazy, rich person's vacation at a villa in Jamaica.

THE MAN'S BUSINESS brought him to New York more and more often. As he could not afford a hotel, Hart named the family's guest room as a suite in his honor. Whenever he could extend his trip to include a weekend, the woman joined him, and the four of them—Evelyn and Hart, Hart's friend and his wife—would see the latest Broadway show and visit the fanciest restaurants. The couple from Chicago became Evelyn's favorite object of derision as they were a hearty stand-in for her husband, whom she could not or would not mock to his face. Then one day everything changed. The man gave a speech at a political convention that attracted a great deal of media attention. He won a prominent position in government, and people began to talk that he might be the first Black man to serve as president of the United States. He was on television constantly, though the first time I saw him, it caught me unawares. I was watching the evening news with my sister when his familiar face flashed across the screen. "I know that man," I said. "He's a friend of Evelyn and Hart's." And then I had a thought that showed how badly I had been indoctrinated with Evelyn's rude ways, I thought, What is he doing on TV? He lives in an itsy-bitsy house in the suburbs of Chicago, and his wife actually thinks Ann Taylor is a big-name designer.

Evelyn no doubt had the same thought the first, second, and hundredth time she saw the man on TV. But it soon became clear his fame was no flash in the pan; it was the real deal. As humble as ever, the man and his wife continued to visit the Porters whenever they were in town. The man, now a regular presence on the cover of magazines, seemed to rely on Hart as a touchstone, a truth teller in an uncertain sea of new friends and overly zealous supporters.

The woman, Evelyn noted, no longer wore Ann Taylor. She now showed up for dinner at the Porters' dressed in Donna Karan and Oscar de la Renta, confessing, somewhat embarrassedly, that whenever she met a designer, the next day he sent over a rack full of clothes in her size. Evelyn's eyes widened, and she began to warm to the woman. I had to admit that her behavior was impressive. Evelyn was not so sycophantic that the woman would recognize her immediately as a fake, but she began to reach out casually, in ways that suggested she was merely strengthening the relationship, not deepening what had been only a very shallow acquaintance before.

When February rolled around, there was no question that the couple from Chicago would join the Porters on their annual jaunt to Jamaica. This time around there was no complaining from Evelyn. Rather, if anything, she seemed slightly nervous about being outshone by the wife. Every day she brought home shopping bags full of what she called resort wear, expensive warm-weather clothes that are sold only in the wintertime. Then the next day she took it all back. She had always seemed so confident in her wardrobe choices, donning the latest looks as easily as her seven-year-old daughter wore her school uniform. But the days leading up to the Jamaica vacation were a flurry of shopping, returns, and exchanges.

Evelyn returned from Jamaica rested and buoyant. During the vacation Hart's friend had told them that he would soon be announcing his bid for the presidency and he wanted Hart to play a key role in the campaign. The Porters were moving to Chicago, where campaign headquarters would be set up. And after the election, if all went well, they would move to Washington, D.C.

"Congratulations," I told Evelyn, and although this meant I would soon lose my job, I was genuinely happy for them, especially Hart, who was being rewarded for being such a good friend.

"Thank you," Evelyn said, beaming. "I want you to know that I'd like you to come with us."

"To Chicago?" I said, somewhat stupidly, since I knew this was where they were going.

"No, to Mars," Evelyn said, affixing me with the full beam of her grin.

I knew she did not remember that I have a sister in New York and nieces and nephews that I love. She did not remember that I have a boyfriend who I hope will one day be my husband. It was not her job to remember that I have a life away from Park Avenue. I imagine it is inconceivable to her that there is life beyond Park Avenue.

"I couldn't," I said quietly.

"What are you staying here for?" she chided. "That chubby little taxi driver with the high-pitched voice? I'm offering you a front seat to history in the making."

I was both surprised that she had remembered Felix and hurt that she had chosen to dismiss him in such unflattering terms.

"You're an attractive girl," Evelyn said. "You could do very well for yourself. I'd like for you to stay with us for at least two more years, until Nick begins kindergarten, but after that I wouldn't be averse to setting you up with a nice lobbyist or policy researcher. You're bilingual, and Washington is a very international city. With the right introduction, it's not inconceivable that you could marry above your station."

I found this interesting, that she spoke of my "station" as if it were a fixed and solid thing, rather than the uneven labyrinth of trapeze bars and swings that she herself had traversed. At any given moment during our acquaintance, she had made it clear that she sometimes thought of marrying Hart as marrying up, but she just as often thought of it as marrying down. Now the couple was on the upswing again, and it seemed only natural to her that what I would want for my own life was some facsimile of hers.

If I had the gift of speaking my mind without filters, I would have told Evelyn that while Hart's friend's bid for the presidency was indeed exciting, I did not need a front seat to that particular portion of American history. If I was bold, I would have told Evelyn that, presidential pal or no, she should treasure her marriage because at the end of the day there really is only one story in the history of the world: You're born, and you spend a portion of your life feeling lonely and adrift. If you're lucky, that time is very short, and if you're unlucky, that time never ends. But if you're average, you meet a man who thinks you walk on water and because of this single, irrational thought, he'll give you anything he's got. It may be half of the bed in the Lincoln Bedroom. It may be a lifetime supply of free taxi rides for your sister and all of her rambunctious kids. It's not history in the making, like Hart's friend and his presidential race, but it's how we live our lives. It's all the history I need or care to know.

At first, Evelyn was hurt, offended even. But as winter turned toward spring, and Hart became a regular presence on television and in the newspapers, she softened toward me again. She found a way not to take my rejection of her job offer personally. I imagine it has something to do with her fantasy of me as the noble immigrant, that she came to see as rooted in a Brooklyn she has never seen, the way the Statue of Liberty stubbornly plants her stone feet on Liberty Island.

As for me, the evening that Evelyn offered to take me to Chicago, to give me the opportunity to sit with and serve greatness, Felix came and picked me up from work. It's not something he did often, but somehow he seemed to always know when I was just too weary to take the subway and then a bus home. No matter that he could have cleared a hundred dollars in the two hours it takes him to drive from Tilden Avenue to Park Avenue to pick me up and back again. He sat in the car, straining to listen to some Haitian station he would lose if he drove even two more blocks north. The smile on his face when he saw me emerge from the service entrance let me know this was a man who would carry me, from borough to borough, by piggyback, if it were my pleasure. I am not my grandmother. She was the type of woman that men feared and women envied. But I do have the sense that my grandmother gave me. She would consider me a portrait in foolishness to make myself a willing exile from this land called love.

Coming Clean

NICOLE BAILEY-WILLIAMS

IT WAS A WEEK AWAY from my wedding, and I was scared witless and shitless. I had been with Laurence since our senior year in high school when the star football player had guided us to a teeth-clenching, on-the-edge-of-our-seats win, and I, a pageant princess, walked away with another title, Homecoming Queen. It was that night, when he was coasting on the dizzying vapors of victory, and I was sedated by the satisfaction of collecting another trophy, that I held his gaze when he smiled at me. And I smiled back.

I'd never liked football players. I'd thought that they were shallow, dumb even, so although I'd found him physically attractive, I'd never thought that he was anything more than a decorative shell. I, on the other hand, was actually proud of my reputation of being pretty, intelligent, talented, pleasant, and yet untouchable.

I prided myself on being every freshman's dream—the girls' silent envy and the boys' overt desire. But they saw only the shell. The beautifully decorated Fabergé egg. Inside, I was flawed, but I never let anyone get close enough to see that.

But that night when he smiled at me, the clasp came undone, and I was thrown wide open. Vulnerable, unburdened and surprisingly happy.

We'd sat in the bleachers and talked for hours after the dance. With his football jacket draped over my shoulders, we mused about the colleges we were applying to, our hopes for the future, and how we wanted to change the world. With youthful optimism and suburban kids' security, we were confident that we'd make a big impact on the community and the world.

He kissed me that night as we stood on the step in front of my door, and I knew we were on the verge of something that would change the rest of my life.

We were inseparable for the rest of the school year, and we compared notes as college acceptances poured in. Hampton? Yeah, but only a partial athletic scholarship. Howard, yes. Money, nope. Duke, yes, and a full ride. North Carolina, here we come.

And off we went hundreds of miles away with each other as our only support system. His mother had spent the past five years floating in and out of his life in a hazy, smoke-filled world, leaving him and his two siblings to be raised by a reluctant aunt. At eighteen, he still didn't know who his father was. My mother, who was dripping rich and on husband number four, seemed more than happy to have me out of the house so that she could continue her perpetual party without any interruption from me.

My real father had died of lung cancer when I was six, and the parade of men my mother had trotted in to act as his replacement had been worthless to me. They'd been a gold mine to her. That's what she drummed into my head.

"Honey, keep yourself up. No man wants to come home to a cow unless he's a farmer."

She'd started me in the pageant circuit when I was almost ten, saying, "You really need to improve your walk. You look like Igor lurking around here. And lift your chin. The only thing interesting down there are my Prada boots."

She didn't know that the reason I kept my head down was that husband number two had filled me with shame one drunken night while one of their parties roared on below my bedroom. That was something no charm lessons, Borghese products, or tennis bracelet could ever erase. And silently I carried it with me for years.

And Laurence was the only one I'd ever told. I'd carried that burden so long, and he bore witness to it. So whether he liked it or not, he was stuck with me forever.

Duke was just as lonely for me as I expected. Laurence was happy, though. He had friends from the team, and tons of people on campus knew him directly and me by association. I'd been used to being a standout on my own, but as Mom had told me countless times, "There's always someone prettier."

That advice had done absolutely nothing for my self-esteem and had only bolstered my seemingly absent but realistically present insecurity. And vultures started swarming as soon as we landed on campus.

He smiled and laughed them off at first, holding my hand a little tighter, but the rumors began during sophomore year.

Black students were few and far between, so that enabled me to keep people at arm's length, maintaining the superficial relationships I was used to having. So there was a lot that got by me. But then I overheard two female students snickering as I passed them on my way to a finance class. (I'd selected finance as a major, as my mother suggested, so that I knew how to handle a rich man's money.) A few days later Laurence was waiting for me after class, and some guys were giving him high fives and dapping him up. When I approached him, his smile froze, and the guys grinned broadly and nodded hello to me before walking away.

"You look like you've just seen a ghost," I teased, standing beside him.

"Naw. You just threw me for a loop, sneaking up on me like that."

"What am I supposed to do, wear a bell around my neck?"
I joked.

He smiled absently but said nothing as we walked out of
the building.

"Let's go off campus to get something to eat," he suggested.

"What's the occasion?"

"Our win over Louisville," he said.

"Okay."

As we walked to the parking lot where my BMW X5, a gift
to me from Momma via husband number three, was parked,
people congratulated Laurence on the team's away game. More
than a few of them called him a nickname I'd never heard
before.

"So what's up with the name Pancake?"

"It's because I flip 'em over like pancakes when I'm on the
field."

"Cute," I said.

But over the next week I heard a different reason. I had
just entered the suite where I stayed, and I overheard my suite
mates talking.

". . . and when he's done, he flips them over to hit the other
side. Like he's flipping pancakes."

"Oh my God. Do you think she knows?"

"I doubt it. She's such a rigid ice princess she'd never let
him . . ."

"You never know what people do in private."

My breath caught in my throat, and I felt my heart thump-
ing like it wanted to break through my chest.

I backed quietly out of the living room and rushed down
the hall to the elevator. I tried to maintain some semblance
of poise, for Mom always said, "Even if you have to cry, do it
behind Chanel frames."

I made it to the parking lot, jumped in my car, and screeched off the campus, having no idea where I was heading. I drove for hours with tears blurring my vision, and I wished that I had someone to talk to. Laurence had been my best friend for the past two years, and it hurt like hell not being able to reach out to him since he was the one responsible for my anguish and pain. The only other person who I could think to call was my mother.

Her cell phone rang and rang, and I cursed every time I hung up. "Why have a cell phone if you're not going to pick it up?" I shrieked, throwing mine into the passenger seat. I was sitting in the parking lot of the mall, and the backseat was loaded with shopping bags—a lesson in therapy I'd learned at home.

Finally, my cell phone rang.

"Mom," I said into the mouthpiece after checking the number on the incoming call.

"Darling, is there something wrong? I see that I missed your call."

Call! It was just like her to minimize my seven frantic calls, condensing them into one.

"Laurence is cheating on me," I said.

"Wait a second, honey," she said.

I heard her murmuring hellos and other greetings to people as she moved to a quieter place.

"Sorry, sweetie. I'm at a dinner party at the Nelsons'. I only saw that you called when I looked in my purse for a pen."

I was silent as she blathered on.

"Now what did you say, sugar?"

"I said that Laurence is cheating on me."

"What does that mean?"

"It means that he's fucking someone else."

"Cheyenne," she said calmly, "did I teach you to curse like that?"

"No."

"Is it appropriate for you to curse at your mother?"

"No."

"Be glad that you're all the way down there."

"Yes, ma'am."

"Okay, so is he having these dalliances with any one particular person?"

Dalliances. Leave it to my mother to turn into Danielle Steele while my heart was crumbling.

"I don't know."

"Is he doing it right under your nose?"

"Not that I know of. I think it's happening on road trips for football."

"That's good."

"What's good about it?"

"At least he's trying to spare your feelings. He's being respectful."

"Respectfully cheating? You're killing me, Mom."

"No, baby, it's time for you to grow up. Rich men, poor men, young men, old men, all men have the potential to cheat. What are you willing to tolerate?"

"What? None of it, Mom. This is insane."

"Cheyenne, listen. Laurence is a nice guy, and he's got a wealth of potential. Right now he's just—how do you say—smelling himself because he's really popular. Trust me, women can smell money. It's actually not a bad trait—like a sixth sense."

"Mom?"

"What I'm saying is that with a high-profile man, you've got to expect some of this."

"Does that mean I've got to accept it, Mom?" I whined, my voice climbing to a pitch at which a dog could hear it. "I mean, is there an acceptable price tag at which I should feel comfortable selling myself?"

"Honey, you're being irrational."

"Mom, I need real guidance. I need your help."

"I'm trying to help you. You don't want my help."

"You're trying to turn me into some submissive—"

"Who said anything about being submissive?"

"You want me to just roll over and take it as long as the price tag—"

"Cheyenne, I will not do this now. I'm out at a party. I'll call you when I get home."

I was thinking, Don't bother. Instead, I just mumbled, "Bye," before I turned my phone off.

When I returned to my suite, I breezed in with a smile plastered to my face, a good show for my vicious suite mates. Thank God they weren't there. I unpacked my purchases and tucked them neatly away. No one needed to know that I'd tried retail therapy to get over Laurence's humiliation. As long as I could hide my shame, layer myself in perfection, they'd never have to know what I was really feeling.

As I washed off my mask of makeup that night, I still wasn't sure what I wanted to do about Laurence. I loved him, but was love worth my self-respect? I didn't have much experience with love, but I knew that I wasn't supposed to feel like I was bartering my dignity just to be with someone.

I slept fitfully that night, trying to stifle my tears so that my roommate wouldn't hear, and morning found me puffy-eyed and disheveled.

"I tried calling you all night," I heard Laurence say as he stood in the doorway.

I looked at my roommate's side of the room, and I was happy to find her gone.

"I got into it with my mom, so I hung up and turned the phone off," I muttered, pulling my hair down from its ponytail so that it would fluff around my face and hide my eyes.

"Is everything okay with you two?"

"It will be," I said, swinging my legs around to the floor and scurrying around the room, trying to look busy.

"Do I get a kiss?"

"Ooh, it's morning. I didn't brush yet. Why don't you go ahead and I'll meet you after class?" I suggested, heading toward the bathroom.

"Okay. I'll see you later."

"Toodles."

In the shower I cursed myself for my cowardice. My brave self said, "You should have told him to go to hell. You were the one who he called every time his crackhead mama showed up. Your mother brought you both to college. You are the one who types his papers and does his laundry. You've made him who he is."

Yeah, a man who doesn't respect you. I skipped my first class that morning and headed over to an apartment complex near the mall. I filled out an application and wrote out a check for the deposit. I planned a move-in date for the second week in January, a week before classes resumed. If I was going to debase myself by keeping Laurence in my life, I sure didn't need anyone to bear witness to my humiliation. A single apartment with unfamiliar neighbors would help me save face.

The next two years breezed by in a flash, and I was virtually shielded from Laurence's indiscretions. With his own key to my place and a car to get around, we practically lived together. Officially, he had a ratty old apartment, but he kept more stuff at my place than at his own.

But there were moments. Once I returned from a weekend trip to St. Kitts with my mom and found a tube of lipstick under my sofa. Another time I skipped a morning class because of cramps, and I overheard him whispering on the phone in the kitchen. On yet another occasion, when I was finishing a project with a partner, I found him having a "study group" with three female students in my living room. It wouldn't have been so bad if they'd actually had their books open, but a bottle of tequila sat where those should have been. And one of the girls had already had one shot too many.

Over and over I'd swallowed my words and bitten my tongue. My self-esteem was shattered, but I had the official title of girlfriend. Whatever that meant. But during spring break of senior year, Laurence took things to a different level. With a ring.

After the bowl games, he'd been drafted to play in the NFL, and to celebrate, he'd invited me, my mom, and her husband out to dinner with him, his aunt, his uncle, and his siblings. His mom had even pulled herself together for the event, probably smelling the dollar signs from whatever alley she'd been using for her hotel. We were gathered around a long table at the Chart House overlooking the Delaware River. The lights from Camden twinkled in the distance. From the other tables, our scene probably looked most amicable. Celebratory and fun even. But inside, I was as twisted as I had been for two years.

Laurence had been kind to me and decent enough, and we'd had few arguments, probably because I let him do what he wanted. But inside, I crumbled every time he touched me. I'd tried to be more seductive and adventurous, but it came off badly. As poised as I was, I couldn't master hooker heels, and I twisted my ankle trying. I must have given terrible head because he stopped me during my first attempt, telling me, "No teeth, baby, no teeth." I felt like a sexual failure, frigid like my suite mates had said, and part of me understood his desire to find someone more experienced. So I said nothing about his philandering, glad that he was at least respectful enough to always wear a condom with me. If I turned a blind eye to his cheating, and acted as if I didn't see a thing, I could ignore it all.

But there was no ignoring the ring that beamed from the top of the strawberry in the center of my crème brûlée.

"Four karats, princess-cut . . ." my mother began whispering to me as she clutched my hand beneath the table. She leaned over and hugged me before holding my face in her hands, saying softly, "You've invested the time. Now reap the reward." She cleared her throat and said loud enough for all to hear, "Say something."

"He didn't ask," I said, smiling and turning to look at Laurence.

"That's a question if I ever heard one," his mother said, smiling and showing all of her gums.

Laurence said, "So what do you say? Do you want to jump the broom?"

"Yes," I responded with a slightly embarrassed smile.

He stood and walked over to me, pulling me in for a kiss.

My mother had kicked into socialite gear, setting a date for us to be photographed before we went back to finish senior year. She sent announcements to every newspaper and local magazine within an hour's drive. The engagement party was planned for the weekend after graduation, and she'd host it at the hip new Sino-French restaurant in Center City, Philadelphia.

She was in her element, calling florists, doing tastings at various reception sites, previewing wedding souvenirs, sampling wedding cakes, and beginning the search for a gown. In between our appointments, she doled out advice.

"No long engagements. You don't want to give him too much time to think about it.

"Get pregnant right away. You'll secure your place early on.

"Cut off any of your unmarried associates. You don't want to invite temptation right into your door."

Her excitement was infectious, and I could almost see myself getting caught up in the anticipation of it all. But something was missing, and if she had stopped and focused, she could have seen the vacancy in my eyes.

A month before our February nuptials, the round of bridal showers began. The first one at church for the congregation members who watched me grow up. The second one for family and old friends, for surely they couldn't mix with the new, polite, highbrow crowd who attended the third shower. I was glassy-eyed through it all, and Laurence was blissfully oblivious. He just signed checks, for Mother smiled, telling me, "You have to show him early on what his role is. Check signer."

But none of it felt right, and even with my minimal experience, I knew that.

So a week before the wedding, my bridesmaids, a motley crew of my peers who were the children of Mom's friends, and I sat in a spa in Center City. Mom had cornered the wedding planner, twisting her arm into coming too, and the two of them sat, reviewing the dizzying details of my wedding, which was sure to be the social event of the season. With her face scrubbed clean, my mother looked angelic, like Dante's Beatrice leading him on a journey. And watching her, I felt my throat closing as the lower rims of my eyes filled with tears.

"Mommy," I whimpered.

She looked up from her conversation with the wedding planner. "Give me a moment, Vivian," she said to her.

When Vivian left, my walled-up emotions completely crumbled, and tears splattered into the plush robe that was the spa-goers' uniform.

My mother rushed over and sat on the divan with me.

"What is it, baby?" she cooed.

"I . . . I . . . don't want to do this," I sputtered.

I'd been envisioning what my life would be like as Laurence's wife, and the thought of it terrified me. During the season I'd be the dutiful, perhaps even enthusiastic wife at the games, proudly watching my man do his thing with the pigskin. If I followed my mother's advice, I'd have a baby early, so I'd be stuck at home while he traveled to away games because, nanny or no, my conscience wouldn't allow me to leave my child out of my care for too long. And while he was away . . . hell, it wouldn't have to be while he was away from me. He'd been doing dirt right under my nose for years, and I hadn't said a word. And in my silence, I'd lost my self-respect and his respect too.

My mother looked into my eyes before looking down and grasping my hands.

"Baby, I'm sorry that I haven't always given you the best advice about love. The truth is, I don't know a lot about it. Hell, you see that. I'm on husband number four, and I don't know how long he's going to be around. He hates me, and I suspect that his attorney is trying to find a loophole in the prenup before he serves papers on me."

"I'm sor—" I began.

"Don't be. I'm a big girl. I'm finally figuring it out, after all of these trips down the aisle. So after all of that instability, I owe you some love lessons because I want you to be luckier in love than I was."

"If this is more of your advice about marrying well and living like a diva—"

"No, no. What I'm about to share is the real stuff. The stuff that love legacies are made of. Are you ready?" she asked with a smile.

"Mm-hmm," I sniffed.

"Okay. Thing number one—the way you start off is the way things will stay for a very long time. That's with house-work, sex, everything. So you've lost a little ground with turning a blind eye to his loose-zipper syndrome. First things first, make him get tested and you go too. Acknowledge that you know about it, and tell him that with the ring, you expect that things are going to change.

"Thing number two—the only third person in your marriage should be God.

"Thing number three—communicate constantly. Men don't know what you're thinking, so you have to make it plain for them. Spell it out and don't make them guess. Also, talk about your day—simple stuff as well as big stuff. That way you'll be involved in each other's lives.

"Thing number four is to make sure that you make time for yourselves individually, as a couple, and as a family. He needs time with the guys, but make sure that you know who his friends are and let him know whose friendship is unpalatable to you. That means he needs to cut off some of those single, ne'er-do-well friends as well as the married ones who make it a habit to cheat.

"Thing five—don't let the sun set on your wrath. You don't know what can happen during the night, so don't go to bed angry.

"Thing six. Even with a nanny and a housekeeper, make sure that you share household responsibilities.

"Thing seven, stand up for yourself. Don't be passive or let anyone walk over you. Some folks will have you, as the wife, submitting all over the place, but you're no one's doormat.

"The final thing is to love each other. It's so easy to get caught up in these rules and work and life, but if you're going to go through with this wedding, you have an obligation to God, yourself, and each other to make it work. I'm dishing out all of this advice, and I hope that it's good. Maybe next time around, I'll get it right."

I reached out and hugged my mother, and she kissed me on the forehead.

"It's your choice, baby. You do what feels good to you. Laurence is a great guy, but don't marry him just because you have a past together. History is history, but you can make the future right."

"Okay."

The next Saturday was Valentine's Day, and as I sat at the vanity, looking at myself in the mirror, I took a deep breath.

"You're beautiful," I said. "And you deserve the best. So go out there and claim your man."

I pulled the veil down over my face, stood up, and said a prayer.

An Act of Faith

DAVID ANTHONY DURHAM

*J*OYCE HAD JUST TURNED twenty-one when she first met Calvin, in the fall of 1967. It was a fair day at an outdoor shopping center, where she worked in a flower shop. She stood behind the counter, her concentration focused on the cash register, whose jammed drawer she was trying to pry open with a screwdriver. She moved gently, eyebrows close together in concentration, scared of scratching the paint and yet angry because the stupid thing was always messing with her.

Business had been light all day. Perhaps that was why her head snapped up so forcefully when he strode through the entrance, bringing with him a gust of air that ruffled the leaves of the plants around the door. He held a clipboard in one hand, a small package under his arm. A pencil stuck out from behind his ear. He was a slim, dark-skinned brother in his early twenties, with an athletic body like a mid-range sprinter. His tight-fitting brown slacks hugged the muscles of his legs and outlined the firm shape of his behind. Joyce took him in with one quick glance and then shoved the screwdriver under the counter.

He skipped-slid toward her and handed her the package. "Hey, girl, you working here or tossing the joint?"

"It's jammed," Joyce answered. "Should I sign?"

Their hands touched as he handed her the clipboard. Though Joyce was shy by nature and circumstance, she found her gaze lingering on his for a few long moments. His eyes pressed heavy on his lower lids, but instead of looking tired they gave off a bemused sensuality, as if he were watching her from under the bed sheets, contemplating her after a moment of intimacy sprung on her by surprise. Joyce suddenly remembered that she hadn't brushed her teeth after lunch. She feared that a bit of lettuce was wedged between her lower front teeth. With her lips shut tight, she looked down to sign for the package. She could feel his eyes watching her, almost like a physical touch that slid down her arm and focused on the bones of her wrist.

Joyce handed the pad back to him. "I have something I'm supposed to mail out with you-all. I just need to find the address." She searched through an address book below the counter, then began filling out the tab. She again felt the touch of his eyes on her. She couldn't fight the urge her eyes seemed to feel to look up. When she did so—just for a moment—he was indeed gazing back at her, with the oddest look of enchantment in his eyes.

He said, "I'm having the strangest feeling watching you. It's like . . . I mean, it makes me think . . . I just might fall in love with you." He waited, as if he knew Joyce would need a moment to weigh the full import of the statement. "I don't know if you'll believe me on this, but I have this sort of sixth sense. My grandmother used to call it the touch. It means that I always know my destiny. All I have to do is keep my eyes open, and if I do, sometimes I can see my future clear as day."

Joyce cast her voice dry and humorless. "You're telling me you're touched, are you?"

"I'm saying something just hit me like a flash, just when I was watching you." He eyed her for a moment, ran his fingers over his chin, and seemed to consider his words carefully. "When I look at you, a bunch of different things pop up in my head. I see us getting old together. I see me scraping the bunions off your toes. I see a whole mess of grandchildren around us, and a big ol' dog sitting at our feet as we watch the sunset, thinking about how fabulous our life has been, and how glad we are that we didn't let the love slip through our fingers back in '67 when we met straight out of the blue. Same thing didn't occur to you?"

Joyce finished writing and handed him the envelope and mail form. "What makes you think I have bunions?"

"Okay, I'm not sure about the bunion thing, but . . . do you like dogs?"

"Allergic. One whiff and I'm spitting and hissing."

He smiled thinly and acknowledged his tactical error with a shrug. He reached out a finger as if to touch her chin. He didn't do so but motioned as if he were lifting her face up toward his. Which, in fact, was just what happened.

"Listen, I don't know your name or anything about you, but I'm not hustling you. My name is Calvin Carter. I'd like to know you better. That's all. People gotta connect in this world, and sometimes it takes a little faith to let that happen. Sometimes you gotta pull out a couple blocks in that wall and let some air through and look a brother in the face and just give him a moment. That's all I'm talking about. I could tell you my life story; you could tell me yours; then we could see what comes of it. Think we could do that?"

Joyce, as if she heard this question regularly, said, "Let me think about it." And despite the fact that she told herself Calvin could only be another young hustler doing what young hustlers do, and despite the fact that his invocation of the word *love* was as subtle as knocking on a door with a battering ram, and despite the fact that her common sense told her she should handle him with the curt, cold civility that she usually reserved for religious fanatics carrying clipboards . . . Despite all this, think about it was just what she did.

For each of the next five days Calvin waited for Joyce after work. He would rush into the store breathless, still in his work uniform, pluck a flower from one of the bouquets by the door, and present it to her with courtly formality. The first time she charged him for the flower and refused to let him walk her home. The second she allowed him to walk with her but wouldn't let him touch her bags. The third she told him he was getting on her nerves. The fourth she asked him if he knew what he was getting into. And this day, the fifth day of his assault, she allowed herself to laugh out loud and look, for long periods, straight into his eyes. They were the kind of eyes that had a certain glint to them, as if the light were always catching them just right.

A few hundred yards from her apartment building Joyce stopped walking. "Where did you get eyes like that?" she asked.

He grinned. "Eyes like what?"

"Eyes like . . . I don't know like what. That's why I asked."

He stepped closer, shifting the grocery bags that he carried tucked under his arm. "Why don't you describe them to me? Maybe we can figure it out."

Joyce opened her mouth as if to say something but then shifted her jaw a little to the left and resumed walking. "You are vain. Get something a little good and it goes straight to a Black man's head."

Calvin kept up with her. "They come from my momma if you want to know the truth. People say she was part Indian."

"Where was she from?"

"South Hill, Virginia. Tobacco country."

"You're a country boy?"

"Born and raised. Most of my family still lives down there. That's where I'd be if I hadn't come up here to find you." He flashed his smile again, but Joyce just pursed her lips.

When they reached the steps to Joyce's row house, she took

one step up and paused. Calvin glanced up at the large structure behind her. The house sat on the corner and was shaped
in a strange, triangular design, like a wedge cut out of a cake of
red brick. He stepped up as if to look into the lower windows.

"You live here? You share it with someone?"

"It's my parents' house," Joyce said, her businesslike tone
returning.

"Uh-oh, you still live with your folks? I guess that makes
you one of them wholesome-type girls. That's the kind I like.
You gonna let me meet them? I got a way with parents."

Joyce reached out for her bags. "Let's not worry about that.
Now, I suppose I should tell you that I don't work tomorrow.
So don't go showing up there worrying Mrs. Goldstein with
your crazy self. She will call security on you."

Calvin shifted both bags to one arm and stepped forward.
With his free hand he gently reached up and touched the
chilled skin of her cheek. "I'm not crazy," he said. "I like to
joke and all, but about some things I'm right serious. Like I'm
serious that your face may be the only face I'll ever need. It's
that beautiful."

Joyce's lips crinkled into a crooked smile, defensive even
though her words were plainspoken. "How can you be so sure?
I can't see things beyond tomorrow."

"Faith, baby. You need to open yourself up and let what has
to happen happen. How about this? From now you don't have
to be sure. I'll be sure enough for both of us. Okay? All you
have to do is do what you know you want to, and I'll take care
that everything else is all right. Okay?"

Her head moved in the tiniest indication of a nod. "Maybe
we should start getting to know each other."

Calvin straightened up and inhaled the cool evening air
through his nose. "Yeah. That's what I'm talking about."

After parting a few moments later, Joyce stood alone inside

the house. She leaned her back against the door and listened to the uneasy silence around her, hearing the fading tones of Calvin's voice. When Joyce said that she lived in her parents' home, she spoke the truth, but a somewhat incomplete truth. She lived in her parents' house, but the old couple had passed into the next world some nine months before. Robert and Caroline Johnston had had their daughter late in life. They raised her in that drafty old row house that they had correctly prophesied they would live in until they passed on. They had aged into one of those old couples we might all wish to emulate, so used to each other that they seemed to speak from different regions of the same mind, move with different limbs of the same body, and look upon each other with the casual acceptance that one looks upon one's own reflection. They dealt with life's trials with a resigned reliance on each other, on their daughter, and on God. If there was any irony to their lives, it was that they produced a daughter who seemed incapable of inheriting any such trust.

For Joyce, her faith in most things ended one breezy winter night. The house's rattling windows had been sealed with plastic, and the doors stuffed with old rags. These were their customary insulations, and that fateful night they worked so well that the old couple slept their way into death, quietly asphyxiated by a carbon monoxide leak. Joyce had stayed the night at her friend's and would never truly come to terms with why her life was saved by something as frivolous as a sorority dance. Guilt gnawed hard at her, the unshakable belief that she could have saved them had she been home. For many nights she dreamt of waking to the smell of gas, rushing through the house, crying warnings and throwing open the windows, finding her parents sound asleep and shaking them, shaking them, shaking them . . .

Upon waking from these dreams she often wished that she

had been allowed to die with them, instead of being left alone in this empty house, with all her memories, with the vague fear that the world was not to be trusted and that love was a burden too heavy to bear. Thoughts such as these were just a few of the many things held trapped inside her, the bits and pieces of the real her, the things she wished desperately to get beyond, but that she could never imagine sharing with another living person.

Joyce walked alongside Calvin through the damp air of the Capital Mall. She wore a light blue knee-length coat, whose large collar spread across her shoulders. Her face was carefully made up, her straightened hair wrapped tight around the top of her head, pinned in the back with a seashell brooch. Her eyes studied the Washington Monument as they approached it, several hundred yards ahead of them. It was near sundown; the sky was dim and overcast. All day long it had threatened to rain, but they decided to walk anyway, as the streets were less crowded than usual. The air had a moist taste to it that was almost sweet to inhale. As usual, Calvin talked.

"I was over at my buddy's house yesterday watching the Jets game. One of the hardest things for me to do is watch a football game these days. I should be out there myself."

"Out there yourself doing what?"

"Playing ball! I was good enough. I was better than good enough. I played varsity from the time I was a freshman. Had the fastest hundred yards in the county—would have been a state record, but they didn't recognize my time 'cause they said it wasn't official. I even had some colleges coming out to look me over. Can you imagine that? Coming all the way out to South Hill?"

"So, what happened?"

"My knee blew. Some fool slammed into me from the side." Calvin indicated the blow with a chop to his left knee. "And that was that. Ripped the joint apart, tore up the cartilage, did a job on it. You can't mess with a knee, not when you're talking about going pro. Man . . . It's a shame too. When I was on my game, wasn't nobody that could touch me. It was like I was moving at a different speed than everybody else, always a step ahead."

For a moment, Calvin hunkered down into a running position. One hand came up before him, and his body indicated slight, subtle weight shifts, as if the walkway before them were full of invisible opponents. He dropped the stance when he noticed Joyce smiling at him. "But I guess that's payback, or something. That's the way the world comes back at you for your sins."

"What did you ever do that was so bad?" Joyce asked. "You act like you did something unmentionable."

Calvin looked down at the ground. "Eventually I did. I left South Hill. That was all I had to do to hurt my momma. I ran away, like a thief in the night. When my oldest brother, Marshall, was alive, everyone figured that he and Jefferson would take care of the farm, and I might be the first one to get out and travel or go to school or something. There's some beautiful things about living at South Hill, but it feels so far from the world. Nothing's happening there but small things, close-in-on-you things."

They had reached a cross street and stood waiting for the light to change. Calvin shoved his hands deep into the pockets of his jacket. "I haven't told you about Marshall, have I?"

"No."

"He got killed."

"Murdered?"

"That's the word. Murdered the old-fashion way—out in a field at night, a good, honest southern lynching. After that everybody just knew that I was supposed to stay, help Jefferson and run the farm and get married and that would be my life. But shit . . ." The light changed, and they started walking. "When I was little, we got *National Geographic*. I used to read that magazine from cover to cover. All those animals, and countries, and naked little African girls. I spent all that time reading that stuff and just waiting to get out and see it all, and then Momma just expected me to forget about it. How was I supposed to forget? It just never felt like farming was supposed to be my life. So I packed up a handful of stuff and snuck out one night, caught a bus up to D.C., and I've been here ever since. I guess I didn't get that far, really."

A moment before, when she'd named the method of Marshall's death, Joyce had felt a quick tingle in her lower back, the fear that this was where the truth began to come out, the secrets that might begin to chip away at the image she'd built of Calvin. She'd never been as near to crime as she was with his casual mention of a killing. But a few sentences later he'd moved the conversation along and she'd followed. This was not a man to be afraid of. He'd done nothing to others, and yet the world had done violence to those close to him. She felt her shoulder brush his and had a sudden desire to slip her arms inside his coat and press herself against the heat of him and tilt her head and open her mouth to his, to break through that wall he mentioned and to start consuming and being consumed.

Instead, she said, "That's not that bad, Calvin. You have to live your own life."

"That's not the way Momma sees it. I started writing her letters as soon as I got a place to stay, trying to explain to her and tell her about all the things that were going on around here, the Movement and all, being in the center of everything. She never wrote me back, not once. I don't even know if she read them." He stopped walking and looked Joyce in the face. "It's been three years. Three years. And it feels like it'll be forever. Like I can't go back there and she'll never come to me here. That gets to me more and more. People got to have connections, don't they?" He reached out, took Joyce's hand, and held it loosely in his. "What do we have without connections? Sometimes I know I had to leave; other times I feel unhinged from everything that made me who I am. You ever feel that way?"

Joyce didn't answer. She looked down at his hand and then intertwined his fingers with hers. "Come," she said, and pulled him on.

Calvin and Joyce's next date began well enough. They ate dinner near Dupont Circle, in a restaurant that specialized in tomato dishes. Afterward they walked to a movie theater and caught a cheap showing of *Doctor Zhivago*. Calvin enjoyed the film more than Joyce. He liked its grand scale and its focus on one man moving through large historical forces. And he liked the fact that—despite everything else—it was still just a love story.

Joyce nodded as he spoke, agreeing mutely with his enthusiasm. She wasn't thinking much about the movie. Rather, she found herself wondering who this man was, where he came from, and why she so enjoyed listening to his voice, why her eyes so liked to wander over his backside, and why she felt that his hand fit so naturally into the small of her back. She recognized in him many of the same traits that so turned her off in others. It was obvious he liked to hear himself talk. He had a certain vanity that he showed when he smiled. And he, like so many men, looked at the world with a boyish naïveté that he both disguised and betrayed by his musical flow of words.

But with Calvin each of these traits struck her as endearing. She found herself questioning her own pessimism. The more she questioned, the more she felt herself to be pale next to his color, tired where he was energized, dull while he was inspired. She began to wonder why he liked her and if he would continue to. Each passing moment made the evening more difficult for her.

After the movie they went to a nightclub nearby. Once settled at the bar, Calvin turned to Joyce and smiled. The blue light that lit up the back of the bar reflected off his teeth and sparkled in the liquid of his eyes, tainting the whites with a warm indigo. Joyce realized she didn't know the exact color of his eyes, even though she'd spent so long looking at them.

"I don't know why people complained about the movie being too drab," Calvin said. "I mean, it's kind of gray, but then when there is color, it's like, bam! The whole world just burst out in flowers. I like that. I like it when things hit you by surprise. I do fault the man for cheating on his wife, though. I understand what it means to have passion, but you gotta do right by the ones you commit to." He paused and studied Joyce for a moment.

She knew he was waiting for her to say something. "So you're claiming your eye doesn't wander?"

"Well . . . You can't tell where an eye may move, but it's not the eye that matters. It's the heart. An eye just looks at the world. It's the person behind it that has to decide what to do with what it sees. On that you can always trust me."

"How do you know you can always trust me?"

Calvin grinned. "Girl, once you've swum in this sea you won't want to go anyplace else. This here's deep water, and you're a fish that likes to swim." Joyce began to laugh. "I'm serious. I am, even if it's a fucked-up line. Don't laugh. Joyce . . . Can't you see a brother's trying? But anyway, I'm talking too much. Now it's your turn. Let's have the full history of Joyce Johnston, starting with day one. Gimme all of it."

Joyce looked over and nodded at the bartender, who was strolling toward them. "How about we get a drink first?"

For the rest of the evening, Calvin continued asking questions, and Joyce kept deflecting them. As they talked, Joyce put down drink after drink. She drank hoping that alcohol would relieve her nervousness and allow her to loosen up. She actually wanted to be honest with him about the pain in her past, wanted to explain herself to him. But before long she lost—along with her nervousness—most of her inhibitions, her motor functions, and, eventually, a chunk of the evening's memories.

A few hours later she awoke from a rambling, fluid dream of twirling ceilings. She opened her eyes and realized that she was lying stretched across her couch, with a towel tucked under her chin, a low stream of tomato-based drool dribbling from the corner of her mouth. Calvin sat at her side, wiping her vomit clean with his handkerchief.

"Hey, baby," he said, with a familiarity she had not heard before. "How about that? We've gone and spent the night together."

"What?"

Calvin leaned in and whispered, as if sharing a secret, "Well, I guess you had a little too much to drink. I walked you home. I helped you change your clothes. And then I just took care of you. I just sat here and memorized your face."

Joyce closed her eyes and covered her face with her hands. Her head still swam and sloshed as if it were full of liquid. She could only half put meaning to his words, but she understood enough to feel shame creeping into her crowded thoughts. "I just wanted to talk," she mumbled.

Calvin smiled. "You did talk, Joyce. You told me everything. We've got no secrets anymore. You even convinced me to go home and introduce you to Momma."

It took a few moments for Joyce to respond. She cautiously pulled her hands away from her face. Calvin's smile was still there, his teeth as bright as ever, and his face still held that childish enthusiasm. But it seemed to Joyce that something about him looked different. She couldn't be sure whether the expression on his face had changed or whether the way she looked at it had changed, but she did know without a doubt that he had seen her at her worst, must have heard the things that pained her, must have pushed her limbs through the motions of life—all this, and still he looked upon her and smiled. He never told her exactly what she said that evening, but he also never spoke of it with anything but fondness.

The following evening Joyce accepted this man into her bed. She wouldn't remember later just how it happened. She didn't know which of them initiated it, whether they spoke about it first or if they acted without words. But none of this mattered. Once together, it felt to her that it had always been this way. He had always been there above her, inside her. She knew every portion of his body, every swell and depression, the curve of his muscles and the softness of his backside. With her arms cinched around his back she took in the whole of him. She felt each contour of his penis inside her, gripped so tightly she committed it to memory in the very first moments. She pressed her palms against his sweaty skin and brushed her lips across his shoulders, tasting the salt scent of him, knowing in those moments no sweeter scent, nothing more right.

She had a strange thought then. She remembered reading once that by comparison to the possible variety of organisms in the universe, all of the earth's living creatures were quite similar, made of the same simple elements. She'd never given this much thought before because the world seemed so full of difference. But with his flesh gripped between her teeth she knew that on this one thing science was right. The two of them were of the same material.

And Lord, it was good to finally realize it.

"JESUS . . ." JOYCE SAID. "How far back here do you-all live?"

"It's not far now," Calvin said. "It's just starting to look like home."

They had been driving for the past four hours. First down the interstate, then onto increasingly smaller and smaller roads. For the last several miles their rental car bounced along a dirt road, beneath bare trees, through a countryside of farms and rolling hills. They hadn't actually needed to come down this road, but Calvin chose it for scenic value, what he called "the complete country-fide experience." He spoke almost nonstop throughout the trip, recounting his youth in the country. He tended to exaggerate the backwardness of country people. He claimed that none of them had figured out how to keep their teeth and urged Joyce to pretend she didn't notice. He argued the virtues of inbred marriages, focusing on how simple it made inheritance. And he told the tale of some local man who, in old age, took to exposing his erect penis in public, apparently proud that the years had not weakened the flow of blood to this vital organ.

He joked, but often Joyce caught a deeper tone to his voice, some pain in his remembrances that his laughter couldn't disguise. This was his first trip home since he ran away three years before, and she could tell that the call, and the cries, of home weighed more heavily on him with each passing mile. She began to wonder why they were here. Hadn't this trip been her idea? Hadn't she proposed that she meet his family? The idea had seemed novel, almost brave, in the safety of her apartment. Now she felt her fear growing at this endless list of names that Calvin produced, the strangeness of his stories, the tone of his voice, and the image she had conjured up of his mother, a woman who seemed as hard and cold as steel, who towered, in Joyce's mind, like the great trees they drove under.

Joyce grimaced with each jolt of the car. "How hard is it to pave a road?"

"No harder than plucking a chicken," Calvin said, grinning.

Joyce looked askance at him. "What does that mean?"

"Nothing." Calvin shrugged. "Just, you ever pluck a chicken?"

"No, I never plucked a chicken."

"Well, plucking a chicken ain't easy. Matter of fact the whole chicken killing thing'll mess you up. Grams only tried to make me kill a chicken once. I must have been about seven—"

"Seven?"

"That's old enough to kill a chicken, if you have the stomach for it. We always used a hatchet. Just lay its little neck across the chopping block and—" He chopped precisely at the dashboard. "Thing is it scared me to death because sometimes the chicken would get up and run around the yard headless. And there was this one rooster, Mr. Charlie, that I used to have nightmares about. We called him Mr. Charlie 'cause he was so evil. Fact is that Mr. Charlie spent too long watching us kill his hens. That would have to get on your nerves, all them plump thighs . . ." Calvin glanced over at Joyce. "Anyway, I didn't do it. I broke down crying. Grams had to take the hatchet from me and do it herself. I just knew that if I did it, I'd never stop dreaming that Mr. Charlie and a flock of headless hens were coming after me."

They eventually stopped on a hill overlooking the valley that the Carter family owned. They walked a short distance through the tall grass and climbed up onto the stump of a large tree. The valley that spread out before them seemed as dry and barren as the winter air. The hills rolled off as far as the eye could see, cut up into geometric plots, with different shadings of brown, yellow, and gray. One dirt road carved its way hesitantly through the valley. A lone hawk floated high above.

"You should see it in the spring," Calvin said. He wrapped his arms around Joyce from behind. "It's so green you wouldn't believe it. Imagine all those trees in full bloom, and the fields bursting with little shoots. Look there, I think that's my uncle Pete's place." Joyce followed Calvin's finger to where a thin stream of smoke trailed up. She could just make out the roof of the house through the trees. "We'll need to stop there on the way in. That's the way people always did it when they visited—stopped first at Uncle Pete's, then Uncle Levert's and on down the line to my momma's house. By the time they got there word had already been sent down and Momma would be out in the yard waiting. I suppose that might happen today. It's hard to sneak up on my mother."

"Calvin, you make it sound so . . . nice, I guess. All that family. All those stories. I don't really know why you left. I mean, you told me, but . . . I don't know."

Calvin ran his tongue across his teeth and thought for a few moments. "It was just too small a world, with too much in it. Everything that happened seemed right up in your face, cramping you. I saw my father just a couple hours before—" He drew his shoulders together like he was shivering, then relaxed them and looked out over the valley. His eyes settled on the hawk. "Do you know sometimes I used to wish him dead? When I was young, I used to think how different it would have been if he were gone. He wouldn't be around to get at us the way he did, and Momma would be different. She had to carry so much because of him. He lost half the land she owned, gambling, I guess. Things just went through his fingers."

The hawk suddenly dipped and dropped downward for several seconds, only to check and rise again.

"It was a Saturday night, late in the summer. Me and some

friends had gone into town to one of the little joints they had. I walked in there all ready for a night out and guess who I see? My father, acting like a man half his age, with his mouth all over some woman that sure as hell was not my mother. I froze dead in the doorway. Everybody in the place stopped and stared at me, hoping there'd be some sort of scene. I just stared at him. I could see he was stumbling drunk. I can still picture it now: the grin across his face, the way his hands were groping over her, all of it. I just had to turn around and leave. I remember my friend James said I should go in there and grab him and take him home so he didn't end up driving like that, but I didn't care. Right then he could drive himself straight off a cliff for all I cared. And that's just about what he did. Just what he did . . ."

Joyce turned and slid one arm inside his jacket. She laid her cheek against his chest.

"They found him the next morning, about a half mile from the house. There's this turn in the road . . . Always was a treacherous turn. He drove straight off into the field and drove the car up the base of a big old tree. It looked like he was try-ing to ride over it, like he thought, I'll just take a shortcut over this tree here . . . So then there's that to mess around in my head as well. And then Marshall gets killed the way he does. All that stuff just starts crowding you. Like the hills keep it in, like family never really leaves. Either dead or alive, they're all here, buried over on that hill, rambling around in this valley. How could I stay when I had to see that tree every day and wonder why God had given me the choice to save his life? It felt like James had whispered right into my ear. He said, 'You shouldn't let him drive like that.' But I did. I sure enough did." He sniffled and stroked Joyce's hair. "Anyway, I had to leave to find you. That's all I really wanted."

Joyce listened to his story and recognized the pain that it

caused him and wished it weren't so. But still—selfishly, hungrily—she wanted nothing else at that moment but for him to truly find her. She understood that you never know a person completely at any one moment. She didn't need to have all of him at once, and she didn't have to tell him everything from her own life today, or tomorrow, or at any specific moment. The sharing between two people could go on always, evolving each day as the world pressed against you with different currents, as they grew more confident with each other, as their eyes learned to look ever deeper into each other. She believed that she'd finally found the other person in front of whom she could slowly strip piece by painful piece her facade away. She would one day stand naked before this man, her true self exposed, as he would before her.

At that moment, feeling the chill rushing up from the valley of South Hill, hearing the whispers of the ghosts that haunted Calvin, Joyce signed her name on some imaginary dotted line. She agreed to take a journey, to accept the slow revelations that, she hoped, would stretch into two long lifetimes. It was a gesture as great as if she'd lifted her arms and thrown herself into flight like that hawk. An act of faith.

Outwardly, she said only, "Then let's go home." She whispered it into the collar of his coat.

Calvin stood silent. His nose was running, but for a few moments he stopped sniffling. Joyce kept her cheek pressed to his chest. A truck passed on the road behind them. Something rustled in the grass.

"Okay," Calvin said, and without another word they drove the five hours back to the District.

Barking in Tongues

KENNETH CARROLL

I

"Man, don't be ah fool." Melba snatched the letter from Ezra's hand and bounded playfully across the carpeted bedroom. She drew deeply on the cigarette dangling loosely from the corner of her mouth. The blue light from an early-morning sky gave the ascending smoke an ethereal quality as it drifted hazily around her naked body. "You look like an angel standing there in the light," said Ezra, his voice low with desire.

"Ain't no Black angels, Ezra, a good Christian like you should know that; now be quiet while I'm reading." Melba laughed, her stomach convulsing in amusement. Ezra stared at Melba with what she scornfully called his "let's get married eyes."

"I got the letter right after I finished praying," said Ezra, his voice revealing his Carolina origins. "I've memorized every word of it. Some people who saw him last time he was here said he truly is a blessing prophet, just like he say." Ezra's voice was an annoying buzz in Melba's ear. She cut him off by reading the letter aloud, drowning out his words.

My Dear Christian Friend:

This letter may come as a suprise to you but it is a blessing straight from Heaven because I am on my way back to Washington, D.C. for another very special Deliverance,

*Blessing and Healing service on this Sunday night coming
and every living soul what sees me will get a straight one-
way blessing for Monday so help me God in Heaven.*

"You can't be taking this letter seriously," said Melba. Ezra
grabbed his robe from the headboard, carefully concealing his
naked body. He tied the robe so tight that Melba thought he
would slice himself in half. "You afraid your mama goin' walk
in," said Melba, shaking her head and looking out the window
at the sun rising from the bottom of the avenue.

Melba loved her body and enjoyed parading around her
apartment in the nude. Her body was thirty-nine years old now
and round and soft in places where it used to be flat and tight,
but it still turned heads and could even make this preacher's
son forget his religion. Melba looked down at the letter again.

*I am that great Prophet that people is talking about all
over the country because I gives out two and three straight
blessings everywhere I go. As you know they call me the all
seeing Prophet from Texas and I now have headquarters in
Baltimore, Md. plus I have branch offices in many areas
and thousands of folk is being healed and many folks is
getting rich off of Gods blessings so if you want help in
a hurry see me this Sunday night coming and I double
guarantee you that you can be blessed in one day only.*

Ezra moved in measured steps toward Melba. Despite his
expanding waistline and his thinning hair, he excited her with
his unselfish gentleness and an almost manic desire to please
her. But like any good medicine, Melba could only take Ezra
in small doses. She did not doubt his proclamations of love for
her; he was always caring and, so far, trustworthy. But Ezra's
love was a box where he would keep her in comfortable noth-

ingness. She wanted to live, and living didn't have nothing to do with marrying a born-again square like Ezra.

He stood behind Melba and stroked her shoulders. "I know it ain't your way to believe in things, but people told me they've seen the Prophet perform miracles," Ezra said.

"I know he perform miracles, he got you fools coming to hear him." Melba laughed. "Ezra, if he so blessed, why can't he get a decent secretary or some spell-checker software?"

"Melba, you got to believe in something or someone eventually—we all do," said Ezra, his voice calm and soothing—very deaconlike, Melba thought.

"I believe in me—period. No men, no gods, no gimmicks. That's why I ain't getting married and having kids. I've seen what a ball and chain men and babies can be." Melba, resurrecting a deep and bitter hurt as she talked, crushed out her cigarette butt in the Jesus Saves ashtray that Ezra had given her. "I wanta have the good things that my mama didn't have. She waited for Jesus. Every minute—waiting on the Lord to deliver her out of Egypt, which was my father's house." Melba stood naked in the window; she cupped her hands in a mock prayer. "Oh, Lord, deliver my black ass; deliver me, great savior of Jerusalem—" Melba stopped abruptly to view Ezra's frowning face.

"Melba, honey, don't blaspheme like that."

"Jesus failed her, Ezra, like all the other men in her life and mine. I refuse to spend my Sundays shouting and waiting with you fools and believing in a prophet from Texas who can't write an intelligent letter. But if you really believe this stuff, then *tain't nobody's business if you do*—just leave me out of it." Melba tossed the letter at Ezra and lit up another cigarette.

"One day you goin' need the Lord, Melba," said Ezra, picking up the folded letter from the floor.

"What you hoping, Ezra, is one day I'm goin' need you,"

said Melba, "but I don't love out of need, and I don't believe out of desperation."

"Just come see the Prophet with me, so we can ask him for our blessings," said Ezra. "Deacon John Hawkins at Miracle Temple asked me to carry the Prophet around when he arrives. Saturday night we having dinner at my house—"

"You goin' take this fool to your mama's house? Maybe that's God's punishment for his lying ass—he got to meet your mama," said Melba.

"My mama ain't a bad woman, she just got her ways—"

"Yeah, and she can keep her ways," said Melba, lying back on the bed.

"I ain't asking you to make a decision on it now, Melba, just think about it," said Ezra. "I got a good feeling about Prophet Bates. I think he might have what we need. And even if he don't have what I need, maybe he has what you need." Ezra stroked Melba's shoulders. She untied his robe and pulled him toward her on the bed. Something told her the Prophet could be dangerous; something else made her long to meet him.

II

Everywhere I go people get quick action and fast results to their problems especially if you have money problems because I always find out what the blessing is going to be before I come to town and you can always get it straight if you follow what I tell you in fact I was in Washington, D.C. on last Sunday night and I told all of my followers and their friends to read Psalms 79:5 for they money blessings on Monday and God did bless everybody who followed my instructions with cash money and folks is still counting they money and on this Sunday night coming I

will be back in the city of Washington, D.C. so that you
can do the same thing and put some money away for a
change.

"Hurry up, Melba, the Prophet over there alone with Mama," Ezra said.

"Don't rush me," said Melba, frantically searching her closets, trying to decide what to wear. "Jesus—Ezra, don't you want me to look good for Prophet Bates?"

"Please, Melba," said Ezra softly, "don't use his name in vain."

"You mean Prophet Bates," giggled Melba.

"I wished you hadn't told those friends of yours," said Ezra, dressed to the nines in his pin-striped, double-breasted suit with matching pin-striped suspenders and black leather oxfords. Melba had been through ten outfit changes already without a decision.

"It ain't like I ran out onstage last night passing out flyers," said Melba, digging deep into her closets. "How this look?" she asked, not waiting for Ezra to comment before she grabbed another dress. "I just told Brazil—how 'bout this one?" Melba was already leaving the bedroom with her outfit, a purple suede dress that accentuated her ample hips and a matching jacket that did the same for her breasts. Ezra followed Melba over to the full-length mirror in the bathroom but walked out when she began undressing. He talked to her from the bedroom, raising his voice in an effort to be heard over the running water.

"But the letter said specifically," Ezra began:

May I say to you please keep your busines—to your ownself
until after you get your blessing as some folk talk too much
but an old follower of mines whom I helped a many time
in the past told me about you and they also said that

you needed money and could keep your business to your ownself, but you may bring a close friend or a loved one that you know needs help if you think you can trust them and they will keep their business to their ownself because I am going to upset Washington, D.C. again when I get there an everybody what sees me on Sunday night will be blessed dead straight Monday so help me God or you can get every dime of you money back.

"Brazil ain't exactly the kind of friend the Prophet was talking 'bout," said Ezra.

Melba rushed out of the bathroom butt-naked, wet, and angry. She paraded up to Ezra until her nose touched his chin. The smell of fragrant soap flooded his nostrils. "Listen, Ezra, Brazil may not sing in the choir at Mount Calvary, but she's my friend—and I don't care how holy and righteous you get, don't you ever insult her," said Melba, her hands on her hips. Ezra stuttered before squeezing a feeble apology from his lips.

"Maybe you should see Prophet Bates alone."

"I said I was sorry, Melba, I wasn't trying to—"

"Yes, you were, but you remember, Ezra, I ain't never dragged you into my bedroom, this is where you *beg* to be. Just 'cause you met Prophet Bates don't make you a disciple. According to your Bible, you a fornicator—a sinner like me and my friends. And if they goin' burn in hell for dancing naked, then so am I—and so are you for loving me." Melba stomped back into the bathroom.

Ezra stood next to the open window, hat in hand and sweat rolling off his forehead. When Melba came out of the bathroom twenty minutes later, fully dressed, Ezra was still standing like a small child sent to a corner for punishment. "You look beautiful," he mumbled.

"Come on, we got a Prophet to meet," said Melba. Ezra smiled, scurrying out the door ahead of her, with his blessings already halfway granted.

III

Ezra, who couldn't persuade Melba to breathe if she didn't want to, certainly had not changed her mind about meeting the Prophet. It had been Brazil, her best friend and fellow dancer at the Penthouse Lounge who had explained to Melba that the Prophet was really a con man. "Shit, girl," Brazil had said, "he ah jackleg preacher who claims he can give out the winning lottery number to people." Melba had been reading the letter to her friend as they changed for their Friday night performance. Brazil, who once had a scandalous affair with one of D.C.'s most prominent preachers, had also been involved with a priest in Atlanta and a rabbi in New York. "Shit, it's just something 'bout religious men—they the biggest freaks," she said. Melba read the letter again, this time with Brazil pointing out the code words that indicated to the knowing faithful that the Prophet Bates would be performing a *numbers offering service.* "Why the hell would a preacher tell you to read Psalms 79:5 for a *money* blessing?" Brazil asked. "What he saying is play 795 straight."

> *Yes my dear Christian friend on this Sunday night coming I will be back in Washington, D.C. and if I was you I would come early as I am always crowded whenever I comes to town for everyone knows what I can do and it is always straight and one-way the very next day. Along with a straight Psalms for money I am also bringing a generous*

*supply of my special Mojo Hands that will make you hold
money when you get your hands on it and also special
annointing oils for the sick and afflicted and once again
I say to you this is it you dont have to look no further this
is it. I have the thing for you Washington that God told
me will fall and bless your right away and you can win as
much cash money as you want to.*

"Let me call that fool before he gives away his soul to this
hustler." It was just like Ezra, Melba thought, to invite a con
man to his house. But before Melba called Ezra, she suddenly
decided that she wanted to meet this Prophet. Brazil tried to
warn her against it. "Somebody who steals in the name of the
Lord ain't to be played with, girl." But Melba ignored her;
something about the gall of the Prophet's hustle had sparked
her imagination and interest. Whoever Prophet Bates was,
Melba was sure he didn't cover his body when he was in the
bedroom or sit around waiting for his blessings to arrive. He's
probably a good-looking Reverend Ike type who can charm
the skin off a snake. Now, like Ezra, Melba believed something
was in store for her upon meeting the Prophet.

*Yes my dear Christian friend on this Sunday night coming
which is September 14, I will be back in Washington,
D.C. at the Miracle Temple of Divine Faith located at
1000 G Street N.W. at 8:00 A.M. sharp in the greatest
blessed and Healing service ever held in the city of
Washington, D.C. I want you to know that I am a man of
God and I don't believe in playing with God or trying to
fool folk so I am saying to you right now if what I tell you
is not right you can get every dime of your money back or I
hope God to Paralyze me stone cold dead.*

IV

"I see you finally hunted down Jezebel," said Mrs. Johnson, Ezra's octogenarian and obnoxious mother. Decked out in a bluish gray wig, apron, and brown orthopedic shoes, she turned her back on Ezra and Melba and walked toward the kitchen. Ezra looked pleadingly at Melba, begging her with his eyes not to make a scene. "You better talk to her now; I ain't goin' have that all evening," said Melba, removing her coat while Ezra hurried into the kitchen. She could hear him arguing with his mother. Mrs. Johnson's gravelly voice crushed Ezra's sheepish whispers. Melba hung her coat in the closet and noticed a full-length camel's hair coat. She checked the label: "100% camel hair imported directly from Morocco for Steinberg's Haberdashery." All right, Prophet, thought Melba, show me what you got. She straightened her dress and applied a fresh coat of purple haze lipstick, which perfectly matched her outfit. She walked confidently into the dining room, expecting to finally meet the Prophet, but the room was empty. "He in the toilet," said Mrs. Johnson, brushing brusquely by Melba. She sat a bowl of mash potatoes and gravy on the large dining room table. "Can I help you with something?" asked Melba, instinctively being polite, but wishing she hadn't offered. Mrs. Johnson stopped in the dining room doorway, her lips parting quickly, poised, Melba thought, for another acerbic remark. "Well, come on, since you here," she said, handing Melba an apron. Melba followed her into the kitchen and brought out the greens and candied yams, followed by Mrs. Johnson, who labored with the roasted chicken. Ezra, bringing the lemonade, passed Melba in the kitchen and stared at her. "You look good in that apron," he said, smiling brightly.

"I'll wear it the next time we make love," said Melba. Ezra

blushed and looked for his mother, then hastily exited. Melba set the rolls on the table and removed the apron, giving it to Mrs. Johnson, who handled it with the tips of her fingers as if it were diseased. She sat across from Ezra and Melba. The three waited quietly for the Prophet. Ezra broke the awkward silence. "You say he went to the bathroom, Mama."

"I said he was in the toilet," replied Mrs. Johnson.

"Maybe I should go check on him," said Ezra.

"What you goin' do—go for him?" asked his mother.

Melba restrained a laugh. Before Ezra could get up, the Prophet came strolling triumphantly into the dining room, patting his protruding belly. Ezra and Melba stood up to greet him. The Prophet was short and stocky, in his early fifties, Melba figured, and though he was nattily attired in a black silk and tweed suit, he looked plain. His hair, thinning and slicked back in a Jheri curl, reminded Melba of black telephone cord. He looks more boring than Ezra, she thought, instantly regretful about her decision to meet him. "Ezra's been pontificating about how wonderful you are," said the Prophet, "and looking at you, I know he speaks with great veracity." Melba was surprised at the Prophet's proper speaking voice. Unlike his letter, he sounded intelligent. Melba barely concealed her disappointment in a cheery reply and settled in for a torturous evening.

The dinner turned into a painfully long "praise Jesus tournament," which Melba thought was won by Mrs. Johnson when she thanked Jesus for her hysterectomy. Melba spoke only when spoken to, and then said very little. All she could think about was how the Prophet turned out to be a frog and the money she was losing by taking off on a Saturday night. Only when the Prophet asked what she wanted for a blessing did her mind return to the dinner. "Well, Prophet Bates," said Melba, sarcastically, "I just want Jesus to deliver me from boredom."

"Why would a fine woman like you be bored?" the Prophet asked, his face contorted by a lecherous grin.

"She need ta ask Jesus to deliver her heathenous soul from dancing naked for mens," said Mrs. Johnson.

"Your son don't seem to mind," said Melba, getting up from the table. She had had enough of this charade. This is how life would be with Ezra, thought Melba, boring dinners with members of Miracle Temple Church and his ornery mother.

"My son's goin' burn in hell if he keep walking behind you," said Mrs. Johnson, following Melba into the living room.

"Mama, Melba, please," said Ezra, "let's not spoil the Prophet's dinner."

"I ain't spoiled nothing," said Mrs. Johnson, "this Jezebel come in my house and don't say two words to nobody all during dinner—'cause she don't know the Lord."

"I know you, you old witch," said Melba, heading for the closet to get her coat. "I know how you rule over your son like a warden, how he ain't goin' get nowhere in life long as you cast your shadow over him."

"Mama, Melba, please," said Ezra, chasing behind her.

The Prophet slowly trailed the combatants into the living room, enjoying the melee.

"Melba, please don't go," said Ezra.

"I don't care how many dime-store Prophets come to town, ain't nobody disrespecting me goddamn it," said Melba.

"Don't you cuss my Lord," said Mrs. Johnson, advancing on Melba. "I'll get my pistol if you don't leave my house."

Ezra gingerly grabbed his mother's arm to keep her away from Melba, who was already in her overcoat. "I'll catch a cab home, Ezra," said Melba, heading out the door.

Prophet Bates hurriedly grabbed his coat and ran after her. "Sister Melba, let me give you a ride home."

"That's awright, Prophet," said Melba, "I know you got souls to save and numbers to give out."

The Prophet laughed heartily. "You something else, baby," he said, his voice sounding suddenly unprophetlike. "You better get your fine ass in my ride before Sister Johnson sends you a couple bad ones from her thirty-eight." Melba stopped and turned to look back at Bates. He was smiling, looking more like an aging hustler than a prophet.

She laughed at him, "Okay, fool, where's your car?" Bates reached for Melba's arm and led her toward his large Pontiac. A damn rental, Melba thought as she got in.

"I figured another few minutes and old Sister Johnson would've had me performing an exorcism on you," said Bates.

"Somebody need to perform one on you."

"Aw, baby, don't be so mean."

"I ain't your fucking baby, and my house is in the other direction."

"We ain't going to your house yet," said Bates. "We're heading to my hotel for a nightcap—which I'm sure we can both use after dealing with Sister Johnson."

"Look, you country dog, don't get yourself hurt," said Melba, sliding her hand menacingly into her purse.

"Lord, Miss Melba," said Bates, laughing like a department store Santa, "chill with your fine self. My hotel's a short ride from here. If you don't want a drink, you can get a cab out front." Bates pulled into the driveway of the Jefferson Hotel. Two hotel employees in tuxedos opened the lobby doors, and the desk clerk handed Bates his messages. He tucked them into his black appointment book. Hell, the damn night's blown anyway, thought Melba, might as well see what this fool is about.

She was impressed at how classy everything was. "Damn, they even got a leather couch in the elevator," said Melba.

"Baby, you know the Prophet only goes first class, just like the Good Lord wants me to," said a grinning Bates.

"You sound more like a pimp than a Prophet," said Melba.

"Hell, pimp, prophet, preacher, prostitute, we're all about bringing relief to a suffering American public," said Bates, opening his room with an electronic passkey.

"Room 725," said Melba. "Should I play that straight, Prophet?"

"Two dollars straight," he replied. They both laughed. Bates's suite was larger than Melba's entire one-bedroom apartment. He led her to the living room and turned on the compact disc player. "Love and Happiness," crooned Rev. Al Green. "Pardon me, need to make some calls, only be a second," said Bates. "But let me get you a drink first." He put his appointment book down, pushed a button on the remote control, and a stocked bar appeared from behind an oak panel. "What you drinking?"

"Scotch and soda," replied Melba. Bates poured the drink and hurried toward what Melba thought was his favorite hangout—the toilet. He left his appointment book lying open, and Melba immediately picked it up. She looked at Bates's appointment calendar and saw that he planned to be in ten different cities within two weeks. Good Lord, why are the wicked so strong? thought Melba, whose last vacation was a bus trip to New Jersey with Brazil. Melba dropped Bates's book and a wad of hundred-dollar bills and traveler's checks fell to the floor. She felt like a jackpot winner in Atlantic City. Hell, Bates was stealing from people with his lies, Melba quickly reasoned; this is fair play. She tucked five hundred dollars in her purse and pushed the rest back into the fold. While putting the money back, she saw a check from Ezra. He was giving Bates twenty-five hundred dollars. On the check memo he had written, "blessing for me and Melba." What a chump, Melba thought, tucking his check into her purse and closing the appointment book just as Bates returned.

"Sorry for leaving you alone, just be another minute," said Bates, picking up his appointment book and going into the bedroom to make some calls. He returned five minutes later with his jacket and vest removed.

"So, Melba," said Bates, sitting next to her on the couch, "how did you end up with Deacon Ezra? I figured that square to be dating a reject from the animal shelter, but I'd tear down the Walls of Jericho just to get a look at you."

"You ain't exactly what I'd imagined either," said Melba.

"You thought I'd be some handsome, pious, country-talking, Bible-beating, chitling-eating scoundrel," said Bates, pouring himself another vodka and orange juice.

"Exactly," said Melba. "You didn't think I came to hear that bullshit you wrote in that sorry-ass letter to Ezra."

"Touché," said Bates, clinking glasses with Melba as they both laughed. "I've found that folks like a more homey response from their miracle workers, and believe me, those letters are highly effective," said Bates. "But enough about me, dear," said Bates, leaning forward. "When you, Ezra and his mama goin' to get married?"

"Shit, what I look like, one of your dumb-ass followers?"

"No, you look like a woman in search of something," said Bates, moving closer to Melba and looking deeply into her eyes. "What you looking for, Melba—and don't tell me nothing—I specialize in recognizing the faces of those in need, and sister, you are in need."

"What I need," said Melba laughing nervously, "is another fucking drink."

Bates poured her another. "Seriously," he said, "what you want?"

"Why should I tell you? You ain't got it," said Melba.

"If I ain't got what you want, then what's the harm in telling me, especially since you ain't got it either," said Bates.

Melba's head was light from the scotch; she enjoyed the sensation. She took a long swallow from her glass and looked into Bates's eyes. "Shit, you really believe you a prophet, don't you?" asked Melba.

"I'm a nigga from Houston's Fifth Ward who hustled my ass out of Texas," said Bates. "I stay in the finest hotels in America, have two homes, a Jaguar and a Mercedes. Folks feed me when I'm hungry and make love to me when I'm horny and all I have to do is give 'em what they want—salvation in a neat, uncomplicated package. But that ain't what you want, is it, Melba?"

Melba walked over to the patio window; the view of the city was breathtaking. The sky was clear, and the stars flickered over the Potomac River as it coursed behind the Washington Monument. It saddened her to think that if she hadn't met Bates, she might have never seen the city this way. "I want—" Melba started and stopped. It frightened her to talk beyond generalities about what she wanted. She was used to talking about what she didn't want: her job, a boring life with Ezra, marriage, children, poverty, and old age. "I want to be happy, I want more life, I—" Melba began to cry, she leaned against the patio glass and sobbed.

Bates sat Melba down on the couch and took her drink from her. He held her hands. His voice was soothing. "Melba, you can have more; in fact, you deserve it, and it's all within your reach." Bates's manicured fingers stroked Melba's hands. "If you come with me, I'll show you more life in a week than you've seen in all your years."

"I can't go with you," said Melba, rising from the couch and stumbling toward the door.

"What's keeping you here, Melba?" asked Bates. "Ezra or that chump change you making dancing for them fools, or just plain old fear?" Melba stopped at the door and turned to face him. Bates was standing now, his voice resounding throughout the suite. "Tonight, when I saw you, I thought you were different, but I was wrong. You're scared of life, just like Ezra and the thousands of suckas who keep me in tailored suits and fine suites. You keep praying and wishing and talking while life goes right by you. So you'll stay with Ezra and keep dancing in funky joints and talking about wanting more life, and one day you'll wake to find that you're Mrs. Johnson, praying for the one that got away. But it didn't get away; you just never went after it." Bates called the front desk for a cab and helped Melba into her coat. Bates was no prophet, but Melba knew he was right. "This wasn't about sex," said Bates, "the Prophet gets more ass than toilet seats, you dig. This was about imagining the possibilities."

"What would I do if I went with you?" asked Melba.

"Make love in fine hotels, travel to new cities every week, help me spend my money, meet the rest of the world, and learn to live," said Bates.

"And for this you just goin' give me money," said Melba.

"Hell, yeah," said Bates. "What you think them men in that strip joint give you money for? You've got something, Melba, that a square like Ezra could never appreciate. He just wants to put you in a pumpkin shell. I want to teach you to fly. Maybe, after a few months, you'll leave me, hell, maybe I'll make you leave, but you'll never put up with Ezra or his mama again, 'cause you'll know that there's real life in the world." Melba removed her coat; Bates smiled and canceled the cab. Melba followed him into the bedroom. "You can always change your mind," said Bates.

Melba was silent; she looked blankly down at Bates's smiling face and sat on the bed next to him. "Show me something better, Bates," she whispered. Bates began unbuttoning her blouse. Melba closed her eyes and prayed silently for a miracle.

V

Melba could hear someone calling her name. The voice exploded in her aching head. She opened her mouth to respond, and the smell of her breath caused her to recoil. Her eyelids felt as if they had gravel in them. A hand on her back shook her. "Stop," she moaned, but the shaking continued. She opened her eyes, and the sun slammed into them like a punch. She shut them tightly and very slowly inched them open again. Ezra was standing beside the bed in his black Sunday suit.

"Ezra, what you doing here?"

"I came to take you home, Melba." Ezra's voice was strained and unnaturally calm.

"Hell you mean, I'm already home," replied Melba.

"You ain't home, you in the—" Ezra stopped, his voice cracking with emotion, "you in Bates's hotel room."

Melba sat up. Fully awake, though still groggy from her hangover.

"Where's Bates?"

"He's gone," said Ezra. "He left after the healing service. He told me you were here." Melba scrambled nude across the bed to the dresser, searching frantically for her purse. Ezra turned his head away from her naked body. Her purse had been emptied out, the contents resting on the dresser. The money, including her own few dollars and Ezra's check, was gone. A card from Bates lay next to her purse:

Mind your wants cause somebody wants your mind. Sorry, but I decided last night when I saw that you had taken Ezra's check (along with my five hundred dollars) from me, that maybe you weren't ready for life with the Prophet. It was noble of you to take Ezra's offering, but I got the check back. Wish we could have worked things out, (Lord have mercy woman you sure make good love!) but me and the Lord moves in mysterious ways.

Spiritually Yours,
Prophet John C. Bates

Melba let the card drop to the floor. Her head was spinning and she felt nauseous. She leaned against the dresser for support. Ezra held his head down and extended her clothes toward her. "Look at me, Ezra," Melba commanded, "goddamm it, look at me," she screamed, knocking the clothes from his hands. Melba grabbed his face, forcing him to look in her eyes.

"You can't make me share your shame."

"I ain't ashamed."

"You slept with him," said Ezra, forcing the words from his mouth.

"Yes, I slept with him," said Melba. "He promised to change my life, and God knows I need my life changed. You want me to wait on you and your Lord, who don't even love you enough to keep you from being taken by bastards like Bates. Your Lord ain't shit!"

Ezra grabbed Melba's shoulders and shook her. His chest heaved and tears cascaded from his puffed cheeks as he raised his right hand above her. "My Lord, my Lord loves me you—"

Ezra's voice was a whisper between clenched teeth. His right hand trembled above his head. "My Lord is the only one who loves me." Melba waited for him to slap her or say something mean. It was what most men would do. Ezra sat down on the bed and sobbed, holding his face in his opened palms.

Melba took her clothes and ran into the bathroom. She slammed the door shut and began heaving violently. She rested her head on the commode and cried. When she was sure she was finished vomiting, she got in the shower. The water felt good, and Melba instinctively began to sing. "If you wanta help me, Jesus, it's all right," she sang, remembering her mother's favorite spiritual.

Melba, fully dressed now, found Ezra in the living room. He stared blankly out into the D.C. scenery from the patio window. "Why'd you come here, Ezra?" asked Melba.

" 'Cause I'm cursed to love you," replied Ezra, "even though you ain't no good."

"Please. You don't love me, you want to marry me so you can turn me into your mama—is that love?"

"That's all I know to do with my love," said Ezra, his words emerging in full breaths.

Melba stood quietly behind him, trying to fight the urge to apologize for breaking his heart. As bad as she felt for herself, she felt worse for Ezra; he had been betrayed by her and Bates in the same evening. Yet he had come for her, here in another man's hotel room, and she knew that was some kind of love, though she was not sure it was the kind of love she wanted.

"Bates was right about us; we're suckers, chumps who wouldn't know what living was if it walked right up to us. You say you want to live, but you're afraid to even leave you mama's house. And you certainly ain't goin' leave it to marry a sinner like me," said Melba. "And the bad thing is, Ezra, you the best prospect I got."

"I ain't nothing to you no more," said Ezra, putting his hat on and heading for the door.

Melba grabbed him and pulled him close to her. "Listen, Ezra, the Prophet showed us something. He made us pay dearly for this miracle of sight, but he showed it to us."

"He showed how wrong we are for each other."

"No, Ezra, he showed us something far more important than this thing we call a relationship. He showed us how desperately we want to live. That's why I ain't ashamed, Ezra, I won't be ashamed for trying to live."

Melba put her arms around Ezra and held him tightly. She felt the familiarity of his arms sliding gingerly around her waist. He suddenly pushed her away. "I got the car double parked," said Ezra, opening the door and bolting out the room ahead of her. Melba put on her coat and took one long last look at the gorgeous view of D.C. Then followed Ezra slowly to the elevator. She made a note to play two dollars on number 725—straight.

Wilhelmina

JONETTA ROSE BARRAS

*I*T STARTED with the mirror. Johnny swore that much on the day he lay dying at New Orleans's Charity Hospital. He had been taken there one Saturday evening after losing consciousness during dinner at his older sister Louisa's house.

Louisa had triple washed the greens, meticulously stripping leaves from each stem, and boiled ham hocks on the electric stove, which she hated because invariably the food heated too quickly. The electric stove was her husband's idea of spoiling her; gas is better, she asserted, but didn't dare tell him to take it back to Sears—although she thought about it each time she burned her gravy.

She had rounded out the meal with candied sweet potatoes, cornmeal-coated fried trout, fried green tomatoes, and peach cobbler. Mouths salivated even before she told everyone to sit down and asked Louella, Karen's oldest girl and Louisa's grandniece, to say the grace.

Everyone was filling his or her gold-trimmed porcelain plates with seconds, and pleasant chatter filled the air like a quiet gospel hymn. But all of that stopped when Johnny upped and passed out in the hallway, on his way to the bathroom. The cobbler and ice cream hadn't even been served.

Some of the relatives, thinking the fainting spell a minor event, threatened to hogtie him for messing up a perfectly good dinner with unnecessary theatrics. If he acted like everybody else and ate like an adult instead of a bird, all of that could have been avoided.

But Johnny wasn't putting on, as some had suspected. Despite a battery of tests for illnesses of which neither he nor Louisa had ever heard, doctors were unable to determine the reason for the fainting episode, which resulted in him being unconscious for three hours, prompting emergency room attendants and the first doctor on the scene to suggest that he had entered a diabetic coma. That was a false diagnosis.

Louisa promised, in colorful and less than Christian language, to sue the hospital until her younger sister, Alberta, stepped in: "Stop it! You vexing Johnny, sister. You oughta be ashamed, trying to make money off his misfortune."

Alberta sucked her teeth and turned her head, a habit she had picked up from her now-deceased great-grandmother that served notice to anyone in listening distance that she was upset; one step further would cause her notorious temper to be unleashed.

"Alberta, you know that's not true. You know these doctors treat us poor people different from how they treat other people. They just tell us anything. I like 'em to know we poor, we're not stupid or retarded."

Alberta didn't say another word on the subject. Her teeth sucking was the final comment. The chastising quieted Louisa. The internist assigned to the case smiled as he continued poking and pulling at Johnny.

After a full week of examining every crevice of his body, taking so many tubes of blood that some joked he would need a transfusion, and collecting so many stool specimens that Johnny lost all desire to use the bathroom, Louisa offered her own diagnosis and dared the doctors to dispute it: "The man's suffering from grief. Plain and simple, grief."

She swore Johnny was witnessing his last days and began

making preparations for his wake and interment at LaBatt Funeral Home near the underpass on Claiborne Avenue.

"That's absurd," said one of the six attending physicians, looking around to see the affirmative head shaking of his colleagues. The team, which included three specialists, couldn't decide exactly what ailed Johnny.

"They just working on him for the insurance money," Louisa asserted. Alberta sucked her teeth and looked out the window.

"Bunny, you know it's true," Louisa added, using her sister's nickname, hoping to curry favor.

"Everything is about money to you. Sometimes I don't know how we're sisters."

The bickering and confusion went on like that, even as other family members were notified of Johnny's hospitalization. They came in droves during visiting hours, believing themselves capable of divining his illness, although trained doctors from as far away as Dallas, Texas, had been unable.

ON WHAT WOULD BE Johnny's last day on earth, his first cousin Antoinette was at his side. A tall, slender woman, who, even at forty-five years old, turned the heads of young boys, Antoinette had never married. She adored Johnny. If they hadn't been cousins, the family teased, Antoinette would have roped him into marrying her. When she was twelve and he was thirteen, Louisa caught them kissing under the magnolia tree and ran into the house, interrupting her mother's community meeting without even excusing herself, and blurted out, "Mama, they kissing right now. Johnny and Antoinette. Like they boyfriend and girlfriend."

Ruby Ann turned nearly beet red, which was a whole lot of embarrassment given that the woman was so high yellow she looked white, her red hair didn't help to dissuade the nonbelievers who questioned her racial origin. She begged the ladies' pardon for her rude daughter and returned to the chatter of the moment, as if nothing had been said. Later that evening she picked up the telephone and called her brother, Winston. "I want you to do something about that girl. You gotta get her away from my Johnny. She's corrupting the boy, Winston.

"They like each other too much. We both gonna be sorry, if you don't do something. I can't watch these children every minute of the day. I have my meetings."

After that, Antoinette's visits to her first cousins became more infrequent. She and Johnny saw each other in the park, outside of school, at ball games, however.

"They still acting weird," Louisa reported to her mother.

"Relatives in the bayou marry each other all the time, and nobody thinks they're bad," Johnny argued one day when his mother returned to what had become the saga of Johnny and Antoinette.

"I'm not raisin' you to be like those heathens, speaking in tongues, eatin' possum, and bathing once a month. This is New Orleans, we civilized down here.

"I'm gonna talk to her mama this time; your uncle Winston thinks this is funny. It's not."

After that conversation, Antoinette's mother, Janine, announced to the family at the next monthly Sunday dinner that her daughter was going to a nice Catholic boarding school for girls in California next year.

"It's such a fine school, and she'll be around more refined young ladies than those at Claret public school where she is now. It's a little expensive, but me and Winston only have two children, we should offer them a chance that we didn't have, don't y'all agree?"

"Janine, what a great plan," Ruby Ann chimed in.

Nothing but forks and knives hitting plates could be heard

for a few seconds after their comments. Everyone knew why Antoinette was being sent away. Johnny and Antoinette made the best of the next two months. They were, in fact, inseparable. No one worried any longer; the problem had been taken care of.

This was all before Johnny had that terrible accident on Chef Menteur Highway; everyone believed he would die, but he didn't. Ruby Ann attributed the miracle to the power of St. Jude, to whom she had made a twenty-one-day novena. Normally nine days was enough to move mountains; Ruby Ann said she wasn't taking any chances with her only son.

The accident happened three months after Antoinette left. Johnny was riding with his friend when they had a head-on collision. The friend died, and Johnny was left partially paralyzed. He never went back to school. The following year was filled with a series of agonizing operations and rehabilitative treatments.

Whenever she came to town, Antoinette visited him. But Johnny was uncomfortable and embarrassed by his physical condition; sometimes he couldn't contain his anger. She had a soft gentle southern way of picking up his spirits and making him smile. But she couldn't persuade him to return for his last year of high school. Eventually she stopped trying. So did everyone else.

Three years after the accident, Johnny moved to one of those assisted living apartments for people with a disability. The government paid his rent and he received a Social Security check.

Maybe to supplement his income, maybe to keep himself busy, maybe to meet other people, he started selling clothes, purses, sunglasses, pencils, and other items on the corner of Galvez and Saint Bernard streets. He seemed to enjoy his life despite the worry it caused his mother and sisters.

LOUISA CALLED ANTOINETTE, telling her Johnny was in the hospital and it didn't look good. Antoinette took the first plane from Oakland, California, where she had moved after graduating college. She told her employer she had a family emergency and didn't know when she would be back. "If you can't hold the job, I understand." Antoinette had money; she wasn't rich, but she was a smart investor.

At New Orleans International Airport, she took a limousine straight to Charity Hospital. The driver waited as she raced to Johnny's room. He was watching a rerun of *Matlock* on the television suspended from the ceiling just over the foot of his bed.

"Johnny, honey, are you okay? Are they taking care of you? What can I do for you?"

"Antoinette, don't make a fuss. Get me some red beans and rice."

"Well, I declare," said Louisa. "We been here for weeks."

"Been here all day," interrupted Alberta, also visibly annoyed by the request and by Antoinette's failure to acknowledge her and Louisa's presence, "and he didn't ask for one bean lessen on a bowl of beans."

"Johnny trying to make it seem like we're not good sisters," Louisa said. The pout of her mouth was even more pronounced than usual.

"Don't feel that way. How y'all doing, anyway?" Antoinette said, making matters worse, not better, with a statement that both sisters felt dismissive. "Johnny knows I like to feel needed. Anyway, I'm coming back tomorrow with those beans. If you need me before then, I'm staying at the Roosevelt Hotel. I wanna get a little rest. Here's the telephone number." She wrote on a pad near his bed and then leaned over and kissed him solidly on the lips.

"Some things never change," Louisa said sarcastically.

"Louisa and Alberta, why don't y'all come for dinner?"

"We're gonna stay with Johnny, Antoinette. Thanks for the invitation, though," Alberta said, answering also for Louisa.

The next day Antoinette arrived as promised with red beans and rice. She had gone through considerable trouble to showcase her culinary skills. She persuaded one of the porters at the hotel to purchase a hot plate, two pots, some plastic storage dishes, a Styrofoam ice chest, a five-pound bag of rice and beans, along with a small slice of sausage. (Who would cook beans and rice without a little meat?) Then she sent him to borrow cooking utensils from the hotel kitchen, after they both realized they had forgotten them.

She brought the same meal day after day during that last week, although she knew Johnny would complain.

"They not like Wilhelmina's. I don't know what she used to put in hers, but something's missing. Maybe you could try a little more butter." Antoinette would spend that evening making the adjustments.

"They still not right, Antoinette. Don't worry 'bout it."

"No, Johnny, I'm going to get it right. Let me try one more time. I know you really want this and, well, I want to make you happy."

"Try putting a little more sugar. Not too sweet, though."

"I'll try that."

But the next day Johnny set the bowl aside, allowing his gray-green eyes to rest inside that fateful May morning.

HE WANTED to meet Wilhelmina eye to eye, embrace her without the intrusion of crutches under his arms. That morning, with indescribable deliberateness and determination, he skillfully hooked the handle of one of the two canes he kept in the bathroom onto the shower curtain rod and then hoisted himself like a weightless sail up and over the edge of the tub. He had cleared every anticipated obstacle when he slipped on the blue mat that Wilhelmina insisted gave a *Home* magazine elegance to their drab bathroom. He tried breaking his fall: He reached for a corner of the face bowl, the edge of the tub, and the rim of the toilet seat. But all he broke was that "damn mirror," as it came to be called.

Wilhelmina dropped her pot of grits on the kitchen floor and almost slipped, rushing to the bathroom. Johnny was splattered across the cold linoleum. The blue mat was bunched in the corner near the toilet. Pieces of the broken mirror were scattered around. Saying nothing, she backed out of the room and reached for Johnny's crutches, which he kept in the hall on the floor just near the bathroom door. Retrieving them, she stepped inside the bathroom, once again, and placed them near Johnny. She walked back to the kitchen, without saying a word or even asking if he had been injured. Making any comment might trample his pride, which she was certain had been significantly bruised by the episode, especially since she had to provide assistance.

Johnny placed his hands at the bar of each crutch to lift himself to a sitting position. Then he pulled himself up until he was fully standing with the wooden supports under each arm. Finally, he slowly made his way to the kitchen, his upper body and crutches arriving slightly before his legs. Wilhelmina was on her knees, wiping up the grits.

"What happened, baby?" Johnny asked as he eased his bruised frame into the chair near the table where Wilhelmina had set their two plates for breakfast.

"Silly me. I dropped the pot. But I'm making some more."

"Let's just have coffee."

"No, Johnny. You know what they say about breakfast being so important."

"Okay." Johnny reached for his coffee and smiled.

Wilhelmina was right. He didn't need to prove anything—not to himself and certainly not to her.

WILHELMINA AND JOHNNY had lived together for four years. She had been impressed that first day they met at the corner of Galvez and Saint Bernard streets. His crutches buried under his armpits, he stood with a stately air near his folding table filled with sunglasses, T-shirts, and small leather wallets he made himself, along with pencils and ink pens, which were his hottest items.

"You had all this hair, all over your head, and I kept thinkin' of those pictures of Frederick Douglass in the history books in the library," Wilhelmina said months later after they had gotten to know each other. "Mr. Douglass was so brave and handsome . . . But I didn't want to say nothin' 'cause you might'd saw me as some fast woman, which I wasn't."

Johnny hadn't delayed his compliments. "If I had you for my woman, I wouldn't have to sell this stuff. I'd already be rich," he told her the day they met, exquisitely reshaping into a work of art the ordinariness that she knew had been her personal property since she learned her name.

Wilhelmina continued to pick up one pair of glasses, then another, ignoring what she later called Johnny's "freshness."

"None of them do you justice. You're too pretty for them," he continued. "Plus, they can't protect you against the sun like I can.

"A man couldn't help but feel he'd inherited the earth and all that was good and priceless surrounded him, if he had you."

Finally she smiled. It took a lot of confidence for a man on crutches to flirt. She lingered longer, listening to him call people at the bus stop by name, as if he were operating a store.

Wilhelmina was striking—not New Orleans striking. Her skin wasn't red, honey gold, or near white. Her hair wasn't straight, though it did dance softly just above the top of her shoulder. Her hips were far from full. She was a plume-dark woman, thin as two rails, with a knack for fracturing verbs when she spoke excitedly.

The first time Ruby Ann met the woman at their monthly Sunday family dinner, she followed Johnny as he went to the bathroom and begged him to leave her alone.

"You need a smart wife, son. How are you going to get anywhere with her? Just 'cause you on crutches don't mean you have to settle for less than you deserve. Plus you a good-lookin' man, you can get a better-looking woman. She's too skinny!"

"Mama, you gotta let me live my life. You can't tell me all the time what to do and what not to do. That's why I moved out. And if you keep acting like this, I'm not coming back no more for dinner."

When Ruby Ann whispered at the next family dinner yet another disparaging remark about Wilhelmina, Johnny grabbed his crutches said good evening and walked out of the door. He came back two months later, only after Ruby Ann apologized to him and Wilhelmina—although Wilhelmina had never heard any of the dark comments that had been made about her. "I'm not going to say another word about that skinny black gal," she told Louisa and Alberta. And she didn't. Ruby Ann died from a heart attack two years later.

PERSUADING WILHELMINA to live with him wasn't an easy feat. What man ever finds the direct path to a woman?

Johnny saw her every day. Wilhelmina caught the bus at Galvez and Saint Bernard streets on her way home from the hotel where she made beds, cleaned toilets, changed towels, and pretended to be invisible whenever she came face-to-face with one of the White guests. He often fashioned a ring of words and hung them delicately on her ears, like diamonds, hoping to convince her to be his woman. While she agreed to join him at the Sunset Bar for Irish coffee, at the Circle Theater for a movie, and at Corpus Christi Church for ten o'clock mass, it was seven months before she went to his apartment in the Florida Avenue Project and another six months before she climbed into his bed.

It wasn't that she didn't want him. She wanted him from that night they sat in the balcony at the Circle Theater and he wrapped his arm around her shoulder. She knew, even on crutches, with legs nearly as stiff as two-by-fours, Johnny could protect her. She knew too that he wouldn't flirt in her presence with Creole girls the way Lawrence had done.

Wilhelmina had hoped to marry Lawrence, a college graduate who taught elementary school. "No, you didn't think that. I never said that. What gave you that impression?" Lawrence said the day she confronted him about his roving eyes and how she thought they were planning for a future together.

"Wilhelmina, you are a nice woman and all, but I have other plans."

"You take yo' other plans and get yo' black butt out my place," she said, standing with the door open but refusing to cry.

Things went from bad to worse when she met William, who kept her a prisoner in his apartment. He never invited his friends over to meet her and didn't take her out. She finally allowed herself to consider he might be ashamed of her; she moved in with a girlfriend from the hotel.

With Michael, Wilhelmina swore it would be different. It wasn't. She bought him shoes and shirts, cooked dinner, and did everything she could, but he took what she offered and left nothing on the table. "Didn't even leave me a decent tip," she told her girlfriend when she arrived home one day to find all of his things missing from the closet and a note that said simply, "Thanks for being such a good woman. I know you gonna meet the right man one day."

When Wilhelmina met Johnny, she actually had sworn off the male species. "Too much trouble, child. Too much trouble." But she knew Johnny wasn't like the others. Her only worry was whether he would be able to satisfy her in the bed. "Not that I'm trying to sleep with him right away. But you know, I wonder if he can do it with his legs messed up and all," she said to her friend Freda from the hotel.

"Girl. That's what you worried about. Me, I be thinking if he can take care of me. You know, pay my rent, and buy food and stuff like that, so I can quit this hotel and don't have to spend another day picking up dirty towels and cleaning dirty tubs behind people."

"Freda, I ain't like you. I dream of love. Why you don't dream of it?"

" 'Cause it ain't nothing but a dream, that's why." They laughed; there was nothing in either of their experiences that would dispute that conclusion—except Johnny, maybe.

Wilhelmina wondered if she and Johnny could spend a long rainy weekend together without any possibility of escape, not even through the dull, dated movies on television. She learned how silly she had been.

A week after she climbed into bed with Johnny, she moved into his apartment. She agreed to quit her job, after he asserted that it was a man's pleasure and duty to care for his woman. If she needed to go someplace, she could. If she needed to work, Johnny told her, they could work together. And they did.

THEY WERE AN ODD PAIR: He, short and ruddy-faced. She, tall and plum-dark. He, serious, bordering on melancholy. She, gay and smiling. Wilhelmina's magnetism pulled people to their weather-beaten table and prompted them to leave money in the couple's worn cigar box, even when they didn't buy anything.

Johnny's family took offense at them standing on the corner selling red, green, and blue pencils at twenty-five cents each, and sunglasses at five dollars apiece.

"It's begging. Lord, I'm glad Daddy not around to see you on the street like that," Louisa said during one of the family dinners.

"We ain't beggin', Louisa. We're independent business-people. They got people like that all over New Orleans," Wilhelmina shot back in defense of Johnny.

"I know that, but Johnny's better than they are. Maybe you don't know that."

"I know it all right. I think you mad 'cause he's with me. That's why you sayin' this stuff."

Then Louisa stopped talking, turning her attention to someone else or some other part of the room, which hurt Wilhelmina even more.

"Don't pay her no mind. She jealous that's all," Johnny whispered in Wilhelmina's ear. "She doesn't have what we have."

"What, Johnny?" Louisa asked, half angry because she couldn't hear what he was saying. He pulled the same trick on her, though: He looked around the room, never answering her question.

Wilhelmina and Johnny were at Galvez and Saint Bernard streets nearly every day. During the week they watched young girls in plaid skirts, knee-high socks, and white blouses march into Corpus Christi School. At lunch, those same girls, loud and laughing, spilled onto the playground. Sundays, after mass, Wilhelmina and Johnny walked the two blocks to the Circle Theater. At the window, Johnny paid the three dollars for their admission, stopped at the concession stand for popcorn, sodas, and the Junior Mint candy Wilhelmina loved. She carried the refreshments, walking behind him as he placed his crutches on the step ahead of him and then swung his legs up to repeat the same action. It was a ritual: Sunday at the Circle.

Their whole life was a series of rituals: grits and cheese with scrambled eggs for breakfast during the week; fancy banana fritters on Sundays. Wilhelmina chose Johnny's clothes each morning. He brushed her hair at night—one hundred strokes.

FOR THREE DAYS BEFORE that fatal May day when Johnny fell in the bathroom, he had insomnia. He tried watching television, reading and even talking to himself. Nothing worked.

On the third night, as he sat at the kitchen table, looking out the window as if searching for the thief that stole his sleep, he felt something was about to happen to him. He always had insomnia before some major event, even when he didn't know a major event was about to occur.

"Ruby Ann said it was my guardian angel telling me to pay attention," Johnny confided in Wilhelmina, who sat at the kitchen table, drinking coffee with chicory, so she could stay awake with him.

"Just before the accident, I couldn't sleep for a whole week. I mean, I'd go to bed and just lie there, my eyes wide open.

Sometimes I hummed a song in my head. Mostly I just looked up at the ceiling. I did that for a whole week.

"Something bad's going to happen, honey. Something real bad. I can feel it."

"Johnny, stop that! This ain't no omen. You just got things on yo' mind keepin' you up, that's all."

Johnny sat in his wooden straight-back chair, his legs out in front, his crutches on the floor nearby like an obedient dog. An image of himself splitting in three flashed before him. He jumped, almost falling from his seat were it not for Wilhelmina reaching for him. He grabbed his crutches, tucked them under his arms, and stood before the full-length mirror, assuring himself he had not actually divided.

The next morning he tried the stunt in the bathroom, breaking the mirror Wilhelmina always kept on the floor near the bathroom tub. Johnny's reflection could be seen inside the shattered glass, just as he had seen it the night before.

After he collected himself and sat down at the kitchen table, he pleaded with Wilhelmina to stay home. Breaking a mirror was a bad omen, in anybody's book.

"It's not like we need the money. We get a good check from the government; it pays our bills. We're not going to hurt if we miss one day."

"But, Johnny, people depend on us. Those children at Corpus Christi when they forget their pencils, they know they can get another one from us. And people used to seein' us. Sometimes the day ain't right when we not there. Miss Thompson told me that one day. She say she came by on Thursday and we had gone. She say she was worried, wonderin' where we was."

Wilhelmina placed Johnny's plaid shirt on the bed along with his black pants. Then she put on her favorite lime green knit suit.

"I feel like a flower, Johnny. Do I look like one?" She hugged him, hoping to ease his fears.

"Yeah, you do. That's why we oughta stay home and get right back in bed."

Wilhelmina smiled. She picked up the two shopping bags filled with sunglasses, shirts, a few purses, pens and pencils, and placed them near the front door. Then she cleared away the dishes from the kitchen table and went back to wait for Johnny as he dressed.

"You ready?" she called from the front door. The two walked out together, leaving behind the bathroom fall, the broken mirror, and the days of insomnia.

AROUND NOON, when the girls at Corpus Christi spilled onto the playground, Johnny admitted to himself he had been foolish. There was nothing to worry about. They had done well for a Wednesday. They could make their goal of twenty dollars earlier than usual. He decided to take Wilhelmina out to dinner. It was four in the afternoon when he told her, "Let's call it quits."

Wilhelmina had been full of smiles all day. A couple of the regular customers raved that Johnny was lucky to have a wife so happy and peaceful—full of joy, they said.

"That kind of woman makes even the poorest man think he's rich," Johnny remembered Frank Stanton saying before he boarded the bus going home.

I am rich, Johnny thought as he watched Wilhelmina packing their things, signaling the end of the day.

The two of them were standing on the corner, waiting for the light to change when they heard what sounded like a car backfiring. Wilhelmina looked, hoping to locate the source of the noise. Instead, she saw people all around falling to the ground. She placed herself in front of Johnny, putting her arms around him while easing him to the ground.

When Davis Angelin, another regular customer, pulled Wilhelmina off Johnny, she had a bullet in the base of her head. They had to pry her arms from around him. Johnny lay on the ground, his face awash with tears.

The police never caught the men who, looking for fun and excitement that day, shot into a crowd of people at Galvez and Saint Bernard streets. Three other people were killed. Mr. Thompson, a man Johnny didn't know, and sweet old Alice Loften, who used to walk to the corner every day for exercise and to talk with Wilhelmina, who she always said she wished had been her daughter. Ms. Loften died an old maid. She had spent most of her life teaching school and when she retired, she said she had grown too comfortable to let a man interfere.

Johnny never went back to that corner. A month later he went to live with his cousin Rayford in the house on Bienville Street in the French Quarter. Johnny didn't leave that house for six years until the day he went for Sunday family dinner at Louisa's. She persuaded him to come out because his nieces and nephews were all begging to visit with him. "They miss you, Johnny. Can you come just for them? You haven't even seen a couple of your grandnieces."

In the middle of the meal, Johnny excused himself to go to the bathroom. That's when he fainted in the hallway. The ambulance arrived, taking him to Charity Hospital.

ANTOINETTE, I WISHED you had met her. She wasn't no real pretty woman, not like you. But she had this way about her. You would've liked her. I know that."

"Johnny, I'm sure I would have—even if she did steal you from me."

"Yeah, she did. And Antoinette, she could cook some red beans and rice, way better than Ruby Ann, and we all know that woman could cook. But Wilhelmina, well, she might not have been able to do fancy cooking like you and Louisa and Alberta and Ruby Ann. But beans . . . she was a master. She could make grits with cheese too.

"That last day, that's what we had. Grits with cheese . . ." Then Johnny went silent. Antoinette had finished shaving him and moved to clip his hair, but she didn't hear him breathing.

"Johnny? Johnny!"

"What you shoutin' for, Antoinette, something the matter?"

"No, you stopped talking, that's all."

"I was thinking of that day. Wilhelmina was absolutely gorgeous. She had on that lime green suit she had found at the Goodwill; it hugged her small hips. And she was standing at the door, waiting on me with this huge smile. She could make a whole room glow with her smile—"

"Here, Johnny, take a look," Antoinette said, holding the mirror before him. He turned away. After that Wednesday, he had never used a mirror.

"Thank you, Antoinette. Thank you," he said, before returning to the nightmare of that Wednesday.

When Louisa and Alberta came to visit that evening, Antoinette was in the corner reading. Johnny lay in the bed. His eyes wide open. His face streaked with dried tears.

"Hey, Johnny," Louisa called out as if she were in some parking lot, instead of a hospital. Alberta always had to tell her to lower her voice.

"Johnny," Louisa called again, causing Antoinette to put down her book.

"Johnny!" Alberta said, before walking to the bed and placing her fingers on his neck to check his pulse. She put her hands over his eyes, closing the lids.

"Is he dead?" Antoinette asked. "What happened? No one came in. Aren't they supposed to come in when a patient stops breathing?"

"Don't worry." Alberta put her arms around Antoinette. "It wasn't anything you did. It wasn't anything anyone did. The doctors never found out what was wrong with him."

"Y'all didn't believe me. Doctors didn't believe me," Louisa asserted as tears streamed down her face. "I told you he was suffering from grief. Plain and simple grief."

The Story of Ruth

VICTORIA CHRISTOPHER MURRAY

*T*HEY'D KISSED at least a million times, but each was better than the first.

Ruth pulled away, taking a moment to catch her breath. "We've got to stop." She peeked through the windshield. "Your mother might see us."

"So what?" Mahlon shrugged with a grin. "We're grown and we're married."

He aimed his lips toward hers again, but she leaned away. "Sweetie, your mother's waiting."

He sighed. "Okay, you go in. I'm gonna make this run, pick up the pies."

"Don't worry, baby, we'll get back to this tonight."

"Promise?"

She blew him a kiss, then jumped from the car before he could reach for her again. With a smile, she watched him drive their Honda away. Almost two years, and he still made her feel as if today were their beginning.

She trotted up the steps of the two-story house, but before she could knock, the door opened. Naomi stood, beaming as if she'd been waiting all day. "Baby girl!" she exclaimed, and pulled Ruth into her arms. She stepped back, looked toward the curb. "Where's my son?"

"He ran to the store to pick up dessert."

Naomi waved her hand in the air. "He didn't have to do that."

"I wanted him to," Ruth said. "We never bring anything."

Taking her daughter-in-law's hand, Naomi said, "I don't need you to bring anything but yourselves." She led Ruth into the living room. "But at least this will give us a chance to catch up." She sank onto the couch and then patted the spot next to her. "Tell me about your promotion."

"I'm so excited about being an assistant editor. I have to pull double duty; I'm still an assistant too. But at least now I can acquire my own projects."

"I'm so proud of you." Naomi hugged her. "You've worked hard and today we're going to celebrate."

"Thanks, but you didn't have to do this, you know."

"Are you kidding? Anytime I get the chance to show my daughter-in-law how much I love her, I'm going to do it! And anyway, I don't get to see you and Mahlon nearly enough."

"Sorry about that; we do have to make more time. How're you doing?"

"Really well. My asthma is under control and in every other way I'm in good health. This is a happy time for me." Naomi leaned back and her eyes shone as if she'd just been told a joke. With her head tilted to the side, she said, "I saw you and my son in the car."

Ruth bowed her head.

"I'm teasing." Naomi chuckled. "It's just wonderful to see Mahlon happy. And that makes me happy." She paused, and the glow she wore dimmed a bit. "There were days," she began, her voice softer now, "when I thought neither Mahlon nor I would smile again." Her eyes wandered toward the center of the room to the mantel above the fireplace where the pictorial history told the story of the Hendersons: Naomi, Edmund, and Mahlon, their only child. Naomi began again. "But you've returned the sunshine to our lives."

The words were the same; every chance Naomi had, she

thanked Ruth for bringing back joy after they'd lost their beloved husband and father to cancer three years before.

"I love you for saying that."

"It's true. You've come into our lives and made it all better. You take care of Mahlon, take care of me. You've taken away all regrets that I once had about never having another child because I have you."

Ruth's eyes watered like they always did when Naomi spoke such words. She had girlfriends who told tales of wicked mothers-in-law who'd stepped straight out of horror novels. But Naomi had opened her heart to her from the moment they met. She loved this woman as much as she did her own mother.

"Well, let's not sit here being all melancholy," Naomi said. "Let's check on dinner." She pushed herself from the sofa and paused at the window. "What's taking Mahlon so long?"

"You know my husband. He probably picked up a few other things besides the pies. He'll be here in a minute." She hooked her arm through Naomi's and led her into the kitchen.

There Ruth watched as Naomi pulled pan after pan from the oven. Dishes filled with macaroni and cheese, baked chicken, and candied yams. On the stovetop, collard greens simmered and vegetables steamed. And then there were Naomi's famous corn muffins that Ruth insisted could get her mother-in-law a show on the Food Network. Ruth moaned with pleasure without taking a single bite.

Naomi smiled. "That must mean you're hungry."

"I wasn't, but I am now." The knock on the door stopped her from grabbing one of the muffins. "That's my husband." She rushed toward the entry. "Honey," she started before she swung the door open, "why didn't you use your—" She stopped, stared at the man in the uniform. "Can I help you?"

"Are you Naomi Henderson?"

"I'm Ruth Henderson. May I help you?"

The officer motioned to step inside, and she scooted to the left so that he could. Behind her, she heard Naomi's soft steps.

"Mahlon, what took you—" When Naomi stopped, Ruth knew that she was standing right behind her. "Ruth," Naomi said. "What's wrong?"

"Mrs. Henderson?"

Naomi nodded at the officer.

"Do either of you know Mahlon Henderson?"

Ruth grasped Naomi's hand. "He's my son," Naomi responded.

The officer nodded. And before he uttered a word, his slackened face told the story. "There's been a shooting . . . at the grocery store. And we found a driver's license with this address."

The women gasped together.

"I'm sorry, but Mahlon is dead."

Ruth heard the cry from Naomi before her own world faded to black.

RUTH SQUIRMED, then stretched. She opened her eyes and wondered why her body felt so heavy; why did she feel as if she'd been sleeping for a week?

She rolled over, and her eyes focused on the chair across from the bed. What was Naomi doing in her bedroom? Then she remembered.

She hadn't been sleeping for a week, but she wished she had. She wished she had been able to sleep through all the pain—the pain of the police officer reviving her, of having to identify Mahlon's body and then plan a funeral. And then the final pain—of walking into the church with Naomi at her side, and listening to others speak about the wonderful man

Mahlon *had* been. And then watching the gravediggers lower the man she loved into the ground. This was not the way her fairy tale was supposed to end.

She moaned and Naomi sprang up from the recliner. "Are you all right?" she said as she sat on the bed's edge.

With a sigh, Ruth nodded. "I don't even remember coming up here."

"Your mother and father convinced you to lie down after everyone left. It's been a couple of hours."

Ruth glanced to the windows. She remembered her father encouraging her to rest just a little before four. And now the August sun had almost completed its daily bow to the night. "Are my parents still here?"

Naomi shook her head. "They were exhausted too. I sent them home and told them I'd call the moment you woke up."

Ruth swung her legs over the side of the bed. "I hope you weren't sitting in the chair all this time."

Naomi shook her head. "No, I cleaned up."

"Wish you hadn't done that."

"I had to do something."

Ruth nodded and fought back the ever-present tears that had accompanied her since this nightmare began. She couldn't cry now; she had to be strong for her mother-in-law.

"Go ahead, let it out," Naomi said as if she heard Ruth's thoughts.

"How do you do it? How are you so strong?"

She shrugged. "Don't be fooled. I'm not strong. It's just that I've been through so much I don't have many tears left." She gave a small smile. "And I have to be strong . . . for you."

"It's supposed to be the other way around."

"We'll make a deal; we'll be strong for each other."

Ruth nodded, but a moment later she turned away, trying

to hide the single tear that crept down her face. "I might need a little time to hold up my end."

Naomi pulled Ruth into her arms. "Take all the time you need," she said as her daughter-in-law wept in her arms. "I promise we'll get through this. We'll get through this together and we'll get through this with God."

THE DAYS TURNED into weeks; the weeks twisted to months. And like everyone said, time made her loss more bearable. The ache of missing Mahlon was always there. But almost five months later it was different now, sometimes her pain was accompanied with a smile.

Ruth always smiled more when she was with Naomi. Her parents were her rock, keeping her steady through the toughest of times. But Naomi was her pillow, a soft place to rest. She found special solace being with the woman whose pain was as deep as hers. Their shared loss drew them closer, and they found comfort in taking care of each other.

Most mornings Naomi would drop by, bringing Ruth breakfast before she left for work. Many evenings Ruth would stop at one of Naomi's favorite restaurants and purchase dinner for her. And in the in-between hours they shared phone calls.

"How's my favorite editor-in-chief," Naomi would always say.

Ruth would laugh. "I'm only twenty-four; I'm not there yet."

"You're on your way." Naomi spoke with such confidence that Ruth began to believe that truth herself.

They shared much of their weekends as well, both fearing the long, empty hours. Sometimes they shopped, took in a movie, strolled on the beach. Sometimes they did nothing more than sit and cry together. But always they loved each other.

Now, as Ruth slipped her purse strap onto her shoulder, she checked her phone once again for a message from Naomi. There were very few mornings that she missed stopping by. She probably slept late, Ruth thought. That was good. Over the last few days Naomi had seemed tired, and Ruth had encouraged her to rest today. *Maybe she's starting to listen to me.* She smiled with that thought and rushed to her car. Inside, she paused as she always did. Closed her eyes, inhaled, and imagined Mahlon in her place: sitting behind the wheel, looking over at her, smiling and loving her with his glance.

Her ringing phone startled her from her reverie, and she flipped her cell open.

"Ruth?"

She frowned, not recognizing the voice.

"This is Madeline."

"Oh, hello, Ms. Madeline," she said. But her forehead was still creased with confusion. *Why was Naomi's neighbor calling her?*

"I just wanted to let you know that Naomi was just taken to the hospital."

"What!"

"Now, don't worry, honey," the neighbor said as if she couldn't get the words out fast enough. "It's her asthma. She was having trouble breathing."

"Why didn't she call me?"

"She wanted to, but I wanted to get her to the hospital. I told her I would call you once the ambulance came. They're taking her to Daniel Freeman."

"I'll be right there." She clicked off the phone and punched the accelerator. The engine roared, but the car stayed still. She paused. Took a deep breath and inhaled calm. She couldn't afford to get into an accident. She had to get to Naomi.

She put the car in drive, edged from the curb, and drove as

if her heart weren't fiercely pumping. Drove as if she didn't fear losing someone else she loved.

"Please, God," she began her prayer. "Please, don't take Naomi away from me."

It was only fifteen minutes, but it felt like hours had passed when Ruth finally swerved into the emergency room parking lot and then dashed into the lobby.

At the information desk, she tried to control her trembling as she waited for the woman who examined her nails as she chatted on the phone.

"Excuse me," Ruth said again to the woman.

The woman held up her hand, motioning for Ruth to wait.

Isn't this a hospital? she wanted to scream.

"Ruth!"

She turned toward the voice. "Ms. Madeline, how's my mother-in-law?"

Madeline smiled. "She's fine." And then she added, "Really," knowing that was the part that Ruth needed to hear. "She's in the emergency room. Come on."

She followed Ms. Madeline through the double doors, down a long corridor, past patients on gurneys, scurrying nurses, and doctors dressed in scrubs. Ruth marveled at how easily they moved through the chaos. Finally Madeline stopped and pointed to a small space partitioned off by curtains.

Taking a breath, Ruth stepped inside.

"Hi." Naomi greeted her as if she were stretched out on the couch at home rather than on the flat padded stretcher.

"I was so worried about you." She hugged Naomi.

"It was just my asthma."

"So, you're fine?"

"Yes." But she paused, as if there were more.

The pounding in Ruth's chest had settled, but Naomi's hesitation made her fear rise again.

"What is it?" she asked. Silence. "Tell me," she insisted.

Naomi said, "I have to leave Los Angeles. It'll be better for my asthma. I'm moving to Arizona."

"Arizona?" Ruth whispered.

She looked into her daughter-in-law's eyes. "I have to. The asthma, it's been so much worse."

"But . . . do you know anyone in Arizona?"

She shook her head. "But I'll be fine. It's not like I have much of a life here anymore." She paused, reached for Ruth, and took her hand. "Except for you, of course."

Ruth looked down at her fingers entwined with Naomi's. Their skin tones blended together like they were meant to be. How was she supposed to live her life without Mahlon and now without Naomi? For just a moment she closed her eyes, talked to God. And He told her what to do.

Slowly, she said, "Okay. Then we're going to Arizona."

Naomi reared back at those words. "We?"

Ruth nodded.

"You can't do that. Your family is here. And that great new job. Your life. It's all here."

Ruth paused, considered for a moment Naomi's words. And then God repeated what He had just said: *Go, blessings await.*

Ruth said, "My family has each other. And my job . . ." She paused and thought about how long she'd worked for the promotion, then said, "I'll probably find a better job in Arizona." She squeezed Ruth's hand. "But my life . . . I know my life is with you."

"But what are you going to do in Arizona with me? It's not like I can have another son and then raise him to marry you."

Ruth laughed. "Now wouldn't that be something?" But then, serious again, she said, "Anyway, I'm not thinking about that. I just know that I'm supposed to be with you."

Naomi's mouth was still open wide with surprise. "I don't believe this."

Madeline stepped from behind and took Naomi's other hand. "Believe it," she said. "Ruth is giving you the gift of love—the kind of love that God wants from us. Naomi, you are blessed with this wonderful young woman. One of her is better than you having seven sons."

With watery eyes, Naomi nodded. "Then that's the way it will be."

RUTH HUGGED HER MOTHER one last time. "Mama, I'll call you as soon as we land."

Her mother nodded, but she couldn't speak through her quivering lips.

"I promise to take care of her," Naomi said to Ruth's mother.

"We know you will." Ruth's father spoke for both of them.

It still took a moment for Ruth to turn away. She took Naomi's hand, and together they strolled into the terminal. Through the long security line they both stayed silent, each inside her thoughts. Each saying good-bye to Los Angeles and the life that to this day was all they knew.

Ruth pressed down her rising fear. *Go, blessings await.* That's what she held on to. That's what she believed.

When they settled in front of the gate, Naomi said, "Before we get on this plane, I want you to know that I won't have any problem if you change your mind and want to stay. I will still love you. I will always love you."

Ruth's chin jutted forward. "My place is with you."

"Then that's the way it will be."

"Excuse me."

Both lifted their eyes to take in the sight of the man who towered above them. He was dressed in a pilot's uniform, but that did little to hide the muscles that made him a man.

"Ms. Naomi, is that you?"

Naomi peered, but only for a moment before her lips spread into a smile. "Bo Gaines! Oh, my goodness."

He pulled her from her seat. They hugged. And Ruth stared, soaking in as much of him as she could. First, she decided that it was unfair for a man to have eyelashes like that. But it was equally unjust for him to be walking around with so many blessings on the outside. It seemed ridiculous that this man wasn't starring in somebody's major movie.

"Ms. Naomi!" He stood back and with his light brown eyes gazed at her some more. "It's so good to see you."

"I didn't know you were back in Los Angeles. I spoke to your mom a few months ago; she didn't tell me."

"I'm not. I'm just flying through. I live in Phoenix actually."

"Really? That's where we're going." She paused. "Oh, excuse me. Let me introduce you to my daughter-in-law."

She turned, but before she could say anything, Bo took Ruth's hand. "Wow." Seconds passed and then: "It's nice to meet you."

It took Ruth a moment to recover from the electrical bolt that raced from her hand, through her arm, to her heart. Inside, she tried to shake away all that she still felt. What was that? she wondered.

Naomi explained. "Bo was like a son to me before he and his family moved away." She asked him, "How many years has it been?"

"Too many. Listen, I have to get on the plane, but wait for me when we land. I'll catch up then"—he turned, stared at Ruth once more—"with both of you."

She was so glad that the rich Hershey color of her skin hid the heat that rose beneath. With his stare still on her, she decided that she needed to find something in her bag—her lipstick, her tissue, a quarter, something. But when he strolled away, she stopped her search and watched him. And marveled at the way he strutted to the door—like he owned the whole airline.

"My."

It wasn't until her mother-in-law spoke that Ruth remembered that Naomi was there.

She needed to say something, but there were few words that she could think of at the moment that would sound like English.

Naomi said, "Well, I guess you liked what you saw."

"What?"

"Don't what me." Then Naomi grinned. Leaned closer to Ruth and whispered, "But the great thing is—he liked what he saw too."

"I—I don't know what you're talking about."

"Oh, yes, you do." With her smile still in place, Naomi nodded her head, as if she were responding to a voice she heard inside. "I get it now. I know why God told you to go with me to Phoenix."

Her skin heated again. "What are you talking about?"

"You heard him. Bo lives in Phoenix."

"And?"

"And he is going to be your husband. I'm going to make sure of it."

For a moment she sat in the middle of that wonderful thought. Soaked it in. Then realized that she didn't know a thing about the man. And there were other challenges as well. "First of all, how can I get married? I just lost Mahlon."

"Yes, dear. But, Mahlon would want both of us to go on with our lives."

"And second of all," Ruth began, wishing that she weren't so interested, "how do you know that Bo isn't married?"

"He's not. His mother told me that he broke off an engagement about a year ago. And he told his mother that it's difficult to meet women in Phoenix." She lowered her voice, leaned closer. "I think he meant *Black* women."

Now Ruth smiled, even though she didn't want to. "Thirdly, how do you know I'm interested in him?"

Naomi leaned back. "My asthma hasn't affected my eyes. I saw the two of you. Neither of you could help it." Naomi's eyes shone in a way Ruth hadn't seen in months. "Mark my words. You and Bo." She shook her head. "I'm on my way to being happy again."

"Flight thirty-seven to Phoenix is now ready to board." The announcement came over the loudspeaker.

"That's us." Naomi stood, glanced at Ruth. "Come on, daughter, it's time for us to get on with our lives."

Ruth handed the attendant her ticket and then followed Naomi down the jetway. Her heart fluttered when she saw Bo standing at the door.

"Just wanted to make sure you two made the flight," he said to Naomi, but smiled at Ruth.

"We're here," Naomi said, taking Ruth's hand. "We'll be waiting for you right at the gate once we land."

They had moved only a few feet when Ruth glanced back over her shoulder. Bo stood at the entry to the cockpit, watching her. He tipped his hat, and for the first time she smiled at him.

Blessings await.

She smiled, knowing all of God's promises were true.

A River to the Moon

ANTHONY GROOMS

In the moonlight, the shadows seemed to twirl about the bed, and the breeze, foretelling storm, rushed in through the windows and billowed the light curtains. Jimmy Lee watched Beah's breasts bounce against her ribs; they were round and had edible color, and he could feel their movement resonate through her body and vibrate in his thighs. The air, drying up sweat, tickled like fingers on his back. His body felt like milk in a half-full milk can or water in a well bucket. She threw her head back onto the mattress and moaned and at the same time clawed his chest. For a moment his concentration waned. The wind had picked up and the branches broke the moonlight into flutters. Then the intensity began to build again, like weary legs striving toward a summit, a summit that shifted its distance and shape with each step toward it, until suddenly he was stepping on it. He fell on top of her and let out an exhausted laugh into her ear. He felt oozy, drugged, and for just a moment, he slept. Then she pulled his penis out of her, turned, and pushed her back into his side, and he rolled over and cradled his body around hers. Together, they seemed to float. The bed was a raft, and they were floating on a river of moonlight, rippled by the shadows. It was a river to refresh them and a river to carry them away.

JUST A MONTH BEFORE, at the time of the first cutting of timothy, as he drove the rake over the mounds of cut hay, he had
thought how much the smell of the hay reminded him of a
woman, freshly bathed and doused with talc. Then he couldn't
imagine who the woman he was daydreaming about was,
though he could smell her and he could feel her weight pressing against his thighs, pressing his back into the soft mounds
of the ripe timothy. He wouldn't have minded if she had looked
like Dinah Washington, the singer, whose picture he had seen
in a magazine. She was a big woman with a pretty, round face
and a wide smile. When she sang, "He's slender, but he's tender; He makes my heart surrender," Jimmy Lee imagined she
sang about him. She had been born in Tuscaloosa, just fifty
miles east of where he lived, and then she had moved up to
Chicago. One day he too would move up to Chicago and live
in a tall building and ride on a streetcar.

It was at that moment, the moment of that particular day-
dream, that Mr. Jacks, his boss man, had flagged for him.
Deacon Thompson, one of the older workers, had suddenly
fallen senseless, and Jacks wanted Jimmy Lee to drive him
to the clinic. At the clinic, the doctor said the old man had
had a stroke and he sent Jimmy Lee to find Beah, Deacon's
daughter.

It was dark and moonless when Jimmy Lee drove Beah
home from the clinic, where they had waited for hours in the
basement, where the colored were seen, until the nurse told
them that nothing more could be done for Deacon and to go
home. As they approached the house, the trees blocked out
the sky on either side of the driveway, creating the effect of
a bright, jeweled swath of sky directly in front and overhead
of them. In the swath Jimmy recognized Jupiter, swimming
against the Milky Way. He knew it was a planet and had a
vague notion from pictures how it looked through a telescope.

But he couldn't say a lot about it, except that he knew its route through the sky from observation. He knew the routes of most of the bright planets and stars even if he didn't know their names. He knew some of the bright constellations—Orion, the Big and Little Dippers from the winter sky, and the Scorpion from the summer sky. Still, most of the bright patterns remained a mystery to him. He drew his own constellations from the things he knew, not mysterious queens and monsters, but haystacks, mules, and pine trees. One thing he knew well, that the heavens were mysterious and glorious. Many a night he went to sleep with a crick in his neck from staring into the sky. One day, he thought, he would get himself a telescope, just a little one, so that he could see the mountains on the moon and the canals of Mars.

Suddenly, a meteor streaked across the open swath. It filled him with wonder and privilege. "Did you see that?" he asked Beah.

"What?" Beah said, distantly.

Jimmy Lee remembered Deacon, now, and the meteor seemed a bad omen, Deacon's soul departing from earth.

"Just a falling star."

"Oh." Her voice trailed off. She had said only a few words on the half hour drive from town. She sounded tired and scared. Then her voice brightened. "Did you make a wish?"

"Uh-uh. What you supposed to wish for?"

"Haven't you ever heard of wishing on a star?"

Jimmy Lee thought a moment. "I heard of wishing on a turkey bone. I didn't know you can wish on stars."

"On falling stars."

"Well, then, I wish Deacon will be all right." He listened to Beah's breathing, strained but even.

"That was nice of you to say."

"He'll be all right."

"I hope so," she said, her voice getting soft and distant

again. "But I don't want him to suffer. I'd rather the Lord take him quickly and not let him linger."

"He'll be all right. Won't he?" Jimmy Lee parked the truck in the driveway and turned off the engine.

"I don't know. Doctor doesn't know. Only the Lord knows."

"Well, he will be all right."

Neither moved nor spoke for a while. Jimmy Lee was thinking he had never spent any time with Beah. He had seen her at the Normal School and at church, but he had never attended either often enough to know more than her name. He had always thought she was an attractive woman, full-bodied, but not heavy, and dark-skinned, but not so black that people would make fun of her. She had long hair, which he found attractive. It wasn't quite Indian hair, it was a little nappy, but she kept it pressed and twisted on her head in some style or the other. She had a clean smell about her. That was the remarkable thing, the thing he could only know by being this close to her. Even though she had been cooking all day at Maribelle's Diner, she didn't smell of fried fish or grease. She must've washed up before she left work.

"You must be tired?" she said at last.

"Not so much tired as hungry. I didn't get no lunch or supper."

Beah got out of the car. "Come on in. I'll fix you a plate. That's the least I can do."

He sat at the table in the large kitchen as she moved about in the lamplight. She decided aloud not to light a fire, but she found him plenty of cold foods: fried chicken and cornbread, sliced tomatoes and onion, and a tall glass of sweet tea. For dessert she gave him a slice of pound cake. As he ate and watched her move about the kitchen, taking plates from the cupboard, unwrapping and rewrapping foods as she placed them in storage tins, a sense of peace began to settle over him. Somehow, in this kitchen, he was feeling that things were the way they were supposed to be. Things had never felt this way in his own home, filled with siblings. In his own home he was always on the verge of exploding, always resisting the urge to tear everything apart because nothing was right about it. But here there was a woman preparing food in the lamplight. She had a quiet, sturdy build, and she moved lightly and confidently about the room. She smiled. She sat food in front of him. For his own part, he sat at a table and was eating with a fork and drinking from a real glass, not a jelly jar. In the center of the table was the oil lamp; next to it, ceramic hen and rooster salt and pepper shakers. At the end of the meal, he thanked her.

Before sunrise he was in her yard again. She came down in her robe to open the door for him. He apologized for coming so early, but he said he wanted to make sure she had firewood and he would see that the chickens and pigs were fed. When he came back from feeding the animals, she invited him to sit down.

"Don't mind if I do," he said, not playing the customary game of politely refusing at first. She served him fried eggs, salted meat, biscuits, and a bowl of canned peaches. He ate with his mouth close to the plate, stopping once in a while to breathe and look up at her. At the end of the breakfast, he thanked her.

"Now, if you drop me off by Mr. Jacks', I give you the pick-up back," he said.

"How are you gon' get about? You got a car?"

"I can get around all right. But—" He paused and hung his head. "If I had the truck, I could get around a bit easier and be over here to help you."

She shook her head no, and he thought she was saying that

she didn't want his help, but then she smiled, parting her teeth and biting the tip of her tongue. "Keep the truck for now," she said. "My work woman carries me to work."

The pattern continued for the next few days, supper and breakfast. She seemed to take pleasure in watching him eat her food, rarely eating much of it herself. She was around food all day at the diner, she explained. And he enjoyed talking to her, shyly at first, and then about stranger and stranger things, things he had only thought about and had never said to anyone. He told her about the various trees, about the insects that sang in the trees, about the stars that shone above the trees. In August, he told her, just a few weeks away, for a night or two, the sky would rain falling stars, great yellow streaks that sometimes fizzled and left shiny dust on your skin. This happened like clockwork, every year. In December, it would happen again, only this time the shower would be farther away and the falling stars whiter and briefer.

On the third evening, she finally asked him, "How do you know so much?"

"I just notice things," he answered, biting into the peach cobbler she had made just for him. "I've always just noticed things about the outdoors." He laughed. "Course, even when I was indoors, I was mostly outdoors—the house being nothing but a shack."

"I've never paid that much attention to the things right around me," she said. "It's really funny. You know, I was good in school. A straight-A student. But I can't tell you the names of any of these trees except, of course, for oak and pine. The obvious ones. I don't even much know the names of all these flowers around here. Mama planted them years ago, and I just keep them up from time to time."

"Sometime," Jimmy Lee confessed, the setting sun casting a shadow across the bridge of his nose, "I dream I'm going up into space. Like Buck Rogers or somebody. Going up and exploring the moon."

Beah laughed, then caught herself. For a moment her laughter sounded derisive, and he felt ashamed. "I'm sorry," she said, and she patted his hand. She let her hand linger on his. "I'm sorry. I think it's wonderful to want to go places. But the moon!" She looked away from him, out of the window to the yard. The sunset was coloring the sheets on the clothesline. "I've just been trying all my life just to get to New York City."

"That's a long ways away."

"It's a lot closer than the moon!"

"I reckon so, but nobody's been to the moon before."

"So you reckon you will be the first?"

He hung his head. "Maybe not."

She still held his hand and squeezed it. "Maybe you got just as much chance of going to the moon as I got of getting to New York City."

"Don't say that," he said. "Don't say that."

She took her hand away from his and rubbed the inside of her other palm. "I don't reckon so. Not really so. You and me and all the rest, we stuck here, Jimmy Lee. This our life for real no matter what we dream about. You working for Mr. Jacks and me cooking for Maribelle's. Seem like God didn't give us much of a life. I sometimes wonder why, 'cause it ain't fair. And Papa, worked all his life right here."

"Don't say that." He took her hand and held it for a long moment, until she smiled and pulled it back.

In the week after they brought Deacon home, Jimmy Lee had continued to come to help, morning and evening, and Beah had continued to feed him. He couldn't say exactly when it happened, but it began to feel just right—unnecessary, but unavoidable at the same time. He went to her place early, fed her pigs and chickens, milked her cow, and then came to the house with the half-full milk can swaying in one hand, fresh well water in a bucket in the other. She had breakfast ready. He washed his face and hands, and they both sat and ate as the sun peeked above the trees and began to brighten the rooms. Then he worked for Mr. Jacks—all day long in the sun—caring for his animals, raking his hay. The tenants and sharecroppers worked the cotton, cane, and soybean fields; he worked Jacks's stock. In the evening he returned to help Beah. He cared for her animals, chopped wood, weeded the garden, made a repair or two. Then he helped to bathe and feed Deacon. Later she'd have a supper ready. Then he'd wash and she'd give him a clean shirt, either one of Deacon's or one of his own.

The first time he was shirtless in front of her, he had wished to make love to her. He was embarrassed the moment the thought crossed his mind. She had held Deacon's shirt out to him, and as he took it, he felt the need to have her admire him, to say he had a strong body, that he was good-looking.

She had said nothing. They ate. He went home.

For more than a week, things went that way. Then one evening when he came in from the chores, she had a bath waiting for him in the mudroom. He took off his shirt, but she did not leave the room.

"Give me your pants, Jimmy Lee," she had said matter of factly, as if she had always been asking for his pants. "I'll wash them for you."

He hesitated. "Ain't you gon' turn your back?"

She smiled. "I think we know each other well enough." Then her throat trembled. "Jimmy Lee, there is something about you that makes me feel good. I don't know what it is. You're a handsome man, but that's not it. I never took much notice of you before, but having you here, helping me, I have gotten to know you. I like you, Jimmy Lee."

He had nearly choked on a sudden rush of emotion. It wasn't passion, exactly. It was like a rush of something warm and so happy it made him want to cry. "I like you too," he said, hardly breathing.

She had taken a step back. "Now, you know people gon' say this is wrong, but it feels right for us, I think."

He loosened his belt. Already he was getting hard. She pulled the waist of his pants over his rump and down to his knees. "People gon' talk."

"They are already talking," she said.

NOW, HAVING MADE LOVE, he nestled his chin over the back of her head and his hands cupped her breasts, which rose and fell with the rhythm of her breathing. Slowly, his breath fell into rhythm with hers, and he began to dream of water.

A stream rose up in his dream. First as a metronomic dripping, a lovely tenor with a hollow core and a melodic rippling, each ripple a blossom, until the blossoms were a field swaying with the chorus of dripping, a pleasant rain shower or a night full of tree frog song. Then everything went into motion and he and Beah were drifting on a river, moving in the moonlight and through air heavy with the scent of summer rain, swinging around the stones, sliding down the riffles, and floating across the flats. In the distance were the silhouettes of willow oaks and sycamores. The slanting moonlight shone like silver paint of the old bridge that crossed the Tombigbee, just down the road from Jacks's Plantation. They were floating on the Tombigbee, the so-called undertakers' river for the Indian undertakers who used to live on it. He chuckled to himself when he recognized where they were in the dream, first by the old bridge where the road ran into town, and then by the little Tupelo swamp, and then they were in the big bend. They could meander all the way down to Mobile on this river. He had never been to Mobile. He had heard it was a great city, something like Chicago. From here, he was dreaming, they could go anywhere, he and Beah, to New York City or to the moon, or to anywhere in between.

PART TWO

Ties That Bind

Poetry

Why I Will Praise an Old Black Man

HONORÉE FANONNE JEFFERS

for Herman Beavers

Who lays in the cut, leaning back
in the dusty front seat of a long car he bought
on ancient credit, Al Green or a song
even deeper playing on the eight-track,
song about a working brother's calloused
pain, dismissed but throbbing the same.
This is the countrified, steady paycheck
man who braved sorrow song days, toiled
until his bones protested at last.
Who will die clean and grieved
like Charlie and Ambrose
and Vess and Lil Jinx.
I look to meet them in the yonder,
souls whose rheumy squints
have glimpsed tall trees over my head.

I have known some ugliness
but never at these hands that know how to whittle
from the wood's heart, that can gentle
a bad dog's growl with a slight wave.
That's why I got me a weakness
for the sharp-as-a-mosquito's-peter
creases in pin-striped pants, the Stacy Adams'
side-zipped shoe blues dance
of a dapper, old Black man.
Yes, his musty do-right smell of cedar,
yes, his deacon's bass resting
in his throat on fourth Sunday morning,
yes, the way he calls me *daughter*
and then I can sleep
unbroken through the night.

Acts of Love

KWAME ALEXANDER

You never know he loves you
You overhear that he works like a slave
And that freedom is expensive
So you pay the price

There are no hot dogs and soda pop summers
Because there are no baseball games
Your tongue is not sweet on cotton candy
Because there are no moonlit carnivals

Time is money, smiles are seldom
Home is serious business
With little time for little things like
Card games and Ping-Pong and talking

Conversations become instructions:
Write all messages here

Clean the gutters as such
Mow the lawn like this

You crave his touch
Some small ritual of precious contact
Perhaps a drop of water in noonday heat
Even a forehead scratch would do

You never know he loves you
You overhear that he works like a slave
And that freedom is expensive
So you pay the price

Family Meetings become trials:
Who took this message? Guilty
Why isn't the grass cut? Guilty
Did you finish up on the roof? Guilty

You never hear he loves you
Even in the car
Engine battling the hum of silence
Questions you're afraid to ask

Then one day in your Sunday proper
His sermon ended, the pews empty

You shadow his stillness
Hoping for some movement on this desert island
You look up into blinding sun
Cling to high mountain
His face, a golden moon, now beams
His hands, spring rain drizzling scalp

And then you know.

Nonfiction

When There's Trouble at Home

LONNAE O'NEAL PARKER

Don't start none, won't be none
SCHOOLYARD TAUNT

LAST NOVEMBER, I watched a nightmare sequence on the ABC television drama *Desperate Housewives*. The character Lynette is a former corporate type who gave up her high-powered job to stay home with her four children, and in the sequence, the kids were crying, beating pans together, and ratcheting up the stereo. Lynette yelled at them to *"Stop, stop, why don't you listen, why won't you stop?"* She slammed her fruit bowl to the floor and threw a jar of peanut butter out of the window. When she snapped back to reality and realized she was on the verge of a breakdown, she handed the kids off to a neighbor and sped off in her minivan.

Last year, in an op-ed column for the *Washington Post*, Ellen Goodman wrote that Lynette was a woman of her times:

> *It's Lynette who speaks truth to power—the power of the updated and eternal myth of momhood.*

This "truth" is that even a woman who purposely chooses to be a full-time mom can be one nap away from losing it. The "truth" is that mothers who would throw their bodies in front of a truck for their children also fantasize about throwing their kids in front of a truck. Okay, a little wooden truck.

I related to that *Desperate Housewives* scene because sometimes I feel on the verge of a nightmare sequence of my own. Sometimes I wonder if I'm the only one in my house with vision powerful enough to see the socks lying on the dining room floor or the cornflake fossilizing in the corner of the kitchen. Sometimes there are so many people tugging at my hand, so many chores that require my attention, I can almost feel my body chemistry changing, telling me urgently it's time for fight or flight. There are times when my husband needs so much of my attention, he attacks even my briefest periods of quiet with a constant barrage of words. There are mornings when all three of my children call me so incessantly that I hate the sound of myself coming from their lips. *Mommy! Mommy! Mommy! Mommy! Mommy! Mommy! Mommy!* they call over and over again, until I want to scream *What? What? What? What? What? Shit! What?* Then, in my nightmare, my six-year-old cries and I want to comfort her because I know she's feeling hurt and abandoned, but in that moment, I cannot, because my margins are overrun. Because there is not enough air in my lungs for the measured softness of comforting words, there are too many programs open in my head, and patience requires more memory than I have available. Then I start to cry too, because now I know how my mother must have felt, but, my Lord, don't I know how my daughter feels as well.

The episode of *Desperate Housewives* ends with Lynette crying in the arms of her girlfriends. "Why didn't anybody tell me?" she implores as they try to soothe her. In her 1998 *Washington Post* essay "Nobody Can Tell You," writer Cecelie Berry talks about the hard, lonely parts of motherhood we're not supposed to mind. She gives voice to her depression, the "bastard child" of her affair with domesticity, she says, and rages against a slow, agonizing erosion of herself. It is true of marriage and true of motherhood as well: There are some things you don't know until you're well into it. And sometimes that feels way, way too late. Sometimes, when there's trouble at home it is run through with ache and bitter disappointment. I always swore my household would be free from fights with my husband and hollering at my kids, but too often, my very best efforts aren't nearly enough to stifle the angry words rising in my throat.

Growing up, there was weekly yelling in my house. Momma yelled at Daddy for drinking and running around and Daddy yelled at Momma because he was an alcoholic and a paranoid schizophrenic and his sickness always caused him to see her with men who weren't there. In good times, my parents bragged to relatives that I was bright and they affectionately called me Fifi because Momma says I was always such a prissy thing. But when I was reluctant with Saturday chores, or I needed Momma to listen to me when she was tired, my parents would sometimes snap angrily, cutting me with their words, accusing me of being lazy and too demanding. Still, both the yelling and the praise were secondary to the sustained periods of being largely unnoticed. Of being mostly unable to compete for attention with my father's alcohol abuse and mental illness and my mother's depression. Of getting so little feedback that sometimes I would hurt myself, just to double-check that I had mass and took up space. I also wasn't yelled at a lot because, until adolescence, I was too timid to do anything that would get me into trouble. And I sometimes try to explain to my own kids how easy they have it—how when I was a child, there was zero tolerance for attitude or protest in the house I lived in and all the places I visited. "Mommy, what would happen if you talked back?" my ten-year-old daughter Sydney, acting as her own attorney, once wanted to know. Because she actually, sometimes, gets to enter into negotiations with her parents and often lobbies for more favorable terms.

"We didn't talk back," I told her.

"But what would happen if you did?" she persisted. And even after thinking hard, I could not come up with an answer. I didn't know what would have happened, I tried to tell her, because talking back was not something that existed in the realm of the possible when I was a child. It was not even a concept, so any violation felt beyond my capacity to fathom. That nonconcept is part of a couple of distinct schools I come from when it comes to discipline in my house now and the one I grew up in. They are schools with some parts I deeply want to keep and other parts I am yet hoping to overcome.

Although whippings are decried and sometimes even criminalized in places where methods of modern, mainstream parenting are debated, except for very recently, I've always known Black families to be harsh disciplinarians. To yell and especially to spank (except in Black places, the verb was "to whup" and it was usually done with a belt). Physicality was an inviolate part of the routine of families: kisses when you were good, pain when you weren't. My momma tells a story about inviting a little White girl from her neighborhood to their house for dinner when she was young and making an exaggerated production of chewing her food and rolling her eyes at the table to make her friend laugh. "Okay, Betty Lou, that's enough," my genteel grandma Mabel warned her. But Momma continued. "All right, that's enough," Grandma Mabel warned again, but after a brief interlude Momma was right back at it. Grandma Mabel didn't warn her a third time. She reached over and slapped Momma's face so hard that the food flew from her mouth and landed against the wall. Then they all finished dinner without further incident.

In her *Washington Post* article "A Good Whuppin'?" my colleague and friend Deneen Brown writes about the commonality, folklore, and ritual of punishment in the houses of Black folks.

> *Go outside and pick me a switch. And don't pick a small one either.*
>
> *That command, for many, is part of being Black in America—part of a cultural tradition that sought to steel Black children for the world, forge their characters, help prepare them for the pure meanness that waited out there, just because of the color of their skin. Many Black parents who whipped felt more was at stake if they did not scourge their children.*
>
> *Don't get it wrong. The wielding of the switch and the belt and the wooden spoon is not a practice unique to Black people. Most races spank their children, especially Southern Whites who are fundamentalist Christians. But the stories of beatings done in the name of love, beatings that were endured by many—not all—Black parents, are like a familiar song. There are some bad associations with slavery. There are some good associations with survival.*

Feminist, abolitionist, and former slave Sojourner Truth had thirteen children and saw nearly all of them sold. That didn't stop her from whipping her kids in the time that she had them. When Truth became a mother, writes Paula Giddings, "she would sometimes whip her child when it cried for more bread rather than give it a piece secretly, lest it should learn to take what was not its own." She whipped because what do you imagine they did to slaves caught stealing? Black families would whip their kids because white people might kill them. Because the streets could consume them, because the police would jail them.

> *Tryin' your best to bring the*
> *Water to your eyes*
> *Thinkin' it might stop her*
> *From whuppin' your behind*
> *I wish those days could come back once more*
> > *(Stevie Wonder,*
> > *"I Wish")*

They whipped because the stakes were high, missteps were costly, and *Stop! Don't!* and *No!* had to mean what they said the very first time since Colored people couldn't rely on second chances (as true for Emmett Till as it was for Amadou Diallo). Sometimes, we kids also suspected they whipped us because it felt good to them, because they were horrible and mean and *I hate you!* and *I'm going to run away!* That's sometimes what we were thinking—we just never, ever said so.

In his essay "The Black Belt," journalist and children's book author Fred McKissack describes growing up in St. Louis on a block where his folks' Black whuppin' belt had reached legendary neighborhood status. He talks about being a schoolboy and hearing a White kid say to his parent, "I don't feel like cleaning my damn room," and marveling that "all" he got was his mouth washed out with soap. "As recently as the last decade, for a Black child to curse at his parent could be reasonably regarded as a suicidal act," McKissack writes. "Indeed, the daring youngster could wind up seeing a child psychologist and facing the following question: 'Did you intend to end your life when you called your mom a bitch?' "

It was one of those generalized pathologies grown folks whispered in our ears about White kids. *They talk back to their mommas and their parents don't whup them.* Adults would get mad just thinking about those White kids, and we were made to understand that none of that would ever be a problem with us. As a child, it was not uncommon for me to be in a distant part of the house and be summoned by my daddy to fetch a glass of ice water, even if the kitchen was only a few feet from where he was sitting, or to change the television channel in the days before remotes. This had to be done quickly, quietly, and, most important, without the smallest semblance of "attitude," or any physical tic that might possibly indicate frustration. That meant there was no looking funny, twisting your lips, or sucking your teeth, and we were not to "even think about" rolling our eyes.

In the book *Fatherhood*, Bill Cosby writes that his wife, the elegant Camille Cosby, used to threaten to knock their kids "into next week" and he once told his son, "When I come home Thursday, I am going to kick your butt." *Today* show personality Al Roker titled his book on fatherhood *Don't Make Me Stop This Car*, after an oft-repeated warning from his own bus driver dad. In his comedy movie *Delirious*, Eddie Murphy recalls his mother's seemingly bionic powers at landing a shoe upside his behind. And an unscientific survey of my own close friends and family reveals certain recurrent themes in the threats leveled against us growing up. Routinely, if an adult didn't appreciate something we were up to, we were made to understand that they could, at any moment: slap you silly, slap you into tomorrow, slap your eyes out of your head, smack you upside your head, snatch you bald-headed, smack your teeth down your throat, smack the shit out of you, knock some sense into you, knock your neck to your knees, beat that ass, whup your ass, wipe the floor with your ass, knock your ass out.

Break your neck, smack the black off of you. Leave you for dead. Said the luminous actress Debbi Morgan to her young onscreen niece Jurnee Smollett in the 1997 movie *Eve's Bayou*: "I will hurt you."

I remember times when childhood was less sentimental and motherhood less saccharine. My cantankerous grandmother Momma Susie used to hold babies while an inch of ash gathered on the end of the cigarette she was smoking, hands free, as it dangled from the side of her mouth. And if, on occasion, some bit of ash fell onto the baby's arm, and the baby started to cry, she just dusted it off, changed positions, and said loudly, "Aw, that baby's all right." And it was. A little smudged is all. There was not a soul in my family who ever read Dr. Spock or subscribed to the "Touch Points" theory by T. Berry Brazelton. Times were different, and even White kids, who our parents told us got everything they wanted and never got yelled at, were deemed less fragile and more subject to a natural order of inviolate adult rule. Accounts of White schoolmasters and parochial school nuns were dense with stories of harsh corporal punishment, and don't you remember when Charmin or Northern toilet paper commercials featured a White child loading tissue down his pants, to cushion the impending spanking that was coming to his behind?

Some of those times resonate with me now, not because of the physical punishments (or cigarette ash) but despite them. From the time we were very young, we were made to understand that adults were in charge. That life had boundaries and consequences for crossing them. We learned that all eyes in the neighborhood were on us and any grown person, at any time, had the right to correct us, to chastise us, to smack our behinds and send us home crying to Momma, who would smack us again because Mrs. Phillips had to get after us. Not long ago, I was listening to National Public Radio's *The Di-*

ane Rehm Show, and author Cindy Post Senning, the great-granddaughter of etiquette maven Emily Post, was talking about her book *The Guide to Good Manners for Kids.* When a listener wanted to know how she should handle a neighbor's or relative's recalcitrant child, Senning advised against correcting other people's kids. I thought to myself: Those women can't know how the world used to look from the South Side of Chicago or other Black places, where neighbors have always relied heavily on each other. While we didn't think anything good about all the folks who could fuss or get us into trouble, even when we were small we could sense that the opposite of love has always been indifference. And all due respect to Ms. Post Senning, but don't I wonder what some of our communities would look like now if everyone was still together, trying to get to the same places, fussing at everyone else's kids?

The harsh discipline was often painful, but in most cases, all that "knocking your ass out" was hyperbole meant to make you think twice about acting up. I never knew anyone who lost facial parts as the result of a good whuppin'. Still, I understand much of that romantic lore is revisionist history and there is a darker, more disturbing side to excessive yelling and harsh physical punishments—to being mostly unnoticed at all. It has shown up in the lives of extended family members who grew up with too little kindness. It has also shown up in my own psyche, in struggles with my family and scars that never fully fade, even with the passage of time. My brother, who was always whipped more harshly and more often than my sister or me, is estranged from us now. It is unclear whether those whippings have anything to do with where he is today, which is nowhere lucid or sane—nowhere anybody who loves him can reach him—it's just clear those whippings must have hurt. And sometimes the cumulative effect of all our hurts makes us too heavy with pain to ever walk with dignity. My house was loud and sometimes unforgiving, and in many ways, that scarred me and made me promise things were going to be different when I had my own kids. I read all the *What to Expect* books and memorized the book *I Love You This Much*. We decorated a nursery from the pages of a catalog and I told myself I wasn't ever going to spank or yell. For years, that worked just fine, until one day my policy changed.

When Sydney was fourteen months old, I returned to the *Washington Post* to work as a reporter for the first time and sent her to a home-based day care a few minutes away. The owner, Mrs. McCorkle, was young, but organized and self-possessed beyond her years. Frequently when I would pick Sydney up, if one of the children was misbehaving, Mrs. McCorkle would just start counting, and that child would cease and desist before she got to ten. Once Sydney misbehaved while playing with a neighbor's child in the cul-de-sac where we used to live. I started counting and Syd chilled out before I got to six. Wow! said my neighbor, Ranae. What happens when you get to ten? I don't know, I told her. I'll have to call Mrs. McCorkle and ask. I think Sydney was about three when I stopped counting to ten and started to spank.

Since then the threat of spanking has always loomed disproportionately large in the back of my children's minds, but while whippings are infrequent, sometimes I yell more than I care to admit. Not long ago I cussed Sydney out on the way back from her ballet lesson. She made us late, she couldn't find her shoes, her body was stiff with attitude, and I spat vicious words until I was spent, and a little ashamed. Good thing there was nobody else in the car with me at the time or I'd have really felt out of control. When I picked her up, I was able to calmly say, "We need to help each other think of ways you can keep your stuff together and we can get out of the house in a more timely fashion," and Sydney agreed. A former neighbor once told me about a girlfriend who called talking about how she was "going to hurt that little bitch." My neighbor asked who she was talking about. Turns out, she was talking about her own six-year-old daughter. We could laugh because that was clearly venting gone over the top. (Kind of like in the old television series *The Honeymooners,* when Jackie Gleason used to tell his wife, "One of these days, Alice. Pow! Right in the kisser!" And that qualifies as classic television.) Because kids try you and cussing out the air or calling a friend to rant gives you time to calm down so sometimes you don't have to say things to your children that are hard to take back. Or frighten them by saying nothing at all.

Try as I might, I don't have the same ironclad authority as the adults I grew up with, and in many ways I don't want to. My house has an appellate process; it has precocious kids who tell me, "Mom, I don't like it when you yell," and, "You hurt my feelings." And I get to say, "Well, I didn't like it when you came downstairs naked." My house has more exchange, more compromise, more kisses, and yes, that often means a whole lot more funny looks and twisted lips, a lot more attitude than ever would have been tolerated when I was young. That's why, sometimes, I've got to get in little people's faces to let them know, "I will knock your eyeballs out of your head." Or maybe I say, "Don't make me tap that sammy," which means "Don't make me spank your butt." I got that one from Vita, in my book club, and it works especially well for the little ones who might find the idea of having their eyeballs violated a little too nightmarish. Later we make up in sentimental e-mails after we've had time to calm down or we go in the living room and try to bring back the love by playing a duet on the piano. Sometimes we're too angry to do any of that, but we move on anyway because, really, that's all we can do.

"I Wish," sang Stevie Wonder, and I have wished I were a

woman who never yells. Sometimes I wish I wasn't a writer, so I wouldn't spend so much time in my head or find it so painful when people tried to pull me out. But mostly, instead of wishing, I find it more immediately useful to know my triggers, to be honest with myself; to work on my patience, and to have people around who can help me vent or check me when I'm tripping. My parenting is a constant calibration of the old-school lessons in accountability and respect (my kids say "yes, ma'am" and "no, ma'am" on the phone ever since I heard a lovely little White girl's impeccable phone manners when I called North Carolina once for a story), tempered by a modern emphasis on feelings and self-esteem. Jacqueline Kennedy once said it doesn't matter what else you do if you don't raise your children well, and I believe that to be true. Beauty fades and the most storied career passes into memory. I talk to my mother nearly every day now, but for a long time our relationship was strained, and it took us years to find our way back to each other. But tomorrow is not promised and I can't count on having years with my kids, so I try to find my way back to them sooner. To say I'm sorry now, in real time, which is the only time we've got, and let them know Momma doesn't always get it right, while they are still little, in the hopes that that immediacy lessens some of the sting. I try not to let our hurts fester long and grow deep between us.

It is something I've learned over long years and painful lessons. They are lessons that apply not only to kids but to husbands as well, because despite my best efforts, despite how different I said my house would be from the house I grew up in, my marriage is one more place where I've yelled more often than I care to admit. And it is one more place where my romantic fantasies don't always square with the wife that I have been. For a couple of years now, I've helped write an occasional column for *Essence* magazine called "Making Love Work." It profiles couples who have weathered hard times and offers their tips on pulling a relationship back together. Friends and relatives often recognize my name in the pages, but Tanzi, a friend of my close friend Stephanie, who sees my husband and me out on occasion, says she skips the column whenever she sees my name. I have the perfect marriage, she tells Stephanie, and who the hell wants to read an article about relationship problems by a woman who has never been through anything? I can see where she might get that. Because as a couple, our public face is always smiling. Because my husband knows my songs and likes to lead me to the dance floor; and I like to walk up and wrap my arms around him from behind. Because we play off each other well and sprinkle color in each other's stories. So I can see where she might think my marriage is perfect.

It's just she's wrong about that.

Losing my rosebushes was what finally sent Ralph and me to seek professional help for our marriage—that and everything that happened along with the move to our new house. When my daughter Savannah was a newborn and Sydney was four years old, my friend Deneen brought me two tiny rosebushes, no more than bulbs and sticks, to plant in honor of each of them. A deep hearty red one for Sydney, and a beautiful light pink for Savannah. I tended those rosebushes and they grew like my daughters, who could each tell you which one was theirs. I'm sentimental and often try to keep living reminders to mark the times of our lives. When one of my best friends and sorority sister, Valerie Smith Reid, died of breast cancer when I was pregnant with Savannah, I took a cutting from a plant I sent her when her cancer went into remission and we all thought she would live. My Valerie plant sits in my kitchen, reminding me of my friend. I loved the joy and celebration that those rosebushes stood for, and I loved that I had a friend thoughtful enough to give them to me.

When we sold our first house in 2002, I asked to take the rosebushes, said I wanted it put in our contract. My husband promised he would take care of it. That he would call the guy who still does our lawn before the move, but he didn't get around to it. I asked the day of the move, but things were so hectic it wasn't a priority. I asked him for weeks after the move, but by that time, he had gotten into a $200 carpeting dispute with the people who bought our house. They were relandscaping, so they just dug up my rosebushes and threw them in the trash.

Those bushes were a part of my first house and my babies and my life as a young married woman. They were a gift of friendship, and why didn't he know how much they meant to me? Why did he leave them so bad-karma strangers could hurt me with their casual disregard? How was it that I was still so unable to make myself heard in this marriage, after so many years? Moving days are always stressful but I had a newborn, and my husband had left all the packing to me and the Señora. It was a busy time for him at work, but I asked him to take a day or two off so that we could make a plan, touch bases, figure out logistics. He wouldn't—but why did I just sit there and play the victim?

By the time we began unpacking, on moving day, I began to realize a lot of things had gone wrong. There were the usual nicks on furniture and in the wooden frame to a tapestry from Guatemala, but it was my grandmother Mabel's broken china that wracked my body with sobs. Dishes that were probably eighty years old had fallen to pieces. They had been passed down from my mother, and after surviving so long, I had let them crumble on my watch. "You should have taken them in the car," my husband told me. "I couldn't remember every damn thing," I spat back. "You should have helped me plan. These dishes meant the world to me," I cried. "Everything means the world to you," he countered, his voice alien and ugly with sarcasm and scorn. After many, many battles, it was in those few months after the move that I finally felt empty and defeated. And my husband was as cold and withdrawn as I've ever seen him.

When I was a young bride, no one told me that marriage had seasons. That the marriage you have at year one is not the same marriage at year six or eight or eleven. That some days would feel like St. Tropez and some days would feel like the Gulag. Like my childhood friend Alicia once said, I thought we'd giggle all day and make love all night. No one ever tells you that sometimes you hold on to the institution because it means far more to you than the man. No one said that to me, or perhaps they tried to, and I just wasn't in a place where I could hear them.

Sometimes it seems like I've been married since I was seventeen. Only a few weeks after my college boyfriend and I broke up, I met my husband on Valentine's Day in 1989 at Howard University Hospital where he was a pharmaceutical representative and I was getting a physical. I was twenty-one years old. We started talking and he mentioned he had a little brother. Said he loved kids, and right then it flashed through my mind: "I'm going to marry this guy and we're going to have kids." And so we did. But for a while at first, there were a few other relationships he was loath to let go of. This left me jealous and angry. Still, like my momma before me, I was young, *and I had to have that boy.* I used to call my husband "The King" when he'd come visit me at work. Used to get a kick out of talking him up to everyone we met. He was smart, he had played college football, he was a Que, and I always did have a thing for the fraternal men of Omega. He left his W-2 on the table when we were dating and I fell in love with his salary and benefits. Before the wedding, somebody I worked with told my friend Stephanie, "Lonnae's not ready to get married." And he was right. But that's something else no one could have told me at the time. I was all packaged like the magazine and television shows instructed, and I just wanted to be taken off the shelf. I had an engagement party, three showers, and a bachelorette party. I had a big wedding and a big ring on my finger. Our picture was in *Jet* magazine. After all of that, I thought marriage would be magically delicious.

We married and Sydney came quickly. Then I became a *Washington Post* reporter. I was meeting people and hanging out after work, and suddenly I wasn't the little twenty-one-year-old who liked to make brief appearances onstage before scurrying behind the curtains, where it was safe. I had a promising career and people who told me I was good at what I did. I was coming out from behind my shadow. I was growing, but my marriage was stagnant. My husband grew resentful of this new wife and her bigger world. He said I wasn't the woman he married. And I grew resentful, because he was right, I wasn't.

(Black Thought)
Yeah, so what you sayin I can trust you?
(Female Voice)
Is you crazy, you my king for real
(Both)
But sometimes relationships get ill
(Female Voice)
No doubt
(The Roots,
featuring Erykah Badu, "You Got Me")

I can't detail all the arguments we had. How many times I'd walked out in my mind and how ready my body was to follow along. I couldn't talk to my husband. That had been one of our recurrent themes, but I don't know if it was because he wasn't listening or because from my daddy's house to my husband's, I had never had much of a voice. I wrote things down so I could know what I thought. I couldn't talk to my husband, so I left a message for one of his best friends asking if we could talk, and I poured all my sadness into my journal, which I carried with me always. Except the day I left it in my bedroom, which is where my husband found it. I didn't want to come home from work that night. I wanted to run away, right then and there, but it's a familiar story to a lot of women. My child was with him, and I couldn't walk away from her or take her from her daddy.

Ever practical, my sister Lisa told me I needed to decide what I was going to do and if I wanted to stay married. She said I should give it a year to try to work things out, then I'd be in a good position to know.

That summer, after a journalism convention in Chicago, I went to see my grandmother Momma Susie, who was living with my uncle Ronnie. My complicated, hard-cussing Momma Susie had always cautioned the women in the family to wait until they were thirty and had done some living before getting settled down. But she waited until late in life to give me advice about my own marriage. As I sat at the side of her bed rubbing her hand, she began: "Lonnae, I was married for fifty years. Some of it good, some of it bad, but I wouldn't change nothing. You stay married. There's nothing out there in the streets for you. You find somebody else, they got the same problems, or different ones. You stay married." I nodded and cried and kissed her cold, fading hand. Fifteen minutes after I left her, my Momma Susie died. And since we hadn't spoken in at least two years, she had no way of knowing that my marriage was in trouble. I decided the universe was trying to tell me something that day. And I decided to listen. With all our cards on the table, things got better between my husband and me. Then Savannah came along, then Satchel, then we moved into our new home.

Not long ago, one of my best girlfriends and I were talking about problems in marriage and she said, "You know, Black people don't go for all that counseling." I took her point. I grew up seeing couples who stayed together for decades, living in separate bedrooms—couples who would be more likely to smother each other than ever see a therapist. But I'm an advocate of counseling. I've had to face down too many dark things I wouldn't have been able to look at without help. Early in our marriage, I had asked my husband if we could talk to someone, but he had always refused. If we needed to talk to someone, we didn't need to be together, he would say. Later, when he was ready, I was not, because things had gotten better. Finally, after the move, we were both ready, and we decided to go to counseling. The experience has given us better tools and a language for the times when bitter words fail us. Although Black couples have the highest divorce rate in the country, says Audrey Chapman, a Washington, D.C., therapist who wrote *Getting Good Loving: Seven Ways to Find Love and Make It Last,* they have been slow to avail themselves of therapeutic remedies. Chapman, who also hosts the long-running radio call-in program *The Audrey Chapman Show,* says men, especially, are more resistant, less inclined to want to have "other people in their business." Black folks "are so hung up on that, it's taken them years and years to come around," she says. Like anything you want to last, marriage takes maintenance, tune-ups, "continual work," says Chapman. "Weekly, monthly, yearly work."

Shortly after we moved, we were welcomed to the neighborhood by the Taylors, a few doors down, who have three children of their own. She's a psychiatrist, he's a nurse anesthetist, and they're very involved with their church. They're busy people, but they reserve one day a week as a date night for just the two of them. Ralph and I were so taken by this idea that last year we adopted the practice ourselves. For five or six years, Friday nights have been family movie night at the Parkers; now Saturday nights are date nights. Sometimes it's dinner and a movie, sometimes just a drive to a furniture showroom or even Home Depot. The point isn't where we go, just that we make time to be alone, together. As writer Angela Ards puts it:

> There are no set roles. We play to our strengths and pick up the slack. I cook the most, because it's relaxing and I enjoy feeding friends, but he burns in the kitchen most regularly. He also washes dishes, the chore I avoid like the plague, and takes the heavy lifting. At times what looks like tradition is more personal sensibility. . . . We say thanks a lot, which sounds kind of formal but is actually very nice because it's a reminder that we're choosing to love.

I'm glad Stephanie's friend Tanzi thinks I've never been through anything. Because I've never wanted my hardest times to linger on my face. If she thinks I make marriage look easy, it's because I work at it. I work at my marriage and my family when it hurts. I work at it when I fantasize about leaving it all alone. I work at it because I've had to work at everything in my life and I have no expectation that it will ever be any different, because, especially for the Black women I've known, it never has been. It is true that there are some things nobody can tell you, but sometimes it is worth it to try.

The move to my new house taught me a couple of things. If you have something that would be unbearable to lose, you have to find ways to take care of it. It's as true for marriages and children as it is for china and rosebushes. I think I've always known that, but it is important and affirming to remind myself daily. We do it with rituals—family dinners, movie nights, and date nights—to sustain us. Sometimes when there's trouble at home, we circle each other warily, waiting to see how it's all going to play out. My husband has a saying for those times, a balm he likes to drop. "Bring back the love," he says. And not always, but more often than not, the love is stronger than all the angry words rising in my throat.

At Its Best

TRACY PRICE-THOMPSON

There's some bad talk going around town these days about Black on Black Love and its certain demise. I mean the statistics are out there and the predictions are grim: the crumbling structure of the traditional Black family, the rising number of single Black female-headed households, the bone-shaking fear of dating a brother on the down low, the startling rates of Black teenage pregnancies, and the staggering numbers of incarcerated Black men.

Unfortunately, much of this negative data is a valid indicator of the erosion of the Black family. As a people, many of our collective behaviors and actions support these figures, and they simply cannot be ignored. And no, we don't have a monopoly on dysfunctional relationships or on societal ills. We coexist alongside of folks of all races, ethnicities, and socioeconomic backgrounds as we struggle to survive in a world where we're increasingly led away from self-love and taught that "family" is just another f-word.

But while there's no denying the fact that far too many of our children are living in poverty caused by single-parent households, and hoards of our young Black women are baring all and gyrating in music videos, and frightening numbers of our sons and brothers are off on extended vacations courtesy of the state and federal governments, can we also give some propers to the sisters and brothers who are out there doing the right thing each day? How do we honor those dedicated Black men who, like seaworthy ships in the night, return dutifully to black ports each evening, bringing home the day's bounty after navigating risky waters to provide for their own? I mean, where is the news flash that heralds culturally conscious Black men and women who choose to love each other, and who celebrate their Black love by living balanced lives and raising ethnically attuned productive Black children?

To hell with all that negative hoopla. I've run across quite a few good Black men in my day. I gave birth to and raised good Black men. My father was one, as was my brother. I was born into greatness in that regard, surrounded by Black men who loved and edified me in all my blessed Black female glory. It was this unconditional love and adoration from the initial men in my life that taught me to appreciate my own worth and helped me become a confident, self-loving sistah from the inside and out.

I used to be a warrior woman way back in the day. Black, proud, fearless, and invincible. I met my husband, Greg, during a time in my life when I believed I could do it all, and do it all alone, if I had to. We were both young soldiers stationed overseas in Europe, and I was racing through life in my usual fashion, full speed and headfirst. He was charming and respectful. Funny and attentive. I was hesitant, playing the field. We explored southern Germany, marveling at the countryside and falling in love.

Somehow we clicked and it was magical. The universe went into a holding pattern. The stars were aligned and the sun shone perpetually. Greg was all man, and life was good.

My parents were thrilled. They loved him on sight. He was infectious that way, still is. They saw in him the same things I saw. His character, the strength of his convictions, his unyielding efforts to do the right thing. Just a good Black man. We set about building our family empire, raising our children and teaching them to love themselves . . . and each other.

The years passed, most of them very good. Life was hectic, the military demanding. The children grew, Greg and I adapted, and my parents aged. There was joy and lots of laughter. Of course there were tears and heartaches, bumps along our road, and at times we faltered, but we held hands a lot and we prayed too. Sometimes we climbed over life's obstacles, and at other times we maneuvered around them. But always, we did it together. Always, holding hands.

I'd always known that my husband was a special breed of Black man. The kind of Black man who was culturally conscious and who believed in the power and worth of his Black self, and that of his Black family. After all, he'd married a spoiled little dark-hued sistah filled with spunk and zest. A superwoman warrior-diva who stood on her own two feet and let her hair grow out naturally, yet one who accepted his role as the head of their family and who understood her role as the family's heart.

Yes, I was experiencing Black on Black Love on every level, and it felt good. But very soon I would learn the true depth of my Black man's strength and love and at a time when I was hurting and needed him the most.

I was standing near my father's deathbed when it happened. Cringing, really. Weeping and shaking. Unwilling to get too near, afraid to bear such close witness to the transition that was occurring before me.

On the bed was the first man I'd ever loved. My rock, my sanctuary, my sword, and my shield. My beloved father. Until this moment I'd never made a major decision without consulting him. Even after I was married, I still clung to him. He was the real man in my life. He'd been such a tower of strength and wisdom in my world, an oasis of comfort and unconditional love. I was fearful of living life without him, had never once imagined it. His breathing was ragged; his chest rose and fell irregularly. My sister and I had finally given his doctors permission to remove him from life support, and watching him struggle was driving spikes through my heart.

See, I'd been spoiled. Raised by loving parents and doted on by my Black father, I was everything the statistics said I shouldn't be. Growing up in the projects, I'd witnessed the phenomenon of fatherless Black families devoid of male guidance and affection, but I'd never experienced it. My father had always "been there" whenever I'd needed him. In every way that I'd needed him. He had devoted his life to loving, providing for, and raising his children, and his character was the yardstick I'd used to measure the worth of every man I met. If a man didn't measure up to the stature of my father, then he wasn't the man for me.

And then came Gregory. He measured up. His character reflected my father's in all facets. With his kindness, strength, and affection, Greg had captured my skeptical heart, and now the love we'd built together was culminating at this crisis point as I stood near my father's head, terrified at the proximity, too close to his death for comfort.

My father would have wanted me right there, I knew. Standing at his shoulder, right in the forefront of it all. He'd spent his whole life preparing me for the day when I'd have to live without him. Strengthening me. And now that it was his time to die, what better way to make one's transition than to be surrounded by the children you'd loved and raised as they prayed for you and performed a laying on of hands, rubbing your limbs and whispering their love in your ears.

But still . . . it was all too raw for me. Too painful. As much as I wanted to be brave and strong for my father . . . I just couldn't. I hung back, shriveled in the presence of death. Sensing my distress, my husband took me in his arms. He whispered words of love, then quietly switched places with me.

He took the place at the head of my father's bed, using his love to create a protective barrier between me and that which I just could not face. His shoulders were broader than mine, his heart beat stronger. And while I trembled in my husband's shadow, he stood tall at my father's side and witnessed his transition on my behalf, serving as a physical and emotional buffer for my pain, standing strong for my father and allowing me, his warrior woman, to be weak.

There were several transitions on that hot June day. My father and best ally in the world departed this life. He left this world completely fulfilled, having been the best Black man, son, husband, and father that he could possibly have been. He left me secure in his love for me, secure in his love of his people, and secure in my love of self. He also passed the torch and left me in very capable hands. In the hands of a loving Black man. In the hands of my husband.

As I look back, I realize that all my life I'd borne witness to the positive attributes of Black on Black Love. I am living, breathing proof that Black Love can and does exist, and in the highest realms imaginable. Of all the blessings that have been bestowed upon me, all of the riches of life, the joys of my world, the greatest of them all is the gift of complete love that I was given by the first Black man in my life and that I continue to be blessed with in my husband.

Of course I've seen the negative ramifications of relationships in our communities. I've heard the statistics. The harsh realities don't escape me, and I'm well aware of today's growing rift between Black men and women, Black fathers and children, Black husbands and wives. The media and society at-large would have us believe that there's no real need to encourage and develop strong Black family units anymore. In this so-called melting pot of America we're supposed to be culture-blind and oblivious to the fact that our Black children still require ethnic edification and intensive lessons in self-love and esteem. True love begins with the love of self, and the love of one's own, but the images broadcast by our mass media lull us into forgetting these principles, and then when our chickens eventually come home to roost, the media slaps us in the face with their carefully calculated statistics and we're forced to acknowledge that we're failing each other and we have no one to blame except ourselves.

Sure, the oceans of Black America have become littered with shipwrecks. The choppy waters are churning with casualties of this ever-raging battle against Black Love. Black men are rejecting us in droves. Declaring as beautiful those women who look as different from their mothers, sisters, and daughters as possible.

Yet I choose to praise, focus on, and align myself with those mighty African-blooded seafarers who love their own and who choose to return to Black ports each night. Bringing nourishment and sustenance to those Black mothers, daughters, and sons who depend upon them for solid leadership and, yes, solid love.

A Polaroid snapshot sits on my desk. A smiling couple, heads close, arms entwined, squint into the sun. The woman is caramel-toned, slender, and very pretty. You can tell by looking at her that she is classy and outgoing. A vivacious and proud Black woman. She has the glow of a diva far ahead of her time. The man stands a few inches shorter than she. Handsome. Ethnic-looking. Strong. Grinning, protective, damn proud of the treasure he holds in his arms. It is a photograph of my parents. Beside it sits a snapshot of my husband and me, embracing in a similar pose. Two complete and colorful pictures of Black Love not only surviving but conquering the odds.

To hell with their statistics.

For us this is Black Love, at its best.

Becoming a Grandmother Becomes Me—Finally

ROBIN ALVA MARCUS

BACK IN MY MID-FORTIES, during a period that was practically crackling with imminent transition and the anticipation of miracles, before I'd even *thought* about *beginning* to imagine how I *might* feel about being a grandmother or what variation of the word I'd want my grandchild to call me or what kind of grandmother I'd be or even whether I was ready for the whole conversation, I became one. Before I'd cleared out my nest and ascended to my place among the ranks of parents who were done with the raising part of the job, before I could catch my breath from seeing my last son successfully launched so that I could begin the next phase of my adult life, *before I was ready, dammit,* I received the frightening news via a strange telephone call from a woman I'd only said maybe six words to in the relatively brief time she'd been in my oldest son's life that instead of coasting away from child care worries for a minute I was actually en route to a kind of Second Coming of it.

I reacted with shock. My jaws flapped open, but I couldn't corral any of the words crowding into my mouth into a coherent or appropriate response. In truth, I wasn't surprised exactly, but I'd shoved the possibility into one of those really deep corners in the back of my mind where thoughts like that reside. Because it scared me, it was unavoidable, and there wasn't a damn thing I could do to prevent it. The minute I'd heard my son bragging about this woman, who was older by seven years (!) and had two children already (!!) and a second husband not quite out of the picture (!!!), I'd squinted down the road and seen their baby coming. Her call confirmed my worst predictions about that relationship. When they'd temporarily broken up at one point, I told him, "You've dodged a bullet. If you get back up in that saddle, you won't dodge the next one."

Maybe I was too metaphoric or naive; evolution, the mating instinct, and the reproductive imperative are far more powerful than any mother's warning. At any rate, they patched their bustup, and I threw my hands up. "It's your life," I said. A few months later the call came.

"Your son says you don't like me but you seem to respect me and I know he hasn't told you but I think you should know that I'm pregnant in case you want to get to know your first grandchild."

Her words spilled through the receiver in a torrent, no commas, no periods, and, surprisingly, no emotion. It was as if she'd rehearsed several times, taken a dozen deep breaths, exhaled, and then sent the words inflectionless into the air to do their work. Her announcement was followed by silence from my end as I felt my universe imploding, the expectations I'd had for my son's (and my) future disintegrating, my relationship with my oldest son shifting. And then this:

"So, I was wondering, as far as medical history, could you tell me . . ."

I somehow managed to say, "I'll have to call you back," before hanging up. I sat on my sofa blinking, stunned, looking at my hands, a grandmother's hands. I went looking for my son and laid his ass out.

Oh, I was a mess. I beat him all upside his head and shoulders with questions. How could he have been so stupid? Didn't he see the trap? How was he gonna take care of a child on a part-time Athlete's Foot salary? And how could he be sure it was his? All his teenage life I'd sworn that if he, or either of his brothers, became teenage fathers, they'd have to move out, get their two little *minimum-wage* jobs at Popeye's, and set up camp with their families in some Section 8 housing somewhere, wherever. Wasn't going to be no "Boys in the Hood" *in my house* with a crib in their bedroom and a stack of Pampers in the closet and they and their baby's mama acting like they got an efficiency apartment, *in my house.* No, sir. My house was like the inn in Bethlehem: no room here. You grown enough to start a family, be grown enough to go out and take care of it. Didn't he believe I was serious? What did he plan to do?

And finally why *her,* of all people?

In the brooding that followed I wondered why that boy always had to go so hard. Why did he force my hand? I couldn't retreat, I didn't know how to redraw the line in the sand; I had two more sons coming up behind him, watching. A precedent was being set; what message did I want to send them? I'd stood at that line with my arms folded over my chest or my finger pointing so many times that I had never considered an alternative. I'd been resolute; now I had to go as hard as he did. *I'd have to put him out.*

But really, I couldn't just throw him into the street. I knew that if I was feeling the way *I* was feeling over the situation, I could only guess what might be going on in *his* head when he tried to rest it on his pillow at night. His world had suddenly become enormously complicated. His dream for his life, at least his immediate future, had changed in that instant, or whenever he got the news, as well. My tirade turned into a conversation about options. He still wanted to finish college, he needed to provide for the baby in every way that the responsibility required. I encouraged him to join the air force, something that, considering my pacifism, I never imagined doing, and he followed that advice.

NOW, FATHERS OF GIRLS may think it's tough to guide their daughters through the throngs of sex-obsessed boys who come sniffing after their daughters, but from my side of the equation, as a mother of only sons, I can attest to the assertiveness, even the aggressiveness of girls. Girls were calling that boy before I realized we had to talk about girls calling. The mother of a friend of his told me that a girl wrote a message to her son in one of those books kids throw together and then autograph at the end of the school year that read: "Hope you're not a virgin when we get to 8th grade!"

Mothers of daughters might cast a wary eye on every "But I love him!" pipsqueak masquerading as a man that their daughters parade through the living room. Fear of pregnancy is probably in the Top Two on their list as well. Usually though, when a girl does become pregnant while living at home, she stays there, right? Usually. That means that mothers of daughters who live at home while pregnant and in the early months or years of their grandchildren's lives get to grow into the role organically. Their choices are limited, relatively speaking. The pregnancy is accepted and accommodated. These mothers often become co-mothers and the babies are equally comfortable relating to both Grandma and Mommy as Mother.

When you have sons, a girlfriend's pregnancy can seem so peripheral to your reality that it's like an idea, something way over there. Because it's not present in your day-to-day life, it's absent. If you're not at all thrilled about the relationship, it's easy to lose track of it and you might not recognize this as a stage of grieving. I did a lot of thinking about what it meant for the dream I'd had for him and assessed how far that dream had carried him. The progression in the dream, the arc of his story, was supposed to end with his being able to take care of himself so that I could let go and move back into the life I'd put on hold when I became a mother. His impending fatherhood, it seemed at the time, threatened to smash up the whole enterprise.

[Cue violins.]

In the dream version my son has finished college, embarked on a challenging, satisfying, and remunerative career first as a teacher while he attends law school, then as a lawyer; he has moved out of the house, established himself in a nice place; burned off whatever wildness remained; maybe in his mid-thirties he has found himself delighted and surprised by meeting a wonderful (Black) woman who fits the established criteria of being able to sit down with my friends and me at the table and hold her own on any number of subjects, but with respect; she "gets" yoga; she is solid, and lovely, and not only perfect for my son but in possession of a vision for the actualization of her own potential; she is socially conscious, politically sophisticated; they marry, invite me and his brothers for dinner often, and on one such occasion announce that they are pregnant; we are all magnificently happy; I buy the layette; we have a baby shower at my house; the pregnancy goes well, is uneventful, as they say; when her time comes, I am called right away; of course I'm expected to be at the hospital when my precious first grandchild arrives, in fact, I'm in the delivery room; if it's a girl, they give her my first name as her middle name, continuing a family tradition from my mother's side; everyone returns happily to their individual living quarters, and nothing much really changes.

[Cue the sound of a needle abruptly scratching the record.]

I needed that boy to live my dream for him—I guess. Her phone call made that dream die twice, and that made me hostile. Besides, I didn't *like* that woman; I couldn't imagine being connected to her for the rest of the life of this child she was carrying. I had no part in the pregnancy; I didn't speak to the mother again until after the baby was born. I withheld connecting until the blood tests confirmed my son's paternity. My youngest son joked that we should go on *Jerry Springer*. He thought that was funny. Then guess what *he* did five years later?

I PAID for my resistance and my bad attitude. The universe sent a veritable barrage of grandbabies my way. They came so fast that by the last one's arrival I was just about numb. Today I have nine grandchildren, people. *Nine.* And at the moment, eight are under the age of five. Along the way they've shown me how to become the grandmother they needed me to be. I've learned that as a matter of fact:

1. They make you earn their affection. They don't automatically give a rat's ass about you. Loving you is not like some birthright. Once they're old enough to have a preference and act on it, about three months, if they don't dig you, they'll holler when you pick them up. You'll really feel inadequate. But then all the tricks you learned about quieting a fussy baby will come flooding back. You'll sing a soft song, doesn't matter what it is. You'll stroke their back or belly. You'll realize that unlike the first go-round, you *know* this business now. The baby will sense the presence of an expert, and your competence will calm him or her. Or maybe not. One of my grandchildren still doesn't check for me, but in time she will.

2. My capacity to love expanded each time, with each birth, the same way it did to accommodate each of my sons.

When each of my sons was born, it seemed as if I grew a new heart with my new baby's name on it: Brandon, Ismael, Rafael. Now, tiny hearts hang off theirs, like charms: Brandee, Taina, Lil Eazy, Jason Juicy Cheeks, Chloe Robin, Amina, Lena, Lil Brandon, Jack in the Sack.

3. Babies are rather, uh, *unfortunate*-looking at birth. And please note, I discarded the words *ugly, funny-looking,* and *pitiful* before arriving at that euphemism. One seemed like he was all head, another as if she was all eyes, one was bald for, like, *ever* but now has more hair than Tressy, one had a tongue hanging out of his mouth almost down to his chin, one looked like a little frog in a dress. Looking at them, I was reminded about the lopsidedness of my first son's head and how I tried to gently smooth it into shape before my friends came to visit. This did not work, so I brushed his few strands in a sort of swoop that drew the eye away from the slope. My friend Cindy called it "the Errol Flynn look." Another friend said he looked like "Howdie Doodie" and I didn't speak to her for a lonnnnng time after. Another son's eyes occasionally crossed when he smiled, but he smiled early and deliberately, he was *such* a nice little fellow. One of my sons was stunningly beautiful, but I know that's an exception. I'm just saying that if I'm going to comment on my grandbabies' newborn queerness, I believe I have the right. A couple of mine had faces—only briefly, but nevertheless—that only their mother could absolutely and un-conditionally love.

I've learned that I get to do the Grandmother Dance my way and that as long as my love is consistent and real, the babies will feel it no matter how often or infrequently they see me. There are grandmothers who can't babysit enough; I'm not one of those. I'm not babysitting babies—period. I might watch him or her while you take a shower, but I'm not floor-walking and changing poopy diapers. I did my time in that vineyard. Babies require more vigilance and work than I'm willing to put in just so somebody can go see a movie. I was a devoted and active mom to my sons; it's their turn to be the same with their children. I like having them with me when they're old enough to hold a conversation and sit in Ben's Chili Bowl after seeing a movie with me and talk. I like quick walks to the store around the corner.

And your parents better be here when we get back.

A LONG TIME AGO I yearned for girls; I hoped with all three pregnancies that I was carrying a daughter. I had more girls' names picked out than boys', and each time I saw a little tiny sack of male genitalia emerge during childbirth my joy was tinged with a little disappointment. After the last one was born and I knew he was the last, I realized that I liked being the mother of sons—you feel kind of queenly walking with your sons in the world, your princes. My experience raising sons has given me a perspective on boys that makes me understand them and love them differently from how I do the girls. Not more than, different from. And I do, I really do love them all. I also love watching my sons grow into fatherhood. They listen to my suggestions and indulge me when I recommend articles about child rearing. I'm not overbearing—I know they have to find their way. But I see my influence in their approaches to parenthood, and that is so cool.

For example, I don't believe in spanking/whupping/beating/"tapping" or otherwise hurting children to teach them a lesson or to punish. Once I heard my son Ismael reprimand his then fifteen-month by looking him in the eye and saying, "Didn't we just talk about this? Do we need to go talk about it some more?" and it worked. The boy settled down. When I watched Brandon hook up the inhaler for his daughter and give her asthma medication, my heart swelled, I didn't *know* the boy who did that; in fact he'd become a man. Rafael suffers with separation anxiety when he takes Jason and Jack home, and the boys who have girls are rising to the occasion—they know about princesses, and Dora, and they sing Elmo songs. . . . They're all great dads and I must have been a great mother because whatever reservations I may have had about the women who would have their babies, they have each been wonderful mothers. They chose the right women, or fate put them together, or whatever. The mothers of my grandchildren have my profound gratitude. They all try really hard. The babies may live under widely dissimilar circumstances, but they're wealthy in what matters, and that includes loving, devoted, involved fathers.

MY TRANSITION from mother to grandmother started off rocky, but each opportunity to do something for or with a grandchild, each time I observe a son changing a diaper with professional skill or patiently answering a question or making a doctor's appointment for a sick child and then attending the visit, with each of these moments I'm closer to figuring out this thing that initially seemed so overwhelming. I'm learning it in parts the way I learned how to be a mother. I had to learn every day, every minute how to do it. You learn by doing.

That phone call almost eight years ago was disturbing, to say the least. I didn't think I was ready; I thought the expectations would be greater than I could handle. What I've learned is that my life has become fuller and that my sons' lives have become more focused. I may not agree with all their choices, but they have robbed this train their way, and I have confidence that since they're working from love, everything will work out. All the consequences and rewards will accrue to them while I get practically nothing but niceness, which I've earned, dammit, from raising them.

When everyone is over now, I admit, it's a challenge. I love the peace and quiet of my empty home. Having everyone there is like being invaded. But then I hear, "It's Grandma!" or I find pictures in my writing room of rainbows and captions that read "We love you Grandma" and I know how lucky I am that all these folks love to come home, to *me*. Sometimes I slip off to the serenity of my bedroom and they sneak in to bounce on the bed or lie there with me. Man! There's nothing better. I put on music and they dance with such infectious abandon. They make me laugh.

I have a feeling there might be one or two more coming; my sons are still pretty young, and that condom thing, they don't seem to have figured that out yet. But at least I got a chance to be on hand when a new grandchild made his grand entrance. I now know how it feels to be one of the folks standing just outside of the delivery room and not lying on the table with all that intense activity directed at me. So if there are more little people in the pipeline headed our way, I'd like to receive them proper. Heads up, guys: no more phone calls! And certainly no more like the one announcing number seven, which went almost verbatim like this:

"Ma? You sittin down?"

"Yeah. Why? Whatsup?"

"Looks like another one's on the way."

"Another what, baby?"

"Yeah."

"When?"

"Today."

"Today! Who? Where? How . . ."

And just like that another little heart began to grow.

Learning the Name Dad

REGINALD DWAYNE BETTS

THERE ARE ONLY two days in prison: weekdays and weekends. You can tell which day it is by the behavior leading up to dinner. If it's a weekday, right after the afternoon count, you can look out into the pod, dorm, or tier and see a series of faces waiting for an officer to turn a corner with a stack of first-class mail. Men brushing their teeth, holding books in their hands or with a mirror bent just enough to show any figure coming or leaving. Once the guard comes, whether the man drops mail in your hand, door slot, or tosses it under the door, your reaction is the same. When he walks away, you walk away: to either savor the letter or move on, bury your disappointment in activity. Some men have given up on the ritual. They spend the moments when other people are waiting for mail consumed in some activity. Staring intently at a magazine filled with pornography or watching *Oprah*.

Mail call reveals secrets. With so many people using names to run from demons they brought to prison from the streets, that moment the guard pauses at a cell is the only time they hear the name their mother called them. Black hasn't been Tyrone Smith since he got his first tattoo, and there aren't three people here who know that Ray-Ray's real name is Todd Jones. Ray-Ray's mother doesn't even call him Todd, but each afternoon he wants to hear Todd Jones sure as he's not eligible for parole. It's a signal, a bridge to another time before pistols and robbery charges collapsed his dreams into a small cell.

Still, when the guard calls out Reginald, I'm not taken back to memories of my kinfolks calling me by my first name. I think about the judge who addressed me as Reginald and realize the start of me owning my given name, if traced, leads me back to the moment a police officer clasped cuffs around my wrist.

I got my name from my father. When it was time to name the screaming newborn, he named me Reginald Dwayne Betts II. "I didn't pick it; your father named you that," is what my mother tells me when I ask how I became the second. If she'd thought of another name in the last twenty-six years, she hadn't told me. My mother had buried it in her head until the middle of the story of my birth.

My family called me Dwayne from the very beginning. They lean on nicknames like they do the weight of the Bible. So many of us were named after fathers or named by fathers that the family reanointed us with something that didn't cause tension. Sometimes we handed out nicknames; other times we made middle names into nicknames. Always we set aside birth names until they could be said aloud without invoking someone else. Kareem becomes Reds, and Leon is Delontae until he's old enough to know what it means to have your daddy's name and not have him in your house. One day in the future I'll introduce my cousin as Delontae, and he will respond to the young woman he's meeting with "Hi, my name is Leon." This naming is only a little less vicious than the playground games that end in Damien's angular skull making him Peanut forever.

I became Dwayne so thoroughly that until the second grade I could not spell Reginald. When my second-grade teacher asked if Reginald Betts was present, I looked around too, wondering who the boy was that wasn't there; and when she called me out on my inattentiveness, I let her know I was Dwayne. No one ever told me that the reason I wasn't Reginald or Reggie or Junior was because of my father's absence. The truth of this was never an issue, because the missing name said it all. I never knew my father. There was never a time when I walked into a kitchen and the conversation hushed with the echo of "father" or "Reggie" in the air. My mother never threw dirt on his name; she left me to make of the man what I could form from silence. I knew him by the silence his name caused and I learned from silence. I had decided exactly who he was and resolved to be the opposite.

Once I was old enough to think about it, I decided my father had to be a drug addict. The strong pull of heroin or cocaine was the only thing I knew that made men disappear into the comedy of *Cops.* At thirteen, what could I know about why relationships broke down, what could I know of men who leave but want to stay? I didn't know how easy it was to erase a man's history and didn't realize how crazy I was for scrapping his to create one for him that fit my ideas. I never imagined him as bad as the neighborhood man I saw beat a woman with a baseball bat. We were a group of about eight playing football in a field when the screams interrupted us. None of us were older than eleven, and all just stood silent as he tried to twist the fat end of a bat around her body. We could hear it thump against her shins, her arms. She protected her head until the police carted him off, but no one suggested he wouldn't be back. Those women weren't weak, but they stayed. I made him a drug addict in my head, because while I knew beating a woman was bad, I also knew the men who did it returned. Some of these men lived in the homes of my friends. It seemed to me that only drugs could drive a person to disappear. Drugs—the only problem no woman in my family tolerated. In my head my father's frame was the one I saw carting off the neighbor's television and stealing anything, tied down or not. When the phone rang, for years I expected it to be him calling from prison. I knew no one in prison. Still, everything evil enough to drive my mother away from a man became a synonym for my father in my head, and I believed this enough to reject my own name, *Reginald Dwayne Betts,* without thought or question. I believed it until the crispness of steel cuffs slipped over my wrists.

It took a nine-year prison sentence to convince me that my name was Reginald Dwayne Betts. In legal documents, suffixes don't carry as much weight as in real life. Reginald Dwayne Betts and Reginald Dwayne Betts II could easily be the same person. The official record usually made no distinction. When I landed on the first few acres of land that housed a collection of cells, which I'd call home, I understood that my name wasn't Dwayne. Every identification card and court paper I'd been given said Reginald Dwayne Betts, and there wasn't a thing my family could tell me to convince me that I wasn't him.

In prison I learned in less than a week that love comes in letters dropped on your cell floor by an indifferent guard. Before the cuffs settled around my wrists, I was thinking of my mother. Not thinking about my name, but what I would tell her. If there was an explanation for the gun in my hand, or my hands gripping the steering wheel of that forest green Grand Prix that still smelled like new leather. I could hear behind her tears, could sense this feeling that I'd failed, grown into the body of a man from whom someone had tried to save me. The official charges made the pronouncement for her, and I never wondered if she'd think it was her husband who was arrested. I never wondered if she'd cringe at the question of whether she had a son named Reginald Dwayne Betts. My full name was known to her from the very beginning, but still, in every envelope that had her careful print, she wrote clearly Dwayne Betts.

My father's name is Reginald Dwayne Betts. The etymology of Reginald is complex. It comes from the name Reynold, which comes from the Germanic name Reginold. Reginold is the combination of two words, *ragin* and *wald,* the former meaning "advice" and the latter "rule." Many sources shorten the meaning of Reginald to "king" or "ruler." Dwayne comes from the Gaelic *dubhan,* which means "little and dark." Various places assign "king" and "mentor" as the meaning of Reginald. When my parents named me, I don't know if they had no idea what Reginald or Dwayne meant. After I went to prison, I had to carry both names. Each letter I received said Dwayne, while the men around me, they called me Reggie, Dwayne, Shahid, Young Music, or Frog. A collection of curious nicknames that didn't name me, but told a story about a place and my relationship to it. Shahid, given to me when I was a seventeen-year-old boy in a prison full of men aged fourteen to seventy, with everyone under thirty looking for some kind of conversion; Young Music, the vision of a friend who said I favored Musiq Soulchild. I learned to listen for the names, and decide what the names meant as I heard them. When the officers called out "Betts," before a crowd of men awaiting mail or while passing my cell waving an envelope, the meaning was clear.

I spent months thinking about mail, about the fine print that could cover a page and tell me the truth about what some woman felt about me. The letters were always from women, from my mother, my grandma, Aunt Tricia, and the occasional letter from a random cousin or one of my little sisters. My father's mother wrote me twice a month for years although she hadn't touched my face since I was a very small boy. The type of love you find scribbled in arthritic print pushed me. Yet still I dedicated whole letters to ranting about my lack of visits, about how I didn't need them. How it took hours to travel to the closest prisons I was incarcerated in at various times: Sussex, Southampton, Coffeewood, or Craigsville, Virginia, and a full day to drive to Pound, Virginia, the mountain site of Red Onion State Prison, the super maximum-security prison where I spent a few months when I was eighteen.

My father started writing after the judge sentenced me to prison. The careful script of his letters laced with a meaning I couldn't understand. Page after page, with only a hint of who he was. I learned his birthday after the sixth or so letter, never learned his high school or if he went to college. There were just scatterings of his soul, between what I considered ramblings. He talked about why things didn't work out as he planned, and how my life arced in the direction of a prison because he wasn't involved. He never told me that he was locked up when he wrote me that first letter.

When I walked into my cell for the first time at Sussex 1 State Prison, I'd been incarcerated for nearly four years. I'd been transferred from Red Onion State Prison, the fifteen-hour drive in shackles and cuffs still deep in my bones. My father showed up in the chiseled lines on my cellmate Pop Spratley's face. I watched Pop fold his 250-pound aged body around a desk made for a boy in grade school. Pop sat at that desk for hours, penning letters to his family, letters that averaged fifteen pages. He'd been in prison for nearly twenty-eight years and was the first man I acknowledged who had a name remotely fatherly. The entire prison called him Pop Spratley, and by the time I met Pop Gray, the second sixty-year-old man I'd share a cell with, I realized that Pop wasn't a name that just came with age. It was the respect earned beyond the violence and pain.

My father showed up in the eyes of the other young men around me. Sometimes I'd know more people with sentences over thirty years than under it, and I saw my father in them. We were all straitjacketed by a past that echoed with the screams of dead men, or women crying because they'd felt the harsh edges of our knuckles. All of us had wronged a woman somewhere, sent her away crying with our child in her arms, or we had just left.

I confronted my father in these men. His face in the center of an argument on who'd win the college football championship. The things I should have said to him, but didn't, the reason why Marquise and I split the tiny square that was a pack of Ramen noodles in half so that it could feed us both.

And still I stopped writing him. I don't remember why I stopped writing. I ripped open his letters with the same excitement that I greeted all mail, only after I read what he wrote there would be numbness. His letters persisted through my stops at a jail and three prisons. Four years' worth of periodic letters that said nothing of who he was, but plenty about what he wanted. He told me that he was manic-depressive and wanted to get back with his wife, my mother, whom he hadn't seen in nearly twenty years. How was I to deal with his collection of reasons for him and my mother to be together still? My mother left him before I remember walking. I couldn't imagine what he had done, and yet he wanted me to understand him. He never told me his birthday, just how much he loved my mother. His anger shared time with this love, seethed through his lines. He wanted me to know he felt wronged, wanted me to understand about streets he ran.

The night I stopped writing him, I called a cell, with a window spanning an arm and a half horizontally and a hand vertically to look through, my home. The sliver of night I could see, seated on the bottom bunk near the toilet, was black. One moment I was reading a letter from him and the next I was standing above the toilet setting every word he'd ever written me on fire. It took eight minutes for the smoke to clear from the cell after the letters burned and he became a presence that was there and not there. I never got to know my father through his letters, never forgave him anything because I never learned what it was that I should forgive. I met my father in the stories of men whose eyes were dimmed by the pain they caused, and although I learned to love them, to treat them as family, I couldn't figure out how to translate that into a conversation with my father. I walked around seeing myself in the eyes of the men around me, just like I saw my father in their features, and no matter how much I wanted it to, the practicing of forgiveness didn't lead to words between a dad and his son.

In eight years, I never awaited the letter of a man, never wondered if an uncle, brother, or running buddy would show. Receiving mail was a ritual, the way I'd let it sit on my bunk for a moment before opening it, being careful not to tear the envelope too much. This was a ritual about women, about getting love from the place it most often came. All the men around me knew it too, got caught up in it. We were like dogs that spent their days waiting for the mail carrier. In isolation, I'd drape a sheet over the cell door and read the letters I'd receive as if it were a date. Men would hold off on reading their mail until they made themselves something to eat. Once I understood the ritual, I knew it was a way to mark time and measure love; less accurate than the sundial, it was what we had. And we used it to usher meaning into our lives, to form a backdrop to who was getting out.

Weekends are different. The wait isn't for the letter, but the body that is the letter. There is less waiting on a weekend. The pattern so slow to form that after a while it seems less a prison-wide dance and more what the few who prepare for the social do. On Saturdays, I would wake up and make sure I was the first to shower. I wanted to have everything out of the way. If I went to breakfast, I'd make sure my meal was light, show a little generosity and give my eggs away to a friend. People who knew they weren't getting visits found some activity to fill the day. Summertime left the basketball courts packed with sweating men, left the track swarming with thinkers and those nodding from the effects of the drug IV of choice. The weight pit would be flooded with bodies, headphones on the ears of some to aid in the oneness with the moment that balancing four hundred pounds of steel on your shoulders gave you. If I saw a man on the weight pile, I knew he wasn't waiting for a visit. He couldn't pray to hear his name called over the shouting, the banging of dumbbells and barbells.

The wait is longer on Saturday and Sunday. No fifteen-minute window after count when you can expect your mail. The bodies that the weekend brings travel long distances, then are stuck in lines until your name is called. So the waiting starts early. The first year at Southampton found me up and ready by ten, mapping out my aunt's trip because I knew exactly where she had to go. It took around fifteen minutes for her to get to my mother's house and another thirty for them to finish talking, add two hours to get to the prison and twenty minutes to get processed, and I figured that if she left her house by seven, I could expect them around ten. The problem was she left exactly when she wanted to and that could be seven or twelve.

Southampton had long tiers full of cells, and you could wait for visits in relative privacy. Augusta Correctional Center was different; it was a prison of pods, rectangular units with forty-four cells each. Aunt Tricia once got to Augusta with ten minutes left in visitation. I'd long given up that she'd arrive with my mother that day and was in the pod doing push-ups. She was so late that I couldn't take a shower or throw on the pants I only wore to the visiting room, so I went with what I had on. That's the day that I was cured of the weekend wait. My mother and aunt were sitting across from me, neither noticing that I smelled like seven days in the heat with no toilet. They just eased on into the conversation asking how I was doing. The stains on my shirt no more noticed than the fine creasing that usually greeted them. It cost two dollars' worth of food to get a man to sweat over an iron and press your state blues until lines jumped from the fabric.

I learned the visits weren't about visits, and the mail wasn't about mail. The visits and mail were about the quiet time when people called you by names you recognized. In a visiting room or in a letter, Trigger became Junior with the care of a magician hiding a nickel under your palm. You'd never know how it got there, but would leave with the sense that it had been there all along.

Although I didn't realize it, after I came home I was still searching for the nickel hidden under my palm. I hadn't written my father in years, hadn't spoken to him in over a decade. One day he called the law office where my fiancée worked. I imagine he said, Hello, this is Reginald Betts. My woman would have responded, "Who?" I'm sure silence followed as he repeated his name slowly, like I do. This time, though, he said it all, Reginald Dwayne Betts. He wouldn't have said that first; like the legal system, people don't refer to suffixes. They talked. And then he and I talked. If it hadn't happened to me, I would have said it was straight out of a movie: My meeting him at her office, and he looking at me with my eyes.

In a way it was like the visiting room. He called me son and I expected to hear it, although I never called him anything. I made talking a circus act where I never initiated words because I didn't know if I should say Reginald or Pops or what. Still, we talked occasionally for a while, and then we talked on a regular basis.

The last time I called him, he picked up the phone on the third ring. It was nearly February, and the air bit like it should in the first month of a new year. The Virginia Department of

Corrections had released me from its roll of inmates almost two years earlier and I'd heard my father's voice as a man for the first time just thirty days ago. He knew I was out of prison and I knew he lived ten minutes from where I worked, but we rarely spoke. I stepped out of Hart Middle School, and the wind whipped, hard and certain against my black parka. I dialed his number because I no longer knew how to avoid dialing his number. When his voice sounded in the wireless earpiece draped over my ear, I responded, "Dad." There was question and answer in my voice. This day full of the twenty-six years I'd been living on the planet was the first time I'd called this man who shares my name Father, Dad, or any other affectionate term that hints at our biological connection.

When I called my father Dad for the first time that late January day, nearly two years after I'd been released, I was finding a name I never looked for. My release made the rituals of visits and receiving mail a backdrop to my life; it changed the role I played in that particular drama. Suddenly, I was the one sending letters to prisons, getting letters stamped with red ink that marks it as coming from a correctional center. The situation had changed. There were no prison bars between us, and I was, in a way, continuing the conversation I stopped long ago. When the letters went up into blue flame, I had no intention of talking to my father again. And even as I began to recognize the threads of his story in the men I did time with, recognized it in the tales I told about myself, I still had no intention of searching him out. Still, when the opportunity presented itself, I called him. The air was empty the first few times, as we had no words.

Someone told me to tell my father I love him each time I speak to him. I have never told my father I love him. I did call him Dad. I spoke with the hawk at my skin that day, January's air telling me that some days might feel like May but it was still winter. I remembered the conversations I had while gripping steel bars and screaming out into a tier of tired men. We were all tired and angry, but there was love. No one ever said it. Your friends would just send you a meal when the letter with the money didn't come, or send you a cup of wine when you found out somebody died. I never told my father I loved him, but I called him Dad. He understood that having a son call you by a name that only he can use was like getting a visit.

My African Sister

FAITH ADIELE

THE FIRST TIME I VISIT my father's bungalow at the University of Nigeria, I perch on a vinyl settee in the parlor and drink milky tea while my father rambles on about the student riots, the military government's Structural Adjustment Program, his college years with my mother, what he recalls her saying about the family farm in Washington State—never a pause for me or anyone else to speak.

Meanwhile my stepmother, another stranger, flits about the room, dipping forward with black market sugar and tins of Danish biscuits, slipping coasters under our cups the instant we lift to sip. From the darkened hallway comes the slap of flip-flops and giggles.

"You have children?" I ask politely, as if this were a question for a daughter to be asking her father, casually, as if it were not the question I've traveled halfway around the globe to ask. My bag bulges with shiny American goods: books and toys, watches and Walkmans, scarves and perfume. No matter their age or sex, I've got it covered.

WHEN I WAS NOT QUITE TWO, my father, a graduate student from Nigeria, received an urgent summons to return home. He left forty-eight hours later, clothes and books scattered across the floor of his rented room. He was to attend to family business, scout-out job prospects, and come back. Though my parents had split, and my mother was raising me alone in Seattle, her Scandinavian immigrant family having thrown her out for bearing a Black child, they maintained relations for my sake.

"I want you to know that this is not a good-bye," he wrote to us from a ship in the middle of the Atlantic, nervous about reports of ethnic and religious tensions awaiting him. "I shall look forward to our meeting so long as we are all alive."

My mother never saw him again.

MY STEPMOTHER NODS at my question, glances at my father. She is light-skinned and solicitous, with a wide nose and a voice like the breeze of the fans she angles at me.

"Yes, yes." My father waves his hands. "You'll meet them later."

He is short like me, his weathered skin dark as plums. A strip of wiry black hair encircles the back of his head. There's a space in his mouth where a tooth should be. I don't see the broad-shouldered rugby player who stared out from my wall all those years. The only feature I recognize is that round nose.

A blur flashes tan and red in the hallway. I glance up to see a velvety brown girl in a scarlet school uniform receding into the dimness, familiar eyes stunned wide. A face I could swear is mine.

It's not possible, I tell myself. Even if the girl in the hall is my sister, we have different mothers of different races. How can we look alike? For twenty-six years I have been an only child, the only child. The only New World African among Scandinavian Americans. The only Black member of our family, our town.

My father is explaining that during Christmas we'll travel

to our ancestral village, where I will be formally presented to the extended family and clan elders.

Christmas has always been White. After my mother and grandparents reconciled and we moved to their farm, I grew up hearing Finnish spoken, with a wreath of candles in my curls on St. Lucia Day. Mummi, my Finnish grandmother, and I spent all December at the kitchen table cutting out *nissu,* little Swedish pigs, and six-point stars from the almond-scented dough. Before baking, we painted them with tiny brushes like the ones she used for tinting family photographs, and the world we created, with its blue snowmen and yellow pigs, was equally whimsical. Sheet after sheet of cookies emerged from the oven transformed, the egg paint set into a deep, satiny glaze.

Each night Old Pappa, my Swedish grandfather, and I set candles in the windows or built snow lanterns in the yard for the *tonttu,* farm sprites, and I imagined that we were conductors on the Underground Railroad, lighting the way for runaway slaves.

I spent my childhood searching for anyone who looked like me. Wedging myself into the back of my grandparents' closet among board games, paint-by-numbers kits, and jigsaw puzzles, I sifted through shoeboxes of photographs. Monochrome snapshots of morose White relatives in black clothes. Portraits hand-tinted with Mummi's ice-cream colors. These were the extras that didn't make the cut; I'd already looted the official family album, sliding out the only two photos of my father.

I developed interest in Great-Uncle Vaino, a quiet fellow who always eyed the camera as if from a great distance, the forehead beneath his dark, slicked-back hair perpetually wrinkled from squinting. His broad, swarthy face with cleft chin and hooked nose evoked the unknown origins of the Finns. In his face lay the possibility of Turkey and Hungary. He looked more Inuit than Scandinavian, and when he laughed, the dark slits of his eyes disappeared completely.

Into the box beneath my bed he went. He didn't look like me, but at least he was different and dark.

The sharp bite of Mummi's *limpa* bread bloomed at the mouth of the hallway, reminding me that it was time for our baking, but at twelve I was pushing my way out of childhood, wondering what I would become. My grandparents had thrown out my nineteen-year-old mother, after all, for being with a Black man and only took her back because I was so cute. After the golden skin and dark eyes my mother rhapsodized over, these curls my grandmother twisted around her fingers, this round nose my grandfather tugged before hanging me upside down, then what?

I studied my African folktales and Norse legends and waited at the window for Anansi the Spider and Loki the Half Giant, the tricksters, to come scuttling over the purple mountains that ringed the farm. They would say, "Welcome, sister!" in a special language that only we understood. But no one ever came. No one has ever looked like me.

IN TRUE AFRICAN FASHION, my father and I move slowly, circuitously, as if conversation were a tribal praise song or highlife dance with instrumental flourishes and digressive harmonies. Eventually my father calls, "Emekachukwu, Okechukwu, Adanna! Come and greet your sister!"

Before the words even leave his mouth, the three are quivering in the center of the parlor. Grins split their faces. The eldest, Emekachukwu, is already languid with teenage charisma. Behind him stoops a lanky boy with yellow skin and glittering, feverish eyes—Okechukwu, the invalid. Pressed close to him is me, fourteen years ago.

"Okay," our father says, the Igbo chieftain making clan policy, "this is your older sister from America. She's come to visit. You love her."

He is wrong. It is I who love them, I who have grown up twenty-six years alone. Up to now family has always meant being the focal point. Now, in one day, with one sentence, I go from being the youngest, the sole daughter, niece, grandchild, to being the eldest of four, the one with the responsibility for love.

He is right. Adanna reaches me first. She is twelve, with a personality that shoves her brothers to the side. She is exquisite—luminous skin the color of Dutch cocoa; heart-shaped face with high, rounded cheekbones, slimmer than mine, darker; a mouth that flowers above a delicate pointed chin. I can see myself for the first time; we are exquisite. We come face-to-face, and the rest of the family gasps, *Aieeeee!,* steps back, disappears, makes way for our love.

THE FIRST THING my sister does upon meeting me is drag me into her room. She pushes me onto her bed and dumps her photo album in my lap. I smile, thinking of the album in my bag. My mother has always laughed at how I hoard photographs, especially the black-and-white, the older the better. Half my collection is unidentified, snapshots of scowling Scandinavians no one can remember. Who was that rotund Elmer always standing next to Bessie, a creamy-faced cow?

My sister, who has lived all twelve of her years in my absence, hands me the images to accompany her life, this language we share. Still shy of my eyes, she huddles close, her head on my shoulder, the African seeking warmth.

She whispers that she's been lonely all these years, the only girl in the family. The house is full of women—young cousins come from the village for schooling, orphans my father inherited after the war—but I know what she means.

"I was so glad to learn about you," she says. Her pulse throbs against my shoulder, a flutter of life working its way inside me.

"When did you find out?" I ask, touching her curls.

"Yesterday."

I twist around on my new sister's bed, winded as if I had run all the way here from America. Inhale, I remind myself.

Adanna beams.

"He never told you that he had a child in America?" I want to add: *That until I was twelve, the age you are now, he wrote to me? That for months beforehand he knew I was coming to Nigeria, and that I've been here, just kilometers away, for weeks already?* Only, it comes out as "Are you sure? He didn't tell you before?"

"No." She shakes her head, her eyes soft. She repeats: "I learned about you yesterday."

It's the logistics of the betrayal—rather than the betrayal itself—that stun me. I wonder how a twenty-six-year concealment of a whole daughter is even possible. It's quite a feat, even half a world away. I try to breathe, the thick Nigerian air a helpful reminder. Scoop it up, heavy and green, draw it in warm, circulate it through the blood and lungs, send it out cooler. Stay alive.

I leaf through Adanna's album, amazed at how she and I have always looked alike, from infancy onward, despite different mothers, and gradually the stitch in my side subsides.

I smile. I could almost swear that her baby pictures are mine. I too posed for the camera, mouth open in a silent, show-stopping exclamation of delight. I too was all brown eyes and blooming bud mouth.

On the fifth page I find an actual photo of me in front of

the *Joulu* tree in my grandparents' living room. Like Adanna in her photos, I am dressed in red—stretch stirrup pants. A halo of tinsel laces my short Afro. I see another snapshot that I recognize from my mother's collection back home: me piloting a shiny red tricycle in the driveway. Slowly I realize what I am seeing: Her photo album is a blend of her photos and mine. Our lives intertwined.

I tap the corners of my photos, relieved to find myself. This is not America with its books and magazines and television shows and movies that refuse to reflect me, its glossy surfaces that for twenty-six years have been telling me I don't matter, no one needs my image. I have always been here in Africa. I exist.

"Yeah," I marvel, "Mom used to love to dress me in red." Adanna was mistaken. I was cherished, perhaps even longed for.

Now it is Adanna's turn to stare. "B-b-but," she stammers, "I was the one they loved to dress in red. These are *my* pictures."

She palms our images, her fingers the brown tributary linking the same face, same stubborn personality, fourteen years apart, half a world away. Her eyes train on mine, widen. "I found them in a drawer and just assumed . . ."

At my shaking head, she gasps. "All these years I thought these were me!"

THE VILLAGERS LOOK at my sister and me and start to cry. Time and again it happens. We are strolling down a village road at dusk, hand in hand, quiet, our feet red with dust, and some woman stops pounding yam in mid-thrust, the heavy wooden pestle suspended above her head, and drops her jaw.

"Chineke," she gasps, looking from Adanna to me to the

sky, where Chineke resides. "Can she be *mmo*?" A ghost or an ancestral spirit reappeared from the land of the dead.

Adanna and I laugh, hurrying down the path before the others can hear her shouts to "Come see—o!" and run out of the house, wiping their hands on their bright, Dutch-printed *wrappas*, ululating like a wedding party.

Or we are lounging in the embrace of the giant iroko tree, chewing on bright mango pits and waiting for the afternoon heat to pass, and some distant-distant cousin will drive by in a battered Peugeot belching a halo of sour diesel and smack his long pink palm against his inky forehead.

"Oh-ho!" he shouts, nearly piloting the vehicle into the ditch, a move my father is famous for. "Are there suddenly two Adannas now?"

I accept this attention as I have always accepted attention, with the tight, unspoken greed of the addict, the flex in the heart muscle, the warmth spreading out through the bloodstream. This time it is not about being female, but the hunger, the expectation, is always the same: to see myself conceived, given shape, in the mirror of another's eyes. Loki the Trickster, Shape Shifter.

I accept these laughing and sobbing women, these nearly smashed cars, as confirmation that I belong to this family. Yes, I may be the American, missing for twenty-six years, raised without language in the Land of Efficiency. I may be the secret my father keeps hidden in the compound until he can explain to the clan elders. But my face is the password, the key unlocking the door to family.

I HATE HER. She lies curled asleep with her head in my lap, breath thick and milky as an infant, wearing my name. Our shame is evident every time someone calls her. *Ada*—the senior daughter of the lineage, *Nna*—father. *Adanna*. Father's firstborn daughter.

"If she's Adanna," any Nigerian must surely ask, "then how can you be?"

Exactly. Her very name denies my existence. As does Emeka's. After the birth of a child, parents are thenceforth known by the name of the firstborn: Papa-Emeka and Mama-Emeka, not Magnus and Grace. I keep waiting for a correction, a memo to be sent out: *Dear So-and-so, up to now you've known me as Papa-Emeka, but I'm actually Papa-Faith. Please adjust your Rolodex accordingly.*

Faith. "Your mother named you well," my father muses. He is full of praise. For my mother for naming and raising me well. For me for traveling all this way. "She found us herself," he announces to the countless stream of singing-clapping-dancing guests that come to witness my miraculous arrival. "She's the one!"

Adanna stretches like a cat in my lap, unshutters thick lashes. She sees me: elder sister. The one who spoils. The exotic American. Her passport to what lies ahead, what she might become.

I stare back. I see: younger sister. The one who adores. Exotic African. The passport back home. Who I might have been.

She is popular, quick to laugh, not afraid of math and science. Her eyes speak. "I missed you." She gleams.

Isaiah 9:6[1]

BRIAN GILMORE

I never named names . . .
HOWARD FAST[2]

1.

My children have unique names. African-American names. This pronouncement requires some explanation.

But first, let me advise the reader that what I want is for my children to know they are special and that the African-American experience is new each day and always in a state of being created. Perhaps that is the greatest thing about being African-American: More so than any other racial or ethnic group in America, we "African-Americans" can define ourselves newly every day in America because of our peculiar history of becoming who we are right here in America, for the most part. There is no old country or old village somewhere for us where we know where we are from; for the most part, it all happened right here, through chattel slavery, Jim Crow, and now onward.

---

[1] Isaiah 9:6 reads "For unto us a child is born . . ."

[2] Howard Fast, 1914–2003, writer, is considered a "literary phenomenon." He is the author of approximately eighty books, including *Spartacus,* the legendary story of a slave rebellion against the Roman Empire. However, Fast is also known for being labeled a Communist during the Red Scare period of the 1950s and being jailed for refusing to testify at hearings convened by the House Committee on Un-American Activities.

For that reason, when it came time to name each of our three children, my wife, Elanna, and I tried to give each child a name that was unique and meaningful. The name had to infer confidence within the child, a sense of self. As African-Americans, no matter the name, it is an "African-American," so the emphasis, to me, is on the special nature of the name.

2.

We once loved predictable names. Tyrone, Leroy, and Chantay ruled my youngest days. These names are slipping into history.

In the sixties and seventies, thousands of Black people got rid of their birth names and adopted Arabic or African names. The sixties and early seventies were all about redefinition and self-determination for Black people, so their names were changed as well as the names of their children. As a result, Bobby is Ahmad. Calvin is Jabari. Their children have similar names.

Next was the period where African-Americans, in attempting to create an authentic Black identity, simply made up names. Keisha, Tamika, and Diante ruled the world. This is still prevalent.

My parents, born during the Great Depression, kept it simple: American names for their children. I have an Irish name. It has served me well. I cannot tell you how many times I have walked into job interviews and the mouths of the white interviewers dropped open. They were certain I was a white public interest lawyer with publishing credits after reading my résumé. I remember sitting down at one interview before four Whites grinning inside as they sat there in shock. A Black woman walked into the interview; she was an office assistant.

"Welcome, Mr. Gilmore," she said with a huge grin on her face. She placed a cup of water in front of me, and wished me luck.

3.

A job applicant with a name that sounds like it might belong to an African-American—say, Lakisha Washington or Jamal Jones—can find it harder to get a job.

—NATIONAL BUREAU OF ECONOMIC RESEARCH, 2006[3]

4.

Our first child is Adanya, meaning "her father's daughter." The name is West African, Ibo, and neither Elanna nor myself is Ibo. Everyone loves the name mostly for its meaning.

It took us forever to find "Adanya"; ours was the endless search through every baby name book ever published. The hospital representative from D.C. Vital Records came to our hospital room a half dozen times seeking our completed birth certificate application.

"Not yet," we said in unison.

Eventually, our first child did become Adanya a few hours before mother, child, and father were discharged.

Elanna always agreed: Our children should have unique names that tell them they are special. The power of the African-American experience is that we are becoming who we are right

[3]http://www.nber.org.

here, right now. All of our names are "African-American," but the names should possess meaning for them and for us.

Adanya was born in 1999, February 23, the same birthday as the Black intellectual W.E.B. DuBois[4] and Chicago Black Arts poet Haki Madhubuti.[5] DuBois, born in America, 1868, eventually left America in self-imposed exile in the early 1960s, died, and is buried in Ghana, West Africa. Haki Madhubuti, the poet, was born in America, as Don L. Lee, in 1942. In the renaming movement of the sixties and seventies, Haki changed his name in 1973.

5.

Adanya's godparents are from India. Her godfather, Dev Kayal, is a good friend whom I met many years ago. Dev once related an interesting story to me about the significance of naming and names.

According to Dev, when he was born, and in his country's tradition, he did not receive his permanent legal name for a year. He was observed for a year and then received a name. This is an East Indian tradition. His given name was Devashis: that means "from the divine with blessing." The name, in my view, was simply beautiful.

This is what happened to his name:

When Dev was a young teen, his parents immigrated to

[4]W.E.B. DuBois, the great writer, sociologist, political thinker, and race man, was born in Great Barrington, Massachusetts, on February 23, 1868. He died in Africa in 1963.

[5]Haki Madhubuti, poet, writer, and cofounder of Third World Press in 1967, was born on February 23, 1942.

America to become citizens. When Dev legally entered the country, his father had to submit a name for him. It was, as he recalls, like the unverifiable stories from Ellis Island when Europeans claim that their names were changed when they entered America. Dev says the name he received as a one-year-old was changed when he came to America. He was, thereafter, Dev Kayal.

An excerpt from the poem "Dying with the Wrong Name," by the Arab-American poet Sam Hamod, captures it as well:

> *Na'aim Jazeeny, Sine Hussein, Im'a Brahim, Hussein Hamode*
>   *Subh',*
> *all lost when "A man in a*
> *dark blue suit at Ellis Island says, with*
> *tiredness and authority, You only need two*
> *names in America and suddenly—as cleanly*
> *as the air, you've lost*
> *your name . . ."[6]*

6.

Our second baby girl was born May 28, 2002. It was my fortieth birthday. Elanna proclaimed immediately she would select a name. Thank God.

After Adanya, I knew finding a special name would be complex. But I also knew that if one child has a unique name, all of your children should have unique names. You don't name one child Spartacus and then turn around and name the next one Jim.

But what name? I kept wondering. I was out of names. Another African name? A name from a famous African-American?

[6]Sam Hamod, *Dying with the Wrong Name* (Anthe Publications, 1980).

What about Harriet Tubman Gilmore? Maya Angelou Gilmore? Fannie Lou Hamer Gilmore? It was mind-boggling. Years ago I met a Black guy named Crispus Attucks Davis. He was very proud of his name. He also told me he had just got out of jail after doing nineteen years.

Elanna warmed up to one name eventually: Lirit.

She came across Lirit in one of the many name books we had been carting around. *Lirit* means "poetic" in Hebrew and is the name of a Hebrew Writers' Association and its online literary journal. It caught both of us. I am a poet, so the name was alive. I had not heard of it either.

My second child, born on my fortieth birthday, is named Lirit because her father is a poet.

7.

On Easter Sunday, April 16, 2006, Elanna gave birth to another African-American baby girl. The child experienced some minor complications and was admitted to the hospital for a week in the neonatal intensive care unit (NICU). This gave us time to think about names.

I told Elanna days before that I only had one name and that if she did not like the name, she could name the child anything she wanted. It was her show this time; it was tough. I knew now why there were millions of Ashleys and Hannahs in the world.

After just two days in the NICU, the wonderful hospital nurses fell in love with Baby Gilmore No. 3 and wanted to put her name on her incubator. We had no idea what to name her. We stalled them.

Finally, Elanna asked me for the name I had written down weeks ago.

"Are you sure?" I asked.

"What is it?"

"Pannonica."

She was speechless.

That evening Baby Gilmore No. 3 finally had a nametag outside her crib: "PANNONICA." She was released a few days later, doing well.

The week she came home, I sent out a mass e-mail telling our friends and family the significance of the name:

> *"Pannonica" is a song composed by jazz pianist Thelonious Monk & named after Pannonica de Koenigswarter who was named after a butterfly that her father had once tried to catch. A descendant of the English branch of the Rothschild family, the Baroness Pannonica de Koenigswarter, or "Nica" . . . was considered as one of the most important patrons of modern jazz musicians. Not long after marrying Jules de Koenigswarter, a pilot during the war who joined the French diplomatic corps, Nica and her husband moved to Mexico City. She quickly became disinterested in Mexico and, evidently, her marriage, and in 1951 headed to New York City, where she rented a suite at the Stanhope Hotel on Fifth Avenue. She plunged into the New York jazz scene, attracting scores of musicians to her apartment for rest, relaxation . . . and impromptu jam sessions. Quickly she became somewhat of a patron to jazz musicians. . . . Her suite at the Stanhope, unfortunately, is perhaps best known for being the place where Charlie Parker died in 1955. Because of Parker's death, the baroness was forced to leave the Stanhope, so she took up residence at the Bolivar Hotel, where she lived for many years. Thelonious Monk's composition "Ba-Lue Bolivar Ba-Lues-Are" was named for the hotel. . . . Nica*

*first met Monk in Paris in June 1954 . . . introduced to
Monk backstage by a mutual friend—pianist Mary Lou
Williams. . . . In 1972, when Monk became so ill that
he needed special attention, he moved into a room in the
baroness's New Jersey home.*

8.

My girls will get calls for job interviews. When I tell people
what Adanya means, they immediately fall in love with the
name. People will think Lirit is Jewish because her wonderful
name is Hebrew in origin. Pannonica will fool them all; they
will wonder if she is, in fact, one of the Rothschilds. Some will
think she is a jazz lover.

Our girls do not have to worry. They love their names;
their names love them. We, African-Americans, are all becoming something more each day here in America, and now naming, for special meaning, is still the ultimate statement of love
and freedom.

Grandpa Dutstun

SIMONE BOSTIC

It took me twenty years before I could think of my paternal grandfather as Grandpa. It took twenty years for me to feel compassion for him, to view him as a person and acknowledge that though we never had a traditional relationship, he made a contribution to my life and to the person that I have become. Twenty years after he was cold and dead I saw him staring back at me from my mirror. I had to first face the sting of life, love, and loss too, though not absolve him from his sins, forgive him and understand the factors that could have made him the person he was and how he related to the person that I am. The majority of that time my view of him was through the eyes of a child and overshadowed by one especially vivid memory of him that I have relived in one form or another in my nightmares over thirty years.

I was five years old and I loved to count.

"One. Two. Three. Four." I counted aloud each narrow step that led to our house at the top of the hill. I already knew that there were eighty-five—eighty-seven if you counted the triangular step at the turn and the extra step that I had to make on the side because my legs could not make it up the knee-high step in front of Ms. Linda's house. Sometimes I forgot to count the sixties and seventies and so ended up with over a hundred. One day, I would bound up the steps two and three at a time like my sisters, Tonia and Anne; then I would only have to count up to twenty.

"Eighteen. Nineteen. Twenty. Twenty-one." I waved at my mother. She was almost to the top, being better at navigating the rough, uneven risers, some little more than stones held in place by poorly mixed concrete or a piece of lat or anchored by rebar and filled in with dirt. With a houseful of work and two other children, Mummy did not have the time to count steps with me, though she sometimes took time-out to humor me.

The narrow passage was little more than an alley linking Barton Lane and Layan Hill, parallel thoroughfares that would otherwise be half an hour apart. In most places, two grown people could not pass each other abreast without either rubbing shoulders or having one step up onto the drains that ran most of its length on either side. Short, stubborn tufts of grass and shining bush sprang up close to concrete walls rising like a bull run on either side, effectively channeling travelers forward.

"Twenty-six. Twenty-seven. Twenty-eight." I was not the most graceful duck on the pond; dirt was attracted to me, and on more than one occasion, I had tripped and fallen on these steps. This time, however, I kept my eyes on my feet and my hand stretched out to one side to keep my balance. I did not want to fall or dirty my dress and shoes because I had promised my mother to make a special effort to keep myself clean—especially the shoes that she had had my sister Anne whiten with liquid polish till they glowed.

"Thirty-one. Thirty-two. Thirty-thr—" Something made me raise my gaze to locate my mother. It was not so much a noise or a movement as a ripple that runs over the surface of the soul, a sixth sense, like a gazelle has when a lion materializes out of the shadows. He stood there. Eight feet tall. He was dressed in the black three-piece suit and felt hat ensemble that he wore when he went out—whether it was to the doctor, a funeral, or out drinking in the local rum shop. How many

times had he used this hat's predecessors to beat us or chase my siblings and me away, like stray dogs begging for scraps? He called out a greeting to Ms. Linda and began his descent. A chill caressed my skin. Sweat prickled the back of my knees. My belly spasmed and bubbled. Gas seeped from my body. Spittle crept down my throat, choking me, like strands of hair accidentally swallowed. I searched for my mother. My eyes locked with hers, and I found them a mirror of my emotions. She stood there—frozen. She had already passed his gate and he was sandwiched between us.

Like an agouti cornered by the venomous Mapipire Za-nana, I searched in vain for an escape. I pivoted to head down-ward, but he was gaining on me like an avalanche. There was no way that I could make it back down fast enough. I was trapped. Panic fluttered in my chest and gripped my throat in its vise as my body shivered under the blazing sun. I stepped into the canal, pushing myself against the sloppily white-washed wall in an attempt to make myself flat. Or disappear. Anything but just stand there! My shoes slipped and skidded in the mossy muck of the canal, and I clawed at the wall to regain footing. Rough, broken, clay bricks audibly rasped the cotton of my dress, scraped the backs of my thighs, and pulled at my hair; they bit into my little palms as I forced myself back against them. I could go no further. I bowed my head, closed my eyes, and waited.

To the rhythm of his falling feet and my heart pulsing in my head, he brushed past me. I smelled him more than I felt him. A musky mix of male, must, and mold with the sickly-sweet smell of the rum that my father swore ran through his veins in such quantities that he "would take a long time to rotten when the devil called him." The scent seeped from his pores, assailing me as surely as the sting of his hat. It lingered, mixing with my sweat and sticking to my skin, to the walls

of my nostrils, filling my mouth and throat even after he had long since disappeared from view.

I opened my eyes. He was gone. Swallowing the taste of his smell, I inhaled deeply. Did he look at me? Did he look at her? Did he even notice me? What had transpired in the couple minutes that it took for him to pass me by? I didn't know.

"Come on, Moonie babe," my mother coaxed.

I slowly disengaged myself from my perch and dusted the tiny concrete chips from where they were embedded in the soft flesh of my burning palms. I examined the grid of scrapes and welts that crisscrossed its surface and wiped the blood and grit on the back of my skirt. My hands came back white—coated with dust and flakes of paint that marked the back of my dress where my body made violent contact with the wall. My white shoes were now green while milky rivulets streaked the canal, slowly mixing with wastewater. Hot tears pooled between my eyelids. I looked toward home, lowered my head, and swaddled in a blanket of shame, silently resumed my ascent, accompanied by the warm, rhythmic swish of the urine puddled in my shoes.

This incident epitomized the relationship between my grandfather and me. His mere presence was cause for terror. In the years to follow, my mother often recounted this incident while I actively avoided any close contact with him, limiting our interaction to my peeking at him through the crack in the curtains. When inebriated, which seemed more often than not, he would empty his small two-room house of all furniture and, lining them up, proceed to give them a sound whipping while he informed them or one of his invisible nemeses, of what he intended to do to their mothers' reproductive organs. Some days he would turn his attention upward to where our house stood and berate my mother, who remained stoic and unresponsive to his barrage of venom. He seemed to have a hate for my mother and would encourage my father to mistreat her and, by extension, us.

When sober, he was a workaholic who, having nothing else to do and for reasons known only to himself, manually cut the banks that bordered his property, terracing the hill and expanding his boundaries at the expense and irritation of his neighbors. With the speed of a tractor and without the aid of machinery he tirelessly moved tons of stone and earth from the high bank on one side of the yard to the other. My father called him Dirtstone—pronounced "Dutstun" for emphasis.

The only knowledge that I had of his past was what I quilted from stories that I had overheard or was told by people who knew him as a human being. He was born Gladstone Bostic in St. Lucy, Barbados. His father, a European, after marrying and raising a family with "an acceptable woman of his own social status," in his old age married a Black woman young enough to be his daughter. The family lived on preabolition lands, to the chagrin of the gentile community. As was the state of justice in the turn of the century, when his father died, his young wife and their two dark-skinned sons were disinherited by the claims of his full-blooded White siblings who were decades his senior. When his mother passed, the two brothers migrated to Trinidad. I was proud of my heritage and especially proud of my great-grandfather. In an age where it was acceptable for a man to have a Black mistress but totally unheard of to marry one, he defied society. I wondered how a man of such strong character could spawn the likes of Dutstun. Now, as I have faced discrimination, I can only imagine how growing up a "molasses mulatto" in colonial society could be damaging to a person's psyche.

My cousins, however, were blessed with Bostic looks with their "good" tawny hair, light eyes, and café au lait coloration. Every day they hustled up to my grandfather's house, where they each got a quarter for tuckshop money while our little fingers scrounged in the recesses of the clay bricks and corners of our house for stray pennies to take like trophies to my mother, who used them to purchase rice or sugar to sweeten our flour porridge. He would become enraged if we played with his other grandchildren, so we devised a sign to warn of his approach. The lookout would signal "Cross Coming," and they would scamper into their house while we would retreat up the hill to the safety of ours.

"These children who you chasing like strangers," I overheard Ms. Linda warn him gravely, "these are the selfsame children that you going to be begging for one day."

When asked why he favored one set of grandchildren over the other when we looked more like him, he told her, "My daughter's children I know are mine. I can never be sure about my sons'." I, however, believed that we were a constant reminder of his shortcoming though he seemed to fail to realize that his children leaned toward his chocolate coloring more than to the cream of his wife. One day, from my vantage point lurking in the shadows, I overheard someone gossiping that "the African woman's blood" was strong in us, but in my childhood's over-imagination I concocted that, denied her rightful place in life, she refused to let the family forget that she was here in death, and secretly I reveled in being her coconspirator.

Ms. Linda was the only person that I knew who knew both my grandparents when they were young. She had lived in the neighborhood since she got married at the age of fourteen. The only immediate neighbor not related by blood, she piled me with warm coconut tarts as I begged her for stories about my grandmother. She filled my head with her memories, insisting that in their heyday my grandparents were the star couple. She was the architect and he the contractor that brought her visions to life, and she was his life. I had seen her pale face staring back at me from a faded black-and-white photograph, but it was in the houses that she designed that I felt her presence. She was from a good family in Panama and to her mother's horror married my grandfather. From all accounts she was happy and he was a totally different man from the one that I saw every day. She was headstrong and fun-loving and ambitious. In the few years that they were married she had a house built for each of her children during her pregnancy so that each child was born owning property. It was this determination that eventually killed her. While moving into their new house just before the birth of their fifth child she lifted a heavy object and hemorrhaged to death, taking her unborn baby with her. My grandfather was never the same. Both my grandparents died that day; his body continued respiration for thirty-plus years more, but his heart was buried with her. The rest of him he buried in drink.

Dad said that his father quit his job in order to stay at home and take care of his four young children, who then ranged in age from two to six. He spoke of how he tried to get married again in order to give his children a mother, but he and his bride had a legendary quarrel at their wedding reception about her cake; she left him after less than two weeks of "wedded bliss." The family became locked in a downward spiral. The children were left to raise themselves whenever he worked, and increasingly larger portions of the money went to drinks. He systematically lost the family's property—and status—in games of cards except for one house that my aunt was able to buy back from a debtor with the earnings from her first job.

Their stories were contradicted by the monster that I saw before me, so in all good sense, I decided to keep my distance. That was until my mother called us three girls and informed us that our grandpa was sick and no matter how we felt about him or what he had done to us in the not-so-distant past, he was family and it was our duty to take care of him. We three, with my sister Anne in the lead, dusted, scrubbed, and swept. We cleaned every corner of his house, washed his clothes, and ensured that his mug was clean every morning. Ironically the grandchildren whom he showered with affection scorned having anything to do with him in his illness. Grudgingly, one of the girls would take him a mug of hot chocolate every morning and, unceremoniously, pour the piping hot beverage into the cold, curdled remains from the day before.

I didn't mind the cleaning too much. I tried to do whatever chores I had to do as fast as I could and get back to whatever book I was engrossed in at the time. My greatest fear was when he was decked out in a fresh pair of pajamas and I was forced to sit with him and keep him company. Given a choice, I would have preferred a whipping. He would always begin by slurring in his thick Bajan accent, "Come, Annie, sit here." I never could figure out if he called Tonia and me by our eldest sister's name because he could not tell us apart due to old age or, worse yet, he had never taken the time to learn our names in the first place.

He sat to the left of the doorway in the dark mahogany morris chair that was low to the floor, lower than looked comfortable for a man his age. Of the three chairs in the room, that was the only one that I had ever seen him sitting in. That chair and its mate were from the 1930s, when he was married to my grandmother, and except for dust, a few dings, and rings on the arms marking where he routinely rested his enamel cup, the wood still looked pristine. It was an antique; my dad said that they didn't make them that way anymore, with wood so well cured that it would last forever. The cushions showed hints of vivid blues, greens, and reds deep in the seams, where time was unable to reach in and dim their vibrance. Everywhere else the fabric was stiff with age and had been weathered and worn into a pattern of overlapping stains in shades of amber, yellow, and sepia. He seemed to notice neither the stains nor the scent of half a century of splotches, spills, and the various accidents of children and grandchildren that did not come out—no matter how often the cushions were beaten, washed, and put out to dry on the low galvanized roof. My mother said older people did not notice these things. I did, however. To me he just smelled like old people, so I practiced holding my breath for as long as I could and was able to hold up to a count of twenty-five or until I started daydreaming or got lost in his story—if it was particularly interesting that day.

I remember once sitting with him. I reached down to shoo away the horde of mosquitoes dining on my exposed calves and for the first time took a long, hard look at the man who had once struck me with terror. Sunken deep within the embrace of the chair, he no longer looked like a giant ogre. He looked rather small, smaller than I was, like a child dwarfed by the chair's heavy lines. His frail arms conformed to the contours of its arms. His bony hands were almost the same color as the wood, and when I squinted, they blurred into one—just as the drone of his voice blurred into the background noises along with the lazy buzz of the insects attracted to the sugar in the mug of lime juice that sweated on the table next to the poorly tuned radio that looked as if it were bought at the same time as the chairs were and played more crackles, pops, and bleeps than music. I turned at the sound of shouting outside. From where I sat in the doorway I could see my cousins chasing each other. Whenever I was forced to sit with him, I placed the wobbly dining room chair, one from the set that my aunt threw out last Christmas, across the doorway just in case I had to make a run for it and so that my mother could see me from our window and know that I had gone above and beyond the call of duty. His chair faced the only window. It opened out to the back boundary and was covered by BRC wire for burglar-proofing. It did little for improving light or ventilation, but it was the only thing that saved the tiny room from feeling like a cave. As he recounted a story about life in the old days and family members long since dead and gone that I had heard at least three times before, he stared out of it with an unwavering gaze as if watching reruns of his life on a TV screen. I turned to see what was so interesting out that window, but all I could see were fronds of razor grass, as tall and thick as sugarcane stalks, gracefully dancing in the warm breeze, cut up like a jigsaw puzzle by the squares of the BRC. Then he started to talk about his wife, my grandmother, Lenora. He spoke as if she were in the other room and at any minute she would come out to meet him; from his withering form it was more than likely going to be the other way round.

A few days later my father took my grandfather to the hospital. He never came home. I didn't cry at the funeral. His two-room house stayed empty and abandoned for fifteen years until it was torn down because of termites. The antique morris chairs and the mismatched furniture were eventually burned for the same reason. The piles of stones remained where they stood until they were used to build the retaining walls on either side of the property. Except for memories and a few pictures crackled and dimmed by age, all traces of my grandfather have disappeared. It was not until I was myself an adult and had had to face the same demons of class, race, and love that I could understand his pain and in my mind transform the monster into a man. I learned to forgive and to return goodness even to people who had not first extended goodness to me. His boring stories about his life taught and gave me a sense of history from which I forged my future. They left in my heart the determination to someday restore my branch of the family to its former glory.

Silence . . . The Language of Trees

ABDUL ALI

It was an unseasonably warm November afternoon. Washington's pigeons were more phantom than bird, since I hadn't seen one all day. The temperature belied the postautumn skin of the trees: the leaves that changed from squash yellow to plum red and later, pumpkin orange, all within weeks—a festive yet dreary time for tree-watching.

My grandfather once told me to trust trees. They knew things like if you wanted to know what kind of neighborhood you're in, "Look at the trees," he would say. "If there ain't any, get lost." If you wanted to know if it was okay to stop during a long drive in a southern town, look at the trees. "If there's bloodstains on any, move like the wind."

The trees spoke to me that afternoon. They had already shed all of their gold, red, and brown leaves. The sun came out, touching my brow until beads of sweat traveled the length of my mushroom-shaped nose. Moments passed before I felt the buzz from my cell phone. A voice introduced itself: "Your grandfather has passed." It took me a few moments to register what this actually meant. Maybe he was in a car that just rode by and "passed" in that way. Or maybe he wanted to surprise me for the holidays, and I had inadvertently "passed" him on the street. A big balloon swelled in my throat. Not only did I fear the worst-case scenario, but a knowing feeling set in.

Losing a grandparent is like losing two pieces of a jigsaw puzzle. A grandparent knows not only the kind of person you are but the kind of person you came from, so the loss is multiplied. I learned a valuable lesson from my grandfather's passing: that it was difficult to count the men in my life who let me know that I mattered to them, that I had a part of them in my blood, and they had a part of me in theirs, that my children had a part of them, and part of me, and themselves . . .

I knew of several women who loved me: my mother, grandmothers, neighbors, girlfriends, and now my daughter. It didn't matter how young or old, women, up to that point, seemed programmed to love me. My daughter memorized my footsteps, squealing whenever I entered the house, calling out *dah-dah,* her arms making the letter *Y,* motioning for me to pick her up. Aside from my grandfather, there weren't many opportunities for me to know that it was natural for men to care about their sons (or daughters).

The men in my family love differently. At family gatherings, watching fathers hug their sons is festive. Without saying anything, handshakes become preludes to conversations. If you hold on too long, then it is assumed you are in need of something. If you let go too fast, then you must be hiding something. We speak silently, look deep into each other's eyes for the truth, and, after that's confirmed, our ears open. We listen to how the other chooses his words. We measure their laughter. An open-shut laugh is not a good sign. The theatrical ones where you can see the inside of someone's mouth, maybe even get a slap on the knee—this is a sure sign that everything is fine. It's never a real silence; if you listen hard, you can hear the inflection in my grandfather's unspoken thought when I got accepted to Howard. Grandpa, born during the Great Depression, had learned the value of thrift, so imagine the psychic obstacle he overcame to send me a check every month so I wouldn't have to worry about money.

A common refrain growing up was: Actions speak louder

than words. We walk carrying the world on our shoulders. It happens in the slap across the back during visits, three-minute-long laughs, or a heavy sigh that turns to a hum. We do not write cards. Silent missives move about the room during the holidays in the form of stares. "So what did you say you're studying?" a distant cousin would ask.

MY GRANDFATHER had an elegant way of expressing his feelings. He would sit me down and tell me things that happened before I was born, or even before my mother was born. He'd talk about how he'd take my grandmother up to Harlem to the Apollo to see Ella Fitzgerald, Billie Holiday, Dinah Washington, and Sarah Vaughan. The watch that he pawned to buy my grandmother summer dresses when he was broke, and all about the extraterrestrial sounds I made when I was a week old.

Grandpa always called me son. He colored his hair black so he appeared thirty years younger, never carrying himself like the octogenarian that he was. I used to think he was old-school, and he was, in the gentlemanly Ossie Davis sort of way. I picked up a few of his mannerisms: his pensive nature, never making rash decisions, worrisomeness, and frugality. There was something symbiotic about our natures—how I'd call him when I got a bad feeling; how he called me the night before he died to tell me how special I was to him.

Little did I realize that he was like a father to me. Of course I still longed for one like other people had—most people my age didn't have fathers in their eighties. It didn't matter, though. In the twenty-one years that I knew him, he measured and passed along his eighty-six years of stories, lessons, jokes, mostly picked up through his vast travels, like how he lived in Germany during the Second World War; that he visited most African countries before they became independent and changed their names; that both of his parents died before he was thirteen, forcing the abrupt end to his formal education; self-educating himself through reading several newspapers, circling unfamiliar words and looking them up later (sometimes calling me, putting my knowledge to the test), training his ear to foreign languages when he traveled abroad; how his parents were probably slaves; his escaping the Panama Canal. How he wanted better for me . . . All of this prepared me for fatherhood, learning his language, how to say a lot using few words, an economy with words whose value lay in action: a fine way of being close to someone you love without saying very much.

My grandfather would take me places with him, all a part of my grooming. Whenever we'd go out to eat, we'd turn on our silent language. If we had a waitress who was extraordinarily good, he'd rub his thumb against his index and middle finger. This meant she wants a big tip. How we'd laugh conspiratorially. He was funny that way. When my cousin got married, we flew to Chicago, my first time on a plane as an adult, and I fell in love. There was a special feeling going somewhere on a plane that Greyhound or Amtrak simply could not rival. At the reception, Grandpa wore a tuxedo and I wore a new suit. And I saw Grandpa dance with a doctor from Silver Spring, Maryland. They danced in a way that I thought only people my age did in the music videos. The crowd had encircled him and this woman, who was probably thirty years his junior. I never saw my grandfather so happy. All I could do was cheer him on.

I SERIOUSLY DOUBTED the existence of "unconditional" love until my daughter was born. I can still feel her hour-old self squeeze my index finger as a phalanx of nurses poked, prodded, and vaccinated her. At first she screamed, probably at the bewilderment of leaving her mother's womb to being in a sort of outer space. Then there were all of the unfamiliar faces giving her needles and affixing nametags to her tiny arm. I was speechless at the bigness of the moment. All I could do was watch. Eventually, when she opened her eyes, our eyes touched. I held out my finger, and she grabbed it, slowly quieting her lament. Even today she grabs my finger and falls asleep on my lap. For me, there's a psychic attachment to that moment; we were linked from the very first hour. I'd like to think that although there weren't words exchanged during that early moment between us, so much was said, our own quiet speak, where I said that I was going to be there for her, that I loved and welcomed her, and that we too would develop a special language that placed a higher value on actions than just words.

WHO WOULD HAVE ever thought that through my grandfather I would receive my biggest lesson about language: how to read between the lines, that there was something important to be had from silence; how to watch the man who's speaking, look him in the eyes, see if those eyes travel or sit steady; listen to their inflection, and measure a man's handshake. How to show, rather than just say, you love someone. I can hear his voice in these lessons like when he suggested that I listen to Nina Simone: Have a reverence for things old, that there was something to be said about things that survived the test of time. Take the first chance to get travel; pay off credit cards monthly (still working on this one); take care of your family; make your presence felt without being next to a person; not to be afraid to be sensitive; eat lots of plantains and mangoes and rice and peas with coconut milk; laugh hard and often. I remember as if it were yesterday how he reprimanded his friends for laughing at my dream of becoming a writer as we drove past a Porsche dealership and I said, "And I'm gonna drive that car." I forget what exactly they were laughing at, my wanting to be a writer or being able to afford a Porsche or trying to do both.

That fateful November afternoon my grandfather, like the leaves on the trees, left, ceremoniously, obedient to nature's call. Trees change colors. Not Grandpa, though. He remained true to form, calling me the night before, saying, "I love you, son," leaving me an inheritance of memories that spans over one hundred years. My memories and his washed into our own language, like leaves from the same tree. I couldn't help but think as the wind blew a flurry of leaves, feeling like skin across my face, that Grandpa was still speaking.

Two Cents and a Question

L. A. BANKS

*L*OVE—THE GREATEST EXPRESSION of it and my earliest experience of such a heavenly phenomenon—was being protected by a vast, warm blanket of family as a child. Many hands and hugs made up that big-breasted, jelly-rolled love that came from aunties, and grandmothers, my mother, plus her girlfriends as second and third mothers, good teachers and church ladies, neighbors who looked out for your welfare, and oh, yes . . . most assuredly my father, who called me his baby girl, his princess, along with many doting uncles, layer upon layer of adults who cared. Indeed, I was blessed.

These people gave emotional shelter, gave children a chance to be just that—kids. Not that these folks were perfect or didn't have the same problems that people face today. Oh, yeah, there were divorces, relationship dramas, job layoffs, funny money, folks that drank too much, folks that ate too much, some folks with hypertension, some had "sugar," some had wayward children, some had wayward spouses . . . but that was grown folks' bizness.

They seemed to say without words, "That don't have nuthin' to do with you, baby," just by guarding you from the rigors of gaining adult awareness too soon. Even those with so-called funny money would find a dollar to put in your hand at a barbecue, just 'cause you were a kid and had run past them. Adults in the family could even be fighting like cats and dogs with your momma or daddy (as many of our family folks did from time to time) but still would hug you up if you were a child, because by being a child, you were exempt from whatever the family dispute of the moment was.

So, don't get me wrong, I'm not painting the picture here of the perfect family. Not even close. I wouldn't know what that was if it jumped up and bit me. But I do know I was loved and that was the counterbalancing weight to any and all ills, much of which I was oblivious to until later. That was not by chance; that was by design—because somebody loved me enough while I was a child to shelter my young psyche from some of the things that it wasn't ready to handle.

For a magical and protected time, because of that profound love, they let children have a childhood. Now, with a number of years under my belt, and hindsight being twenty-twenty, I know in my soul and based upon what I've witnessed that what they gave me was the most profound expression of love one can offer another human being. A chance to grow up knowing you were loved.

Here's two more cents: I personally don't believe that kids need to see everything and/or be a part of everything adult. I know we have this new open-society thing going on, and I'm not alluding to dirty family secrets either. I'm not talking about sweeping things under the rug that will one day land a person on a therapist's couch, uh uh. What I'm talking about is general-purpose sheltering. Perhaps a better word is discretion. Some conversations, again, just one woman's opinion, are not for young ears.

Maybe this process went out with high-buttoned shoes, as they say, but I don't remember hearing adults "talk their business" in front of children back in my day. Just sitting on the bus, train, or subway, I hear women describing, in great detail, *all dey bizness* with wee folk on their laps, and I can't but help scratch my head. Same deal in the supermarket or walking through any department store, loud conversations abound. Whether it's a sister talking into a Bluetooth to her friend with a toddler in tow, or she's walking with a girlfriend, nobody lowers her voice to speak on *anything,* it seems.

I cringe and keep asking: Don't you love that baby enough to speak in code or to be a little discreet? Aw, girl, don't say that about that child's daddy in front of the boy. . . . Why you gotta go there in earshot of a tyke?

Is it me?

I'm not saying that folks didn't have the same types of business to discuss then as they do now. Frankly, I'm of the mind that the dynamics that went on between man and woman, as well as the domestic dramas that go along with any relationship, ain't changed since Adam and Eve. Yet there was a protocol, it seemed, to when and how this information spilled into the minds and ears of children. Sure, women laughed and hooted about a hot, steamy lover too. A lot of the who-shot-John-and-how was communicated in a meaningful eye-cut, a swivel of the neck that would make a girlfriend double over laughing, and a hand placed on the hip in a way that made a statement. One-word exclamations, *Chil'!,* said it all.

In short, women spoke in metaphors, much like the songs of the masters; the soulful crooning balladeers sang about some hot topics (all I have to do is say Barry White and Marvin Gaye; Luther is in there, too, with Smokey et al.), but it was done with style and class. I can't account for men-talk; I wasn't in the room with them growing up. They pulled a quarter out of my ear and sent me on my happy way with a kiss. I was primarily in the company of women.

Lemme tell you how it used to go. You had to get delicious information in layers, like a butter-rich homemade cake. It took time, was offered by degrees when you were ready for it, and once fully iced, you were fully grown. My family was a lively bunch too, so it wasn't all shrinking violets or women with no experience, no, siree. These ladies had much to tell, I later found out. It just wasn't for my consumption until I was allowed to be in their sphere. Only then could I dip into their conversation, and only laughing at first. Had to wait till some of them died, literally, to be able to have anything to say.

Sounds crazy, but it was the truth. I think it served me well, but you decide. All I can do is explain it the way I heard sensitive information spoken around children. Perhaps their methods were too extreme, but I think somewhere on the continuum of truth-telling lies a happy medium. But here's the way I remember it.

When I was younger, people spoke about this thing called sex in hushed tones. It was grown folks' business. It was an entity, something that could possess you and make you lose your mind. From snippets of conversations I'd eavesdropped on, this *thing* could have you talking in tongues and calling on the Almighty. Chil', *yes*. And my aunties and older cousins would be laughing about this very mysterious thing that could take you over and make you act a natural fool. Something so powerful that it could actually make you love somebody's last week's dirty drawers. Eeeiwww!

That was my reaction as a child listening to conversations that were way over my head. Nasty. Disgusting. I was *never* gonna let that thing take me over, eva. Nope. Even though I didn't know what it was. And I was more than happy to go on playing with my toys and cousins at these events that drew family together, because they were talking about some ol' yucky stuff I didn't wanna hear nothing about.

But as time wore on and I graduated from being shooed out of the bean-breaking sessions in the kitchen to becoming a part of the all-female crew, I started to learn how to decipher this verbal code. My body was changing too. I was getting older, boys weren't so foreign a species, and my ear became tuned to hearing what this mysterious and seriously fine creature was all about.

Graduating to be in the company of women was a process of position changes, though. You didn't just get right in to be a part of the conversation, oh, no. First, when you got old enough to carry something important, you were on coat check. You had to run up and down the steps with coats, so you heard virtually nothing. Then, if you were efficient, you got promoted to set the table—not the good china and certainly not alone, mind you, but you were allowed to handle any flatware and items that, if they were broken, you wouldn't stop your momma's heart.

However, being sent in and out of rooms made sure that you were in and out of sensitive convo and could only get information in fits and starts. When a child crossed the kitchen threshold, the old dolls went back to speaking in code or just went dead silent with Cheshire cat grins until you left. Occasionally if you slowed around too much, one would come hug you, laughing, and say, "Baby, now git on. Whatchu want?" You were busted. Had to go on and mind your beeswax. Then, as soon as you were gone, the kitchen would erupt in peals of laughter again.

Finally, you were put on KP, kitchen patrol, helping to do the cleanup. By then you were a teenager, and a lot of the discussion ironically centered around the misfortunes of those caught up by this entity. By then they were close to calling it a beast, glimpsing at any budding young lady in the kitchen with a meaningful glance—and you knew you didn't want to get caught by this thing, turned out so badly that you didn't know up from down.

Alas . . . but human nature being what it is, and raging hormones being what they are, it does catch you. Oddly, these wise women of the pots and pans seemed to know that too, no matter how discreet you'd been. That's when the discussion, ironically, took another twist, and a new entity got talked about, this one came as a duo—love and heartbreak. Hmmm . . .

I watched huge military-sized pots bubble like cauldrons and trays of sumptuous dishes come out from the oven piping hot as stories of yet another being taken over by these entities were told. You waited your turn like rites of passage. Older girl cousins, maybe just your senior by a year, got picked on first. You knew your time was coming, especially when all the female griots got wind that you had a boyfriend. They ganged up on you at family dinners, summer barbecues, holidays, and they had no mercy. They warned you of pending doom from these things that could take you over. I have to call them entities, because to anyone listening, the women spoke as though a third party had done the deed.

It was all told in parables, never saying the young man's name, and they talked about the teen kitchen initiates as though they weren't even in the room. I remember when they got me; it was my initiation into the conversation, to be mentioned. It was just before I was about to go on my junior prom. I should have been ready for them, but I wasn't.

"You know what got her."

"Uhhhmmm, hmmmm. Knew it would."

"See, that's what I been tellin' that girl. But she let it roll right up on her."

"She need to go to church."

"Well, church might help, but you know when it hit ya, ain't too much you can do but—"

"Ride it out." (Sassy auntie—drawing hoots.)

"g. But she too young to ride nuthin'." (General agreenods and smiles.)

"Don't listen to them, chil'. You just be strong." (Confusion for a minute, slow on the uptake; then your cheeks burn and you look away.)

(Laughter.)

(If you could disappear, you would. If you could slide into the toes of your shoes and be gone . . . oh, Lord! They know you've been making out, and the conversation keeps going.)

"True, true, but when you get a little older, it'll make you call, Jesus." (Sidebar from the auntie at the stove.)

(More laughter and several high fives.)

"Y'all best not be blaspheming!" (This from the eldest auntie, who was laughing, nonetheless.)

(You really want to die now, wondering how much these wise women can see.)

"You need to leave that po' chil' alone. She'll be all right, and she ain't no different than when y'all was her age." (Bless you, Nana 'Re—always had my back.)

"Go put the ham on the table, chil', and get on outta this kitchen." (Momma's salvation, once her child had been teased enough. Knew you were chastised enough to let you know they weren't stupid.)

Slowly, and very surely, and as I listened very carefully, I saw the magic wisdom that got sprinkled in by the elders. By the time I'd hit my twenties, they revealed more, gave advice about what to do with a wayward man, laughed harder, let a little more of the veneer come off the conversation, but never enough to be entirely specific. Love, sex, makeups, breakups, money, affairs, and fights, all was cataloged between the pots and pans, told while folks moved and provided. But little ears were none the wiser. Even good and grown women had to let their own creativity be their guide. The group just offered parameters. Nobody talked about things in graphic detail.

That's my serious two cents. My real question is: When did we get to the point where we talked about what we've licked, sucked, humped, and bumped with babies of cognitive age on our laps?

I know I'm dating myself, showing my age. I confess that now, as an old doll of forty-seven, I'm one of the main kitchen infantrywomen in my family. Got young girls at my behest to go fetch me this and that off the table as I stand with my cousins barking orders so that a meal fit for royalty can be served. Just did it this holiday season, in fact. Watched my po' chil' (sixteen years old) get run out of the kitchen, her face red, from my cousins getting on her—and I let them with a chuckle in my heart and swallowing a mother's appreciative smile. History repeating itself. I was inducted like that, so she may be. That's love.

But when did we let babies hear how a no-good SOB got his tires slashed, and how we sought our feminine revenge when we caught him with that skeezer? (*Nary* an expletive edited out for young ears.) When did the four-year-old on the hip while we're on the telephone with a girlfriend get allowed to hear about how that man gave it to us doggie style, uh-huh, and went downtown? Or when did it come in vogue to let a little kid know that the reason he was being sent over our girlfriend's house to play was so that we could *get ours*?

Don't get me wrong. I've been a single mom too. I ain't saying I haven't done any or all of the above—no, siree. That's not what I'm talking about. I've had drama over affairs, wanted to cuss a brother out (and have), got mine, all of that, but not in earshot of a child. Old-school.

My issue is trying to understand when children suddenly became inanimate objects, like plastic dolls that couldn't see, ~~h~~ar, think, or process anything we said, so it was all right to ~~do~~ thing in front of them . . . and then we still want the old-school respect we used to give mommas? I'm just curious. How does that work?

Then I wonder what will happen to those little kids on hips, on laps, and in earshot of this very, very visceral adult reality that is so commonplace. I worry about obscure topics like how will young persons who weren't privy to grown folks' business find another like themselves out there in the world? How do they ultimately find a mate who will raise their children as children (not mini-me adults), value them, respect them, and have a little decorum and discretion? I do not envy teenagers or young adults today. It's gotta be like finding a needle in a haystack. If the standards are gone and the standard-bearers have all died off, then what? Where do we go from here?

See . . . I'm having a problem, I admit. I try to mind my business and try to subscribe to the theory of to each her own. My bad. Maybe because I'm a writer I have this affliction with listening to what folks say. I can't seem to turn a deaf ear and a blind eye to the things I hear and see on public transportation when little children are involved. Can't shake off what sisters walking out of church service are talking about (so let's not go there: Church folks are just as sloppy with their conversations). Can't shake off what assaults my sensibilities in the stores. Can't help grabbing my teenage daughter's arm when we hear it while out together, and I don't have the personal discipline to keep from threatening her life—telling her that if I *ever*, God as my true and only witness, hear her talking in the street like that about her business, I will kill her.

Yes . . . admittedly, maybe it's just me. But I just don't remember all of this. We ain't showing children no love if we're showing them all of this, are we?

That's more than my two cents, maybe a quarter's worth, and it's definitely more than one question involved . . . but you feel me. I know you do.

Love Is a Verb

KIM McLARIN

ERE I STAND, slightly more than a decade into this mothering gig, and what have I learned?

The usual things: how to change diapers and burp babies, how to install a car seat like a professional and cut a child's hair so he doesn't look too much like a refugee. How not to panic when the blood is gushing from a son who's going to need stitches, or not to panic when a daughter shivers so fiercely her little lips turn a striking shade of blue.

What I have not learned is many of the things I had expected, many of the things I was told, with great assurance, I most certainly would. I have not learned patience. I have not, I'm afraid, learned selflessness. I have not learned to slow down and look at the world through the ever-wondering eyes of a child. On the way to school each morning, when my son wants to stop and examine every pinecone that we pass, I shamelessly tell him the principal is waiting, standing at the door, clipboard in hand.

As for that thing which mothers are most expected to learn from this experience—The True Meaning of Love—well, I'm still struggling with that one too. I do, however, believe I've picked-up on something important in that regard, something critical I did fully understand before having children. I've learned that love is a verb.

This idea is not original with me, of course, but even the commonplace can be profound once you finally *get* it. Love is a verb, which means it is an action. Which means you can act it whether you feel it or not.

Love is a verb and you can act it whether you believe it or not at that particular moment; whether you want to act it or not, whether your own parents were able, in their struggle, to do the same. Love is a verb, and if you act it, in the acting, if you're lucky, love itself becomes reborn.

Here's an example.

Yesterday my daughter did something that pissed me off.

It was silly, really, scarcely worth mentioning. I'd been running around all day, as usual, fifty or sixty balls tumbling through the air and about to drop. I'd been dealing with bosses and deadlines and bills and other adult concerns, and then it was time to pick the children up from school and rush my daughter to her orthodontist appointment, where I would shell out some ridiculous amount of cash to straighten teeth that are already better than my own.

When we got to the appointment, however, my daughter found out that she was not, as I had told her, getting braces that actual day. She would get them the following week. No big deal—except it meant she had to go back to school the following morning without the braces she had bragged about getting (braces having become, mysteriously in this generation, a declaration of maturity and a source of pride instead of embarrassment). She would have to face the mean girl brigade. This, naturally, embarrassed and worried her. She burst into tears, stomped down the stairs, hurled accusations my way. *Why did I tell her the wrong thing? How could I make such a terrible mistake? Why, oh, why was I messing with her life?*

This is typical preteen, preadolescent behavior, of course, and I know much worse is yet to come. I should have laughed it off. I should have just taken a deep breath and let the clouds roll right on past. Instead, I got furious. I stomped right down the stairs behind her, pulling my poor son along. I raised my voice. I yelled at her. I wanted, with all my heart, to make her cringe.

Most people would be happy for another week to eat bagels and candy, why are you crying, I get so sick of you guys crying every time I turn around, it drives me nuts, if this is the worst thing that ever happens to you, you'll be lucky, if I had ever spoken to my mother this way she would have smacked me from here to kingdom come!

Even as I was yelling, some part of me realized that my anger was all out of proportion to the misdeed at hand. These maternal moments of madness worry me sometimes. I know that mothers are human, that just because a woman produces a child it doesn't mean she turns automatically into some kind of saint. Still I worry, during these moments when I look at my children and feel something much closer to a word I cannot even, in this context, bring myself to write than to love, that something is terribly wrong with me. I wonder if I should have ever become a mother in the first place. If I am somehow constitutionally unfitted for the job. Are people like plaster, malleable when wet, brittle when dry and unable to shift? And if there's a hole in that plaster, can it ever be smoothly filled?

But that's a pretty labored metaphor. Here's what it really is: Do I have enough love to give my children? Do I have all the love that they will need?

BUT I NEED to be careful here, because someday, perhaps sooner than later, my daughter will be reading this.

Somehow this is a late-breaking revelation to me; it occurred two years ago, when the hot-off-the-presses first copies of my latest novel arrived in the mail. My daughter was beside me as I ripped open the envelope and stared at the books in that moment that always encompasses such possibility and hope. Together we looked at the cover and ran our fingers over the binding and grinned at the letters that spelled out my name. My daughter clapped her hands with delight. But then she did something she would not have only a year before. She asked, "What's it about?"

That made me step back a little bit.

The novel, called *Jump at the Sun,* is a novel of motherhood. It is also a novel of race, of love and sacrifice, of contemporary life and the continuing legacy of slavery, of the costs and responsibilities of living the dream for which our parents and forefathers fought and several other things, but primarily it is a novel of motherhood. And whatever else it may or may not be, it is not a Hallmark card.

When I began the novel, my daughter was three, my son just months old, and the hormones of early motherhood still held me in their grasp. During the long, sometimes painful, sometimes tedious four years it took to complete the book, I worried some about what my mother would make of it. I wondered what my sisters and my aunts might think. It never occurred to me, however, to wonder how my children would receive the book. Their favorite piece of literature at the time was *Goodnight Moon.* It hardly seemed possible that they would one day advance beyond finding the mouse on the windowsill.

But one thing every parent eventually gets, and gets hard, is that children grow up—and fast. My daughter is ten now, my son a bit younger. Both are reading; both are curious; both may someday read my books. What will they think of them; what will my daughter, especially, think of this work, especially? Will she wonder if, in fact, Grace, the heroine of *Jump at the Sun,* is just a stand-in for me? If her feelings are not really my own?

Because of course they are not. Because of course they are.

I SAW A BUMPER STICKER once that read "Motherhood: A Noble Profession," or maybe "Motherhood: The Most Noble Profession" or maybe "Motherhood: The Most Important Profession in the World." Something like that. I don't remember the words exactly; this was years and years and brain cells ago. I do, however, remember my reaction. I laughed.

Motherhood is many things: a job, certainly, and a tough one, perhaps the toughest one you'll ever love. Motherhood is a challenge, an expansion, and a responsibility. It is a blessing, a burden, and most certainly a gift, but it is not a profession. There is no education required, no advanced degrees, no training or testing or licensing. There are no standards one must meet, no peer review, only minor regulation, which varies across culture and society. There's no way to tell, really, how good or bad of a job one is doing in the role, not for a long, long time anyway and maybe not even then—though Lord knows, we hate to acknowledge that possibility. Kids turned out well? Maybe it was you or maybe you just got lucky. Kids turned out like crap? Maybe the same.

It may seem churlish to make so much of a piece of paper slapped on the back of someone's car. In all likelihood the woman behind the wheel was a stay-at-home mother seeking acknowledgment and respect for her choice in a society that does not always grant as much. We're schizophrenic in this way: We propagate a Cult of the Child, arranging our lives around the little ones, abandoning all adult sense and interaction, denigrating any mother who dares skip out on a soccer game now and then, while at the same time turning our noses just slightly upward at the women who choose to make house and home the center of their lives. No wonder that woman wants to equate her day job with medicine or architecture or law.

Still, it feels important to question this idea of motherhood as a state of being and as somehow more noble than anything else. Because this idea still permeates our culture, though we pretend otherwise. And those who don't experience motherhood in this way can end up feeling strange, broken, wrecked.

SOME DAYS my daughter comes up to where I'm standing and bumps me like a colt.

I know what this means: She wants to be hugged. She wants to feel, without having to ask, her mother's arms around her for a few minutes, wants to be embraced and made to feel safe. Which I do, and as I do, it occurs to me that my mother rarely hugged us when we were young. There were too many of us, and she was too busy trying to feed and clothe and shelter the lot, trying to keep us warm in the wintertime and get us off to a decent school and protect us from predators and teach us about God and not lose her mind in the interim.

My mother too was of that generation that did not believe in petting up a child, in stroking her like a horse about to balk. That generation did not believe in playing or petting or praising children, believed more in rearing than in raising kids.

So we grew up without much touching, and I never thought about it much until my own first child was on the way. Early in the pregnancy I decided I would force myself to breast-feed—*force* being the operative word. Breast-feeding was largely foreign to me, despite the La Leche exuberance of my sisters-in-law. As far as I knew, my mother had not breast-fed us, my oldest sister had not breast-fed her children, and neither had any other woman in my family. When I was younger and watching over baby siblings and cousins and other such, it was bottle, bottle, bottle all the way. We never really talked about it, but somehow I absorbed the notion that breast-feeding was no longer necessary and slightly disgusting. Nasty, almost, in the Black southern sense of that versatile word.

Watching women breast-feed on the video in my child-birthing class made me queasy. Watching women do it in public made my stomach curl. When my turn came, I knew enough about the health benefits of breast-feeding to the baby involved to bite the bullet, but I did not expect to like it much. I would endure for the sake of my child and her future IQ.

So I was surprised to discover—once the first few hard and painful weeks were over—how much I liked this oldest way possible of feeding my child. All the stuff women gush about was true: the bonding warmth of it, the closeness, the feeling of accomplishment (and, yes, power) that comes from being able to nourish a human being with only one's body, oneself. I loved it all.

Still, by nine months, when my daughter started to lose interest and the hormone high began to wane, I was ready to let it go. I was ready to take my body back, to not be touched so much.

Things only intensified when my son came along. Suddenly there were two little people, both voraciously clamoring to be held, to be hugged, to be changed and diapered and picked-up and put-down and brushed-off and bathed and washed. Some days, walking to the park or to the car or to the store, my daughter, three years old and sensing displacement by the baby, would grasp automatically for my hand, and I would have to force myself to let her take it. If it was a question of safety, of crossing the street or navigating a busy parking lot or a cavernous store, that was one thing—I grabbed those little fingers and I held on tight and that was simply that.

But sometimes, just walking along the smooth and open path at the park, she would want to hold hands and I'd let her, but only for a minute. I'd do that squeeze-and-let-go routine that people do. Then she grabs again, talking all the while, on autopilot, and I let her hold a little longer this time. I find something to distract her and let go. She grabs again. The pattern repeats.

I know my mother loved us. I know my mother loved us because she sacrificed every hope and dream she ever held for herself that we might live and even prosper. I know this now, and it breaks my heart with sadness and gratitude.

Still, I cannot say—cannot honestly say—that I ever *felt* loved when I was little. Holding my daughter in my arms, I wonder: Is it the being loved or the feeling loved that matters most?

So, let's start again.

Yesterday, I got pissed at my daughter. I got pissed and I acted like a child myself. I was having a bad day for lots of nonsense reasons, unimportant, and then I was supposed to just shift all that to the side and focus on the needs of my children, and I couldn't do it. Not seamlessly. Or maybe I didn't want to do it, not at that moment, not on call, which is what motherhood demands. In that moment, I didn't want to be the mother, didn't want to have to walk with my daughter through the slings and arrows of adolescent girlhood (again!), didn't want to have to care about her emotional needs.

We drove home in silence, and she ran up to her room. I went into the kitchen, poured myself a cup of orange juice, drank it down for fortification.

Had I been my mother, that would have been the end of it. If her generation did not believe in petting children, it also did not much believe in sitting down to discuss things, especially emotional moments. Giving the children a good talking-to—absolutely. But listening to what they had to say or how they were feeling? Considering it? Maybe even apologizing in the end?

Right.

Someone said to me once, "You're a good mother," and I just laughed because I know good and damn well that I am not. A good mother is so far out of my reach it's not even amusing. A good mother is like Jupiter.

What I hope to be is a good enough mother. Good enough to keep them away from Burger King and to teach them why, though I let them eat the super-sugary yogurt most of the time. Good enough to stay in a city I dislike because it is better for them, though I do not always keep my disenchantment to myself. I gripe. What I hope to be is just a better mother than my mother, not because my mother was a terrible mother—she was not. But because that's what we're supposed to do, isn't it? Make things better for our children. Do better for them. Every generation improves. We usually take this to mean materially, but that's not even important, not really, the material stuff. Not by comparison.

My mother was not loved as a child. Or maybe she was loved—everybody gets some love—just not nearly enough; not enough and not from the people from whom she wanted it most. I know this now though I didn't growing up myself. My mother was left behind by her own mother, and so later, when it came time for her to do the mothering herself, she made sure she stayed. She refused to abandon us, though staying would, in the end, cost her a great deal.

Still, she stayed, and that was huge, though we didn't understand it then. She did not leave—not when things got bad, when the marriage to my father fell apart and she lost her job and poverty settled in. Not when the days and weeks and years became mostly about clawing and scraping to survive with five hungry children. She stayed. She stayed, and that was huge.

But lovelessness always leaves its mark. In the neighborhood of our lives lovelessness is the first broken window, the first strip of graffiti, the first shattered glass. The worse the neighborhood looks, the more people stay away; the more people stay away, the worse the neighborhood becomes. Lovelessness leaves a mark that makes it harder to get love and to receive it, which leaves a mark, which makes it harder, and round and round. The people who most need love, the ones with the biggest holes in their hearts from childhood wounds, are the ones least likely to get it, because those same wounds create in them attributes and personalities that frighten or drive love away. How fair is that? But this is life, isn't it? Life don't care from fair. The song says, "Them that's got shall get. Them that's not shall lose."

I was thinking: What a different person my mother would have been had just one person in her life truly loved her at some critical moment, some formative time. And what different people my sisters and brother and I would have been, because our mother would have been different in raising us. And what a different mother my children would have—someone who did not get so angry sometimes, so resentful, so less of this and more of that and maybe they too would be different and their kids and so on and so on. Lovelessness rolls downhill, gathering momentum, breaking roots and splintering branches, wiping out everything in its path.

So my daughter pissed me off, but after I came home and regrouped, I took a breath and went upstairs to her room.

I had to make myself do it. In truth, I wasn't feeling loved, not at that moment, just acting it.

I went up to my daughter's room and knocked on her door and went inside and sat down on the bed next to her and put my arm around her shoulders and apologized. Said I was sorry I had yelled. Explained that I was tired and frustrated and that she needed to understand that. Said I understood she was just disappointed. She was worried about how her friends would react, and friends, at that age, are everything, every single frickin' thing. Made some suggestions for handling the situation. Hugged her again and made her smile. Got up and left the room.

Lovelessness rolls downhill, gathering momentum, breaking roots and splintering branches, wiping out everything in its path, but one person can stop it. One person can raise his foot and stop the rolling. One person can bend and catch it in her heart.

Missing You

PEARL CLEAGE

$\mathscr{F}$EBRUARY IS A MONTH that looms large in my life. Not because it is the month when the country we're marooned in celebrates the birth of two White male presidents we weren't allowed to vote for since we hadn't been declared people yet. And not because it is the month when we demand that attention be paid to *our* history (as if we could even begin to understand our history in 28 days out of 365!).

Not even because the most cursory look at the events that have happened in February might lead us to check the position of the stars, study the configurations of the planets, and believe in black magic, *good and bad,* although I am the first to admit that February has something special about it.

Consider the possibilities of a month in which we celebrate the births of Frederick Douglass, Eubie Blake, Leontyne Price, Langston Hughes, and Marian Anderson *and* the founding of Morehouse College. What can we surmise about a month where we witnessed the assassination of Malcolm X in 1965 *and* Nelson Mandela's release from prison after twenty-seven years in 1990? What kind of energy is contained in a month that saw the first organized emigration of African-Americans back to Africa from New York to Sierra Leone in 1820 *and* the beginning of the Sit-in Movement in Greensboro, North Carolina, in 1960?

But those aren't the reasons this month means a lot to me. I like February because it's the month my mother was born:

February 12, 1922. It was always easy to remember her birthday because she shared it with Abraham Lincoln and we got a day off from school. She always said the holiday was really a celebration of *her* birthday, not his, and while we knew she was kidding, we really weren't. We figured she deserved it at *least* as much as he did.

The odd thing is that I can't remember the date she died. I used to feel guilty when people would ask me and I'd have to mumble something inconclusive. I could see how surprised they were that I clearly didn't remember such a painfully important date. But the date refuses to stay in my mind, no matter how many times I call my sister or check my journals.

After a while I realized that my inability to remember it was not the result of carelessness or callousness. I realized that *how* and *when* she died was not the most important thing to me. The thing that matters to me was that she *lived*. That's what I want to remember, not the false hope of medical miracles and the feigned concern of distracted specialists.

What I want to remember are all the things that were the *essence* of her. The things that shaped my own ideas of what a Black woman could and should be, to herself and to her family and to her people. The things that made me love her. The things that make me miss her more, not less, as the years go. The things that still make me wake up wanting to tell her something, show her something, ask for her advice or her affection.

So February is mostly a personal celebration for me, although I always set aside enough time to say a prayer for Malcolm and thank the Goddess for Leontyne Price and W.E.B. DuBois. Mostly what I try to do is spend enough time by myself to conjure up her spirit to sustain me during these difficult days.

Mostly what I try to do is remember brushing and braiding her hair, or her brushing and braiding mine.

Mostly what I try to do is recall the warm ripeness of those impossibly red tomatoes she used to grow in her garden every summer.

Mostly what I try to do is play my *Madame Butterfly* records because she always liked to play Puccini, even when everybody else in our neighborhood (including me!) was worshipping Motown.

Mostly what I try to do is remember how mad she was at me the one time I lied to her and how seriously I took the promise I made to myself never to do it again.

Mostly what I try to remember is her pleasure in sitting around the kitchen talking and eating fried fish she'd caught and frozen the summer before.

Mostly I remember her delight in her grandchildren and the sound of her laughter that day we made a lopsided snowwoman by the edge of the lake and tied her apron on it.

Mostly I try to remember the cold floor under my feet that wonderful late-night moment when she woke me to come look at the deer nibbling delicately through the moonlit snow of the frozen front yard grass.

Because in the face of my memories, the date she died loses some of its power, even if it doesn't totally surrender. And I'm old enough now to understand that it's important to take what comfort you can in the fact of the Big Questions about life and love and what happens after.

So I'll settle for remembering her laughter and sending her a happy birthday wish from her wild child, still struggling down here. *And missing you . . .*

Finding Martha's Vineyard

JILL NELSON

Who wants to run me over to Tony's?" my mother asks most nights from the time she arrives on the Vineyard in May until she leaves in September.

Tony's is Tony's Market on Dukes County Avenue, right down the street from the baseball field and in back of Circuit Avenue. Founded in 1877 and family owned, Tony's is Martha's Vineyard's equivalent of a New York bodega, the small, cramped store that thrives in cities and towns across the country. Wherever they are situated, these stores open early, close late, and sell a little bit of everything. They are where you go for a cup of coffee and doughnut at the crack of dawn, diapers, aspirin, or ice cream at night, and everything else in between. Here you can get just about everything you want: hairpins, butter, syrup, a sandwich, eggs, wine and beer, film or a disposable camera, produce, newspapers local and national, batteries of all sizes, condoms, toothpaste.

What Tony's Market and, in my experience, most other stores like it also have are the machines necessary to play the state lottery and rolls of one-, two-, and five-dollar scratch tickets. It is these that my mother is interested in.

"Leil wants to go to Tony's. Can you drive her?"

"I'll take her, but I'm running a bath. Can you watch my water?"

"Whoever's going, can you bring me some garlic for the fish?"

"We're out of juice too."

"If they have any double-A batteries, would you get me some?"

"And some coffee ice cream," someone calls out.

The round robin of voices, requests, and desires that a trip to Tony's evokes on a summer evening at the Vineyard ebbs and flows. My mother's request passes from person to person, room to room, an unannounced game of intergenerational telephone in which the initial request is embroidered and changed as it moves among those of us living in my mother's house.

As likely as not she sits on the porch in a bathing suit or shorts, a pair of randomly selected enormous shades covering a third of her face, filling out her number slips. Her wallet lies on the table beside her, or almost obscured by a pile of slips from losing and winning numbers previously played. Rising above the debris of bad combinations and successful hunches, there is usually a glass of champagne or Jack Daniel's and water.

After fifty years, my mother is familiar with the chaos of that time in the evening when everyone returns home at once after long days spent at the beach. One grandchild whose bathing suit is not quite dry is tired and shivering; another, hungry and tired, is slightly fussy. Low tubs of water are run for the children as adults rush to the showers, vying to be able to rinse the salt from hair and skin before the bathtub overflows or the child left with a relative erupts in a fit of cranky exhaustion.

My mother has lived through this many times: as a young mother herself, as an older woman, now as a grandmother. She does not often spend the whole day on the beach anymore, preferring to go across the street and "take a dip" in the morning before the crowd arrives or in the evening after they leave. In that hour or so before twilight the air is still warm and the bright light of summer slowly turns from gold to orange to blue. Then the crowds of people with the paraphernalia of children, sand toys, picnic lunches, and, brought by the more obnoxious, ringing cell phones and boom boxes, are gone. At worst, all that remains of them is the garbage they were too lazy or ill trained to take with them, but most of the time there is not even that.

After five o'clock on most evenings the characteristics of beaches all around the island change. Islanders or summer workers come down for a swim after work. Adults not interested in the midday noise of families with small children appear for an evening swim. The serious sun worshipers, those without children to tend or meals to prepare, remain on the beach talking among themselves and enjoying the growing quiet and fading of the day. Noisiest and always present is the familiar contingent of gulls. They stalk the beach on their awkward legs or fly above it, ancient, jaded-looking eyes alert for the curl of a potato chip, scrap of bread, or pretzel left behind. They swoop in with yellow beaks and snap up what has been forgotten or discarded, feeding on what has been left behind.

In the evening when my mother comes down to the beach for a last dip or just to sit and smoke a cigarette, she joins a group of women I affectionately call the diehards. Most days they sit alongside the jetty, facing the ocean in one direction, the Oak Bluffs ferry terminal in the other, with the sun lowering in the sky behind them. My mother's old friend, eighty-three-year-old Pauline Flippin from New Rochelle, New York, owns a house on Midland Avenue in Vineyard Haven and raised her children and grandchildren during summers spent here. Her husband, Wilton, a doll if there ever was one, drops her off at the beach around two o'clock and returns to pick her up just before sunset. Sandy Hamilton, fifty-five, from Hartford, Connecticut, who owns a condo in the Sea View, a stone's throw away, spends five months a year here. Eloise Allen from Philly, whose house is always crowded with the children of her lawyer son, Wes, and doctor son, Mark, and guests, comes down for a late swim or just to relax after a busy day.

Bob Jennings, who runs the children's summer basketball clinic next to the tennis courts, whose mother, Betty, owns a house just up the street on Narragansett Avenue, and his young daughters, Cheyenne and Quiana, their house less than a block away, stay as long as possible too, playing in the water. Bertha Blake, a nurse at Martha's Vineyard Hospital, is often there too. She has raised her two sons, Daniel and Aaron, as water babies, and they spend long days on the beach. These people are often among the last to remain, leaving when the sun is almost below the horizon.

Others come as they please, as their time on the Vineyard or in a day allows. Ann Parsons, a retired teacher from Sharon, Massachusetts, whose yeast rolls are out of this world; Delores Littles from New York, whose husband, Jim, is a wonderful artist; assorted children, grandchildren, family, and friends temporarily join the group. All are welcome, the only rule: Don't bring no bad vibes.

This is the time too when those who live and work on the Vineyard year-round, the people who make it possible for summer residents to do little or nothing as much of the time as possible, come down for a swim. The water washes off the stress and grime of a hard day's work. The carpenter, plumber, farmer, chef, waitress, fisherman, realtor, landscaper, clerk, shop owner, teacher, house painter, electrician, nanny, all come to the water. Some to swim, others to simply sit on the sand and watch the tide; all to be cooled and rejuvenated.

The beach is a constant, but luck is fleeting. My mother is feeling lucky and numbers close at seven forty-five each night. "Who's driving?" she'll finally call out. "It's six-thirty. I'm on the porch, ready when you are."

Someone always takes her. We know that Leil is lucky,

have learned that the sometimes inconvenient trip to Tony's is a small price compared to the hell to pay if we don't take her and her number comes out. Children are watched, bathed, pots stirred, dishes washed, table set. My mother sits in the car, wallet and plastic folder holding her number slips in one hand, likely a cigarette in the other. One of her hard fingernails taps the folder thoughtfully.

"You know, Jillo, I feel lucky tonight," she says.

"Leil, you feel lucky every night," I tease, making the right turn from Ocean Park onto Sea View Avenue.

"That's true," she laughs. "But sometimes I am lucky."

After six, Tony's is always crowded, not only with gamblers but also people who need something at the last minute. It's the only game in town besides Our Market on the harbor.

After years of driving "the Tony's run" with my mother, the faces of most of the other last-minute gamblers are familiar. We know the drill; get in the line specially designated for numbers players in the corner, have your slips properly filled out and ready, and hope the person in front of you isn't playing dozens of numbers, all combined differently.

Now, my mother, she's gotten this whole thing pretty much down to a science after all these years. Most of the time she plays the same numbers each day, although occasionally she'll add a new one for a day or so, inspired by the birthday of close family or friends, or the appearance of someone she first met in, say, 1979. (If she truly liked them, that'd warrant a two-dollar bet, one straight, one boxed. Otherwise, it'd be two fifty-cent bets.) My mother's numbers are all, like her, personal and subjective. She didn't play O. J. Simpson's license plate number the summer he got in that white Bronco and drove around for hours, causing the interruption of the NBA playoff game between my mother's beloved Knicks and Houston. On the Vineyard August 8, 1974, when Richard Nixon resigned, she didn't play the date of Tricky Dick's birthday, although she did pop a bottle of champagne and pour everyone a drink while Dennis McRae, a family friend, played taps on the battered bugle that still hangs on the porch.

My mother plays her family and friends' birth dates, street addresses, usually some combination of 828, the house on Indianapolis's California Street where she grew up. She does not play the flight numbers of planes that crash or the dates that disasters occur or the number of people killed when something goes terribly wrong. Even though she sometimes announces, "Damn it, I should have played that number," on the rare occasion when it comes out, she never does. My mother does not gamble on the bad luck of others. Instead, she banks on the good luck of family and friends, coming out ahead in the end.

My mother was a wonderful storyteller, at her best on the Vineyard, on the porch overlooking the water. She loved to tell the story of the response of some people when she and my father purchased their house for the low five figures. "Oh, these people thought we were crazy," she'd laugh. "No Black had ever paid that much money for a house here, for all I know no one in Oak Bluffs ever had. They told us we were nuts, would make it difficult for other Blacks, drive the prices up." Then she'd laugh, lifting her arms, bent at the elbows, up, palms out and hands spread, a frequent gesture combining exasperation, supplication, and who gives a damn.

"But your father always loved this house. From the first summer we came here, 1955, he wanted this house. And I loved the view. There's plenty of room and it's solid; it has stood here for a long time. But most of all it was the view. There's just something about that water . . ." Her voice drifts off, comes back. "Look at that," she'd say, her hand broadly gesturing across the front of her body, a motion that encompasses the ocean in front of her, sailboats in the distance, people passing by. "What we paid for this house was a lot of money in those days," I can hear my mother saying as she finishes her story, looking out at the ocean. "But we had to take the chance."

Leil's porch, her favorite spot. A few months after she passes I call Priscilla Sylvia of the Friends of Oak Bluffs and arrange to purchase and inscribe a bench for my mother. I e-mail Priscilla the specifics of exactly where I want the bench placed, along the water right across the street from her porch, in the middle of the view she loved. She is sympathetic, patient, helpful, and assures me that she understands where I want it to sit. I am not so sure, but what can I do, I'm in New York; I've got to take a chance. It is the same with many of those who now own homes and spend time each year on the Vineyard, and will probably be the same for those yet to discover this wonderful island. People who came here by chance, casually invited by friends who they took up on the offer of a weekend visit, sometimes reluctantly, people like my parents who fell in love with this island and took a chance on getting a piece of this rock.

Now it is virtually impossible for a working-class or middle-class family to purchase a home on the Vineyard. Cottages that were purchased for four or five figures thirty, forty, or fifty years ago are now worth upwards of a half million dollars. The price of buying and maintaining a summer home here necessitates, for most families, that both parents work. Today, Martha's Vineyard is one of the "in spots," with no sign of cooling down.

After decades of being off the radar of the popular culture following the heyday of the late nineteenth century, over the last three decades the Vineyard has revived as one of the hot summer destinations. Some say it began with the Kennedys, others say it was Bill Clinton and his family summering here when he was president that put the Vineyard into the national consciousness. Others say the island's revived popularity is just a natural part of the cycle of the place.

The growing popularity and expense of existing here have changed the island in fundamental ways. There is a housing crisis for those who live here year-round, many of whom can barely afford to rent, much less purchase or build, a home here. Each spring many islanders must scramble to find a place to live for the summer when the owners of the homes they rent in the winter return or rent their houses for increased summer rates and income to pay their mortgage. Some who live here year-round move out of their own home and rent it in the summer to get ahead. A small cottage that might rent for five hundred dollars a month in the winter can fetch several thousand dollars a week in the summer. Demand for services, from water to sewage to garbage pickup and disposal, has radically increased, straining the fragile ecosystem of the island. Taxes increase steadily. There are people on the island whose annual tax bill exceeds the original purchase price of their homes. According to tax assessors on the Vineyard, for the last five years property values have increased 24 to 36 percent annually.

Many, many island residents are leaving because the cost of living and raising children here is too high, and their loss weakens the fabric of the island, the very thing that made it so wonderful. What is being lost is the class diversity that made the Vineyard such a special place. Chatting in the spring of 2004 with a reporter at the *Vineyard Gazette,* she comments that the word on Nantucket is that the billionaires are driving out the millionaires, adding that the rule of thumb is that the Vineyard is ten or fifteen years behind Nantucket. This is a profoundly troubling thought for many, many reasons, particularly for all the hardworking thousandaires like me who call this island home.

Some days it seems as if the stress level I come here to escape has followed me. Impatient drivers honk horns and refuse to yield. Yuppies of all ages and colors descend on island-grown produce at the Chilmark Farmers Market on Saturday morning as if in a religious frenzy. Parking is so scarce that in August it is difficult to go to the supermarket, the bank, sometimes even the beach. Each year when I return there are new roads, many new houses. Some of the most beautiful vistas on the island are suddenly gone, an enormous trophy house plunked down, it seems, overnight.

What is always amazing is that through and underneath it all, although it is increasingly more difficult to see and find, Martha's Vineyard remains beautiful and magical, a place of grace. It is the suspicion many of us have that perhaps magic wears thin, grace goes elsewhere, the surety that we cannot take this small and fragile place, or the liberating psychic space it offers us, for granted that makes us protective of this small island. Even though we perhaps cannot imagine the Vineyard without its natural and spiritual beauty, we know that the loss of these things is possible. We must each do what we can to protect and treasure this place that is so special to so many of us.

In September of 2001, the year my mother's body dies, with my daughter, Misu, pregnant with my first grandchild, I return to the Vineyard, clinging to the last of summer. "Mom, come see the bench," my daughter calls from Leil's porch soon after we arrive. I join her, look across the street at the bench. There is a couple sitting there. "When they leave, we'd better run over there," Misu says. "Someone's always stopping to sit down. A few minutes ago a couple drove up, parked, and went and sat on Grandma's bench. Then before I could get over there, those people came."

I'm not surprised. When I look out the window of my mother's favorite porch, there's the bench—planted firmly on the edge of this wonderful island that my mother loved and so many others love so much, looking out over Nantucket Sound and, beyond it, the Atlantic Ocean—perfectly placed. There's her bench, as chance would have it, right where my mother would want it, smack dab in the middle.

Love Lessons

PATRICIA ELAM

ALL THE EVIDENCE POINTS to one thing: I'm not so good at love. At least I haven't been thus far. I'm not bitter about this revelation, though. My life is rich with my children, family, friends, work, and play. I take full responsibility for the choices I have made over the years, and I forgive myself for the ones that didn't serve me well. My favorite explanation to myself and others about a questionable relationship is: "At the time it seemed like a good idea." I refuse to beat myself up or feel regret about them, particularly the marriages, because otherwise I wouldn't have my three amazing children.

In retrospect, I was attracted to particular men because of the fast and furious moments they brought me, the heady feelings that I often mistook for love. In high school I dated guys my father usually referred to as "clowns" (sometimes to their faces) rather than by their given names. He had good reason. I wanted authentic thug boys who were usually missing something, like teeth and/or brains. During my college years, I convinced myself I really didn't care about love. I was so glad to be away from home and parental restrictions (no more of my father randomly showing up at parties wearing pajamas under his trench coat). I was just a girl who wanted to have fun, a kind of "playa playa." I got my feelings hurt, though, when the guys I liked did the same thing to me, but I G'd-up and ignored the hurt. "Love is for sissies" was my motto back then and all the way through my first year of law school.

I confess it was my once faint and then louder biological clock that got my attention and made me consider settling down. I wanted a child, but I didn't want to be nobody's baby mama. (I did have some standards, after all, warped as they were.) The idea of marriage was appealing because it seemed grown-up and responsible, like wearing a suit to work instead of jeans. I don't know that I thought much more beyond how many to invite and what my dress should look like. In any case, I was determined to have a wedding no matter whether it was good or right for me and even though I had no clue as to who would make good marriage material. I chose someone who had a solid profession (a doctor), came from a middle-class family, and I enjoyed making love with. I ignored the fact that we weren't friends and had no other interests in common. I also ignored his bad temper and his drug habit, both of which of course only got worse. After two years of misery, I left my knife-wielding husband with my young son in tow and my clothes hastily stashed in trash bags, escorted by those men in blue, called to the scene by my frantic best friend.

The next marriage produced two more children with a man confused about his strong desire to be with other men rather than, and in addition to, me. At least, I told myself, he was my good friend (a step up from the first husband), wanted to be a father to my first son, and was supposedly ready to leave the gay life alone. Which was kind of true, for a time. The question was why did I say yes to something most women wouldn't have even considered. Both times I chose men for whom I was not a priority. I treated the love I had to offer like it was charity. Maybe enduring love just wasn't in the cards for me.

My parents, still in love and married fifty-seven years, should have been role models. During a recent visit my father recounted for his grandchildren the story of how he met my mother and knew instantly that he wanted to spend the rest of his life with her. He heard her make an announcement at church about an upcoming penny sale. Not quite ready to talk to her then, he returned on the scheduled date for the penny sale, and lo and behold, she didn't even show up. I guess that endeared her to him more as he returned the following week and there she was. Their courtship, he says, consisted of sitting in her parents' living room, while her mother rocked in a chair nearby. Now that she at seventy-nine is in declining health, and he is doing well for eighty-five, my father is devoted to her caretaking as well as cooking, cleaning, and transporting her to numerous doctor appointments. This is for-real love, love in all its permutations. They raised four children, buried a fifth, lost loved ones, established successful careers, supported each other's dreams, suffered hurt and pain, experienced great joy, traveled the world, created a life together. I clearly saw that my parents' marriage hadn't been plagued with anxiety and heartache like both of mine. For one thing, my mother always knew where our father was, something I rarely knew when my husbands weren't with me. I figured I either misunderstood my parents' example or rebelled against it or both. What I did learn from them about love is that it isn't supposed to hurt.

Therapy (and nine years without a romantic relationship) showed me I had to look further within. I came to understand some important facts: You can't change anyone but yourself, and I didn't love myself enough to look for the right kind of love or demand it for myself. I know this sounds cliché, but clichés usually have some truth to them. My truth is I had repeatedly invited in the same kind of furtive, desperate pseudolove from the outside as I was giving to myself on the inside. Exploring, talking, and crying about these realizations helped me understand the need to love myself completely before I could find someone to love me in a whole and healthy way.

I am not alone in this dilemma. The inability to love one-self may be the biggest issue most women suffer from in love relationships. When we don't love ourselves completely, we try to fill ourselves up with what feels good for the moment but is ultimately toxic: drugs, alcohol, overspending, and the ever-popular bad relationships with men. I write an advice column for an online magazine, and most of the questions come from women and most revolve around relationships. Here's an excerpt from one such query: *We've been having sex for three months, but he doesn't want a relationship—help!; I'd rather have a little something from a man than no relationship at all, what's wrong with that?; Why am I only attracted to men who don't love me back?*

When I read letters like this again and again, I am grateful for my experiences in this arena even though they were very painful. Knowing I may be helping someone else makes it feel like it wasn't all in vain. I wrote that young lady back and told her the importance of self-value and suggested she create a set of vows to herself. I shared mine: I vow to love you and not let anyone harm you emotionally. I vow to take care of your heart and not allow it to love precariously or recklessly anymore. I vow to protect you from those who do not value you completely. I vow not to enter you into toxic relationships.

Lately, I've been hearing that some women want to function more like men and have sex just for the sake of having sex. The premise, I suppose, is that these women won't get hurt because their hearts will not be involved. I have trouble believing that deep down inside they don't mind being objectified. Usually when a woman isn't interested in love it's because her last memory of it was a painful one. At the ripe and rich age of fifty plus, I want so much more than sex with someone who wants only that from me. I know I deserve a several-course dining experience and not just an appetizer to tide me over. As a dear friend says, "I'm on my way to becoming a phenomenal woman, and I need a phenomenal love to match." With my past experiences noted and tucked away, my parents' time-tested devotion emblazoned in my heart, and self-infatuation at long last, I'm determined to find that rock-solid love, the one who'll know, without being told, to come correct this time.

The Heart Does Go On

DEBBIE M. RIGAUD

ON THE NIGHT my cherished godmother, Madone "Dada" Nicaisse, took her last breath, the full moon was luminous and low to the ground.

It was September of 2006.

My godmother was my mother's aunt, my maternal grandmother's big sister. But in our clan, there is no distinction between grandmother and great-aunt, immediate family and extended family. Before their 1960s migration to the States, my mother's family lived together in one house in Haiti, the island republic from whence my parents hail. Therein adults regarded each household child as their own.

Dada carried out this tradition, even as relatives settled in different addresses throughout Brooklyn, New York, and East Orange, New Jersey. When my maternal great-grandmother died in the mid-1980s at age one hundred plus, Dada—her firstborn—inherited the crown of eldest member in our extended tight-knit family.

Dada was our royalty. Everyone held her in the highest esteem. As a child my eldest sister christened her Dada when she could not pronounce *ma tante Madone.* This became a cherished moniker, affectionately uttered by the family's generation of American-born children delivered into Dada's care in the 1970s and later.

From Brooklyn, my parents and sisters moved to East Orange, New Jersey. Dada moved with us. We felt blessed that

Dada lived in our house with my parents, three sisters, and me for over fifteen years. She could have chosen to stay with her son, her only child, who lived in Brooklyn with his wife and children. Throughout our childhood, when our parents headed across the river to Manhattan for work, Dada sprang into action. Her signature wake-up call of *"l'école, l'école, l'école"* rang out like a school bell, piercing our sleepiness and prying our eyes open each morning. She then prepped us for our day, combed our full heads of hair, and embossed us with "I'm-Haitian" talcum powder on our collarbones. Later she was there to greet us when we returned home.

My cousins lived next door, and we all walked to school together. Dada usually stood at the top of our home's walkway to watch us until we disappeared around the corner. She'd float a silent prayer over us as we headed to the school building a mile away. I felt her wrap us in a cocoon of love and safety. Dada's prayers were that powerful. In fact, she was the family's designated prayer; everyone called Dada before taking a test, traveling on a flight, or anything in between. There was nothing like knowing you were on Dada's prayer list. Her physically frail, elderly body was twisted with osteoporosis and afflicted with asthma, but it housed a mighty spirit. She was like a force of nature that you feel rather than see.

My mother, Viviane "Mummy" Rigaud, and Dada were very close. This is mostly because like my mother, Dada was an outwardly gentle, shy, reserved Haitian woman, but also equally strong-willed, proud, focused, and completely in charge. Along with my mother, Dada was like a study of a distant era when dignity, not diamonds, was a woman's best friend.

Dada's passing was heartbreaking because for long I'd considered her my soul mate. I never stopped flooding her with letters, postcards, and phone calls professing my adoration and appreciation. She loved me unconditionally and treated me like a princess. We even had a special nickname for each other, Bou Bou. Growing up, my unconventional personality had often placed me at odds with my mother. I kept my hair natural, moved out of the house before marriage, and broke other Haitian traditions/expectations that my elder sisters upheld. But Dada accepted me still. She comforted rather than criticized, soothed rather than scolded. I never felt judged in her presence.

I learned how to celebrate Dada from my mother. My sisters and I followed Mummy's example of placing Dada on a pedestal, giving her the utmost respect, value, and appreciation. Mummy revered Dada as an elder and as the matriarch of our growing extended family.

Mummy had been in Atlanta undergoing chemotherapy when she received the news of Dada's passing. I called her for help with the bio I had to write for Dada's funeral program. Even though my maternal grandmother was Dada's sister, my mother remembered the details and milestones of Dada's life more vividly than she did. Dada's position as family griot and historian seemed to have passed down to my mother. Even though my mom lived in New Jersey, she chose to get treatment in Atlanta in the privacy of my elder sister Judy and her husband Jerry's home. An intensely private person, Mummy didn't want an audience to her hair loss and side effects. So Dada's funeral became a reunion of sorts.

At the services, I remember people complimenting my mother on how healthy and radiant she looked. "I juice veg-e-ta-bles," she revealed in her Haitian New Yorker accent, stretching the word into four audible syllables.

Two months later we tried to keep the Thanksgiving mood festive in honor of Dada. My younger sister Golda, her one-year-old son, Xavier, my husband (then fiancé), Bernard, and

I flew to Atlanta to spend Thanksgiving with our mother and sisters. After dinner, my mother played with her six grandchildren and we took family portraits. Everyone then danced to my mother's favorite songs in Judy's living room, laughing at baby Xavier's great sense of rhythm.

We celebrated through our grief.

Those moments of joy were short-lived. Barely two months after that Thanksgiving, Judy called from Atlanta. It was a Thursday night. "Mummy's not eating, and she's getting weaker," she told me, fearing the worst. "We're taking her to the hospital in the morning to get some fluids." My sister is a doctor of internal medicine and her diagnoses are usually spot-on. "I think she may have three to six months left," she said.

I couldn't believe what I was hearing, so I brushed it off as negative talk. My mother had been fine the week prior. These symptoms had surfaced only over the last few days. And now I was supposed to believe that her days were numbered?

I told Judy that I'd fly out the following weekend, which was eight days away. The next morning, Friday, Judy and my eldest sister, Shirley, took Mummy to the hospital. They called us often with updates. By then my father, maternal grandmother, and aunt had flown down from Jersey.

On Saturday, Judy called me at nine o'clock. "You guys need to fly down here today." She sounded emotionally weary from spending a precarious night beside Mummy's hospital bed. "Her blood pressure is dropping fast. I had the hospital chaplain give her her last rites."

Clenching the phone, I looked over to where my sister Golda was standing, her pregnant belly extended and round. My sisters and I had tried to shield Golda from the hard news. We didn't want to worry her too soon. And so Golda didn't realize the gravity of Mummy's condition.

"I'll book the next flight out," I said before hanging up.

Golda reacted nonchalantly to the news. In fact, she didn't think she'd be able to fly out that day. "I have to clean the house, so I'll book a flight for tomorrow morning," she said. I remembered the defeat in Judy's voice and urged her to come with me. We booked a flight leaving at 1:30 P.M. that same day. When I told Judy that Golda couldn't prepare the baby in time for the 11:30 A.M. flight, Judy sounded worried that we were cutting it too close. "Okay, but get here as soon as possible," she said.

By the time we got to the airline check-in, it was 1:05 P.M. "It's too late for you to make the flight," the woman behind the counter told us.

"But our mother is dying," I said, panicking.

The woman rambled off something about policy and tapped her keyboard in search of seats on the 3:30 P.M. flight.

And then something miraculous happened.

"The one-thirty flight has just been delayed by ten minutes because of a mechanical problem." She stared at the screen in disbelief. "You can still make it, but you better hurry." Golda and I grabbed Xavier and rushed to the security checkpoint to oddly find no one waiting on line. Because we purchased our tickets the same day as our flight, security pulled us aside for a closer check. We got through the whole process in mere minutes. A passenger transport vehicle was waiting on the other side of the checkpoint. At our request, the driver sped us to our departure gate in no time. Upon boarding the plane, all the passengers, including my cousin Natasha and her grandmother (Dada's youngest sister), who were also flying down last minute to see my mother, were anxiously awaiting takeoff. Golda and I took our seats with gratitude in our hearts. Somehow, and for some reason, we had made the flight.

Once we arrived in Atlanta my father and brother-in-law picked us up and drove us straight to the hospital.

It was jolting to see Mummy in such a state. Her covered legs were the first thing that came into view as I entered her room. I was eager to be by her side but wasn't sure I was prepared to see more of her. Our entire lives my mother had never been admitted to a hospital. It was a strange feeling to be visiting her there. She lay on her back, semiconscious and unable to speak. A Haitian church group was in her room, praying and singing hymns.

"We're here, Mummy," Golda and I said, rushing to her bedside, masking our shock. "We're here."

When we touched and spoke to our mother, her eyes fluttered in response. She tried to focus on our faces but couldn't completely control her eye movement. The whites of her eyes were jaundiced because, we'd learned, the cancer had spread to her liver. Judging from her eye flutters, she knew we were there. Although he is a toddler, Xavier seemed to understand that this was a somber moment. His eyes were watery and replete with sadness. Golda held him to the side of her pregnant belly. As she bent over to kiss my mother, Xavier lowered his head to my mother's chest and stroked her gently with his little hand. Mummy gasped in shock and widened her eyes at Xavier's obvious comprehension.

Golda and I voiced encouraging words in my mother's ear as we kissed her and comforted her. My father and cousin stood at her bedside in tears of disbelief. Gripping grief seized my great-aunt and chased her to the hallway, where she broke down.

"It's okay, Mummy," I heard Golda bravely whisper, giving Mummy precious peace of mind. "You can go."

When Mummy's panting relaxed, we knew she felt soothed by our presence. We then sang "His Eye Is on the Sparrow," one of her favorite hymns. Everyone formed a circle and held hands around her bed and prayed.

Seconds after the prayer ended, Mummy took her last breath and drifted away.

It was January of 2007.

A high-pitched wail traveled from my core and escaped out the top of my head. "Mummeeee!" Golda's shriek merged with mine. For that brief moment we let the sorrow overcome us fully.

Not fifteen minutes had passed since we'd arrived at the hospital from the airport, and Mummy was gone. Had we not made that flight, we would have tragically been too late. God cleared the way so that we could spend one last moment with our beloved mother. It was clear to everyone that although she was slipping fast, she held on for this long because she was waiting for our arrival. My older sisters, who returned to the hospital from home minutes after Mummy's passing, told Mummy all day that Golda and I would be flying in. And she waited.

This struck me as an amazing act of love. And she waited for *Golda* and *me,* her younger two eccentric daughters who were known for unconventional philosophies that strayed from some family standards.

My mother's final act was to express her deep love for her daughters. That was her way. I have never come across a mother as maternal and nurturing as mine. She was such a "mommy."

Her overprotective parenting in childhood gave way to a wonderful camaraderie as we entered adulthood. When she visited me in London (where I lived for two years), Mummy was adventurous and full of curiosity. She saved the British Airways menu as a keepsake from her first transatlantic flight. Her excitement energized her as we toured London and Paris. As expected from any tourist, Mummy was awed by world-renowned sites like the Eiffel Tower, but she especially marveled at quirky standouts like the miniature elevators or the *bonjour*-greeting shopkeepers in Paris.

A week after she returned home, I received a card from her in the mail. In it was a photo of Mummy and me in front of the Arc de Triomphe. Her handwritten message on the card thanked me for the great time we shared together. "I am so proud of you," she wrote. I was overjoyed to read those words. I was touched because she was proud of me being myself, rather than the me I was *expected* to be.

Days after her diagnosis and surgery to remove a cancerous lump under her right arm, Mummy came out dancing with my younger sister Golda in celebration of my thirtieth birthday. It completely surprised us when she agreed to come along. She threw on something nice over her fresh surgery bandages, and we headed to a low-key wine bar. We were joined by my cousin, her husband, and three other friends. I will never forget how we hit the vacant dance floor and jammed together like girlfriends.

My sisters and I valued my mother. Mummy was a clever woman, an operating room nurse with a passion for books and for pushing us to excel academically. My sisters and cousins all knew that acing school was the surest way to win Mummy over. Still, it was her easygoing personality that we loved the most. Because of Mummy, we knew just as much about manners, self-respect, and discipline as we knew about burping out the alphabet and cracking jokes about the crazies on the New York City subway. She balanced both sides of her personality well. We were able to speak plainly and debate her about our curfew, straight vs. natural hair, and her painfully mismatched outfits. My mother used comedy to entertain, ease tension, and connect with us. The most vivid memories I have of my mom are our laugh attacks, spawned by her hilarious, witty comments about her casual observations.

"I'm not with you," she'd say in Creole with a straight face when we couldn't hold our laughter in public as well as she could.

Days after her passing, as I searched for old pictures of my mom for a memorial slide show, I was overcome with sadness. I felt inconsolable. Then in a box of photos I found an envelope addressed to me from Dada. Inside was a card with a short message written in Dada's distinct handwriting. "Bou Bou my dear," it read in French. "I send you words of comfort: courage, patience, joy and happiness to you. . . ."

I fell to my knees in gratitude. Once again I felt wrapped in Dada's loving and protective cocoon. She had reached through the beyond to touch me with comfort when I needed it most. Dada's love extended from the beyond to comfort me in my dire time of need. It's a love that's everlasting.

At my beloved mother's funeral, my three sisters and I linked arms with each other and began a most agonizing procession down the wide, cold aisle. Everyone in attendance stood on either side of us and watched with leaking eyes. Over three hundred people in attendance were in painful shock. A majority of them, including close family members, didn't even know my mother was terribly ill. She had kept her condition a secret.

We followed our mother's casket out of the Catholic church. Six male members of our family—my mother's two brothers, three cousins, and a nephew—carried her out like spiritual guardians. I wondered how their grief didn't compromise their physical strength. A single tear slipped down my right cheek to remind me to feel and to live in the moment.

My mind had the tendency to wander lately.

Mental meanderings became a survival skill I'd learned to perfect in the past few months. The shock of my mother's sudden death would have been too much to bear otherwise. This, on the heels of Dada's passing four months prior, would've surely sent me forever into orbit. Both women had raised my sisters and me with a lovingly gentle yet steadying hand.

My father and my mother's seven brothers and sisters looked completely destroyed. I could only imagine what my maternal grandmother, Lamercie "Mummum" Joseph, was feeling. My mother was her firstborn. She alternated between dry-eyed disbelief and brief episodes of wailing outbursts. My woeful grieving grandmother followed all Haitian cultural protocol for a mother attending her child's funeral. She wore all white, and she did not attend the burial site after the funeral mass. She waited a few days before visiting Mummy's crypt.

It was hard not to chuckle when Mummum spoke. The woman had such a quick wit and an unmatched sense of humor that you never knew when she was on the verge of a comedic delivery. No moment was too sad or inappropriate for a quality punch line.

"Timoun," she said in Creole to my sister Golda and me. "Children, now I assume the role of mother *and* grandmother."

"And you're gonna be my mother of the bride," I teased her, using our usual mock-threatening tone. I was to be married in September 2007. That was one of two 2007 events that my mother had been looking forward to—that and the May birth of Golda's second child.

The humor in Mummum's voice was gone. My grandmother's blue-gray eyes looked pained. "I'll be too sad to walk down the aisle as mother of the bride," she said.

My sisters and cousins normally crowded Mummum's kitchen for a yummy meal and colorful tales. She was the family nucleus. Mummum *performed* her stories, twisting her face, arching her back, and waving her hands to expand the listener's imagination. Not the average grandma, Mummum rooted for the Washington Redskins and stayed glued to the tube when a boxing match was on. I'd always known her to be much more hip than my traditional mother. Her record collection alone could rival that of a person a quarter of her age. Plus, I always thought it was cool that she gave us Pappy Andre, a doting stepgrandfather, an esteemed gentleman and devoted, loving husband to Mummum for fifty years. After Mummy's funeral, we crowded her kitchen in concern for her grieving process.

When Golda's daughter Zora was born, she was the spitting image of my mother. Mummum sat at her kitchen table, holding Zora in amazement. It seemed to bring Mummum a bit of comfort.

Three months after Mummy's funeral, my stepgrandfather, Andre "Pappy Andre" Joseph, was diagnosed with advanced lung cancer. Two weeks later he was gone.

It was May of 2007.

With Pappy Andre's funeral, Mummum began grieving for Mummy all over again. "She was such a good child. Never disrespected me. Never talked back," she lamented Mummy's famous obedience one day. Mummum raised her arms in anguish and placed her hands on top of her head. I held her as her tears flowed. Mummum never recovered from her gutwrenching grief. Her sister Dada, husband Andre, and most especially, her daughter Viviane vanished one after another. Two months later Mummum was hospitalized and never returned home. She passed away with over twenty family members at her side—my sister, cousins, aunts, uncle, and myself included. Her death was a devastating blow.

It was July of 2007.

After her passing, I wondered what it was that Mummum tried to express in her final moments. She couldn't speak. An oxygen mask fitted tightly on her face. But she struggled to say something. Frantically, Mummum raised her hands and attempted to pull off her mask. She nearly lifted her head off the pillow. What was it she wanted to say? It plagued me.

Recently, my cousin Jessica said Mummum appeared to her in a dream, saying that she tried everything not to leave us.

That answered my question. As she was being called by her Maker, Mummum felt troubled that we would suffer yet another terrible loss.

On my wedding day in September of that year, I was led down the aisle by my weeping father. A front-row seat marked by a single red rose was kept empty in my mother's memory. I heard isolated sniffs in surround sound. It was a bittersweet occasion. I remained mindful of the fact that the Lord had blessed me with three maternal guardians—my godmother, mother, and grandmother—who are now angels guiding me on my journey.

As my husband and I begin a new chapter, it saddens me that my future children will not personally know my mother. But it brings me comfort to feel that indeed the heart does go on. I still feel their love as strongly now as ever. I am their living legacy. And it is armed with their intentions and principles that I move forward for the benefit of the next generation.

Fiction

♥

Geraldine's Song

FELICIA PRIDE

I HAVEN'T SMOKED in almost three days, but I swear I can see the color of hope in Mel's eyes. It's a brown shade, not bright orange or skylight blue like I thought. Brown. Like the thin layer of a sunrise. Like the palms of Grandlovey's hands. The pull of my son's soul, far more superior to the lure of a blunt, is so strong that it takes me in and doesn't let go.

I wonder if Pops saw this same sensation when he looked into my eyes, twenty-two years ago. He might have because he told me this would be the most powerful experience of my life. Powerful. A defining moment. I get what he meant.

Ageless players around the way who double as local historians always tell me that Pops spit me out. That I got his heavy eyes and his defined mouth and that my ears sag just the same. Junior remains my name as I walk the neighborhood.

Because childbirth murdered Geraldine, my mother and the only woman who ever understood Pops, grief was supposed to make him turn to one of the chemical pick-me-ups readily available in The Gardens, my Baltimore neighborhood where nothing green grows except cash.

Cycles dictate that Pops was supposed to bail on me and leave the chore of raising a man-child to Grandlovey. His father did it. Everyone knew through Grandlovey's church testimonies that the Lord kept her when her husband did not. Pops recalled bumping into his father once by accident. On the corner. Their eyes spoke to one another. Grandpops continued on his rolling stone ways.

But Pops was a complex man with a simple view on everything. "Don't fuck with life and it won't fuck with you." That's what he always told me. He read the Bible every day but maintained a healthy contempt for church. Despite the fact that Grandlovey is a preacher and used to house a small church in her basement, he never set foot into a place of worship as an adult. He used to joke around, let out one of his ten-dollar laughs, and tell me that when he was a young 'un with a runny nose, he hated putting on the same gray suit, a hand-me-down from one of the older boys in the neighborhood, because the pants itched his crotch. Grandlovey would slap his hands and scold him that he best stop touching himself in church before the Lord taketh away.

"Love isn't just a feeling, Junior; it's an act." His words echo in my head as I peek in on Tanisha while I hold our son in my arms. We said "I do" in front of Grandlovey ten days after the stick turned blue. The act of loving Tanisha was like living to me. Necessary. Natural. We are a family.

I find myself checking on her often. Making sure she is still there. The blackness of Grandlovey's house shields me from seeing the tightness of Tanisha's lips as she sleeps. I can't make out the twist of her brows or the curve of her femininity. But she remains a snapshot in my mind. Vision isn't important. I leave her to dream about the son she was told she could never have.

It's only a few hours before the sun announces a new day.

Grandlovey's house is deathly quiet. It's hiding from the neighborhood. The low murmur of a helicopter in the distance. The pop-pop of gunplay. The scream of desperation.

I've spent the last two sunrises in my old room that Tanisha and I converted into a makeshift nursery. We moved my twin bed into the basement to make space for a Salvation Army crib. I kept my basketball posters hanging just in case Mel sees a future. I sit with my son in my arms in a rocking chair that doesn't rock. I am a father.

6:18 P.M. Ishmael III's official time of birth.

My son is awake. I call him Mel for short. Let him grow into his name. He's a clean slate. No expectations. No failures. No faults. As close to perfect as he'll ever be. I don't see myself in him and I'm glad. I'll let him grow into his name. I've been awake longer than he's been alive.

He stares back at me. Softly. Intently. With trust. Cycles are funny.

I was seventeen years old when I realized that Pops loved life so much that he couldn't continue living. The guys with the white jackets said six months was generous. Cancer is like the military, it'll recruit anyone.

No sex. No Grandlovey's fried chicken. No going to O'Dell's for a drink. No more long days as a correctional officer. All mandates from the guys with the white jackets. It was simple, really. If Pops wanted to live longer, he would have to give up stuff. But Pops was a complex man. He sabotaged his chances. Overlived. Fucked with life. In his mind, he was already dead.

But he existed for a little while. Confined to a bed. That wasn't living. Grandlovey gave up her room on the third floor because it got better ventilation. Pops was always hot. Sweaty. A nurse would come by and clean him, make him presentable. But he still didn't want me to see him. Weighing less than me.

Patches of thin, silver hair residing loosely on his head. Flakes of skin shedding on his rubber sheets.

I respected that. But only when he was awake. When he was asleep, I'd sneak in like a child afraid of the dark and stare at him. Softly. Intently. With trust. Then I'd leave unnoticed and pretend that I hadn't seen him dying.

The nurse told me that he was sorry to miss my concerts. Her words were always "It pained him that he couldn't attend your affair today."

So I'd give him private performances. Outside of Grandlovey's door, I'd play his favorite, Bach's Concerto in A Minor. My violin was the gateway to his shimmers of happiness. I played to see pride illuminate his face. But I couldn't see him. He was being selfish. It was lonely behind the wood barrier.

Pops bought me a violin when I was twelve. Told me I needed to own my dream. I named her Geraldine after the mother who I can only dream about.

At times, during my private concerts, I was no longer standing on the pale hardwood floor in front of Grandlovey's door. I was onstage. The New York Philharmonic. Evening affair. Solo. Pops is there. Front row.

He used to tell me that my playing reminded him of the voices of angels. I'd ask him how he knew that sound. He'd simply reply, "Because they visit me." I believed him.

The funeral was the last time. The last time that I courted Geraldine. Sometimes I remember the day as a blur of flowers, white gloves, and loud organ playing. Other times I just recall my performance. Sloppy, like I was six years old again and screeching through my first recital. Cycles are funny.

Most times I just remember the day as an abstract vision. A dream? I want to look into my father's eyes, but can't. I want to see the clairvoyance that prevented me from taking a knife to school to shank a kid who disrespected me. Pops knew that stupidity and had a remedy for it. Clothed me in understanding. I want to see love manifested. I want to see what my mother saw.

I look at my son.

Mel is asleep. I lay him in his crib. I'm scared shitless. Pops made it look easy. I need to reconnect with him.

I grab Geraldine from the back of my closet. She's hidden beneath rags and dirty magazines. I unleash her from her cloth case. I hold her like I just held Mel. She looks tired. A string is popped. I replace it and adjust her voice. Alternate between the tuning pegs and the fine tuners, plucking the strings two, three, and four times for accuracy. The exactness of how each of the four should sound is as familiar as Grandlovey's humming.

I tighten the bow. The thin wood feels cold in my hand. Distant. I add a little of the cracked rosin to the delicate hairs. Too much will distort the sound.

I play one note.

A.

Slowly.

Inhale. Eight count. Exhale. Natural.

I continue with scales, giving equal attention to each string. I dive into improvisation, my fingers agile as a saxophone player's. Geraldine begins to take over my movements. I flow with her.

I play "Twinkle, Twinkle, Little Star." The first song I learned. Mel doesn't waken.

Just like riding a bike.

Then I play Pop's favorite. Effortlessly. My vibrato is first-chair worthy. I fall into myself. I fall into the music. I clench my eyes. Surge through Bach's three movements. I can see Pop's smile. I can see Pop's eyes. Geraldine sounds like angels.

Mel sleeps through it. I am his father.

7:27 P.M. Pop's official time of death.

My son was born one hour and nine minutes prior. My mother died thirty-five minutes before that. I was born.

And Geraldine sings.

Be Longing

STACIA L. BROWN

THERE WAS A METEOR SHOWER the night my mother, my father, and I left D.C. for my grandfather's funeral. I barely knew him, but it made sense to mourn him. I'd always kept him in a mental snow globe. When I shook him from the recesses of my mind, a flurry of rumors swirled up and clouded him: daytime drunkard. Acid-addled adulterer. Hapless heroin addict. Beguiler and beater of wives. But when the accusations settled all around him, I could see him standing on stable ground—the most stable ground a girl with parents like mine could grope for.

My mother's mother was one of the many women my grandfather bewitched and left behind. What little I knew of him I'd culled, in part, from her epithets, tossed bitterly about like paint splashes. Gramsy made anyone within earshot her canvas. But somehow, her artful assassination of his character never really stuck to me. I'd never seen him nod out on a street corner in three-day-old clothes. I'd never seen him hit anyone, let alone one of his women. I hadn't seen him do much of anything, and I loved him the more for that.

I saw him as *somebody's* granddaddy—even though he'd never acted as mine. And he was a hip granddad. The kind who wore Kangol hats slightly askew. The kind who talked around the toothpick jutting from the corner of his smirking lips. The kind who bopped around town with a jazz-infused swagger.

Sometimes absence is the only fertile soil for fondness. That's just a little truism I've picked up in dealing with my parents.

LELETI AND JOHN WERE HIPSTERS before there was a clever name for them. Their matching uniforms of obscure rock band T-shirts, jeans with ripped knees, and black Converse All-Stars magnetized them. It was love, pretentious and distant, at first sight. Most people familiar with their work—her art and his prose—feel compelled to correct me when I call them hipsters. "Not hip-*sters*," the overzealous insist, "hip-*pies*."

See, people seem to think my parents are pop culture pioneers or manifesto makers or close personal friends with Joni Mitchell and Ravi Shankar or some such. I suppose they look the part—Leleti with her chemical-free hair shimmying around her shoulders and John with his gray, elbow-length dreadlocks effervescing their sandalwood essences. Leleti with henna patterning her palms, a Black Power fist tattooed on the back of her shoulder, and John with his thick black eyeglass frames, worn only before the semi-well-attended readings of his semipolitical prose.

But no. I'm sure there *were* Black hippies. I'm sure there were politically charged pacifists who handed white daisies to Black Panthers and protested the war and spelled *America* with a *k* and attended Woodstock to hear acts other than Hendrix and pressed their hair with straightening combs and parted it down the middle. My parents were children when all that was happening. No, the seventies were more than half over when they met, and they were indifferent to anything approaching revolution. They were self-absorbed and obnoxiously hip, and they were obsessed with exile.

D.C. had been deliciously dark when we left it. The sky

had a way of blackening over the country's capital that made me superconscious that its complicated streets had been designed by a Black man. It'd been awhile since I'd seen those skies. I'd been boycotting visits to Leleti and John, until I got that one-line e-mail from Leleti three nights before. "Daddy died" was all it said.

I counted five falling stars before we hit Breezewood. I didn't wish on any of them, even though there are a million things I could've wished for—not least of which was a new name. It's difficult to be Black and named Anouk. (It's difficult to be *Black*, but that's hardly a revelation now, is it?)

I'm not sure my grandfather ever knew my name. I may have been just that vague to him. He always referred to me as "the baby"—Leleti's baby, born before she and my father were wed.

I was conceived in '78, during my parents' first trip to Amsterdam. Anouk was the name of the newborn in the family of their study-abroad hosts. I am told that she was a redhead with pinches of paprika baked into her cheeks and eyes like the shorn grass of early spring. I am told that often.

Leleti and John were always fondly reminiscing about the various facets of my conception.

I can't help but wonder if that would've been the case if Leleti had been raised by my grandfather. I wonder if he would've been the type to blurt out, "Don't nobody wanna hear all that! Keep yo' bed-talk in the bedroom." I like to think he would've been. *I'm* definitely the type, and that's gotta come from *somewhere*.

It's the *somewhere* that seems to hold all the import when loved ones are absentee. Anything—any untraceable trait or unsolved enigma—can reside in the *somewhere*, the wherever-they-are when they aren't with you. My grandfather was a shadow whose form was flattened under the cellophane in the photo albums no one ever pulled out to admire.

His name was Evan Garde, and *"he was avant-garde."* That was what Leleti always said about him.

LELETI AND JOHN DIDN'T PLAN for me. Leleti and John don't do much planning. They tell themselves they're like tumbleweed, tossed wheresoever the wind blows. But they're trendy nomads, looking to Fodor's guides and the travel sections of the *Detroit Free Press,* the *Washington Post,* and the *New York Times* for potential relocation spots. We'd lived in the Delta, New Orleans, Molokai, Nice, Baltimore, and Vegas by the time I was ten, bunking with pen pals and hostel-hopping much of the time. Whenever I didn't know the language, they'd home-school me. Wherever English was spoken, they'd enroll me at the nearest public school and gripe every afternoon about all the things the System wasn't teaching me. Even back then they were totally ostentatious, prattling on about the genius of Basquiat when I brought home finger paintings in the first grade.

For the first six years of my life, our family portraits were snapshots of Leleti and John smoking cloves and leaning wanly against the abandoned stone and brick architecture of random international cities. My expression always lingered somewhere between distress and hope. I'd be hovering around their knees, the top of my head a few feet below their swanky orbit, staring straight into the self-timed camera, while they cast their eyes anywhere but.

On occasion, their photography won an award or one of John's travel essays scored a grant, and we'd live on that, following its stipulations to the next city or town. I suppose they thought they were bestowing the greatest of gifts, living nomadically, raising me as they wished they'd been raised, as they still seemed to be raising themselves.

But on more instances than I can enumerate, I'd shake the

Evan Garde snow globe in my mind and imagine a home where a man with skin the color of pinecones, for all his foibles, managed to hold down a factory job most days and find his way back to his house most nights. His was a nice house. Modest. Two floors and a basement with stacks of books and bottles of water where he'd lock himself in for days to detox. Evan seemed like the type of man who knew how to get his mind right when he needed to. I imagined him consistent, whether bingeing or sober, philandering or faithful.

THE BELTWAY was usually smooth along I-70 before the Pennsylvania Turnpike, but not in Leleti and John's emerald Cooper import. It wasn't at all like the new Minis. There wasn't any gloss in the finish. It hadn't come fully loaded with the option of a Union Jack embossed on the hood. It took ratty, thin, doughnut tires, and it had a semirusted bike rack melded to the fender. His blue mountain bike and her basketed and tasseled Huffy Cruiser weighed down the back end of the rickety antique. I hated embarking on any journey with them that couldn't be ended in half an hour. All their road snacks were vegan. The three muffins in the brown paper bag beside me weighed seven pounds.

"Leleti, I need to be back in Seattle by Monday," I said firmly, watching the sky.

"Yes, Anouk, you've mentioned that twice now," John retorted, watching the road.

"Have I?" Even if I'd known that, I couldn't have helped it. Leleti and John have no concept of chronos. Sometimes, you've got to give them a nudge or twelve.

"If you're so hung up on a schedule, why didn't you drive yourself?" Leleti always pronounced *schedule* the British way. It really pissed me off.

"You know why."

I was up to my ears in college loan debt and I couldn't afford to keep a car in Seattle. I'd sold mine before starting the two-year poetry M.F.A. program in Seattle that Leleti and John called "soul-sucking and pointless" when I showed them my acceptance letter.

They'd been painting at the time, painting in matching denim overalls, though the denim was barely visible under the broad splats of olive and orange paint soaking into it. They'd been laughing and kissing and flicking the excess from their brushes onto each other. I'd used my key to get in, instead of knocking. They don't like it when I do that. They say it's because they value their privacy and because there are some things they'd just rather I didn't interrupt. Whenever they say that, I ask them, "When am I *not* interrupting?" And while that's the point in the conversation where most parents would be reassuring and say something like "Of course you're not a burden! We love you! Drop by anytime!" even if they didn't mean it, Leleti and John tend to keep quiet when I ask them that.

That day, in response to their silence, I remember being tired. I remember staring down at the letter, then back up at them. I remember it taking only a second to decide I wouldn't be back to see them for at least two years.

This trip didn't count. This wasn't about them. This was about them being a means to an end. I wanted them to ferry me to family who wouldn't try to section me out of their lives with an invisible velvet rope.

Sometimes I think Leleti chose John to compensate for there being so little Evan in her upbringing. His absence made her long for the ability to exclude. She wanted someone she could gather to herself, someone who wouldn't mind shutting everyone and everything else out in order to have her. John was just that kind of guy. When he met her, his only attachments in the world were to his parents, and he was all too happy to sever those ties for the promise of a life with Leleti.

Leleti and John met on a Black college campus in 1976. His parents were prerevolutionaries—SNCCers and Panthers before there were SNCCers and Panthers—who'd attended Tuskegee and Bethune-Cookman. Gramsy, who'd put herself through college in the sixties just after Leleti was born, was just a firm advocate of a good Black education. So of course they wanted Howard University for their children, because it was touted as the best historically Black college in the country and thus the only suitable choice for the second-generation nationalists they were trying to groom. Neither Leleti nor John seemed to appreciate these parental desires. Leleti had her heart set on expatriation. John was less interested in Howard or Morehouse or Meharry than in Oxford or the Sorbonne or the Peace Corps.

Their mothers would have no such scheming. Leleti's was hoping that the child would find a husband at Howard, a man "as fine and fearless as Huey Newton—but dipped in a much darker chocolate." John's mama had already tried to arrange his marriage to a girl John's father represented at an arraignment for her participation in a violent civil rights protest.

Later, when Gramsy finally met John's mom, the two could do nothing but cluck and complain about the inauspicious match over separate soul food dinners.

By their sophomore year Leleti and John were sipping imported beer in Adams Morgan and staying on for the second and third sets of way-past-campus-curfew performances. Their all-time favorite band was called The Liberia Kightlinger Trio, fronted by a curvy woman so dark that only her crimson nails on the microphone distinguished her from the darkness in the seedy, smoke-filled dives she played. According to them, Liberia Kightlinger, with her Afro wide as an LP and her closed eyelids hiding iridescent sclera and indigo irises, played plenty of instruments but was best known for the sitar. On particularly maudlin numbers, she would strum a mandolin with bare, raw fingers and Leleti and John would hold their breath, letting whatever Liberia felt soak into them like rain.

After the sets, they'd buy her drinks and they came to be known as her "groupie couple." She told them about Brazil and how it was just as color-conscious as America, so they'd do well to concentrate their travels elsewhere, when they finally got around to the sojourn.

THE MINI took the broad turnpike curves sharper than most modern vehicles would have. John was a notorious speeder. It was one of his unspoken contradictions. He was the picture of calm, slow to react, quick to soothe—well, quick to soothe Leleti, anyway—and yet here he was careening rather recklessly up the highway, randomly swerving and hitting his brakes, oblivious to the strain it may have been putting on his passengers. Whenever we approached a turn, and I wasn't holding on to the pocket on the back of Leleti's seat, I was tossed to, fro, and onto the floor. I wanted to yell something, but I couldn't figure out what.

"Watch it!" maybe?

Another option: "Um, hi. This is your daughter. Precious cargo? Yeah, this is the third time you've knocked me onto the floor."

Or the obvious but never voiced: "You really just don't care, do you?"

D'Angelo's cover of "Girl, You Need a Change of Mind" was blaring through my headphones, so I was probably too loud when I called out, "Did anybody ever get in touch with Gramsy to tell her Evan died?"

I knew the mention of Gramsy had the potential to make things even tenser between Leleti, John, and me, but I couldn't help it. Gramsy had been away on a weeklong retreat in the mountains when Leleti got the news. No wi-fi, room phones, or television were allowed up there. It was perfectly understandable that she hadn't found out about Evan yet. But I still thought it was weird that we were off laying her once-love to rest and she had no idea he wasn't still out here, vaguely alive, as she'd last remembered him.

John gave Leleti's arm a little squeeze as she pinched the bridge of her nose and sighingly answered, "No, Anouk. She still doesn't know."

WHEN I WAS LITTLE, I remember staring at one of Liberia Kightlinger's album covers. In the photograph, she was wearing a psychedelic minidress—violet and orange and electric blue. Her thick legs were gapped, forming an upside-down V, and four-inch heels cradled and lifted her slender feet. She stood at the center of a near-empty dance floor, where three or four dancers shimmied under a massive strobe light. Oblivious to the disco vibe of it all, Liberia Kightlinger leaned down to bang her flat palm against the djimbe drum positioned between her calves.

I thought Liberia Kightlinger was the type of woman who might've caught Evan Garde's fancy. Sometimes I watched him strut into the background of that album cover, walking through the door behind her and wrapping his thumb and forefinger around her tiny wrist. I thought of him pulling her away from the drum and toward the edge of the dance floor. It was the kind of move I thought he might've pulled with any of his children's moms. Before a single song had a chance to finish playing, Liberia was smitten, pressing her back into Evan's broad chest, grazing her fingers over his downy arms as they folded themselves around her waist. He'd grin and nestle his stubbled chin on her shoulder. But when I'd lean in closer to look at this animated scene, Liberia's face would start to shine with tears, anticipating the heartbreak that usually followed Evan's arrival.

In his prime, Evan was the kind of womanizer for whom demurring seemed entirely overrated. He didn't bother with the hard-to-get chicks . . . but then again, there weren't many women he considered hard to get. He'd sired six children by the time he was thirty-four to a myriad of mothers. When he slowed down, settling in with a third and final wife around the time he turned forty, he had two more. Restraint was a concept he'd learn in old age.

"WILL WE BE STOPPING anytime soon?" I wondered.

"We need to make it up the road apace, Anouk," John calmly pointed out.

"I realize that, John, but we've passed at least six rest stops—even Breezewood. We *always* stop in Breezewood."

At night, Breezewood was dazzlingly neon, and most of the fast-food eateries popular in every region of the U.S. (Pizza Hut. Domino's. Starbucks. KFC. McDonald's and Burger King. Krispy Kreme. Taco Bell) were crammed into the space of a half mile. I liked the homogenized nature of it all, how unremarkable the choices were, how man-made the landscape. Breezewood made more sense to me than Sicily or Senegal because it was entirely beyond exoticism and thus held no pull for my parents. Strange, but I felt closer to them there. Vegan though they were, they'd always pull into the visitors' center parking lot and take me to Dairy Queen. They'd slide into a booth on the long seat opposite me and watch sort of curiously as I ate an Oreo blizzard. This was the only ritual we shared, the only thing I did that was certain to hold their attention. I relished it, even if all they were thinking behind their wrinkled noses and unreadable smiles was: This girl is nothing like us.

I bet they'd decided, long before I got there, that this time they'd unceremoniously end the whole charade, that watching me eat ice cream wasn't fascinating at all, that my being nothing like them was really nothing to celebrate.

JOHN GLANCED AT ME in the rearview mirror. "Anouk, whatever you want to stop for I'm pretty sure you can hold in."

I was tired of holding things in. But he was right. We'd left our Dairy Queen behind hours ago, I didn't have to pee, and as long as the two-ton muffins beside me remained untouched, I wasn't going to starve. As usual, my wishes held no urgency. I slumped into the space behind Leleti and turned my iPod up to maximum volume.

ON THE FEW OCCASIONS WHEN I *had* seen Evan Garde, he tended to regard my mother with starry eyes, like dewy blankets of night pinpricked with sparkles. That night never cast its cover on me. If he looked at me at all, it was an afterthought. I'd never gotten more than a glance, a wry smile, a stray question here or there for which he'd never awaited my answer. I laid eyes on him in person four times. I was seven the first time, then twelve, then sixteen, and then there was just last summer. I was twenty-five.

That last visit was the one where it began to sink in that access to my grandfather's other family—Wife Three and their two children (three years older and six years younger than I)—may have been something I desperately needed. I was nothing like Leleti and John. Aside from that year in middle school when I shaved one side of my head and dyed the other side platinum blond and listened to nothing but David Bowie, there's been little evidence that any of their traits have rubbed off on me. I had to resemble someone. I might've eerily resembled one of Evan's other offspring, but how would I have known it? Growing up, Leleti had spent a little time with a few of her siblings here and there, but she hadn't kept it up into adulthood. By the time I was born, she rarely talked about them, and visits were even more scarce, so it was easy to forget she had brothers and sisters at all. Maybe their absence was as detrimental as iron deficiency. Now my relationship with them was anemic.

Evan's newest nuclear family was a cluster of strangers. But last summer, sitting in the living room, sipping cold Pepsi from thick glass bottles and listening to them talk eagerly, expectantly to Leleti, they were also family. Especially Evan, because during that visit, for the first time ever, he and I locked eyes.

"Excuse me," he said every few minutes, staring full on at me. "This here nicotine's callin' my name."

I grinned like an idiot by way of response, flummoxed that he'd spoken directly to me at all.

He returned just moments later, his crisp plaid shirt smelling of Wisk and lawn and Marlboros. This happened a few times. He'd look at me, excuse himself, and head out back for a smoke. Then he'd come back just in time to latch on to the end of an anecdote his wife was telling Leleti. When Leleti laughed, so did he, hearty and hopeful. He might have even interjected something, though I can't remember any specific thing he said. I only know that every time he spoke, I laughed like I was listening to stand-up. And then he'd look over at me and I'd catch a constellation shimmering in his dark eyes. I saw the gleam of Cassiopeia as he grinned sheepishly and said only to me, "Pardon me. I'm 'bout to go on out for a cig."

I was surprised at how much I wanted to follow him then. I didn't. I sat close to Leleti instead, silently clasping the cold curves of the soda bottle, listening to Leleti talk to all these people as though she really knew them.

"Wonder what happened to Filene," she mused.

"Giiiiirl," one of her sisters interjected, and the rest of her family would bring twenty years of scandal up-to-date in all of fifteen minutes.

My twenty-year-old uncle, Devin, was the only person who stopped in the middle of all the clamor to notice me. "She's pretty," he said, audibly but also to himself, since no one responded. I think I should've said thank you. I should've said *something* to let him know I was grateful for the acknowledgment. Or I could've reciprocated his observation with one of my own. Devin was handsome and magnanimous, secretive and modestly brilliant. I'd seen the seeds of that when he was a little boy, and I had an anecdote to prove it. Maybe if I'd shared it, he would've stuck around instead of flipping up the hood on his Central Michigan sweatshirt, excusing himself from the chatter, and bounding out the front door.

Evan would be back by the end of family gossip session and he'd laugh and say something like, "Sho' did!" I'd giggle at his exclamation until they all turned quizzical eyes on me and I realized I was the outsider.

THE CAR JERKED and tossed me back and forth against a hard spring jutting through the worn leather seat. John was stroking

Leleti's hair as she hummed absently and turned her head to the window so he wouldn't coo over her tears.

I was still the outsider.

Sighing and lifting one muff from my ear, I asked, "Are you okay up there, Leleti?"

"She's fine," John commented, quietly. "How about you? How are you holding up?" I saw him clench his jaw, like it was an effort to ask. Just two days before, John called to convince me to stay in Seattle. When I picked up the phone, he just launched into a kind of breathless monologue about the cost of cross-country travel and the days of class I might have to miss before ending, flustered, with "I just—I just think it would be best for you to stay on at school."

Leleti pulled her gaze from the window and stared at the side of her husband's face. "She didn't really know him," she answered.

John shot her a look and then fixed his gaze a hundred feet ahead at the sharp curl of the road. I don't know why I expected him to defend me against that comment, but I did. I'd always secretly figured that if I had any shot at all at penetrating their Teflon exclusivity, I'd find my inroad in John. He was the quieter of the two, and when you got him alone, he'd sometimes betray some small interest in the things you had to say. The right lane would end soon, up where John's eyes were cast, but he made no move to veer into the left one. I guess he figured he didn't have to. It was the middle of the night. We were alone out there.

I shrugged, feigning nonchalance and failing. "That's true, Leleti. I didn't." I let the earphone snap back to my ear.

THE PROBLEM with hipsterism, other than its insistence on glorifying the obscure, is the unwritten rule that hipsters must always be moody and brooding and misunderstood. The problem with being raised by hipsters is that they're incapable of overcoming their self-absorption long enough to parent.

Leleti and John were like this single, fused, impenetrable entity. They weren't so much like a mother and father as they were like older twin siblings with a secret language and secret hopes and secret plans. I think they were truly elated when I turned eighteen. I moved right out. They didn't ask where I was going. They weren't the kind of parents who followed you to orientation to make sure you weren't headed to a party school. They were the kind who just handed over their tax information for FAFSA and told you you were on your own.

And you were.

We rode through all of the Alleghenys in silence. Leleti dozed off as we neared the end of the turnpike, and John lifted a lock of her hair, twirling it absently around his finger.

He began to hum a song that of course I couldn't recognize. It was mid-tempo and minor, more melancholy than the music I remembered them listening to. He hummed it through to the end, and the more notes he revealed, the more familiar the melody became. I knew it somehow, suddenly. I felt eager then but decided not to say anything. I joined in, harmonizing the higher notes, hoping he couldn't hear. But as soon as I began, John gave a little start and glanced back. I wasn't looking in his direction when he did, and he turned back to the road, the corner of his mouth slightly upturned then.

"Huh," he exhaled when our song ended. "Huh," he repeated, bemused. He turned his head again and parted his lips. Then Leleti stirred in front of me and John frowned, facing forward.

I'm not sure when I dozed off, but when I finally woke up, we were in Albion and Leleti was at the wheel. John sat sleeping in front of me.

It was still dark when we arrived in Albion, but first light would likely be creeping over the horizon in one or two hours. I was surprised to find Evan's house bursting with gilded light and grateful laughter at four in the morning. Family milled inside, passing the sheer-curtained windows. Friends gathered on the side of the place, in front of the garage, passing bottles of liquor and crass jokes they'd first heard from Evan.

Tan siding, kelly green shutters, brick steps. This was the kind of warm, solid house that forgave and welcomed, accepted and embraced. Relief swept over my arms, legs, and neck, raising the fine hairs there. This was a good place for a man to have died.

I was the first to open my car door. Leleti and John didn't follow. I slammed the door behind me, and John stirred in his squeaky bucket seat. "John?" Leleti tearfully ventured. He went from zero to attentive in about a nanosecond, and they sat staring moonily at each other for longer than I cared to watch. It was cold. I wanted to go in. But I didn't know these people well enough to go in before Leleti did.

I looked back into the Cooper. John rocked Leleti in his arms, sort of shushing and composing her. I didn't have time for all that. I went to the door and knocked.

Uncle Devin opened it. His face, tear-stained and bright, sort of trembled when he saw me. I pulled him into a hug before I had time to think better of it. Strange that under any other circumstances, I would've second-guessed wrapping my arms around him. Strange how quickly death can close the gaps of estrangement.

"You okay?" he asked.

I nodded over his shoulder. "You?"

He sucked in a deep breath and didn't answer. I wanted to say something comforting. Instead, I pulled back, squeezed his arm, and brushed by him.

There were so many introductions, so many opportunities for people I didn't know to explain, "This is Evan's oldest grandchild. Leleti's baby."

Friends of the friends of Evan's family were clasping my hand between both of theirs, cooing their condolences for my loss.

I was an automaton, fixed with a polite permasmile, echoing small hellos.

"Now, which one is Leleti?"

This went on for at least a half hour. Even now I can't remember when Leleti and John came in (or if they did at all). I remember the tipsy anecdotes carried from room to room on a nicotine mist and how tightly they all hugged me, dozens of people whose names I still don't know, people who knew Evan longer and better than I realized possible. They enveloped me, these neighbors and friends and coworkers. I remember how, looking at them and feigning a calm resignation, I started to bawl. I cried until I was possessed, cried until I was exorcised. And then Wife Three, whose name was Dorothy, led me to the kitchen.

I have always loved repasts. Repasts are where I try to get the hollowing of a good cry to fill with folks' offerings of food. I've never succeeded, but it's always a nice redirection of effort.

EVAN'S FAMILY CHURCH was small and genial, just like the town itself. Every Black person in Albion seemed to have shuffled in and settled themselves into the long, crimson-cushioned pews. Most of them had stopped off to view his body. Not many wept. Evan's chrome casket was lined with lavender velvet and stretched out just under the pulpit at the front of the sanctuary.

I sat about five rows behind my parents and waited. I'm still not sure what for. Maybe I expected Leleti and John to make spectacles of themselves by waving the stalks of sandalwood incense to cleanse the air of sorrow or attempting to hum one of Liberia Kightlinger's wordless dirges.

A convoy of acquaintances marched to the microphone, saying the kinds of flat and flattering things that are always said at funerals. No one mentioned Evan's addictions. I was glad that there was such willingness to recuse in a room where so many could choose to indict.

I didn't think I'd cry, but I did. It was Uncle Devin who'd caused it. I watched him throughout the eulogy, bravely sucking in such large gusts of air. He was trying to be the kind of man his father was, a man whose grief was complicated and quiet and tearless. But I saw only the little boy who'd tagged along to visit me one summer, on a day trip with his parents, and proudly emptied his pockets of change, standing in front of me. He let his little six-year-old fists hover over my open twelve-year-old palms before opening his hands and letting the coins fall. As I caught them, he declared, "Here's a little money for you. You know, because that's what uncles are supposed to do." I wanted to reach up and rub his head that day—like I was the Wally to his Beave or something. He was vulnerable and earnest then, so tiny and so deliberate.

Holding composure would be impossible for him now.

He sobbed, his head thrown back in a kind of agony that couldn't exist on its own. We were all pulled into it. *I* was pulled into it, the unrelenting echo of vacancy. His mother pulled him close, but her gesture didn't quiet him. Her embrace freed him to really convulse, and she held him, squaring her shoulders.

I wondered if I'd cry that way when my own parents died.

But it was impossible for me to predict. Hotter tears coursed over the ones already cooling on my cheeks.

When the service ended, I saw Uncle Devin in front of the church, face awash in mourning, and I tried pressing toward him. The crowd was too thick. The closer I inched, the more the gap between us widened with well-intentioned strangers. I wanted to say that I loved him, because I never had before. I wanted to insulate him from the overabundance of condolences he wasn't composed enough yet to hear. But before I got to him, he was herded into the limousine, the last of Evan's immediate family to enter, and with his exit, the rest of us rushed to our cars to join the processional to the cemetery.

I remember standing frozen for a moment, almost shocked by the swiftness with which I'd ended up alone in the parking lot. Everyone had cleared out without noticing me, trembling, planted on the fringe of the asphalt.

Leleti and John were already in the Mini when I finally found them. I thought they'd make a snide remark about my having taken so long getting back to the car, but when I crawled clumsily into the backseat, John stayed still. The engine wasn't even running. Leleti's tears were slowly drying, and John and I listened as her clipped breaths grew steady. The last car of the processional disappeared down a street at the end of the block.

Leleti knew Albion well, even though she'd never lived there. Without announcement or ceremony—maybe without even admitting it to herself—she'd made her father's life an ongoing study. Learning the names of the streets he'd run and the haunts he'd frequented was a big part of her cherished firsthand knowledge about him. I knew she'd have no problem finding the gravesite. Still, I wondered why we had let the group drift into the early-afternoon haze. I wondered why none of her siblings had waited for us and if anyone would miss us when they arrived at Evan's interment.

The swell of closeness I'd felt just the night before receded in the ghostly still of the parking lot and I was grateful for the steady drone of Leleti's breathing, settled by the occasional sigh John released into the silence. I stared at their hands, clasped atop the arm rest, and before long, Leleti threaded her fingers through John's and nodded. He unknit their hands and started the ignition, peeling across the lot with a jolt.

WHEN WE GOT THERE, the minister was finishing his commitment of Evan's body to the ground. Ash to ash. I thought of the nicotine Evan claimed was calling him, the last time I'd seen him alive. I thought of him existing among cigarette cinders, some of which may have once been his own. Evan knew quite a few of the folks buried out here. Albion legend had it that Evan was the only brother in town brave enough to spend whole nights in the cemetery. He'd passed out by his older sister's grave a few times. On one or two other occasions, it was said that he'd deliberately camped there to spare his wife and kids the sight of him haggard and high.

After the congregants dropped their white roses into the grave, they ambled on by Dorothy and Devin and Evan's other, older children, as interchangeable to me as members in a Greek chorus, sitting in metal folding chairs in the first row of the tented interment, offering their last, pat expressions of sympathy.

We didn't even bother to approach the fray or look for extra roses to toss into the ditch. We stood behind it all, watching the crowd thin, watching everyone resignedly walk away.

Leleti and John aren't joiners. It occurred to me then that neither am I.

We meandered back to the Mini and climbed in without saying a thing to one another. John pumped the gas pedal, trying to get the engine to turn over. It wouldn't start. Though I'm certain the last few straggling cars must've noticed that we'd stalled, no one asked, before leaving, if we needed a jump.

When we resigned ourselves to the reality that the car wouldn't start without a call to AAA, the three of us climbed back out of it, but not before Leleti pulled two stalks of sandalwood incense from the glove compartment. We trudged through the soft, muddy grass, back to Evan's open grave. When we were alone, we walked up to the chasm where my grandfather lay and all leaned forward to look, together. Leleti dropped to her hands and knees and just stared and stared and stared.

John pulled out his lighter and burned the tips of the incense orange, then joined his wife on the ground. They waved the stalks around themselves and over the grave, while I stood a few feet off and watched.

"I don't know why I love you," I started to sing, softly, confusedly. "I don't know why. I love you. . . ."

"I don't know why I love you," John joined in. "But I love you."

"Always treat me like a fool. Kick me when I'm down— that's your rule . . ."

Stevie Wonder. He was one of the few mainstream artists Leleti and John played, and this was their favorite of his songs. They used to sing it to me before bed.

I folded my arms around my chest and hugged myself, harmonizing lowly. Neither of my parents turned to acknowledge me, but they didn't have to. It was enough that they'd helped me sing.

Why We Jump

WILLIAM HENRY LEWIS

for Dieudonne

WHEN LYNETTE SIMMONS sees Samuel Cates for the first time in twenty-five years, she is not sure if it is the Mr. Cates she remembers. She's on the train home, Green Line to Columbia Heights, when she sees him. He stands facing the darkness of the Metro tunnel, rushing past the double door windows. He fidgets, clutches his bag, shifts his weight, anxious for the next station. When he lifts his head to look at the reflection of the people in the car, she sees his face. Lynette recognizes the small ears and the thin, carefully kept mustache. Mr. Cates, the man who, when she was twelve, took a running leap from the floor above her apartment and crashed through the deck roof her daddy had just built. The apartments were terraced: The Simmonses' family-size apartment on the fourth floor pushed beyond the outer wall of the fifth floor, where a two-foot ledge jutted out from the large windows of Mr. Cates's single-unit apartment. Talk got around the building that he was trying to make it to the alley, five floors down. That meant a talented leap past the Simmonses' small deck, and though he took to it as if it were his only way out, he never made it. Sammy Cates, whom she hasn't seen since.

He gets off at L'Enfant Plaza station. Before reasoning on the wisdom of it, she follows him as he heads for the Blue Line. Mr. Cates carries a faded Washington Bullets bag under his arm as he rides the escalator from the platform. His wool blazer looks tailored, recently pressed, with whalebone buttons. The back of his shirt collar—for that's all she can see after he has turned from her—is clean but frayed. Too much bleach, she thinks to herself. As he rises, she holds back, takes notice of his shirt collar, blazer, then his pressed, well-worn khakis and running shoes.

She eases onto a bench, rests her grocery bags, catches her breath before she decides to proceed. For a moment she's disturbed: She feels unsettled in having seen him but doesn't know why. She wants to feel that seeing Mr. Cates is a sign—a *revelation,* as folks at church might call it; an *incarnation,* as she'd like to call it—but of what? There are gaps and voids in how she has imagined him. She can't abide by what has slipped her mind for so long, and in this forgetfulness sits herself down longer than she would like. Lynette Simmons gets this way when the what-should-be of her life clashes with the what-is. Like when she finds herself frozen at the breakfast table, spoon in hand, cereal in the bowl, no milk in the fridge. But she has three cartons of juice, five boxes of cake mix, enough canned beans for ten meals—supplies that a fixed shopping list provides. Everything but milk, which, because she always buys it, she leaves off the list, along with tampons and coffee.

SHE REMEMBERS THAT DAY, twenty-five years ago, as a hot one. Most of the days she recalls from childhood were hot, when sweat came from double dutch and bicycle races, when she heard the off-key warble of the ice cream truck more often than the wail of sirens. If she ever explains that day to anyone, she knows she would start with the heat; the day was hotter than most she remembers. It was the heat that made folks crazy: Kids dropping bricks onto Military Road from the Sixteenth Street overpass, rich White folks cursing at each other on the sidewalk in Georgetown. The police were everywhere, it seemed, busy with arresting someone or wanting to. It was hot all over D.C., even up on Meridian Hill, where a breeze might catch you by surprise.

The Orioles game had just gone off the air. Her father was turning ribs on the grill. Her mother had been out for cigarettes and beer to replace what Lynette's father and her uncle Norman had already drunk. Lynette was mixing instant ice tea in the kitchen. Auntie Berthine, from across the hall—more close friend than blood aunt—was over to visit, along with her cousin, Odessa, from down the street. When Berthine wasn't teasing Lynette's father about his sorry Orioles, she was on Lynette about how much she didn't carry herself like the girl she was supposed to be. When her mother wasn't around, Berthine and Odessa took turns working their finishing-school ideals into Lynette. They called it babysitting. On that day they were sitting on the deck like two doves—pretty dark eyes and big breasts on the both of them. They worked the dozens on Lynette's father while he looked after the ribs and Uncle Norman finished off the beer.

Lynette was bringing the pitcher of ice tea out to the deck when she heard heavy footsteps running above their living room ceiling, two heavy steps toward the outside wall, and then down came Mr. Samuel Cates, through the green deck roof and right onto her father's lounger.

All of them looked to the hole in the roof first. Through that hole, Lynette could see the top of the window of Mr. Cates's apartment. He didn't have a deck like the Simmonses' apartment, just a small ledge and a railing.

Then they looked to Mr. Cates. The pitcher tipped in Lynette's hands as she looked him over, and she spilled ice tea down her front before dropping the pitcher. It broke, but no one seemed to care about that.

Blood trickled from the top of Mr. Cates's head to his temple. He kept his hair cut close to the skin, and that made the gash in his head look larger than it really was. Lynette had already made a hobby of observing Samuel Cates. In her little girl's mind, it was spying; that was more exciting. She might catch a glimpse of him in the laundry room of the building, or standing on the elevator with her mother in between them, she would crane her head ever so slightly to stare at his hands. His fingernails were pristinely kept. Her daddy's carried thin lines of dirt nearly every day other than Sunday.

She mostly saw Mr. Cates from behind, awkwardly backing onto the elevator to avoid eye contact, or rushing out of the building and down the street; he was always in a hurry. But now he was right in front of Lynette. Her mother wasn't there to scold her for staring. It seemed to her that she never had a chance to look at anyone for long. But now he was in the middle of her deck, dazed and bleeding. He was wearing a tan suitcoat and pants, a nice tie to match, though the collar of his shirt was red with blood. But right then none of that seemed strange to her.

BY THE TIME Lynette rises from the bench, Mr. Cates is stepping from the escalator to the Blue Line platform. She catches a glimpse of his black socks and running shoes. Those surprise her, the running shoes. More than surprised, she's curious. She heads for the Blue Line.

For years she had imagined him in worsted wool slacks and loafers. She deduces that the running shoes support all the walking he must do from place to place. He doesn't own a car;

it's been years since he stopped driving. She decided this a long while back. She imagined he didn't drive because he is a man who distracts easily, making esoteric the mundane of what's around him: faulty green light, flickering rather than solid; road construction sign, bent so that it reads SLOW MEN; flurry of pigeons across the reflection of a sedan's tinted windows; the wide eyes of four children in a bus, staring at the pigeons; a fifth child, two seats back, fascinated with a feather the flurry has cast to the wind. No, driving would be too risky for Samuel Cates. He'd be watching that feather or absorbed with the child, watching the feather, and sideswipe somebody's car. Then he'd have to deal with that. She's certain he's cut out the risk of accidents he can't afford or attention he'd rather not face.

MR. CATES LAY THERE on the deck, blood staining his shirt collar. But as red as that collar got, no one moved. Lynette remembers how still everyone became. Except for her father, who was cursing into the alley. Mr. Cates's surprise landing had bounced the ribs from the grill into a Dumpster below. Mr. Simmons looked back to Lynette and then glared at Mr. Cates, who wasn't focused on much of anything. Her father threw the grill fork into the alley, and they heard it clatter in the Dumpster.

That's when it looked like Mr. Cates suddenly knew where he was. He rubbed his head. Blood smeared over half his face. For a moment his eyes got big and then rolled back. He shook himself, got his face straight, and said, "I'm sorry."

Berthine began laughing so hard that she fell back in her chair. Then Norman and Odessa busted out laughing. Lynette knew that if her mother was there, no one would be laughing. Avis Simmons was a graceful, serious woman, the kind who, Lynette felt, never did the wrong thing.

She knew laughing was the wrong thing. She was a quiet girl, a child who would get called out by her teacher for getting lost in pictures in her math book more so than the math or the dove-shaped birthmark on the neck of the girl who sat next to her. She would hear the teacher's voice from far off: *Lynette Simmons, close your mouth before a fly moves in!* At recess and lunch, kids would stare at her and mock her openmouthed fascination with things they had missed. She wished she could say something to stop Berthine and the rest from laughing, but Berthine had a sharp tongue that Lynette did not want to challenge.

Lynette's father went to help Mr. Cates. "Sammy Cates! What's in your mind, bustin' up my damn roof like that?"

Mr. Cates didn't answer.

"I just put the damn thing on this past April!" her father was saying, "And look at my chair! How am I gonna fix that?"

Uncle Norman was saying, "How we gonna eat?"

Mr. Cates loosened his tie. He was looking at Lynette, and she was reminded of the stares she received from the men at the bus stop on Georgia Avenue, the way they looked her up and down with tight-lipped smiles, feeling something she did not. They weren't like the boys her age, who were too busy rubbernecking at titties to notice anything special about her. Though his lips were tight, Mr. Cates's stare was different.

Berthine, who was watching this exchange, hooted to Lynette, "Honey, Sammy Cates ain't looking at nothing you ain't even growed yet!" Lynette laughed a little, feeling some tingle there, on the skin of her chest, or maybe just inside, because more than embarrassment or fear, she felt warm with fascination.

She wondered if he knew who she was. There were times when she felt that only her mother and Berthine noticed her, and that was usually to criticize. Surely Mr. Cates had noticed her in the laundry room, on the elevator, or playing in the courtyard of the building.

Now, on her deck, Mr. Cates smiled at Lynette—gently, a pastor's smile—as if he could just smile away her troubles. She thinks now how odd that was: him sitting there, bruised and bleeding, looking certain that everything would work out. She smiled back, but then his face got serious, like he was apologizing again.

THE BLUE LINE HEADS to Springfield. Samuel Cates stands facing the subway door. Lynette sits where she can study his profile. He stoops more than stands. He reminds her of Everton Fox, the weatherman she sometimes catches when she watches the BBC. She's embarrassed that Everton Fox comes to mind—her, a girl from Meridian Hill, Chocolate City born and bred, watching the BBC like some Embassy Row highbrow. If she had a group of Friday-night-at-the-hair-salon girlfriends to trade stories with, she'd tell them, *Everton looks like a filled-out Billy Dee. I know he must love him some ribs and greens . . .* and she'd lean into a friend's hip while they both doubled over, so her TV crush would seem more like girl-talk than fantasy. She smiles for a moment, because she'd like some Fridays to be like that.

But why would Everton Fox come to mind? He's nothing like Mr. Cates—Cates is small-boned and stooped; he has salt-and-pepper hair, with a less satisfied stomach than Fox—and what is she embarrassed about? She can't say for sure.

She puts her grocery bag between her feet. She has just the one now; the meats, ice cream, and milk she left on the bench. She is not sure where Mr. Cates is headed, but it's sure to be far enough for cold foods to spoil. She's particular about such things, how long eggs are out of the fridge, whether potato salad sits in sun or shade. These concerns she's carried from her mother's house, a place where bed sheets were ironed and hair was always pressed, elbows and knees glistened with Vaseline, and children answered with *yes, ma'am* rather than *yeah*. She lives in the same building she grew up in. Sixth floor now instead of fourth. Two bedrooms, with a southern view of downtown. Low-rent high-rise, a few blocks from Malcolm X Park. The city's salary allows her that much. Six floors in Meridian Hill, tallest hill in the city, higher than ten stories near Georgetown. Prime real estate if White folks lived near Brown folks.

Where does Samuel Cates live now? It's just past rush hour on a Friday, so she figures he must be headed home, somewhere along where the Blue Line snakes through Northwest D.C. or Virginia. Or is it north of Georgetown? Does he got it like that? This is a movin'-on-up step she can't reconcile. She has never known what he did for a living, but she also hasn't figured him as a suburban type. She's known folks who moved into Landover, Rockville, Prince George's County, where the cul-de-sacs, condo rows, and ranch styles look like the suburbs, but the people lived it like the best and worst of Southeast D.C. Folks moved out to P. G. County, Bowie, Wheaton when they got their money together or wanted to look like they had money to get together. When Lynette was young, she did not think of Mr. Cates as a man with money. He almost always wore white button-down shirts, no tie, no suit. Sometimes his shirts were wrinkled. On weekends he wore blue button-downs. She saw him in a T-shirt only once. Maybe he managed a store or was an orderly in some clinic. None of that matches up with the Mr. Cates headed into Northwest: That didn't feel right, even when she considers the worsted wool and loafers she has dressed him in for twenty years. Folks don't just up and move from the hood to Georgetown, do they?

But Mr. Cates was always hard to place. He lived alone. He

was a well-groomed man but never wore a suit. No one knew how he paid his rent or could pin down his schedule. When Lynette and her mother would see him, her mother always asked him over for dinner or to visit their church. That was Avis Simmons's way; she didn't like to see people lonely. But each time Mr. Cates would start in with some excuse, his voice trailing off into a mumble that no one could understand.

Lynette used to steal glances as he sorted through his mail at the elevator doors. He had all sorts of mail: cookware catalogs, coupon books, small boxes from music clubs, brightly colored oversize envelopes. Sometimes Lynette would see a stray envelope or catalog on a table or windowsill in the lobby and want to pick it up, but her mother wouldn't allow it.

SAMUEL CATES STARES INTO THE DARK of the Metro tunnel. Lynette watches his face for signs, a scar, furrowed brow, a furtive look of worry or elation. When she was younger she imagined that after his jump, such a man would have a twitch or would hold his head to one side, eyes leveled at your shoes or just past your face if conversation was unavoidable.

Now he clutches his Washington Bullets bag. Lynette has not thought of him as a basketball fan. Or perhaps the bag just suits what he has to carry. *What's in the bag?* Books, old newspapers, empty Tupperware he's left too long in the break room fridge at work, shoes—the loafers, perhaps—uniform, gift for his children, frozen dinner, car alternator, a gun? The bulge against the cloth looks like anything and gives away nothing. *Sammy Cates, what's in the bag?*

SHE REMEMBERS how after Mr. Cates had been smiling at her for too long, her daddy said, "Go on inside and change your shirt, girl," but she knew he said it just to sound like a father. She didn't move.

Her father then tried to help Mr. Cates to his feet, but Mr. Cates said he was fine. Mr. Simmons said he could *give a got-damn* about how Mr. Cates felt, and went on about his lounger and his deck roof. Odessa helped Berthine get up. Uncle Norman picked the last beer from the cooler, went to look at the ribs in the Dumpster, and whistled like he'd just seen a car accident. He rubbed his chest and lifted his nose to the breeze, which brought with it the smell of chicken frying at Wings 'N' Things, over on Georgia Avenue.

Lynette had stretched the tea-soaked shirt from her skin and bent down to pick up the broken pitcher. There was still a little ice tea left in the bottom half. She poured it through the wooden planks of the deck, watched the liquid trickle away into the shadows, and waited to hear it hit the drain at the edge of the deck. Lynette heard the front door of the apartment close and her mother drop bags on the coffee table before she stepped past Lynette and onto the deck.

Avis Simmons looked over the scene on the deck and said, "What in the hell is going on?"

Uncle Norman said, "Sho' ain't supper," and tried to keep from laughing.

Maybe they thought Mrs. Simmons was joking, but she wasn't laughing. She was looking at Mr. Cates, who wasn't laughing either.

Mr. Simmons helped Mr. Cates lean against a post and then stepped back.

All the while Uncle Norman was smiling. He eased against the rail and chuckled, "Maybe if you knowed how to stand the fuck up, you might make it to the got-damn alley!"

You see, Mr. Cates was hard to help. It wasn't that he was overweight or weak, but he was uncoordinated. He was dizzy, and he was bleeding, and he was the quiet man from upstairs whom everyone saw but no one knew. And it seemed to Lynette that since Mr. Cates wasn't dead, Norman didn't care if he was hurt or embarrassed.

Mrs. Simmons said, "Hot today, ain't it?" She could have been talking to anyone.

But Mr. Cates said, "Yeah. It is."

Lynette's father looked up through the jagged hole in the roof and said, "Like that's some damn news!"

Berthine and Odessa clasped each other's hands to keep from bursting out again.

"It's Saturday, Samuel," Lynette's mother said. "Why you wearing your Sunday suit?"

WHERE HAS HE been all this time? Lynette should know about where he's been. Knowing how people are living is her job. She's worked in Children's Welfare at Health and Human Services a long time, long enough to give more instructions than she gets. Last year they promoted her to an office—same desk in the same corner of the room where she's worked the last twelve years, but now the desk sits behind a metal door and opaque glass partition. Lynette keeps scores of cases in her head. Most are difficult. Many impossible. A dozen or so have set her to crying at the kitchen table before she goes to work. A few she carries with her long after they have grown up, moved away, died young, or been locked down. She watches how people live. Though she swears herself from forecasting, she feels she has a keen sense for how people's lives will turn out.

There's not a soul Lynette can think of to call on evenings or weekends, but she believes she is a people person. Not the sort who socializes over cocktails and bid whist. The sort who knows people's cousins, godmothers, and deacons. She knows who's in the hospital, who just got out, who's pregnant, divorced, or both. From the time that she moved back into the building, she has followed the passing of elders, families growing, moving in, moving out. She knows well only the people on her floor, but she knows about most who live in the building. Lynette Simmons, who hasn't a gossip mate or phone pal, knows that Elvin and Tracy, the Brevard boys from the second floor, sneak girls into their momma's place during school hours. She knows that the entire fourth floor had been rented by Salvadorans until Immigration cleared them out. She knows the gossip on the super's new Lincoln: *Somebody's wife bought that car.* She has watched the Elkins family move from the back of the first floor to the front of the fifth, and finally to the large corner unit on the third.

Lynette would like to be certain that she saw Mr. Cates sometimes after the day he jumped. But she has forgotten. After that day she would steel her preteen nerves when entering the elevator and quickly press the button for her floor. Sometimes she hoped for a short trip if Mr. Cates was already in the elevator, riding from the basement where he bundled newspapers or placed wrapped trash at the bottom of the Dumpster. If he wasn't in the elevator, she might hold her arm across the doors for a moment, for sometimes she dared herself to bump into him by chance. But she can't remember when she stopped seeing him in the elevator: Was she twelve? Sixteen? So much of it blurs together.

She has often tried to pin down when he moved out of the building. Sometimes, when she is preparing for bed, she gets it in her mind that it wasn't that she saw Mr. Cates less but that she simply stopped looking out for him. She remembers that it was sometime in her high school years that she began to imagine her own Mr. Cates—Mr. Cates as a librarian or dentist;

grown man with no family, no friends; his weekends spent in the Smithsonian.

METRO CENTER STATION is approaching. Mr. Cates adjusts his grip on the bag before stepping off the train. Lynette follows, quick steps to keep up, a few moments' rest on a bench, to ease her eagerness. It's not the forgetting, she comforts herself. Everybody forgets. It's the misremembering that causes the void. Because she's not sure what to think next, she tells herself that she has *misremembered* this Mr. Cates, mistaken how he should have looked for someone else, Everton Fox, for example—if he were slimmer—or an old professor, or the produce man at the grocery store who smiles but never speaks.

Mr. Cates heads for the Red Line, bound for Shady Grove. Still traveling west and north. Where's he going? Chevy Chase? Bethesda? That man don't live in no Chevy Chase, she thinks. Folks who live in Chevy Chase don't ride Metro. Rockville makes more sense. Red Line to Rockville or Twinbrook. Ground-floor apartment, she imagines, two-bedroom on a row of cinder-block condos. It's full of old newspapers and clumps of cat hair, which explains why he picks at his blazer like a teen obsessed with zits. She checks her watch to time how long he preens his clothes. Lynette smiles at the intensity of his gestures—traits she would find both annoying and precious in a spouse.

LYNETTE SAT at the kitchen table while her father and Norman argued in the living room about what to do with Mr. Cates. Berthine and Odessa were on the couch, watching Lynette's father and Norman do little but talk. Her mother was on the deck, with Mr. Cates.

Lynette watched her mother wipe the blood from Mr. Cates's face. He had taken off his suit jacket, and her mother was working at getting him to take off his shirt, to see if he had any other injuries. He didn't want that. When she reached for his buttons, he took hold of Mrs. Simmons's wrist and wouldn't let go. Mr. Cates looked from her face to her hands and then away, looking for somebody who might be watching. His neck loosened and he ran his forehead along Momma's hand. She gently eased one of his hands from her wrist, and with her other hand she lifted his head up to wipe it.

Norman was trying to get her father worked up. "What if that crazy nigger try something on your wife?" Norman said toward the TV.

"Sammy Cates ain't the man to pull that kinda shit." Her father was talking to the TV too. " 'Sides, if he tried anything, way Avis is, he wish he did hit the alley. Crazy-ass Negro, all he is."

In all her life Lynette saw her father push her mother only once. When that happened, Avis Simmons picked herself up, went to the bathroom, closed the door, and didn't come out until long after supper. But early Thursday morning, long before he woke, she took the bolt key from his ring. Her father never noticed, and after he left for work in the evening, her mother bolted the front door until Sunday. Lynette never knew where her father went, but he came back with cherry blossoms in his hand, singing Donny Hathaway songs from the alley. All Mrs. Simmons ever said was: ". . . on the third day, he rose up and came into his right mind," and Lynette never saw any more pushing.

Norman and Mr. Simmons sipped at their beer and waited to see what her mother was going to do. Berthine and Odessa were chattering back and forth to each other. Berthine said something about hoping Mr. Cates didn't die or else she wouldn't have a good story to tell after Sunday-morning service, and Odessa said Berthine should be ashamed of herself: God was looking down on all of them. But Berthine was already figuring out, come Sunday, who she would gossip to first.

MR. CATES GETS OFF at Dupont Circle. This surprises Lynette, so much so that she nearly misses making it off the train. She was settled in for a longer ride. She had been lost in her thoughts, as people often are on long train rides: lost in spy novels, classifieds, and box scores—eyes closed, bopping their heads to the music spinning from disk to headphones—or sitting blank and glassy-eyed, casting their worries and daydreams into the darkness beyond the windows. Lynette, thinking Mr. Cates's stop was a long way off, was somewhere in that darkness. It was Mr. Cates's sudden absence from the train doorway that snapped her back to focus, and then she was rushing between the Metro car's closing doors to follow where he must have gone.

She stands on the platform, getting her bearings. Mr. Cates is already rising to the top of the first escalator that will take him out of the station. She gives him some time and follows only after he's stepped off the short escalator leading away from the platform. Lynette watches him slip through the exit gates and toward the escalator to the street. With Samuel Cates several steps ahead, she begins to climb the stairs of the escalator, ascending through the long concrete tube of the Metro exit, its end a bowl of dark, bruise-colored sky into which commuters seem to fall as they step off the top of their ride and go their way. Lynette pauses, looks up at the sky, the dimmed haze of city air waiting to meet her as she rises into it. Mr. Cates steps off, and his head dips out of sight.

When she reaches the top of the escalator, he has already

cut across Connecticut Avenue. He's made it to the median, anxious for what looks like his destination: a bookstore and café across the street.

She prepares herself: Dupont Circle. She was just getting used to the idea of the suburbs. She hadn't figured on Mr. Cates living here, where the rents are high and there are more White folks than Brown. Samuel Cates can't live here, she thinks.

Perhaps he is meeting someone, a friend or lover. In all the years that she's imagined him in her mind, she has never thought of Mr. Cates in love. It's only now she realizes that for a long time he's lived in her as sexless, much as she has come to think of herself.

She can't remember the last time she was sitting across the table from a date, worried over whether to talk politics, crack jokes, or make eyes. She can't remember. Can't or doesn't? Won't or chooses not to? Too many trifling men in Washington, she thinks. She's used that one many times, responding to coworkers or the busybodies at church, just before or after she reminds the nosy or concerned how many more women there are in D.C. than men. When she hears, "Girl, you so right," she breathes the pressure out and doesn't worry herself with how long it's been since she last imagined a man in her bed.

But she's envisioned men in many other ways: in the store, wandering the aisles in search of the mysterious products their dead mothers or ex-wives had used to clean and feed them; in the office, bullshitting their way out of casework; on the train, sly grin, furtive eyes over the sports section, and moist, scowling lips when she doesn't smile back. Everton Fox, the portly BBC weatherman, makes her smile with his four-button suits and the gallant sweep of his hand as it passes over typhoons in Australasia; his accent lilts what she imagines as East London, but she is sure she can hear the hint of his Jamaican ancestors' Creole.

It troubles her that she has no image of what Mr. Cates finds attractive in a lover. All she can picture now is what she sees: blazer, khakis, running shoes, now nervously jaywalking Connecticut Avenue. She pauses, takes a breath, heads for the crosswalk, and prepares to enter somewhere she's never been in the city she calls home.

LYNETTE'S MOTHER told her husband to call Leena Morris, from down the hall, for her to help Mrs. Simmons help Mr. Cates. When Lynette would see Miss Morris on the elevator, Miss Morris would tell Lynette to call her Leena, even though Lynette's mother had told Lynette to say Miss Morris. Leena wasn't like Lynette's mother or Berthine or Odessa or anyone Lynette knew. Berthine wore her best hats only to church and managed to carry her 270 pounds on four-inch heels, but still she called Leena Morris "one of them new-style women."

Leena Morris worked late, but no one ever talked about what she did for work. On early summer mornings, when Lynette and her mother sometimes walked over to Sixteenth Street to meet her father halfway as he came from his security shift, she could see Leena's flickering, TV-blue living room windows, the only ones lit up in the building.

Months before Samuel Cates jumped, Lynette had been eavesdropping from the living room couch as her mother and Berthine talked in the kitchen about Mr. Cates: Sammy Cates, who only came to church on Christmas Eve and left early; Sammy Cates, up at all hours of the night; Sammy Cates, who spent too much time by himself.

While the two women spoke, Lynette was imagining Mr. Cates sitting alone in his apartment, maybe looking out the window, maybe looking into the alley. She tried to picture her mother, alone, sitting with a can of club soda at the kitchen table. Or her father, without his wife, sitting in front of the TV, no food on the table, no ball game on, no nothing going on.

When Leena knocked on the front door and slipped in, Lynette could see the get-the-hell-out-my-house look on her father's face. He waved toward the deck and told Leena, "They out there." Mr. Simmons was irritated by this—all these people in his home, from down the street, down the hall, through his roof—and him having no say in it.

Leena nodded to Berthine and Odessa and shot a wink to Lynette before stepping to the deck, and sliding the door closed behind her. Mr. Cates stumbled to get up, but Lynette's mother held him where he sat. She smiled at Leena, pointed inside, and, without much more talk, came into the living room and went straight for the bathroom to get gauze and alcohol.

Out on the deck, Mr. Cates eased back in his chair. Leena already had his shirt open to wipe away blood and see if he was cut anywhere else.

Lynette remembers that when Berthine said, "She don't waste no time, do she?" her little girl's mind thought it was thinking what Berthine was thinking, even though she didn't yet know what that was all about. Berthine said to no one in particular, "I could say something, but I won't," but pulled Odessa close to whisper something Lynette could not hear anyway.

IN THE CAFÉ SECTION of the bookstore, Lynette is on her second coffee. Mr. Cates is nursing his first. He's been at a table by himself since he came in, looking from the bar of the café to the front of the bookstore.

Lynette drifted in a moment or so after, orbited the New

Arrivals table, and wandered into the front room of the café, which is also lined with books. She worked her way carefully through the poetry section, tracing her fingers from Z on back before easing down to the table where she now sips at her coffee.

Samuel Cates hunches over his cup, looks to the street, looks into the restaurant at the back of the café, then back into his coffee. The track lighting warms the room, and in a glow that looks like late-autumn daylight, his features soften. The light shines on the skin of his head, where she had imagined the hair to be thicker. His awkward lean onto the table looks more like a habit his body has learned. His hands hold the cup like a chalice, and he looks around the room with the same keen fascination she sees in the elderly who watch children at play in the park.

This is not a place Samuel Cates knows well, but he enjoys it, the jazz over the speakers, people speaking and laughing loudly, engrossed in the witty things they are saying. For just a moment Lynette watches a small grin flash on Mr. Cates's face, and then it is gone. Perhaps, because he is alone or because she now sees how he's aged, he seems more pitiful. She is not sure why, but Lynette starts to feel that the lines in his face have come from more smiles than frowns. Just as Lynette comes to feeling this, Mr. Cates slips a small nip-size bottle of Scotch out of his blazer pocket and quickly pours all of it into his cup, which he shields with his arm from no one in particular.

The small bottle vanishes, and she marvels at the deft movement of his hands. Without a beat, he is back to his hunch over the table. She is thinking on wanting a little taste too, something hidden, something quick and secret, maybe scotch, maybe rum. She wonders what takes the edge off, the liquor itself or the secret of it, snuck into a coffee cup in a room full of people. Maybe both. She wants to ask him, "How long you been at that,

Samuel Cates? You go to work sauced or is it just at the end of the day? That what gets you home?" But somehow she knows it's just a taste, every now and then. Sammy Cates, with his little taste on Connecticut Avenue. "All this time, where you been?"

LEENA MORRIS had been on the deck with Mr. Cates for some time, the two of them talking as if nothing had happened. Mr. Cates seemed to have cracked a joke, because Leena was laughing. When she smiled, her mouth opened wide, and Lynette could see her teeth, which weren't very white, but they were set straight and apart from each other so that when she smiled she had a warm, inviting face. She was moving her hands around as she spoke. Her fingers were long and thin. She moved them gently, like she was gently brushing away smoke, and Lynette was thinking that Mr. Cates must be watching that too. Those hands, gliding through the air. The sun was bright on her cheekbones and her wide, flat nose. She was beautiful.

Lynette noticed that her mother was now standing at the sliding door holding alcohol, also watching Mr. Cates and Leena. And it was then that Lynette realized that everybody—her mother, Berthine, Uncle Norman, and even her father—was watching Leena and Mr. Cates. Everyone watched them through the sliding glass door and no one said a thing. The ball game was on. Lynette could hear it and nothing else. Mr. Cates and Leena both turned to see everyone in the living room looking out at them.

Berthine was the first to laugh. Mr. Cates was still smiling as everyone stepped outside. Uncle Norman was the last one on the deck, and he was still laughing when he came out. He reached out to give Mr. Cates a beer, but when Mr. Cates took hold of it Norman held on, tugging it, then let go. Everyone laughed at that too.

Then Norman said, "You a weird one, Sammy Cates. Next time you want a date, just call the sister; you don't got to be jumpin' off no building."

Lynette's mother stopped laughing. So did Leena. Everyone stiffened. No one would look at each other at first. Then Lynette looked at her father, who looked to the deck ceiling for a moment and then pulled Norman back inside.

Leena got up and hurried for the door.

Mrs. Simmons ran after her and shut the sliding door behind her. Before Berthine could say anything, Odessa pushed her inside. Lynette was left standing on the deck, alone with Mr. Cates.

Samuel Cates looked at Lynette. She smiled at him because she thought that he might too, but he looked dazed again. Once, as the elevator was approaching her floor, just for kicks, she said, "Hey, Sammy Cates!" instead of, "Hello, Mr. Cates," and that startled him. Her mother pinched her arm, and he turned back to face the door. She wondered what might happen if she got to talking to Mr. Cates. She put her hand on his shoulder. His body was rigid. Her mother had never allowed her to be alone with strangers, but her mother was off chasing Leena Morris, and here was Mr. Cates, left behind with her. Lynette thought about how she felt at recess, when it seemed that no one wanted to play with her; it's easier to be chosen than to ask.

"Hey, Sammy Cates," she said.

He had gauze in his hand. He was unraveling it and balling it back up. When he had several balls of bloody gauze, he didn't know what to do with them.

Lynette put out her hand. "You can't pay no attention to Norman. He says stuff he has no business sayin'."

Mr. Cates shrugged his shoulders.

Lynette took a couple of the balls from his hands, which weren't very big, just a bit larger than her mother's.

There were two pigeons sitting on the balcony railing, and Lynette tossed the balls at them. The birds fluttered their wings and flew down into the alley. Mr. Cates watched this and squeezed the remaining gauze tightly in his hand.

"I think God makes some folks like Uncle Norman so that the rest of us can see what actin' a fool looks like." She reached to take the rest of the gauze out of his hands, and he closed his fingers around hers.

"I'm not much for all that God business," he said. His face was calm. If his eyes were closed, he could have been asleep. He focused in on their hands. The tops of his were coarse, but his palms were smooth, and even though he didn't let go of her hands when Lynette pulled, he wasn't holding too tightly. If she pulled hard, she could have freed herself.

"You okay, Mr. Cates?"

"You don't got to call me that." He loosened his hands.

Then Lynette did pull her hands away, and the gauze fell onto the deck. When she looked up, the pigeons had come back.

Mr. Cates picked up the wadded cotton, stood up, and threw it at the pigeons. He threw the wads one at a time and missed wildly, but he threw them very hard. The birds flew off in all directions. Then he looked back to Lynette.

She suddenly wondered where everyone else had gone.

He went to the sliding door and opened it to leave.

"Hey."

He stopped and looked back at her.

"You not gonna do anything else crazy, are you?"

He smiled and ran his small hand over the cut on his forehead. Then he gave a slight wave and closed the sliding door behind him. That was twenty-five years ago.

———

WHEN LYNETTE SLIPS BACK from this memory, Mr. Cates is gone. All that remains at his table is a ten-dollar bill under his coffee cup. She picks up her bag and walks to his table. The coffee is gone, but he has left his faded Washington Bullets bag. It sits on the chair next to where he sat. She picks it up and runs for the door.

Lynette follows him a few blocks until she stops across the street from the building he enters, a retirement home in a renovated apartment building. Lynette can't help but smile, for this development fits her pity. She smiles and is immediately ashamed for imagining him as a drunk, senile man wandering the city, riding the Metro, collecting meaningless items in an old bag lined with weeks-old newspaper. She stands on the corner, hand on the zipper of the bag, wondering if it will matter to him that she's looked inside it. The thought strikes her that what's in the bag might surprise her, telling her more than she wants to know. She stands under the streetlight, staring across the street.

It is a small building he has walked into. The upper floors have drop ceilings with large square light fixtures. Inside, the fluttering hints of shadows that fluorescent lights barely reveal. From outside the glass door, the lobby looks small. A hallway leading into the back of the building, a long table just inside the door, a few chairs opposite the table. He must be missing the bag, she's thinking, and how long can she stand on a dark corner, in Dupont Circle, Northwest Washington, D.C.?

Lynette crosses the street, rushes in the door, heads for the hallway. There must be a resident directory near the elevator.

"Excuse me, sister. *Excuse* me!"

Lynette turns to see a large woman at the table she's just passed.

"Can I help you?" The woman wears the white blouse, skirt, hose, and shoes that nurses wear. She's got what is left of a sandwich in one hand, some other part of it in her mouth. She moves the food from one side of her mouth to the other. "You can't come in here, unannounced and all. Who you tryin' to see?"

Lynette steps up to the desk. She sees a registration book next to the woman's neat stack of *Jet* magazines. She runs her finger down the visitor's log. She looks down the hall, then points to where "S. Cates" is scribbled in the log.

"Junior or Senior? Junior just gone up. You from the drugstore?"

Lynette is quiet for a moment, sets down her bag, holds on to Mr. Cates's bag. She feels herself getting nervous, unsure of what she knows.

"Senior been waiting on his pills all day. Man call down here four times, askin' after them pills."

Lynette starts to fill her name into the register.

"If you from the drugstore, I know Cates Junior wants to talk to you. And Lord, take his daddy those pills!"

"I can wait for him down here."

"Wait on *who*? Cates Junior? He'll be up there another forty-five minutes! Sign in and get them pills up there. Been waitin' on you, girl. I don't want to hear no more from that old man tonight!"

Lynette picks up her bags. *I'm not from the drugstore.* She is not sure if she has said this or thought it. A panic fills her because she's run out of things to say. She is not from the drugstore, she is not visiting, she has had nothing to say before she walked in. Suddenly she loses sight of what Mr. Cates looks like. All of this is so far beyond what she had considered. Her mind flashes on a faceless, formless man sitting impatiently next to the bed of his father. The both of them are silent, one beside himself with waiting, his octogenarian expectation of the medicine's delivery eating at him worse than his need for taking it; the other, the son, anxious for this hour's visit to be up, thinking more about another scotch in his coffee than anything else. Or maybe their life is nothing like this.

This is what bothers Lynette. She worries that the Cateses, Senior and Junior, may be right now laughing about fishing trips and Momma Cates's collard greens or ribbing each other over dominoes. Maybe their life is like this, not stolid and monotonous, neither of them bitter at the other for something that could not be explained. And she'd rather not ask the nurse "And how's Senior doing?" like some close family friend making small talk, because she hasn't figured on this other Cates, and a bit of socializing might get the nurse talking—and the nurse is the sort who talks—about how good it is that Sammy Cates comes to see his father: *Junior, be in here once, twice a week in the evening, once on the weekends, in for just an hour, and then he gone till next time. You could time the trains on that man.* And a talker like that will get around to some unsolicited reflection. *Lord knows we all could spend more time with family. I'm more bad than good with that, but, girl, I'm tryin'. . . You got family?* And then Lynette would have to answer, bag in each hand—groceries and unknown—weighing the answer: *Yes, girl, I tell my kids the same, we got to get over to see their grands . . .* but she has no pictures of children when the nurse wants to see—the talkers always want to see pictures. So Lynette ponders: *No, my parents passed awhile back, when I was in my twenties. Don't have any kids—no man on the scene—but if I did have children . . .*

Lynette grabs up her bag to leave. She will go back home. No train this time. If she's lucky, a cab will stop. She's just a zone or so away, so it won't cost that much. She will go home, soak beans for tomorrow, take a bath, fix a drink, watch the news—just like any other night. But she's still holding this

Washington Bullets bag, with no idea what's in it, and she's not sure what to think of this Mr. Cates if she doesn't open it.

She's halfway out the door.

"Hey, girl, hold on! Just hold tight."

Lynette sits in a chair, sets down her bag.

"You all right? If you want to wait, then wait."

Lynette looks at the wall past the nurse, then down the hall to the elevators, then back to the wall. She thinks of her parents. She's struck by how little they have lived in her since they passed. They are buried in the suburbs, at a place where the gravestones lie flat, so that the cemetery lawn looks more like a golf course. A place with few trees, but it was where she could afford. She has hung their pictures on the walls of her apartment, but it strikes her that she can't remember the last time she looked at them. She has not been to the cemetery in years—no reason, no explanation behind it.

Lynette thinks of how her mother had been with Mr. Cates the day he jumped through the roof of their deck, and tries to imagine herself doting on Mr. Cates in his elder years as her mother doted on Mr. Cates then. She imagines going to visit Mr. Cates on a Sunday in whatever retirement home he will end up in. Or she would drive Mr. Cates to church when his legs won't carry him to the Metro. Lynette would have called him the Friday before, as she would have done for years. She would help him down the stairs in such a way that he feels he is doing it himself, all the while asking him about the heat in his apartment, the health of his cats, how he liked the casserole she brought the week before.

As Lynette Simmons stares into the wall, she tells herself that she will wait for Samuel Cates to come down. He will be rushing out, looking for his bag. Maybe he will have forgotten. Maybe she will say hello as she gives it to him. She smiles at the thought of saying, "Hey, Sammy Cates!" but instead she thinks she'll catch up slowly: "How you, Mr. Cates? I'm Lynette, Avis Simmons's daughter, from way back. Meridian Towers Apartments. You remember me? I saw you on the train. We used to live in the same building, a long while back."

The nurse has given up on her sandwich and looks at Lynette with a sideways glance. "I can call up to Mr. Cates. You want me to call him?"

"No, thank you," Lynette says, then she eases further back into the chair and rests her bag on the floor. She thinks to say, "You don't have to call him, he's expecting me," but instead smiles when she realizes that there is no need.

Notes on the Contributors

FAITH ADIELE is an award-winning nonfiction writer whose work has appeared in *O, Essence, Ploughshares, Ms., Creative Nonfiction,* and other journals. She has received awards for her work from the Hurston/Wright Foundation, UNESCO, and PEN, and was short-listed for Best American Essays 2002 and 2005.

KWAME ALEXANDER is the author of ten books, including *Dancing Naked on the Floor: Poems and Essays; Crush: Love Poems;* and *Do the Write Thing: 7 Steps to Publishing Success.* He is the cofounder and producer of the Capital BookFest.

ABDUL ALI is a native of New York City living in Washington, D.C. He was educated at Howard University, where he studied English and theater. He has published in numerous periodicals, including the *Washington Post* and *Black Issues Book Review.* He was a finalist for the 2000 Lary Neal Writers' Award. He is the 2007 winner of the Mount Vernon Poetry Festival Prize.

TINA MCELROY ANSA is a novelist, publisher, filmmaker, teacher, and journalist. She is the author of the novels *Baby of the Family, Ugly Ways, The Hand I Fan With, You Know Better,* and *Taking After Mudear.*

NICOLE BAILEY-WILLIAMS is a novelist and freelance writer. Her debut novel, *A Little Piece of Sky,* was a finalist for the Debut Fiction Legacy

Award, presented by the Hurston/Wright Foundation. She is also the author of the novels *Floating* and *The Love Child's Revenge,* published by Broadway Books last fall.

DOREEN BAINGANA is a Ugandan writer and the author of *Tropical Fish: Stories out of Entebbe.* The book won the Associated Writers and Writing Programs (AWP) Award for Short Fiction and the Commonwealth Prize for First Book, Africa Region, and was a finalist for the Hurston/Wright Legacy Award for Debut Fiction. Her fiction and essays have been published in many journals, including *Glimmer Train* and *African American Review.*

L. A. BANKS has written more than thirty novels and contributed to ten novellas, in multiple genres under various pseudonyms. She is the recipient of the 2008 *Essence* Storyteller of the Year Award. She mysteriously shapeshifts between genres of romance, women's fiction, crime/suspense thrillers, and paranormal lore.

JONETTA ROSE BARRAS is the author of *Bridges: Reuniting Daughters and Daddies,* the best-seller *Whatever Happened to Daddy's Little Girl: The Impact of Fatherlessness on Black Women, The Last of the Black Emperors: The Hollow Comeback of Marion Barry in the New Age of Black Leaders,* and *The Corner Is No Place for Hiding.*

WILL BESTER is a writer based in New York City. He is working on a collection of short stories set during slavery.

REGINALD DWAYNE BETTS writes poems and runs a book club, Young-MenRead, for children in the D.C. Metro area. His work appears in *Gulf Coast, Crab Orchard Review, Obsidian III, Poet Lore,* and other journals. He is currently at work on a memoir, *A Question of Freedom.*

SIMONE BOSTIC is pursuing a degree in speech pathology at the University of the District of Columbia. Her love of words was ignited by the stories that her mother read to her as a child. She is in the process of writing a memoir.

GWENDOLYN BROOKS won the Pulitzer Prize for poetry for her collection *Annie Allen* and authored more than twenty-five works of poetry and nonfiction. During her long and productive career she received scores of honors in the United States and internationally for her work, was a beloved mentor and teacher to a generation of Black writers, and served as the Library of Congress's first Consultant in Poetry.

STACIA L. BROWN has written for *Black Issues Book Review* and *Mosaic* magazine. She lives in New York City, where she is working on a collection of short stories.

KENNETH CARROLL's poetry and plays have appeared in *Black Magazine, Hungry as We Are, Fast Talk, Full Volume, In Search of Color Everywhere, Catch Fire,* and many other journals and anthologies. His short stories have appeared in the anthology *Children of the Dream* and the journals *Shooting Star* and *Gargoyle*. His book of poetry is entitled *So What! For the White Dude Who Said This Ain't Poetry*. He is the executive director of DC WritersCorps.

VERONICA CHAMBERS is a widely published journalist, essayist, and novelist. Her most recent book is *Kickboxing Geishas*. She is also the author of the memoir *Mama's Girl* and the novel *Miss Black America*, as well as the nonfiction books *The Joy of Doing Things Badly* and *Having It All?: Black Women and Success*.

PEARL CLEAGE is an Atlanta-based author whose works include six novels, a dozen plays, two books of essays, and two books of poetry. Her first novel, *What Looks Like Crazy on an Ordinary Day*, was an Oprah Book Club pick; her novel *Baby Brother's Blues* was an NAACP Image Award winner for fiction in 2007, and her most recent novel is *Seen It All and Done the Rest*.

DAVID ANTHONY DURHAM is the author of the novels *Gabriel's Story*, which won the Hurston/Wright Legacy Award for Debut Fiction, *Walk Through Darkness, Pride of Carthage*, and the speculative novel *Acacia*.

PATRICIA ELAM is an award-winning writer whose work has been published in the *Washington Post, Newsday, Essence*, as well as in anthologies such as *Father's Songs, New Stories from the South*, and the *O. Henry Award Stories*. She is the author of the novel *Breathing Room*.

W. RALPH EUBANKS is the author of *Ever Is a Long Time: A Journey into Mississippi's Dark Past*. He has contributed articles to the *Washington Post*'s Outlook Section, National Public Radio, and the *Chicago Tribune*. His book *The House at the End of the Road: A Story of Race, Reconciliation, and Identity* will be published in 2009.

BRIAN GILMORE is a poet, writer, and public interest lawyer. He is the author of two collections of poetry, *elvis is alive and well and living in harlem* and *Jungle Nights and Soda Fountain Rags: Poems for Duke Ellington*. He is a columnist with the Progressive Media Project and a contributing writer for *Jazz Times* magazine.

NIKKI GIOVANNI is a renowned poet, writer, commentator, and activist. Giovanni is the author of thirty books for adults and children and is a Distinguished Professor at Virginia Tech University in Blacksburg, Virginia.

ANTHONY GROOMS is the author of *Ice Poems*, a chapbook; *Trouble No More*, a story collection; and *Bombingham*, a novel. His stories and poems have been published in *Callaloo, African American Review, Crab Orchard Review*, and other literary journals.

JALAL's poetry has been published in *Northern Spies Magazine, Apocalypse Diffused or Deferred: Anthology Mirror of the Arts Program*, and *Whitman-Walker Clinic: Poetry and Prose*. His nonfiction is included in the anthology *Fighting Words*.

HONORÉE FANONNE JEFFERS is the author of three books of poetry: *The Gospel Barbecue,* which was chosen by Lucille Clifton as the winner of the Stan and Tom Wick Prize for a first book of poetry; *Outlandish Blues;* and *Red Clay Suite.* A fiction writer as well, Jeffers is at work on her first novel.

A. VAN JORDAN is the author of three poetry collections: *Rise, MacNolia,* and *Quantum Lyrics.* Among other awards, he has received the Whiting Award, the Anisfield-Wolf Book Award, the PEN/Oakland Josephine Miles Award, and the Pushcart Prize.

WILLIAM HENRY LEWIS is the prizewinning author of the story collections *In the Arms of Our Elders* and *I Got Somebody in Staunton,* which was a finalist for the PEN/Faulkner Award. His fiction has appeared in America's top literary journals and several anthologies. Among his many literary honors, Lewis was a finalist for the Hurston/Wright Award for college writers.

ROBIN ALVA MARCUS is a lecturer in the department of English at Howard University. Her writing has appeared in numerous magazines, as well as in *Grace and Gravity,* an anthology of Washington, D.C., women writers.

KIM MCLARIN is the author of three critically acclaimed novels, including, most recently, *Jump at the Sun.* She is a former staff writer for the *New York Times* and the *Philadelphia Inquirer,* among other newspapers, and is the host of *Basic Black,* Boston's longest-running weekly television program devoted exclusively to African-American themes.

E. ETHELBERT MILLER is a literary activist and the board chair of the Institute for Policy Studies (IPS). Since 1974 he has been the director of the African American Resource Center at Howard University. He is the author of several books of poetry and editor of the award-winning poetry anthology *In Search of Color Everywhere* and the author of the memoir *Fathering Words: The Making of an African American Writer.*

SONSYREA TATE MONTGOMERY is the author of the memoir *Little X: Growing Up in the Nation of Islam* as well as her follow-up memoir, *Do Me Twice.* As a journalist she has written for the *Washington Post,* the *Washington Times,* and the *Virginian-Pilot* and has served as an editor at the *Washington Informer.*

VICTORIA CHRISTOPHER MURRAY is the author of five *Essence* best-selling novels, including the number one *Essence* best-seller, *A Sin and a Shame.* She is also the author of the teen book series *The Divine Divas.*

JILL NELSON is the author of the best-selling memoir *Volunteer Slavery,* the novel *Sexual Healing,* and the acclaimed collection of essays *Straight, No Chaser,* and the editor of the anthology *Police Brutality.* She lives in New York City and on Martha's Vineyard, Massachusetts. Visit JillNelson.com, or contact her at FindingMV@aol.com.

LISA PAGE is a freelance writer whose work has appeared in *Savoy, Emerge, The Crisis,* the *Washington Post Book World,* and *Playboy* magazine, among other publications.

LONNAE O'NEAL PARKER is a Pulitzer Prize–nominated reporter for the *Washington Post* and a contributing editor to *Essence.* She lives in Prince George's County, Maryland.

TRACY PRICE-THOMPSON is the national best-selling author of *Black Coffee, Chocolate Sangria,* and *A Woman's Worth,* which was a Hurston/Wright Legacy Award winner for contemporary fiction. She is also the coeditor of *Proverbs for the People* and *The Sister to Sister Empowerment* Series, which debuted with the collection *If the Hat Fits.*

FELICIA PRIDE is the founder of BackList (www.thebacklist.net), a Web site and publishing blog dedicated to keeping books in style. She is a regular contributor to *Publishers Weekly* and is the editor of *Mosaic Literary Magazine*. She has written two books for the *Everybody Hates Chris* series, published by Simon & Schuster, and her young adult novella was included in the anthology *Hallway Diaries*.

DEBBIE M. RIGAUD began her writing career covering news and entertainment for national magazines. She's interviewed celebs, politicians, cultural icons, social figures, and "real" girls. Her writing has appeared in *Seventeen, CosmoGirl!, Essence, Trace,* and *Vibe Vixen*. Rigaud's novella *Double Act* is featured in the young adult fiction anthology *Hallway Diaries*.

Permissions Acknowledgments

ADIELE: "My African Sister" originally appeared in *Rosebud* magazine, Issue no. 21, 2001, copyright © 2001 by Faith Adiele. Printed by permission of the author.

ALEXANDER: "Acts of Love," "Haiku," and "Kupenda," copyright © 2009 by Kwame Alexander. Printed by permission of the author.

ALI: "Silence . . . The Language of Trees," copyright © 2009 by Abdul Ali. Printed by permission of the author.

ANSA: "Chinaberry," from *The Hand I Fan With* by Tina McElroy Ansa, copyright © 1996 by Tina McElroy Ansa. Used by permission of Doubleday, a division of Random House, Inc.

BAILEY-WILLIAMS: "Coming Clean," copyright © 2009 by Nicole Bailey-Williams. Printed by permission of the author.

BAINGANA: "Lamu Lover," copyright © 2009 by Doreen Baingana. Printed by permission of the author.

BANKS: "Two Cents and a Question," copyright © 2009 by L. A. Banks. Printed by permission of the author.

BARRAS: "Wilhelmina," copyright © 2009 by Jonetta Rose Barras. Printed by permission of the author.

ABOUT THE AUTHOR

MARITA GOLDEN is the author of over a dozen works of fiction and nonfiction, including *Migrations of the Heart, Don't Play in the Sun: One Woman's Journey Through the Color Complex,* and the award-winning novel *After.* She is cofounder and President Emeritus of the Hurston/Wright Foundation.